This work of fiction contains material that some people may find offensive or harmful.
Trigger warnings include, but are not limited to, violence, death, suicide, stereotypes, sex, nudity, harassment, politics, religion, strong language.

'Scots' language used throughout.

Glossary at the rear.

To those still fearing the darkness;
Step into the light and set yourself free.

Special thanks to my family and friends.

Tangled Lines

L. M. Pirie

For Alana, the brightest star in my night sky.

Chapter 1 — Isla

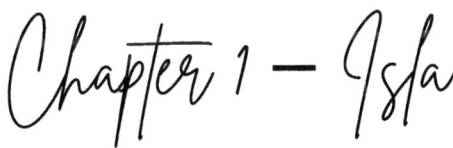

Licking and thrusting against the bow of the Ceilidh, grey frothy waves of the Hebridean sea crash metres from my feet.

A desperate and insatiable hunger consumes my soul as I watch on with a halting perversion.

I'm hooked in a trance by nothing more than the salacious surge.

The irony's uncanny.

I yearn for the touch of another woman, jist one short moment of desire and pleasure. It could be enough to satisfy this agonising urge.

The warmth of someone carrying me off home is matched by the swell now brushing my toes.

Throwing me down passionately and indulging in an unruly seductive temptation; a hot sweaty mess, as our powerful hands explore tangled anatomy.

A drenching of spray meets my face in a sardonic sensation.

'Phwoar, now that would be the perfect ending to such a bloody miserable day.'

It's nae going to happen, but still, there's no harm in dreaming.

I'm craving something reckless and physical, a small moment of unforgettable world-consuming rapture.

God, I really could use some of that… It'll just have to wait.

Biting against my lower lip, the burn continues foraging its way.

I don't even know what I'm waiting for, there isnae anyone here on Skye.

I'm thirty-eight and still alone; no devoted relationship, no grimy children, nothing.

I'd actually need to count back the years since I'd last been intimate— and it isnae for the lack of trying, let me tell ye that.

A few years ago, it didn't worry me; I was career focused, always trying to better myself, but now times shifting on, my loneliness is catching up.

I have needs for goodness' sake, and they don't just disappear. It would be really bloody nice if they did.

Seriously, it's all I can think about nowadays, abstinence was never in my plan.

I need to feel loved and wanted.

Settling for a one-night stand isnae even out of the question, but it's not what I'm longing for.

Love… Love would conquer all.

The puddle at my waders is casting out a pale, red wavy-haired woman with blue eyes.

Dark creases frame her eyes, faint lines lifting at the mouth.

Whatever happened to the young beautiful girl that once peered back?

She was so full of life and lust, nothing more than a goodnight kiss and aspirations of growing content would keep her satisfied.

Now it's all torture and disarray.

A heavy droplet scattered the pool— leaving nothing but myself staring back.

'Eurgh, that's enough, Isla.'

Clinging tightly to the soggy rope, I'm preparing to anchor the fishing trawler; the nylon's cutting deep into the skin.

My tired eyes detect the broody storm resting dangerously above.
Torrential rain is coming— a signal of yet another unforgivable battering.

'Please, jist give me a break, I canna handle any more doom and gloom.'

The Scottish landscape is stunning, but any hope of a heatwave is restricted to around ten days a year.
It's still early February, realistically the chance of some sunshine is diluted to nothing more than an optimistic fantasy... I guess it really is a wet dream.

Small tears finally fall onto my shoulders, hopelessly running down my oilskin coat.
The now unravelling thread-bare, spruce-green tammy no longer protecting my head— It gave up on life a long time ago.
We share that.

The downpour's picking up, and a gale's decided to join my pity party; it's bloody baltic.

Touching my roughened lips, the moaning sea air tastes salty; a stolen kiss would be far more enjoyable, it might settle this soul shaking crave.

'Argh, stop teasing me!'
There's no need to keep tormenting, I'm already well aware no one's coming for a night of passion— Disappointing doesnae even cut it.

Beneath the jacket, my green Aran sweater is soaking up the hurricane; it'll be stinking by the time I get home.

Hoisting my neckband in an attempt to ward off the frost is doing bugger all.

Well, I guess it did accentuate my runny nose and stingy cheeks, but that wisnae the point.

Bloody weather.

Looking back to the surface water, a petite five-foot-four fisherwoman with an exuberant mischievous smile ripples free.

Auch, you maybe still have it Isla, you're just a wee bitty older, a tiny bit saggier, and almost certainly a helluva lot soggier.

The trawlers horn blared out beside me,

'Jesus Christ, Granda! I shit myself!' I screamed with a bounce.

He wasn't nearby— no doubt watching in amusement somewhere dry.

The haunting roar echoed through the barren passage separating Skye from the small island of Raasay.

Gripping tightly, I gave the rope a sharp tug, the boat bounced against the concrete wall; rubber tyres avoiding any catastrophic damage.

A raw shiver crept up my spine as another gust cut and run.

To think I could be sitting in a nice cosy office pushing pencils instead of this.

Drinking coffee whilst some bimbo pumps the heating up to six. Hah, who am I kidding?

That's my worst nightmare, so, so boring and

stereotypical.

Not every woman needs or wants an office job, especially not this one.

I need the waves, the adrenaline, the unpredictability and danger.

Oh aye, danger's my middle name. If I dinna feel alive then what's the point?

This is a job for a strong team, a strong woman, there's men that wouldn't get out of bed to do this… lazy sods.

Anyway, this is the life and soul of my Granda— Alistair, I couldn't allow him to be stealing the limelight without me.

We work as a duo, no strife or worries, just constantly enhancing the MacLeod legacy.

We're bound by bloody saltwater, nothing will tear us apart, we rely on each other like the daylight does the dawn.

My first life goal is to make him proud, there really isnae anything more important, he's my top priority.

Finding my missing puzzle piece is second, but that can take a back seat until one is complete… I mean… unless someone wheechs me away this second— Aye, I doubt I'd say no to that.

'Come on lass, yer hurkle durkeling,' Granda shouted.

His broad droll accent rounding off every vowel, each letter R rolling and rippled.

Granda's stood up top beside the wheelhouse; cheekily peering over the rails.

Auld bugger.

I'm secretly pleased to see he's soaked through too, it

cheers me knowing we share every experience— Well, maybe nae *every* one.

I smiled up to him, he returned it with a wink.

'The tide waits for nae one. Nae even a bonnie lass like yersel.' His resonance carries.

It's affectionate but hardened; much like his tanned and seasoned face.

I hope mine doesn't go like that; it looks way better on a mannie.

The salt-and-pepper beard, wild with whiskers takes up most of his skin— I couldnae imagine him clean shaven; the idea seems unnatural.

Once upon a time Granda proudly owned a mane of dark hair, now his grey friar-tuck appears to be washing out with the tide.

I guess it matches his trawler— The Ceilidh.

Too many harsh beatings will do that to ye, I guess my time's coming.

Eurgh, now that's a thought.

Despite the gruelling workload, Granda never grumbles, he jist lives for his labour.

Man alive, I love him dearly.

'Aye aye, Granda, I hear ye!' The cheeky bugger's always poking fun.

Auch aye, this morning's catch is a fair haul, our nets and chillers are all teeming full of haddock, cod, and some monstrous mackerel.

It's more than plenty to keep us afloat; well, for another day at least.

The fisher life isn't glamorous; it's hard going, precarious, and downright exhausting.

No one in their right mind would willingly choose it... Well, I guess I did, but I doubt anybody normal would bother.

The physical demands never lose their momentum, and the unpredictable climate alone would put most folk off, especially that bloody rain. Vertical, horizontal, rising from below, falling from above... aye, ye need to be mad, desperate for the money or have a death wish. Either way, nae many locals bother applying.

The catch is another story— it's never guaranteed. Some days you go home with aching bones, an immovable headache and clothing that's soggier than a frog's bum.

Other trips are the opposite— returning the catch to avoid overfishing, or our nets tear as they can't cope with the high volumes.

There's never really a happy medium. Mind you, it could be worse.

Back in 2010, a small trawler *'The Alba Torr'* capsized; four souls onboard, my school friend Greg included.

That was the shittiest day.

The only time I seriously thought of packing it all in, but I couldn't bring myself to leave Granda alone— he kept me here.

Two lifeboats and several fishing trawlers tirelessly slogged late into the black.

Granda and I included.

It's maritime law; any vessel in trouble gets assistance from neighbouring boats, but on this night, it wisnae safe.

Life threatening and terrifying, nobody dared to head away without helping.

Granda wouldn't relent, I guess I wouldn't let him— not with Greg and his father out there.

I screamed until my lungs failed.

Soaked and frozen clothing clung to us like a drookit clootie.

Fighting the gales and forty-foot waves, we tried to remain standing, relentless tidal swells threatened to drag us into the turbulent ink.

Icy brine filled our waders, every movement restricted and cumbersome.

I'd imagine treading quicksand feels similar.

Granda kept shouting to stay inside, to keep back, stay out of danger.

Unwilling to take heid, I couldn't watch behind glass as the Torr disintegrated.

I didn't want to be out there any more than Granda, but like him I'm stubborn; reckless and stupid comes to mind too.

Slipping against the metal deck, nets and Granda broke my fall.

If he hadn't known me better or moved in time… yeah. Horrific.

My ego took a hiding— The Ceilidh didn't fare much better.

Regrettably, The Alba Torr met its untimely demise. Its crew swallowed by the endless horizon, where the sea meets the sky.

Churning ninety miles north of the Cape Wrath coastline, jagged merciless cliffs provided little shelter from the tempest.

Greg had only just turned twenty-four three days earlier — we'd joined his final hurrah.

The first and last shindig I've physically grieved; an agonising and bittersweet hangover.

My first day in six years of fishing that struck fear.
I howled for weeks— inconsolable as Greg broke my heart in ways I'd never known possible.
Thoughts of *what if* and *how* haunted me.
I genuinely hope to never experience anything like that again.

Greg's poor mother was crippled; never grieving her son and husband who were misplaced for weeks. Unable to face the world alone, she concluded her misery in the most heart wrenching respect.
Ultimately, it's a tragic tale of one boat, four crew and five deaths.

It could have been us, it almost was.

My heavy heart couldn't cope, it probably still doesn't, but it was a major learning curve.
High-priced lessons were learnt.
No matter the trust and faith you have in modern technology, you can't be ignorant to Mother Nature's unforgivable and ferocious fury, it's not to be taken for granted.
Following instructions also became prevalent.
I learned to listen.

Granda's shuffling fish baskets from below, talk about perfect timing; the rain's just let up.
He processes most of the catch on our way back inland. Naturally I give him a hand, but I always set to work mending those pesky nets.
That's my job, Granda doesn't need the strain.

You know, I really should wear gloves, the nets don't

half make a guddle of your hands, and no bonnie wifey will want me if they're all manky.

In about thirty minutes the local fish lorries will come and collect a cut. They cast fish across the country, but thankfully most of ours is kept fairly local.
Any leftovers are picked up by nearby restaurants and fishmongers, they love the fresh produce.
It sells well, especially in the fancy hotels when tourism peaks.

Granda usually takes payment before washing down the processing area. We have it all figured out, working on autopilot we jig between ourselves. Each of us take on our own wee roles, it's been like this for a number of years… I wouldn't want it any other way.
I just pray I make him proud and continue the birthright. Well, almost birthright.

'That's the nets all done, Granda.'

'Auch, well done lass. Ye'd best get awa, ah'll finish up here and heid for hame.'

'Are ye sure, Granda? I can wait til you leave.'

'Nah, on ye go, Isla. Yiv done ah grand job, ah'll see ye the morn.'

'Thanks, if you need a hand just give me a call.
I'll see you tomorrow, have a good night old man.'

Well, I wasn't going to hang about for nothing. Giving him a kiss on the cheek I moved for the car.

'Yer a devil, Isla, awa ye go. Enjoy yersel.'

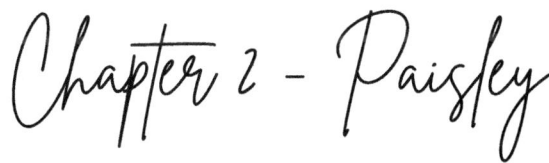

Chapter 2 - Paisley

Reclining in my Herman Miller, I finally allowed myself to take a moment... well, until my next meeting.

Money can't buy you happiness, that's a fact, but it can buy you a very comfortable office chair, and right now that's probably as good as it's going to get.

By trying to clear the headache brewing behind my sockets, I've inadvertently pulled strands of dark mahogany hair from its resting place.

'Where's my brush? I can't look this dogged before the days really begun.
That wouldn't look professional.'

As it happens, massaging my temples hasn't helped, if anything it's increased the ache.

Not really an ideal start to my Wednesday, like I need any more stress; my days are already crammed with enough duress to last a lifetime.
I guess that's the joy of being a Senior Solicitor at Campbell and Cambell... and there's nobody to blame but myself for that career choice.

Collapsing my hands around the oversized teacup, steam mists my face in a hydrating cleanse, it's unfortunate the urine-coloured lemon and ginger provides a nauseating public-toilet-like aroma.

Blowing undulations across the china sea, aging

emerald eyes mirror back in distaste— much like the leaves courting at the base.

'Eurgh… economical tea bags, I'll prosecute management later.'

The ping from my laptop aids the arrival of a new email, no doubt another pleasure cluttering the inbox.

'For goodness' sake, it's not even ten yet.'
A double click fills my screen.

'Auch, not this woman again, honestly what is wrong with people?'

<u>Subject: No money or dog</u>

Dear Ms Campbell,

I still haven't received my divorce money.
Where is it, why haven't you paid me yet?
I'm waiting for £342 and Milo my black
and white dog.
When will I get the dog and money?
Write back soon, I need the cash.
Thanks

Ms Lawrence/Mrs Partridge (divorced name).

'Aye, it's criminal!
How will you ever manage to survive?' An amused smirk tugs my lip.

'Yes, that's right, I've pocketed three hundred and forty-two pounds and Milo's unfortunately consulting with the meatloaf factory.
Bampot, why would I have your cash… or mutt?
Three hundred and forty-two sterling wouldn't even

cover my fees, which by the way, I should be charging extra for; simply to compensate the stupidity of that question.'

It's a shame management hadn't found *'idiot fees'* as a viable solution,

'It's simply not company policy, Paisley.' They remarked in a monotonous drone.

Urgh, morons.

It surely isn't that difficult to run a solicitor's office.

Every emotionally incompetent muppet that burdens my desk, is caught in a complex chain of disputes, discussions and conflicts.

I'm aware no one's perfect, but when will I get my five minutes of peace? Or better yet, a twisted mess of my own I can settle.

That's the one entity I would love.

Someone to relax into, meaningful conversations filled with thought-provoking ideologies and opinions.

In fact, just a woman waiting at home would probably be sufficient. She wouldn't need to be a homemaker— I can manage the basics and I'm not some chauvinistic monster.

All I would ask, is for her to love me as I am.

No grand expectations. No master plans.

Just love me, for me.

It really is that plain and simple. Isn't it?

Day after day, week after week, I defend the underdog.

Reading pages and pages of legal jargon, spitting out black-and-white terminology— which is typically agreed upon by greedy carefree individuals.

The chaos is always settled into order, and yes, without

blowing my own horn, I really am that good.

Except in the romance department— Here I'm the weaker party, it's my greatest injustice.

Nobody wants to invest their love upon me.

Am I really so taxing?

Hmm, maybe it's better if that isn't answered.

How deeply depressing.

The carriage clock clunked past ten— my nails clattering the considerably large redwood desk; unintentionally freeing a tap for each passing second.

'Where is this plonker? He should have been here fifteen minutes ago.'

Patience unfortunately isn't my strongest suit— I detest delay.

My office serves from the heart of Princes Street, next door to the now-abandoned Jenners; a department store from 1838.

Five years of vacant corridors, paint-peeling walls and a decaying roof.

It's a shame really, I found pleasure sauntering the lavish and pretentious halls.

Its perfume-waving dames and tape-measure-wielding tailors always brought an air of sophistication to my day.

The rough internal state now reflects my own; a bleak slow death as millions watch on from the sidelines, unfazed and uninterested.

Noise beyond the large sash windows steals my attention.

Bustling locals and tourists swarming and scurrying the

streets below, tram bells signal their arrival as the 'hop on, hop off' buses hiss and clatter.

So much din, all the friggin time.

There's never any chance of peace in this God forsaken city.

Scanning the room in preparation for my client, the regal wood adds a touch of ostentatiousness.

Ironically a paisley rug dresses the walnut floor, a dark sideboard stacked with books and two antique armchairs scream exorbitance.

Admittedly, the striking expense would appear extravagant to incomers, but I'm silently locked away in a career chasing lifestyle.

Comfort and luxury are one of my few guilty pleasures.

Nothing else really matters when you're at rock bottom.

Trust me, I've been here for quite some time.

My position buys me a first-class view of Edinburgh Castle.

I detest it.

It's become nothing more than a constant reminder of the expectations that accompany my privileged upbringing.

Assumptions and principles my family have forced down the throats of anyone less fortunate.

Personally, I couldn't give two shits about outdated beliefs, or political views.

My only interest is the aforementioned woman— an unorthodox requirement to finally find happiness.

No better than the impoverished, I myself am starved.

Hungry for nothing other than an agreeable cuddle on

the couch, maybe even a dalliance on the side… that would be a benefit, more than that, it would be a Godsend.

The Campbell's of Calder— my family, are very well to do and stappit in tradition.
Every thought or action must be painstakingly planned and executed. They run their lives like a military battalion— Meticulous and immaculate.
Each movement is precise and calculated, very much like a Swiss watch.

Well, on reflection that may be questionable; considering my father passed away fourteen years ago and the baton fell to my mother, there really wasn't much planning in that.
I guess, regrettably, the timepiece ran out of batteries that day.

For some reason, we speak as though he'll walk through the front door in some God-fearing miracle. That would be interesting… and highly unexpected.

You can only imagine the disgrace I bring to the family being a lesbian, at least I can say, I'm the first to my name.

My mother arrives with her own set of ideals, if something's not up to her standard, there's no reason it would be adequate for mine.
Exactness and faultlessness are not up for discussion.

The snotty old bat lives forty minutes away, it's not quite far enough for my liking; even the distance doesn't keep her from meddling in my affairs.

Turning my head to the glass, light beams in.
It actually looks like a nice day— the cast iron radiator

is mimicking the heat as my backside warms.

I'd forgotten how much I enjoy the warmth.

Maybe I should take a holiday, finally relax in the sun and glory in some peace.

Then again, what is a holiday? Do I even know how to relax? Would I travel alone?

No doubt my mother would have something to say about that.

Taking another sip of tea, it's taste has turned bitter and floral— and rather cold.

Eurgh, it'll just have to do, and no is the answer, I couldn't go alone.

Edinburgh might be a shithole, but at least it's home.

Breaking my daydream, James burst through the heavy wooden door, flamboyantly skipping to the tune of Dorothy on the yellow brick road.

I won't tell him it made me jump— he'd use that to a future advantage; the teacup quivers aggressively as I try to steady my hands. Meanwhile the coat dangling from the door's hook appeared possessed as the arms flailed; no doubt looking for its escape.

It failed this time.

Skinny Malinky Long Legs has stopped in his tracks, staring at me like I've got something dirty on my face. Rude.

James gives off the sickening impression that by raiding all of the bakers, he still wouldn't gain a pound.

The ash brown short back and sides are always impeccably groomed, except for his tufty little fringe— it screams effortless chaos.

His dreamy cornflower eyes contrast any room, but the

absence of crow's feet indicates at least five milligrams too much Botox.

A good-looking guy… if you're into that sort of thing.

Fashion follows James, it wouldn't matter if he dressed in a clown suit or a hospital gown, it just always works.

His confidence, well, that never falls short, if self-assurance was an Olympic sport, there wouldn't be enough room in his flat for all of the gold medals.

The string bean has opted for a navy two-piece with a white shirt and baby pink tie.

Very professional— it's just a shame his mouth's about to open and ruin it.

Holding his phone at arms-length, James looks more like a King's Knight ready to defend the castle.

Either that or he's about to cut my head off at the shoulders.

Tempting for us both I'd imagine.

The bloodhound's snout has lifted, drawing in a deep breath, his lips are curling in disgust.

'Paisley, sweetie, I've found her! The perfect answer to your… erm… internal affairs.'

Standing on his tippy-toes with balled fists against his crotch, he looks like a camp baseball player ready to take a swing.

His sadistic smirk is curdling the blood in my veins.

'James, not now. I'm sorry but I'm really busy, I'm waiting on Mr. Stewart; we need to discuss the adjustments to his divorce settlement.'

'Exactly sweetie, and that is precisely why you need a distraction. Mr. Whatshisface is already late, if you don't get a move on, you'll be behind time too.' He tapped his watch for effect.

With the tapping finger and a perfectly plucked arch, he pointed.

'Tea?'

'Yes, lemon and ginger. I'm sorry, what am I going to be late for?'

I let out a slurp— my mother would have freaked.

'Darling, I've signed you up to a pub crawl. Yes, with me.' He rested the hand flamboyantly against his chest.

'Edinburgh Gin Trail, it's a networking extravaganza with unrestricted alcoholic beverages. Won't that be nice? Don't worry, I've paid the admission, this one's on me. I'm treating you sweetie, you deserve it.

It will be excellent for socialising and possibly a bit more, if you'll allow yourself to indulge.'

'I won't be indulging in anything; I can tell you that right now, free of charge.'

James grinned, indicating he'd been holding this horrendous secret all month.

Nope, it won't be happening.

'All right, good,' he agreed with himself, probably without even realising. Tit.

'It's tomorrow night at six o'clock, I need you to dress up and look fantastic.'

Two very effeminate arms bounced in the air.

I couldn't decide on an emotion, so I remained still.

'Darling, I'll meet you at The Royal Mile Tavern at five, we can take it from there… Oh and news break, I'm bringing my newest man Paul!

You can finally meet him, I'm so excited for that!'

Tapping my fingers against the cup, I watched the tea leaves swim.

Oh, good God, no. I don't want to meet the newest shooting in piece. That boy goes through men faster than I change my knickers…

Mind you, I'm impressed one of us is taking them off.

'A pub crawl? No, James… No. I will be going home, getting cosy on my chaise and relaxing with a good book… Oh and a very, very large glass of red!'

I shook my head as he folded his arms.

'I don't do drive-by drinking James, nor do I go on online dates or blind dates, no dates at all, you know that…'

Tinkering with the chair's settings, I raised the arm rest. My teacup still haphazardly resting in one hand.

'…Especially when they've been set up by the biggest gay in the city, and let's be honest, James, you don't manage to hold a partner down any longer than I do.'

Swivelling around on the chair, I turned to face his slimy smirk.

'My mother would have a stroke if she found out I was out on the lash, foremost on a school night. It won't be happening. No! I'm sorry James, that's my final answer.' I concluded with conviction.

His hips swung as he rapidly approached— The boyish face unfazed.

I wish I could tell you mine stayed the same.

'Bollocks! You tell Mama Campbell she needs to liven up.

Anyway, you're almost forty for God's sake…,' he was batting an invisible fly.

'You know, on second thoughts, maybe we should take your mother too.

Now wouldn't *that* be interesting?' James's face lit up.

'Oh, dear God. What the hell did you put in your porridge this morning, James?'

My face crumpled, probably matching the one he'd provided when asking about the tea.

'I'm joshing! Anyway, darling, I choose not to keep them... This one is gorgeous!

I'm trying to get him to agree to a ménage à trois, I can't tell if it's working. Maybe you could help persuade him?'

No words were required to describe the disgust carved onto my face.

Aye, that'll be right. I can't get one person, and he needs two... Greedy bastard.

I placed the teacup down, twisting the handle to face me, nails tapping against the china.

A distraught attempt of implying I wasn't interested.

'Back to the subject, this isn't just any pub crawl, darling. It's curated!

Think artisanal gin, French champagne, and eligible spinsters all ready and waiting *just-for-you*.

I've even arranged for you to be matched up with...' he paused, and my heart sank.

'...Wait for it... a surgeon!'

He did surprise me, I can't lie.

My guise possibly let me down.

'A surgeon?' I asked with a droll tone.

With the theatrics of a noddy dog, James beamed.

Hmm, that might actually appeal to my mother, heaven knows she still couldn't accept her flawed queer daughter.

Twenty years and it still hurt, not that I'm even slightly

bitter about the fact.

Suddenly remembering about the headache, I re-circled my temples; harder and faster than before.

'Does she do brain transplants?' I quipped.

'Auchh,' James feigned an exaggerated look of shock — as though he'd just witnessed a hedgehog standing on its hind legs playing the bagpipes.

Thoughts of steering through tourist-filled pubs, dodging spilt drinks and spewings splattered up walls filled me with dread.

Incorporating a blind date into the mix drove an anxiety induced panic.

My breath suddenly felt heavy and laboured— it wasn't even the good kind of panting.

'James, I do appreciate the thought, but I can't go. The partnership review is coming up in the next few weeks, I'm already bogged down with paperwork and honestly, it just isn't my thing.'

James remained uninterested; he wasn't listening.

'It's at The Royal Mile Tavern.

Darling, I've seen your dating profile; it's drier than a camel's bumhole.'

My hands immediately fell— I forced the chair backwards as I slouched.

I couldn't see it, but I'm fairly confident my face told a story my mouth needn't.

'You need to have some fun, a chance to unwind, Paisley. Maybe you could find someone blind to snuggle up with on that God-awful chaise, wouldn't that be nice?'

Wouldn't it just!

'Please. Sweetie, you're making me depressed just thinking about it. You need a night of heavy petting; your face is starting to sag.

Age, my darling isn't on your side anymore, it's time to shake this mood.' James was physically begging now; his hands clasped together and he hadn't stopped for breath.

Allowing my hands to find my temples again, I rubbed vigorously.

Oh yes, a night of heavy petting is exactly what I need… and definitely the naughty kind.

Cheeky sod— My face and chaise are perfectly adequate. Somebody lying undressed on it would be a cracking idea though. Hmm, I should work on that, try and test the theory. That *could* be fun.

Auch, I'm not going to be able to escape this, he's like a dog with a bone.

What could possibly go wrong?

'Okay, okay! You are unbelievably rude, James.'
Subconsciously I grinned— a stupid rookie mistake, even for a solicitor.

'Let's get something straight for a moment.

If I end up shackled to some butch lesbian who talks about her cat all night… and no, James that isn't an innuendo!

You pair me up with some bore who dresses like my dead great-aunt in an absolutely bogging sweater…'
My tongue poked free during my disgusted grimace.

'…my mother disowns me, or even worse, I lose my job for committing murder.

You'll be marching solo down the Mile to be hung, drawn and quartered by yours truly.'

Picking up the fountain pen, I chewed the end before pulling it free.

'I mean that wholeheartedly, James. I'm taking no shit, I'm single, not desperate.

Oh, and whilst I have your undivided attention, which admittedly is more of a challenge than the dating scene, any kind of filthy three-way will not be influenced by me!

That's a problem for you and Paul.

Personally, I'd be more than satisfied with just one-way.'

Ohh, so satisfied.

The pen made its way back between my lips.

James clapped his hands as he bobbed up and down; the leather brogues creasing at the toe.

The miserable truth that I cannot share with anyone is I am desperate. Undeniably so.

The lack of human contact is stealing my soul from within.

It's not a dirty night that I want, well, not really.

I want the full gift-wrapped package, bow included.

Maybe I'm too fussy or my standards are unattainable.

Personally, I don't think that's the case— My needs might be more refined than some, but I'm not exactly shooting for the stars.

Simply put, someone who is kind, smart and mentally strong would be more than enough.

I don't think I'd like anyone too commanding, or physically strong… but I guess it might be quite nice to be flung around in the throes of passion.

Yes, I could definitely appease that.

A physical attraction would also be very much

appreciated.

Christ, maybe that *is* asking too much, especially now I'm thirty-nine; surely there's someone suitable out there?

Realising the pillock is still standing, I looked back over towards him.

James's grin spread as though I'd handed him unlimited drink tokens to the city's Pink Triangle.

His feet already moving ten to the dozen towards the exit.

Placing the pen back on the desk, I noticed the black ink clarting my hands. Auch, Jesus.

'Oh, and whilst I remember, my chaise lounge is not God-awful... They don't need to be blind either, you're a right cheeky git!' I called out.

Rubbing my lips to check for pen juice, I was convinced I could taste it.

'Five o'clock, darling.' He responded before the coat flailed for a second time.

Turning in the chair, the drab grey castle shared my disgust.

Eurgh, more desperate throw-aways are now leaning in my direction.

I haven't been on a date in years, five to be exact, and that didn't end well.

Lifting my head to the timepiece, my nerves rapidly rose, still over twenty-four hours to deal with the internal meltdown.

I guess he's right, time really isn't on my side

anymore.

Perhaps a terrible, drink-induced one-nighter would be enough to keep the wolves at bay.

Chapter 3 - Isla

Nursing a well-deserved pint of Skye Gold from Uig's microbrewery, the icy hops slid down my throat, light and delicate; it was frankly needed after today's hard graft. I don't even mean a strenuous day— it was all emotional turmoil driving my loins and brain into a frenzy.

My devious needs are advancing far quicker than my ability to sustain them.

The snug but charming Isles Inn with its wood-panelled décor and dull lighting creates the perfect setting for a peaceful afternoon.

A wood burning fireplace heavily scents the air with peat smoke, whilst the hearty laughter of locals mixes warmly.

Trouble's a rare guest in the Skye pubs. More often than not, any arguments that do occur are caused by rowdy tourists— mostly young Europeans eager to see how island life differs.

Blissfully ignorant of the strength stored within a whisky bottle; a couple of drams in, and the water of life starts fighting back.

Thankfully it's not one of those days, the crowd's mellow, everyone's cheerful, and there isn't a single tourist trying to argue with a barstool.

My best school friend and personal confidante, Morag,

is sat beside me; she's a whirlwind of infectious laughter and sharp wit. It's not always the appreciated kind either.

Her filthy mouth and 'take no shit' attitude has kept me going for years. I'm grateful she's stuck around.
My only true friend left on the planet... Well, aside from Granda, but I don't think we'd discuss sex and relationships. That's a bit grim.

Approaching forty with wild thick waves of mousy brown hair, it always gives the impression she's been dragged through a hedge backwards.
I don't doubt she'd enjoy that, dirty bugger.

Her deep brown eyes sparkle like lochs filled with golden heather honey; they're comforting but usually contain untold secrets and gossip.

Standing at five-foot-six with a curvaceous frame, her hugs are both warm and secure. I do enjoy a coorie every now and then... it's not sexual, simply two close friends sharing a cuddle.

There's an unmistakable strength in her stance; strong and powerful. A warning of her unspoken flair—Unless you're me, I can usually get away with murder.

Morag's freckled face blossoms in the summer sun, only for the pattern to fade back into hibernation by winter.

A proud but subtle nod to her Scottish origin is often worn in the form of tartan embellishments; today's homage is a small haggis brooch with googly eyes on her chunky oatmeal cardigan.
She's very much a traditional islander in the form of a young woman.

Morag's nursing her own bottle of dark malty stout, when I say nursing, I mean there's an inch left at the bottom.

A pointy elbow jabbed my ribs. Oww.

'Well, come on then, did you score the catch of the day?' Morag asked, her broad beaming smile showcasing a line of slightly crooked teeth.

'Honestly, Isla, ye'd think a bonnie lass like yersel would be fighting women off with a stick.'

I rolled my eyes and frowned— no words were needed.

Somehow my lack of attachment always became the main subject, and the catch of the day wasn't equivalent to a large haul of mackerel.

Morag pulled a long deliberate scoof out of her near-empty bottle.

Pfft, there's more chance of meeting a mermaid.

'Morag, you know fine well there aren't hordes of eligible women in Skye queuing for a life of fish suppers— I just can't get my hook into anyone.'

I mimicked a claw before hunching down further into the bench.

Morag whipped out her phone.

Oh aye, someone's been plotting… again.

That bloody thing doesn't see sunlight the rest of the year.

'Nonsense! Look, I've signed ye up to this dating app.

'*Highland Hearts*,' you'll be swiping left and right afore ye can say *Nessie's in town*.' Her accent made Highland sound more like heeland.

'I had absolutely nothing better to do this morning, so I thought I'd make a start on the rest of yer life.

Oh, you know me, Isla, I love to meddle.'

'Clearly. I'd worked that out myself.'

Freeing a grunt, I peeled the sticker from my bottle.

For goodness' sake, she's signing me up to more buggering dating apps, do I really look that desperate? Obviously.

I'm officially the local laughing stock, I think I'll need a lie down to get over this level of trauma.

I shook my head.

Morag looked over the phone at me, clearly enjoying the view, her lips spread to her ears.

'Nope, nae happening, Mo.'

'Auch come on, why not?'

'Nope!'

She hit me with the phone, bugger.

'Ye aren't getting out of it, nae until you tell me why.'

Oh really, aye okay. Let's play.

'Mo, the only folk I attract on those sites are a mix of fuddy-duddy women holding kittens, puppies or bearded dragons. Generally, sitting in awful living rooms or kitchens that last seen a lick of paint when God was a boy.

Leaning against a brick wall and staring stupidly into a camera are the half-naked women wearing expensive lingerie. I know you know exactly what I'm saying there.

They often resemble pigeons that have flown into a closed window; their enormous lips squashed together in some daft pout. That's nae attractive, it's repulsive. I couldnae date that!'

'A pigeon? Hah!'

'Or we have the women who, to be honest, resemble

30

porn stars. Their boobs clumsily hang out of skimpy leisure wear, whilst the owner of said breasts sits on their knees in golden sand dunes surrounded by glistening seawater.

I know, before you say it, being on your knees isnae a bad thing, but really? I mean really?'

I stopped mid flow to see the reaction— it was fully engrossed and giggling.

'Auch, Isla.'

'No. Wait, there's more.

The men are on the opposite end of the spectrum with Glencoe or highland moors as their backdrop.

Dressed in ill-fitting kilts and stood in some irksome stance, it only accentuates the fact their balls don't fit between their legs. Eww.

Morag, it's jist wrong!

They find it incomprehensible that I'm nae interested.

Can you imagine such a nightmare? A woman who doesn't want a man, Jesus wept!

Need I continue?'

Morag nodded with amusement.

'The last twelve apps you've set me up on, have all had the same manky brand of mutant. I'm so tired of trawling, Morag… off the water, it's disgusting.'

Not leaving much room for an argument, I let free a huff and shifted awkwardly.

Unusual as it was, Morag was staring at me in silence.

'Look Mo, I'm grateful for the push, really I am, but I'd rather knit fog than go back to online dating; it's just nae for me, I can dilly-dally elsewhere— Anyway, Granda needs me.'

Absent-mindedly fiddling with the stainless-steel saltshaker, Morag's face remained unfazed.

'Auch, awa' an bile yer heid, Isla, I swear this one's different. I'm sick o' hearing about you being lonely.
Except yer age, I hivnae added anything else, I'm sure you'll be able to manage that, yer a big girl!
There's a profile match on there already, that ein looks quite unique, it even has a picture of a heilan coo, I mean can you get any more Scottish than a hairy coo? Personally, I'd start there.'

Morag let out an enthusiastic giggle; loud enough to catch the attention of a man walking past.
He looked over in distaste, presumably under the impression we watched him stumble over the lip dividing the wood and natural stone. We did.

Internally I was howling, but I refrained from letting out a cheer or whistle— I have my own problems.

And what the hell am I supposed to do with a cow? Mind you at this point, a shaggy coo might be the best offer I get.

'Auch, Morag you're such a dafty, my heid is mince!' My arms raised above my head in a defensive surrender.

'Fine. This is the last app. I mean it. Show me how to work the bloody thing.
But let me tell you, if anyone uses the word *bampot*, I'm throwing you into the nearest loch.'

'Isla, just gie it a shot, you never know.'

Paisley

Begrudgingly counting down the hours to James's slapdash attempt at shacking me up, my hands trembled against my forehead.

The thought of tomorrow's impending nightmare already creating a silent apprehension.

My love life's a shambles; everyone can see it, yet the thought of sitting down and having an in-depth conversation with a stranger doesn't fill me with enthusiasm.

A small knock sounded from the door, it's Sharon Silverton— one of the newer members of the legal team.

Popping her head inside, she's giving me a smile that could bounce satellite signals to Mars.

Oft. Hello, Sharon.

This woman is the definition of temptation; letting my hands fall to my knees, I kept them out of the cougars sight.

I provided a polite, non-committal smile; it died away quickly.

Sharon's been working at the Campbell and Cambell office for a whole three months.

The way she struts through the hall, you'd think she personally built the place using gold bricks and platinum filler.

'Hello, Paisley.'

Her husky and sultry voice often sounds like one of those people on the answering end of a telephone sex line.

Not that I've called any… Is that still a thing?

'I was told the best senior solicitor in Edinburgh could be found here, I'd forgotten you were so drop-dead gorgeous.' Her eyes glow as if filled with ten thousand AAA batteries, the unbroken contact is both intimidating and sexy.

I can't stop staring, it feels sinful.

Yip, you've found me, Sharon. Now, tell me I'm naughty and spank me with the bible.

Sharon's holding gaze is burning both upstairs and down.

Okay, that's quite enough, you're making me feel like this morning's breakfast… and you probably drenched that in ketchup before licking your fingers.

Saucy bitch.

My stomach's started doing little involuntary somersaults and my lungs are tight. Not good.

Flaunting a stylish blonde pixie cut, Sharon's porcelain face should belong on one of my mother's finest teapots.

Her long, slender legs could probably reach the moon and despite hitting forty-two, her flawless face gives the appearance of around thirty-five.

Impressive, I must say.

'Thank you, Sharon.

What do I owe this pleasure?' I eventually asked.

Or what kind of pleasure would you like to inflict on me? Is the question I really want to know.

I think I could guess, but workplace romances never end well; especially when the office wildcat would tease and torment before devouring me whole.

I know I'm desperate, but Sharon… hmm, well that smells like trouble, and professionally I'd like to keep my nose clean.

My foot's drumming the table leg.

Fingers fidgeting against my knee whilst heat rapidly skulks into my cheeks.

There's far too much steam in here for one afternoon, and I've still got a pile of paperwork I need to get finished.

The conversation isn't flowing as quickly as I'd like, but I can't open my mouth to push it on.

'Hmmm,' is all that Sharon fills the gap with.

No words spoken, but it was more than enough to make the air feel heavy.

Dangerously, I surveyed the chessboard mini-skirt. She's paired it with a black, tight-fitting, turtle-neck top and boots; patent noir, heeled, and very tightly laced… Damn.

I bet they'd look great sticking out the end of my bed.

Sharon oozes alluring style; it seems appropriate enough for a solicitor's office, but also perfectly adequate for the bedroom.

I wonder who she dresses for.

Oh shit, she's on the move and heading my way with her filthy little swagger.

I need to stand up, remain tactical.

My jelly legs are non-compliant.

Instead, I sit like a rag doll whilst my leer follows every movement— especially the swishing skirt.

Oooh, Jesus.

Standing in front of me, Sharon runs a manicured finger very gradually along the desks beaded edge.

My neck hairs stand on end as I sit watching like a creep in the corner.

Conveniently sitting down on the seat for my clients, she's crossing her moon landing legs. Fuck!

'I'm sorry to disturb you, I can see you are very, very busy.' Sharon spoke, with a menacing amount of effort.

I'm not, disturb me for as long as you like.

'Paisley, I just wondered...' the tone alone signifying a test, '...if you could point me in the direction of some professional development opportunities.'

Yes, old worn-out spinster, ready and waiting to help you with any personal development you need assistance with.

Her thighs are delectable, unclad and very athletically defined. I'm pretty confident they'd also look superb at the base of my duvet.

I don't doubt she'd enjoy remaining at that end.

'I mean, you have been here for... what, fourteen or so years, so who better to ask?'

I believe Sharon's lips are moving, I can hear the articulation, but I'm trapped on the pins.

The skin looks unnaturally soft and tanned— the places I could wrap those...

Embarrassingly I can't remember the statement she just

spoke. My breathing feels weak and deficient… at least my foot's stopped bouncing.

A jazz band's ringing out provocative tunes between my ears.

Wait, it's my turn to speak.

Oh God, what did she ask?

I can almost see her underwear.

Ohh no, this isn't good.

Concentrate on her face, Paisley.

Show her you're not a total imbecile.

Sharon's legs parted ever so slightly— maybe she's trying to give me a hint; either it's my move, or I'm getting the option to admire more…

Christ, you're a pervert, get your eyes up, Paisley. For God's sake, move your bloody eyes back up above the neck!

A few seconds later, I finally managed to drag my pupils into a glare, now very much on Sharon's face. Oh, well done! You're an absolute mess, a hot sweaty disaster…get out of here… go on…she can see right through you now.

The honey trap's still grinning, it's depressingly gorgeous.

Sharon knows how to work a room, that's a fact.

Standing up from the Herman, I tackled the window. Fixed on the castle for a moment, I attempt to cool my fire filled cheeks with the fresh air.

Awkwardly I turned back to the Cheshire Cat.

'Uhhh, I'm sorry.

My mind went off on a tangent; I was miles away thinking about a meeting I have this week.' Liar.

'Oh no, you're fine. If you're really busy, Paisley, I could just come back later.'

Sharon made it sound like an enticing threat rather than an enquiry.

My facade left employment, the muscles no longer contracting as I stared at the teapot.

Clearing my throat, I moved a hand to my forehead.

'Umm, yes please. I'll look into some of the courses and mentoring schemes we have and I'll send them over to you as soon as possible.

Apologies, Sharon, I have a lot on my plate.'

The steam rising from my blouse must be visible from Aberdeen; trying for the authoritative stance I placed my hands on my hips.

Honestly, I'm confident I'd long since surpassed the stage of looking professional.

Sharon stood up, a playful smile and a tormenting set of optics eyeing me from head to toe.

'I'll look forward to seeing what you offer me. I'm available whenever you need.'

Sauntering just as impressively back out the door, it click shut.

'Christ,' I whispered.

Puffing out a long deep breath, and allowing my hands to claw at my face, my breathing was finally returning to its normal rhythm.

Moving back around to the castle, I yanked the window's handle harder— debating whether or not to throw myself onto Princes Street, or take a minute to celebrate the breeze.

Chapter 4 - Isla

The side light perched on my bedside table casts out a bright yellowish hue; basking the bed in a warm cozy glow— despite the frosty exterior.

My only companion is the dark shadow that's rudely dulling the light-wood furniture.

The crisp white duvet tucked around my waist looks grey and depressing.

My remote haven is turning more forbidden with each passing second.

Silence and solitude once sold me on Bramble Brae, but now it's just a disapproving reminder of how lost I've become.

After my third year of trawling, I purchased the bungalow. Spectacular views of the eastern peninsula drew me in, as well as the lack of neighbours and a road that leads to nowhere.

The gravel doesn't churn very often; the only time I see dust rising is when the odd tourist takes a wrong turn.

Usually, they're looking for the Man of Storr rock formation. They can't get to it from here, but I have a secret spot I enjoy visiting— when I can be bothered with the hike.

My one-bedroom home allows my mind to wander, whilst the vast open space surrounding it gives me the freedom to reflect and appreciate the outdoors; it's inside, that's the dilemma.

Replicating my spirit, the emptiness and restricted space longs for the attention of another.

I can't see that happening anytime soon.

Picking up my phone, there's already a barrage of notifications filling the screen.

Three dating suggestions and one text message from Morag saying she was home and waiting with bated breath for a love-hunt update.

'Humph, nae happening and you're not getting a response either, yer nae doubt in bed or running around like a headless chicken.'

Morag has a tendency to over prepare.

The campsite she works at opens in April— it wouldn't be unlike her to be printing pages or filling in diaries just now. Not my idea of fun!

Holding my breath and jabbing a thumb on the screen, the Highland Hearts app opened with some kooky fairground music.

'Great, like I need any more encouragement to join the circus.'

Scrolling down to the *My Messages* button; my first two matches made an appearance.

'Oh Jesus, why am I doing this to myself?'

Tidy Young Lady Looking For Love— 38, Female, Laura— Isle of Lewis.

The photo's of a slim middle-aged woman with greasy grey hair— it looks like it's been blow-dried using a northeast wind.

Prominent buck teeth at the front with two large gaps at

the back of her mouth, presumably from the time her molars had made the joint decision to move out.

Laura's donned a sunflower yellow cardigan with an eye-burning, purple vest underneath.
Gold-hoops dangle at least three inches below the lobes.

The photo's background isn't doing Laura any favours.
Proudly displayed for the dating world to see is a kitchen so disastrously untidy, it's making a war zone look like a wellness retreat.

Cabinet doors hang wide open, they reveal condiments that would be old enough to qualify for an old age pension.

Empty bottles litter the counters like an alcoholic Jenga set, and if I look close enough, I think I'd probably spot a feral cat running a brothel in the basement.

It looks more like a grotesque game of Where's Wally— Except, Wally had clearly packed up and ran for the hills when Laura moved in.

'Friggin hell, definitely nae a viable option.'

The second photo Laura had posted, again, didn't help with her 'still single' situation; it may have been worse than the first.

Imagine Luciano Pavarotti surfing into the living room atop a raging bull, only for them both to be swallowed by a landslide of clutter.

'Jesus Christ, I bet that's bloody stinking.
Yuk, I'm really hoping that photo wasn't planned, why would you even use that as a dating enticement?
Nope, she's nae getting near me, I'd rather tie myself to

the Ceilidh's anchor.
Oh God, my poor eyes.'
Closing the profile, I clicked the next one.
It's not looking much better, but at least the background isn't completely minging.

Fancy a walk on the wild side— 40, Female, Seb—
Inverness.

A short sunglasses-wearing butch woman with a peroxide blonde wolf cut glowered back at me.
To be fair, she probably had a decent enough figure, if it could be seen underneath what looked like a men's XXL brown tweed suit.
   'Come on, Isla, it's nae all about their looks,'
I don't plan on being negative, but the reality isn't doing much for me— I scrolled down anyway, you never know… well, I do… but still…

'Looking for my new stay-at-home wife and/or sugga mummy, someone to treet me gud and make my tea.'

That'll be right, you canna even spell.

'Must like animals. I've got 2 budgees named Bubble n Squeak, a labradoodle named George and 2 cats named after my favourite L Word caracters Alice and Dana. I enjoy walks with George and escape rooms. Not interested in any gold diggin bitches looking for a hot n heavy night of sexual diveance.'

Unintentionally I gagged.
   Covering my mouth tightly with my free hand, I

didn't want to make the situation worse by vomiting on the duvet.

'For fuck's sake, imagine being locked in a room with that, jeezo. That would make anyone try and escape.'

Yet again, I closed the page.

The third match has nothing to go off of except a picture of a highland cow; no information, no age, but Px is printed in the name box.

Odd.

'This must be the profile Morag was talking about. Well, I'm not opening it, I'm confident I've seen more than enough for one night.

It's probably some other poor bugger that's been set up to fail by their overzealous best friend— Either that, or they're completely inept in the education department. Probably unable to work out what their name is, or how to put it into this stupid bloody thing.

Morag's really outdone herself this time.

Wait 'til I see her.'

Closing the app, I threw my phone down onto the empty pillow, turned off the light and yanked the duvet over my head.

Usually, I feel calm and relaxed when sprawling, but tonight feels different.

Reaching over to the vacant side, I touched the glacial cotton between my fingers before slowly moving them up to the surplus pillow— a starvation finding my stomach.

One day, someone will clamber in beside me and steal my heart. If I'm lucky, they might even fill this opening permanently.

My bed has remained vacant for too long, besides myself, no other being has ever lain below this luxurious duvet. Not because I'm frigid, that's nae the case, and I have been intimate, just not in a romantic capacity.

I guess I've created a monster.

An undernourished, un-cherished creature that wants for nothing more than hearts and flowers. Someone who can join me on fishing trips but still allow me the freedom to be my own captain.

For too many years I've protected my ticker; avoided stirring trouble with my family.

Well, I say my family, what I mean is my parents, that and the worry of bringing shame to my grandparents' door.

The thought of causing upset to my mum and dad once bothered me; they couldn't accept me for who I was, in fact, they couldn't even welcome my birth.

My grandparents remained gracious, doting on me through the years, valuing me just the way I am...

I'd never want to bring embarrassment to them.

Closing my eyes in preparation for the drifting rest, my head spins with thoughts of buck-toothed women drowning in oversized suits.

I tightened my lids; it's a miserable ambition to slow the dizzying world with notions of stags wandering the hills, bunnies jumping in the garden grass.

My cosy home shared with a beautiful woman.

We're both curled up on the sofa, reading books to one another with an open bottle of wine, maybe two.

The peaty log fire crackling light into the darkness,

scents of burning wood filling the air while the remaining embers slowly die.

All smiles and laughter lining the atmosphere as we relax comfortably into the other.

Well, we can only dream.

'Tomorrow will be different. Brighter. I promise.'

It's a promise I make every night, but with each fresh dawn, there's a painful realisation that this tomorrow maybe isn't the right one.

Chapter 5 - Paisley

The poky pub is crammed; the smell of stale ale and dirty smoke from the fire in the middle of the room is positively stinking.

My feet are sticking to the wooden floor, no doubt caused by the overflowing drinks and crumbs from lunchtime meals.

The place is a constant hum of noise, mostly chatter from punters enjoying a wind-down, maybe they've had a long hard day at work too… Surely not as dreadful as my two days of suffering.

Looking over to the bar, there's a few drunk sods who must have started drinking at ten yesterday morning. Shouting at their buddies over the din… a couple are swaying precariously on their stools, one's admiring the dregs at the bottom of his pint glass.

I spotted James on the far side; a large stained-glass window of Greyfriars Bobby shining down behind him. Almost angelic in the moment… Oh no, cancel that he's made eye contact.

'Lady Campbell, your throne awaits you.' James screeched, his arm gesturing with an overly exaggerated sweep to an open seat covered with handbags and jackets.

He's dressed in a smart-casual outfit; a pair of dark denim jeans with a folded seam, mahogany brown wallabees and a light blue polo shirt.

It's buttoned up to the very last hole under his chin.

I wonder if one more button would be enough to shut him up.

Oh Christ, the whole bloody pub is now staring, the volume has dropped to zero and James is curtsying like a prized pillock.

Great, my face must match my burgundy blouse, and the stifling heat isn't going to cool that down.

I knew I should have dressed more casually, I think I'm the only one who's made any kind of effort.

There are six sets of eyes crawling over me, watching my every move as I shift towards the table.

Squeezing into the small gap between James and a dumpy little blonde, I positioned myself in the booth. The portly woman kindly shifted the chairs contents; that gained me a tiny bit more space, and she gained a pathetic, half-arsed smile.

They're still gawking, I'm not sure why. Do I have something stuck on my face?

I nodded to them one by one, I don't know why; it felt less effort than opening my mouth.

Oh, now I see it there's a piece of white lint on my coat. Pulling it off and down to the floor, I rubbed my fingers…

Nope, they're still looking.

Maybe they're already pissed.

Clearly the party's already indulged in a beverage or two; empty glasses are dotted around the table— it's giving the impression they've partaken in some kind of satanic ritual.

'My God, darling, for someone who thrives on

punctuality, you do go out of your way to never arrive on time,' James scolded.

'Have you ever tried to get a taxi in this city? It's an absolute shambles…yo…'
He cut me off mid-sentence.

'Okay, okay, I'll let you off this one time, let me introduce everyone.'

James jumped from his seat as if sitting against a prickly thistle, spaghetti arms waving frantically. Nothing new there I suppose.

'This here darling is Michael and Martin. Michael works at the Starbucks down on Leith Walk, and Martin works in Morningside Primary as an auxiliary assistant. They've been together forever.' His arms now reaching for the sky.
I forced yet another humble smile.

'Hello,' I muttered with a nod.
Next to Martin is Amber, an older woman with a tight grey ponytail, she's dressed in a lumberjack-style green check jacket and black jeans.
Both look far too big and I can't help but wonder if she has a Harley Davidson parked outside.

'What is it you do?' I asked.
Jesus, please don't be the surgeon. I'd hate to think you're hacking at somebody's head with a wood axe.

'Ah, a work down at the Tesco, in Oxgangs, do ye know it?' Amber responded in a broad Edinburgh accent — it wasn't the posh kind.
I nodded, maybe too enthusiastically.
Oxgangs isn't really the type of place you wander alone at night… or the daytime for that matter.

Thank Christ.

'Darling, this is my Paul. Isn't he gorgeous?' James shrieked before grabbing Paul's muscular forearm and giving the bicep an excited squeeze.

Well, I have to admit Paul is a good-looking guy.

His hair is well-groomed, dark brown and neat around the sides, a thinning layer with a tousled texture sitting cleanly on top.

The black t-shirt looks as though it's been designed three sizes too small, the muscles are bulging out of the sleeves, whilst the skinny jeans don't leave much to the imagination.

Note to self, ask James how it feels to be slammed on the floor by a man who wrestles grizzly bears for fun.

Paul's smooth chiselled jaw gives his face a light pretty-boy facade, but it doesn't quite match the rest of him. Still handsome, but in a more unconventional way.

He's clearly worked on his appearance for quite some time before attending this evening's masquerade; his body gives off Johnny Bravo vibes, but the head is like something you'd find illustrated on the side of a Fairy Liquid bottle— An interesting concoction indeed.

'Aye, he sure is.' It was the best I could do whilst studying.

'I'm a model for the Gay Times Magazine,' Paul jumped in; his Maryhill Glaswegian accent carrying across the room.

'Oh, how lovely for you.'

Well at least he has a job, if you consider tearing your clothes off for a poofs parade a career.

Luckily, James didn't seem to pick up the hint of sarcasm, no doubt the ménage a trois' was still floating around in his brain.

Degenerate.

Paul sat enthusiastically nodding like a golden retriever waiting on a biscuit— his hand tightly bound in James's.

Shit. That means the crumpled woman beside me is the surgeon.

Well, that's not going to happen, not now, not ever.

That was instant karma.

I looked towards the door— it's still swinging with newcomers.

I've not yet removed my coat, could I reach it before this evening gets out of hand?

'Hiya, can I get anyone a drink? Maybe a couple of shots to kick-start your evening.' The barmaid belted out over the noise, she'd just waltzed over and so far, that was the best offer I'd received.

'A double Hendricks, extra cucumber and no ice please.' I shouted over.

'Aye nae bother, anyone else needing a wee top up?' She spoke again.

I wonder if she's free, hmm, maybe a bit on the young side.

No one else was ordering, in fact, they weren't even paying attention, too busy with the micro conversation regarding a drag queen's breastplate.

I shook my head.

'Aye no worries, I'll be back with your gin in five…'

'Thanks, can you add on two shots of tequila as well, please?' I called out over the racket again— it garnered me a very wide grin.

Definitely pretty, a good smile too. Probably straight.

'In fact, if you could just keep them coming until you're not allowed to serve me anymore, that would be fantastic. Just open a tab and stick them on there.

Don't worry, I won't leave without paying and I'll add a tip.'

At the very least I'd need something strong to handle this rowdy bunch of rejects.

The barmaid's beam grew wider as she gave me a saucy wink.

Hmm, maybe not *that* straight.

Disappearing into the crowd, my head inconspicuously followed her tail end.

In my peripheral, I could see James's brow lift questionably.

'Darling, I didn't get a chance to introduce you to…'

I turned my head back as a dumpy hand was thrust into mine. Giving it a shake, I felt oddly exploited.

'Hiya, I'm Beth, and oh, can I say, I absolutely love your outfit, so classy and stylish. Those black trousers give you a great arse, and I love your stilettos. Stunning!

I'm a surgeon at the Sick Kids' Hospital…'

No chance of that brain transplant then, and please leave my bum out of your thoughts.

'…And… I have just heard so much about you.' Beth stated— Her heavy hand slapped down on my knee.

Ouch.

'James has told me so much about you, a solicitor eh, ohh what a great job. Good for you gal.

It must be sooo stressful and high-paced.

You must have a right big brain in that head of yours.'

The hand crept further up my leg... Absolutely not!

My eyes locked onto Beth's questionably horrific fluffy grey sweatshirt, a pair of very ill-placed blue tits resting on the chest.

I wasn't sure if James had specifically told her to wear it or if this was just Beth's idea of fashion.

Either way, it's giving me the heebie-jeebies and there's no amount of tequila that could equate to such a poor choice.

The barmaid reappeared, a glimmer in her eyes as she handed over the G&T.

Two rather large shot glasses found the free space in front of me— along with a saltshaker and a couple of lime slices.

'Enjoy your tipple.' She spoke again.

'Thanks! Wish me luck.' I replied with a smile.

Beth's glare was uncanny and creepy as she scrutinised my every move.

Lifting the small glass, I threw it back, the second following quickly behind.

The agave burnt my throat— it was still less painful than looking at that damn sweater. It hung awkwardly on her rounded frame, partially riding up towards the belly button, patches of missing fluff on the sleeves made it look like a skinned cat.

Realising I still hadn't responded to Beth, I gave out a feeble smile.

That's a little bit rude, even for me.

'Thank you, and sorry, Beth, I'm Paisley.'

Her ever-expanding grin gave out the impression she had the winning numbers to last night's lottery.

Moving my leg towards James and politely removing Beth's hand from the top of my thigh, I tried to join the conversation on gay-bar strip lighting. Not something I nor Beth seemed to be overly concerned with, but apparently, it's a big thing. Who knew?

'I love being a surgeon, but a solicitor. Oochh, that must be something else.
What kind of soliciting do you do?' Beth asked with wide eyes.
James glared in disbelief.
Paul freed a grunt before checking his phone.

'Darling, soliciting is the job of a common prostitute. I doubt very much if Paisley partakes in any of that.' James replied— his tone frank and sardonic.
For once he was on my team. Unfortunately, I couldn't get the straw dislodged in time to thank him.

'Ohh, I'm sorry. Well never mind then, what do you like to do for fun, Paisley?' Beth asked.
Martin and Michael were now engrossed in the topic— they both stared in anticipation.

I pulled the straw free and placed the glass down, twisting it until the paper pipe faced me.

'Uhm, well, I suppose I like to read.' I answered dryly.
Beth shrugged and took a gulp from her almost empty pint glass before her verbal diarrhoea spilled out across the table— it continued that way for most of the evening.

A couple of drinks in and Beth admittedly was getting better looking. Her dirty blonde hair hung loose in a ponytail, strays caught around elfish ears and a smile so wide, I couldn't help but picture it peeking out the sides of her surgical mask.

She was a slightly heavier woman, plenty of snack handles to hold her down with.

I've nothing against a well-padded lady but this one really doesn't fit my style.

'You really are very pretty, Paisley, but you do have a stern stare.

Do you straighten your hair, it's flawless?'

Beth must have been feeling the benefits of her eighth pint, her chunky fingers fiddled with the hair resting on my shoulders.

'Thanks, I think, and no, it's naturally straight.

At least one part of me is, I guess.' A hint of disappointment leaching through my own reply.

'Darling, she's a purebred.

Shame it's a purebred cow… Only the finest genes for Lady Campbell, not even money could buy you the natural beauty that's been bestowed upon her.' James taunted— No doubt trying to be funny as the prosecco abused him.

'Fuck off, James. You're a twat.'

My retort was probably a bit harsh, but the sixth tequila was holding my tongue hostage.

I cocked my head to the side, watching Beth as the binge started to take effect.

You know, I could probably work with that… If the drink made more of an effort, and the sweater somehow caught fire by a straying cigarette.

A few more drinks, and I might be able to perform at least to the level of a mildly competent human being, but would I be the only one performing?

Christ don't go there, Paisley, you really don't want to know. Could you imagine waking up next to that? Eurgh.

I looked at my phone… for the twelfth time.
The night's dragging and hell's not a fast-paced environment. It's still not even nine.

The pub crawl never went ahead, honestly, I think it was just a ploy to get me out of the house.
James neither confirmed nor denied.

We sat in the same spot for hours, each of us taking turns to try and outdo the other by exaggerating our best qualities and why they were single, well, except the ones who weren't.
I didn't respond, I allowed James to update the table on my lack of qualifications and inability to hold a woman down.

Depressingly, the discussion turned to our hopes and dreams for the future; before doing a full three-sixty— How many marshmallows could be rammed into your throat before you began to gag.
As someone who doesn't attend parties, I didn't have an answer.

Interestingly enough, the men at the table could manage considerably more sugary delights than the women.
Dirty little buggers.

My head filled with all sorts of disgusting images, but I was mostly upset that I didn't get to find out about James and Paul's marshmallow packing abilities!

They quietly sought out each other's most deep and dark secrets. Secrets so heavy, their lips remained locked all night.

Shame, I could have exploited that information later.

The tidy little bar lady reappeared, more Dutch courage strategically placed in front of my chest, a bag of steak and onion crisps along with it.

I crunched my way through them whilst playing a little game of: *how not to let your glass be empty whilst trying to escape HMP Barlinnie.*

Stealing tactical sips, I monitored the droning drivel filling my left ear.

Beth had 'accidentally' fallen into my lap at least three times in the last thirty minutes.

Looking down at the podgy eyes filling my personal space, I couldn't help but glower a disapproving frown.

'Paisleeeyy, do you want to come back to my place? Ohh, you really are very bonnie… I could show you a really enjoyable time.' Beth screeched in a high-pitched whine.

Like hell, I'm not that pissed.

I could feel James's elbow meeting my ribs in delight.

'No, thank you, Beth. I'm not really a one-night stand kind of person. Sorry.' I replied politely.

'It might loosen off that glower, you're very serious. I mean in a hot, attractive kind of way.'

'Thank you, I think, but honestly, I'm… I'm good. I'm probably going to head soon anyway; I have work tomorrow.' The polite approach wasn't working.

'Why don't we escape this misery and go somewhere quieter then? I could make you breakfast in the morning.'

Beth's words were a bit of a slur, I was doubtful she'd

make it home, let alone perform her over keen duty.

I shook my head, still trying inconceivably hard not to be the bitch I knew I was about to be.

Amber was intently watching the two of us.

James's face had turned to worry as my leg twitched in his direction.

Heat was rising through my cheeks, my heart hammering against my chest.

'Beth, I'm nae sure Paisley's after yer body, love.' Amber cut in.

Thank Christ someone did.

'Ohhh, come on, Paisley.

Let's go somewhere quiet?'

'No, Beth.

The mortuary's closed for the evening.

That's the only suitable place I'd like to be taking you right now.'

Oops.

Amber must have left a wet soggy ring on the cushioned bar bench; she howled like a hyena as hops sprayed onto the table.

Michael and Martin quietly sniggered between themselves— wiping their eyes enthusiastically as hush whispers parted.

'That's a bit rude.' Beth clicked back.

My cheeks flushed as I saw red; James's hand came out to my forearm.

'Darling, I know you're going to feel terrible...' James could obviously feel the tension growing.

'You're correct, Beth. I... I was incredibly rude.

I think having to remove your limbs from my body a handful of times, as well as telling you another five... no six, that I'm... that... I have no interest in going anywhere, would be enough.

You have subjected me to... torturous ramblings and managed to point out all of... all my parts you would like to touch or change.

Please desist. I'm not a toy.'

Unfortunately, the tequila hadn't allowed that to be quite as sleek as I'd hoped, but Beth backed off.

At nine o'clock, I made some excuses and swiftly exited the bar.

After four attempts, my lighter finally gave in; lighting the Marlboro, the flame danced in the breeze.

Swaying vigorously and wobbling as the door swung open and closed behind, I watched the stream of drunks passing by.

Taking a long, heavy, drag on the butt of my cigarette sent the ash into a glowing red frenzy.

'Wayyy too much tequila.'

My feet did a little two step as a mass of grey toxic reek met the dark sky.

An Insignia pulled up as I stubbed the cigarette into the overflowing bin.

Narrowly avoiding the ancient cobbles, my heels danced to the Epsom Reel before I gracefully clambered into the back seat.

'Get, in, fuck, get in the car...' My legs wouldn't cross the threshold.

'Take me home, please, Mr. Taxi.'

The voice from my mouth sounded foamy and uncharacteristic.

The driver's lips curled his moustache; the cheery gits obviously had a better night than I have.

A nod from the mirror.

'Aye, I'll just tell you now, if you're sick in the car I'll be adding ninety pounds to your bill.' Mr. Taxi said.

'It's okay, I finished my crips…cirps…crisps inside.' I waved to him.

Crisps! You absolute moron. A perfect example of why people shouldn't drink or procreate.

Oh Jesus Christ, don't wave at him.

'Aye, and… and I said to her, *well that isn't, that's n..n..not… going to happen.* Why… why would I want pancakes? …*Pancakes!* Really!

Anyway, can I take these… bloody things off? My uhhh toes are killing.'

'Oh aye, sounds like you've had a narrow escape. Maybe next time you'll get home with the bird behind the bar.

Aye knock yerself out.'

'Auch… uh … Mr. Taxi… I'm getting too… Too old for this. I jjjust want someone good.'

'Well, hopefully that sorts itself out and you find what you're looking for.

That's us here, do you rent this place?'

'No… no it's all mine… and thanks for… not being ahh creepy… git.'

'Impressive. Well, you get in safe. Oh, and cheers for not destroying my car.'

'Goodnight!' I replied whilst clinging tightly to my shoes, bag and keys.

Haphazardly wiggling my way towards the door; the neighbour's dirty scheming topiary jumped out.

'Bastarding bush.' I shouted whilst punching the leaves from the kerb.

Successfully entering the fortress, my shoes met the floor.

The coat came next.

Slowly sliding from my shoulders, it landed with a pathetic thud.

'Stay! You're bloody stinking of alcohol and smoke,' for some reason I was screaming as if it was a dog; one that had just returned home after playing poker in an illegal casino all night.

Bouncing off every wall and door frame on my way through to the kitchen, I located a wobbly wine glass.

Pouring an extra-large slug from the already-open bottle, some of the plonk met the countertop.

'Whoopsie.'

My rings clattered from the glass, my tongue greedy in its impoverished thirst.

'Bugger...' I stomped angrily to the parquet.

My foot never made it.

'Aahh, ahhh, dirty ... bbuggering dish machine.'

The kitchen appliances are conspiring against my drunken antics.

'That's mmyy pinkie, pinkie toe!' I skirled.

Still holding the glass, the gravitational pull was overbearing.

I grasped tightly to my newly bruised digit, still unsure if I was going to remain standing or bathe the kitchen in vino.

'That was my... one...' a hiccup caused me to bounce, 'one... chance to meet someone and... a... and... I'm partnered up with a... rejects... look like they got dressed in... in... a Littlewoods catalogue... such a handsy little witch... *Fancy coming back to my...to mine*...pffft... scab...scabby cat...'

Stomping again, I made sure to keep my foot clear of the gadgets.

On the move in a two-forward ten-back kind of fashion, I fell into the chaise.

My landing was rescued by a leaking glass and yesterday's DIY guide of *Queer Life: For the Unloved.*

'Thirty... nine, and my proverb... proverbial clock has well and truly ticked its last tock,' I mumbled as hollow juniper giggles escaped.

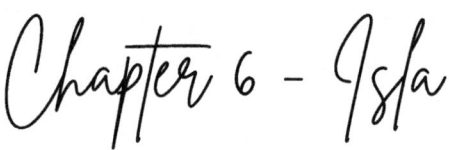 Chapter 6 - Isla

'Christ lassie, did ye hiv a hard night?
Ye look as if ye slept in the shed, oh, and I need yer help with something later on the day.' Granda grumbled, his eyes squinting into the morning sun.

You have nae idea! It was horrific, I'm going to be single forever.

'Ye need to hiv a clear heid if yer working on the trawler. Ye wouldnae want tae end up like poor Greg!'
Looking at him, I couldn't help but feel deflated.

'Aye, I know Granda. I had two pints last night at the Isle and then went home. Morag's set me up on some dating site…'

'Dinna tell me she's pushing ye in tae that crap; those internet sites are full of perverts and weirdos.' Granda crudely announced, cutting me off.

'Granda! I'm on there too!'
I don't want to admit it, but going by last night's window shopping, he's probably right.

'Those computer things are dangerous, lass, wit do ye want tae be on there fir?
Ye could always go oot tae new places and meet folk.'
Unable to look him in the eye, I turned to the water.

'There's no one here.' I whispered.

Once upon a time, Granda would have eagerly sat up front in the church, a traditional man who believed in old-fashioned morals and meeting people face to face.

Ever since he and I had *that* discussion eighteen

years ago, his face had never wavered— He never treated me any different. In fact, Granda's always pushed me to explore; he's my biggest and most encouraging fan.

Even when my parents cast me out as a child, Granda and Granny both stood by me.

My Mum and Dad— Helen & Tam, hadn't been so reliable and understanding; they couldn't comprehend this *phase* I was going through.

Despite the best efforts of my grandparents, especially Granda, my parents couldn't understand a world that wasn't black and white, but for me, that wasn't a viable option.

I live within the grey; honestly, I've been at ease with that fact for more years than I'd like to admit.

My parents manage to create this awkward, pathetic tension, an argument usually trailing closely behind.

I'd like to say it's because of my sexuality, but that would be dishonest.

They never planned on having children, I can appreciate that sentiment, but the issue lies with the fact that they did have a child. Me.

They dumped me on the two kindest souls; and that really pisses me off.

Many discussions, arguments and tantrums occurred over the years. Eventually, my loving grandparents gave up trying with them, interactions became minimal, and I cut my losses.

Granda never returned to the church either.

'Atch Isla, I'm sorry. You're the bonniest lass I've

ever seen, and I'm no jist saying that because you're ma granddaughter.' He sighed out a deep breath.

Lifting my hand he gave it a comforting pat— my features turned towards his whiskers.

'You'll meet someone who'll part the seas for ye lass, and ah'll happily invite them ower tae make them their tea. Fish fingers for three?' A booming laugh following his joke.

Half a chance would be a fine thing— A warmth prickled my neck.

'But lassie, ye need tae be realistic. Only you can decide *what* and *who* will make ye happy.

In twenty years, ye've niver once introduced me tae anyone. That makes me sad, Isla.'

Did he really just exaggerate the 'who' part of that sentence?

'Do ye want tae be fishing for the next thirty-odd years? Honestly lass, I hope ye sell this bloody boat and settle doon, sooner rather than later.'

'Granda…'

'No, Isla, you listen tae me. This boat will be yours when I'm nae here.

The hoose will go along wi' it… It wis agreed with yer granny afore she left us.'

His voice was unrelenting and serious, a most unusual characteristic.

'Yer parents dinna hiv a say in the matter. Fishing wis never in their plan, and ye know, that's alright wi' me. It's nae a job fir the weak. It takes heart, courage, and a lot o' strength.

Something you and I both hae in common,' he paused for a moment of silent consideration. 'Do ye think I'm doing this job because ah need the money, or the worry o' a family tradition going doon the spout?

Well, yer answer is no lass; I'm here every day fir you.

Who else gets tae spend every day wi' their granddaughter? I'm here, so you dinna hae to be.

You're ma family, Isla, it's ma job to see ye alright.'

'Granda…' I tried again.

'Lass, please, jist go out and hiv fun, be free, find a partner, and fir God's sake, dinna be worrying aboot me or this bloody boat.' He smiled again, but it looked tired and weary, the kind that spoke volumes without needing words.

'Granda, are you alright? I've never heard ye speaking like this, it's scaring me.'

'I love ye lass; I jist want tae see ye happy.

Yer thirty-eight and still all alone, I winna be here forever.

Ye need tae open yer eyes tae new opportunities, get oot there and live. I canna die knowing yer all by yersel.'

Oh, Granda, no. I'm not strong enough to deal with those kind of emotions today.

Saline ran down my cheeks, its warmth bittersweet against the cool wind.

I tactically moved my head back to the coastline.

'Granda… I can't survive without you.'

Turning back to look at him, my arms lined tightly around his shoulders. The action was matched.

Just two fisher folk standing in the most comfortable embrace on the pier.

'I love you so, so much old man.'

His protective dominance held my weight.

It brought back memories of being a little girl, riding out on the boat, copying every move he made, sitting on his shoulders as my small hands struggled to cling on.

'You've always kept me safe Granda; from my cruel unloving parents, the tide threatening abyss, maybe even from myself. How can I possibly go through this world without you?'

A deep numbing pain developed above my rib cage, the dull ache behind my eyes creating a migraine of depression. Without even realising, tears heavier than the planet poured onto my knitted top.

'Ye jist dae the best ye can, Isla.

Ye jist hae tae take it one slow and painful step at a time.'

Paisley

Sharon's nude body was smearing the usually empty bed, my duvet tugging lightly against her waist.

It rested delicately below her navel.

The morning sunlight peeking through the curtains bounced around the curves of her delectable stomach and chest.

Ohhh yessss, why don't I remember inviting her over?

Never mind that, what did we get up to?

'Mhmm, good morning gorgeous.' Sharon purred.

That voice, ugh, so silky and smooth, her body perfectly sculpted and chiselled by a Grecian artist.

Their phenomenal masterpiece belonged in the Louvre's private collection, open for every paying visitor to witness and enjoy.

My eyes are enjoying the feast too, eating her up in ways I could only dream of.

Oh, she's on the move— we must have had a good night, I don't even feel nervous.

Rolling over, Sharon effortlessly pinned me down between her thighs.

'Oh, good morning, Sharon.'

The soft mattress secured me in place whilst my arms were hoisted above my ears.

'Hmm, that's a bit rough for first thing, isn't it?' I murmured.

'I've heard that's how you like it.' Sharon replied, a naughty wink before she licked my neck.

I can't fight it— I don't want to.

My lungs are climbing up through my throat.

My drunken eyes can't stop staring at the busty nude—
the tantalising flesh of her breasts drawing a slever to
my lip.

'I've wanted to see what you've been hiding under
that blazer, Paisley. I'm telling you now, I'm taking
whatever I want, and you'll just need to deal with it.
Got it?'

'Take everything…' trying to move my head towards
the floating skin, I can't manoeuvre.

Her plump luscious lips curled into a seductive smile.

She's teasing and boy is it working. I can feel the shift
in my stomach— the butterflies are fluttering.

The flushness of my body has skyrocketed.

God, I'm sweating.

What is this woman doing to me?

'Paisley, stop fidgeting, or I'll need to tie you down.'

'Well, I hope so, you're very much turning me on.' I
replied with a smirk.

Leaning over, an eagerly anticipated kiss was heading
straight for me.

Oh God, yes… YES!!

A flash burst through my eyelids, stinging and biting as
a blurry bookcase came into focus.

Acid burning my tonsils; foggy brain competing with
quivering legs, all in a sorry but frantic attempt to reach
the sink.

Leaning against the worktop, my fingertips clenched
the marble sill, the metallic basin now in view.

I retched and retched as the room spun like a merry-go

ride.

Eye watering heaves burning everything, hands trembling whilst gallons of foul-smelling gut rot lined the stainless steel.

Lifting my head in an unforgivable attempt to reach the sparkling water, I guzzled like I'd been banished to the Sahara.

Greedy harsh gulps— trying to relieve the sting, the agonising pain as bubbles burst against my tonsils.

'Eurgh, my mouth tastes like a badger's arse.'

I stood for a while, waiting for my empty cramping stomach to calm.

Peering carefully at my watch, it dawned on me, I hadn't undressed last night, it was 06:15 am.

'Shit. I was dreaming, that could have been very dangerous.'

Beth and Sharon, both adulterating my drift, as an ache worse than today's hangover overcast my thoughts.

Candidly motivating my feet to the freestanding bin, I pulled the mobile phone from the handbag settled against the lid.

God knows why it was there— I must have dumped it last night.

Unlocking the screen, I scrolled rapidly through the never-ending list of dating apps; I was specifically searching for something. I just couldn't remember what.

My eyes and brain couldn't keep up, the bile silently churning away again.

I thumbed open the Highland Hearts app; God knows I've tried all of the local ones.

Singing its little nauseating tune, a notification for two potential new matches lit the screen.

'Paisley, you can't keep living like this.
You need to make some kind of change, or you're going to die alone and miserable.
Come on girl, get a grip.'
Clicking the newest notification, my fingers ran away without me.

Hello, I'm new to this!
I don't know what I'm looking for,
but I'm tired of being lonely.
Are you single?
Sent 06:34 Friday 9th Feb

I pressed send.

For the first time in my life, I've just admitted my loneliness to someone else.
A tension lifted from my back and shoulders.
Wow, well done you.
What an achievement, you already feel a bit better…
Oh no, cancel that.
Rotating round to the sink again, I gagged and heaved.

Paisley, you'd better start praying for the atonement of bad decisions and cheap booze. Idiot.
Oh, and whilst you're at it, a plea to the dating Gods might not do any harm either.

Eventually gaining enough courage to move back to the chaise, I sat down delicately, the phone gripped tightly as I looked over the profile.

She might look like one of those trolls from the

nineties with spiky blue hair, or worse, it could be Beth.

Either way, the profile has no information other than their age; I'm running blind.

'Your mother will be mortified, Paisley.

Look at the state of you… and internet dating— that's not a Campbell trait, that's common.

Hmm, it's probably best we keep this our own little secret.'

Pulling a cashmere throw from the armrest, I snuggled back down.

My steamy hallucination not yet abandoning my subconscious; the slightly tarnished embarrassment lingering on.

Reopening the phone, I text the office.

'Sick and working from home.'

Wimp.

Closing my eyes a '*buzz*' highlighted a new message. Anticipation eating into me as I rushed to read the response.

'Ahh, it's an email on the work account. Shame.'

Dear Ms. Campbell,

I am writing to request your assistance.

My current solicitor retired a couple of years back and doesn't keep good health.

I'm looking for someone to prepare and update my Last Will and Testament.

Would your establishment be able to fit me in at some point?

I found your company online; any solicitors that near my residence don't have the time or capacity.
I would like for this matter to be dealt with promptly; however, I appreciate everything can take a moment to finalise.
I look forward to your response.

Sincerely
Mr. A. MacLeod

And just like that, the day had begun.

Chapter 7 - Isla

Friday's always a good day; It's the only time I'm not needed at the dock.

Mind you, after the conversation with Granda yesterday, maybe it's not a requirement at all... well, that isnae going to happen.

Usually, Friday's the one day that gives me an option to laze around the house, not that I'm particularly guilty of that and it's a good job too— Morag's just waltzed into my kitchen.

It's only just gone nine.

'Oi, snuggle puss, are ye up?' She shouted through into the bedroom.

'Aye, I'm up,' I replied— Still drying my straying mop with a fluffy white towel.

Clearly, I'm getting no more time to sort myself out; I constructed a towel turban.

The honey eyes are ogling my attire, the tilting chin a giveaway to the questionable style.

'Dinna even say a word, Morag. I wasn't planning on leaving the house. You should be pleased I even put clothes on, I had thought about remaining in the buff, I'm nae sure you'd be impressed with that though.' I answered her unspoken statement.

I've dressed myself in a pair of dark green corduroy trousers and a brown woolly pullover. Definitely not stylish, but I hadn't expected to be facing the masses.

'I didnae say a word, Isla, but now you've mentioned it, what the hell's that on yer feet?'
I laughed before poking my toes out.

'Grey socks with hundreds of little white sheep.
I thought you'd know about socks by now, mibbe yer still living in the dark ages.' I teased with a roll of the eyes.

'Aye, it was a quick verse to avoid thinking about you in the scud... It didnae work!' Morag admitted.

'Trust me, there's nae much to think about, Mo.'
Her eyes glistened as she smiled.

'Well, what's the craic, Isla? Are you all loved up and ready to move on to better places?'

'Hah, if only you'd seen the state of my matches.
I don't think I'll be moving anywhere anytime soon.'
Morag has a way of pushing buttons, but it's a real skill to be able to do it first thing in the morning.

Moving over to where she's standing, I clicked on the kettle; the terry cotton began to slip.

'Hmm, I'll need to try something else then.
I've brought breakfast.'
Morag dumped a paper bag forcibly onto the kitchen worktop.

'Oooh, fresh pastries from the bakers, you're spoiling me!
Mibbe I'll jist need to keep you as my bidie-in, you know, instead of looking for a younger, sexier model.'
I winked and playfully slapped her bum.
Dirty bugger probably liked it.
Going by the grin, there wasn't a 'probably' about it.

'Seriously, I'm no further on, I did have a good chat with Granda yesterday though, that's something I guess.

God, I hope he lives to be a hundred and eighty, I'd be so lost without him.'

Pouring the contents of the bag onto two mismatched plates, one found Morag's chubby hand.

'That would be fantastic, Isla, but we both know that winna happen.

He'd be a right crabbit auld sod if he did.'

It was no secret, Granda wasn't getting any younger and at eighty, he was already outliving several others within his social circle.

'Right, I'll make the coffee whilst ye dry that glorious head o' hair.' Morag stated.

I freed a grateful grin, running my hand teasingly over Morag's shoulder before disappearing into the bedroom.

A '*ping*' sounded from my phone.

Fishing it out of the pocket, the notification indicating a message on Highland Hearts.

Without a moment's hesitation, I pressed open.

Hairy Coo had sent me a message.

Well, that was… unexpected.

> ### New message - Px
> *Hello, I'm new to this!*
> *I don't know what I'm looking for,*
> *but I'm tired of being lonely.*
> *Are you single?*
> *Sent 06:34 Friday 9th Feb*

'Oh. My. God.

What in the world?' Spoken far louder than I'd ever intended.

'Are ye alright?' Shouted Morag.

'Aye, I'll be five minutes,' I called back before stuffing the phone into the corduroy cavity.

Turning the hairdryer on, I balanced against the bed's edge, pondering the cryptic message whilst nonsense filled my senses.

What do I do now? Do I respond, should I ignore it? Calm down. Think rationally.

Dry your hair before anything else. No point catching your death before you've even thought about it.

Munching happily through the pastries, Morag got the full in-depth story on yesterday's outburst with Granda.

'…and just like that, you're free to do whatever you wish?'

'Aye, and it was a wee bitty odd. He asked me to contact a solicitor in Edinburgh to update his will.'

'Do you think he's sick?' Morag asked.

'No, no, I don't think so, maybe he's just aware that age is now working against him.'

I hope.

I took another bite.

'Mind you, Isla, since Auld Bruce stopped working at the Portree Solicitors, we haven't seen anyone new filling that office.

Maybe he's jist being cautious.' Morag chirped in. Her face watched mine intently but she didn't say anything else.

Would Granda tell me if something is wrong? Surely, he would. But what if he doesn't want to worry me?

Oh God, now I'm thinking.

'Right, you, I need to go and take Angus to work;

that's ten o'clock. I'll give ye a text later in the week. Happy hunting and dinna give up!'

Still lost in thought, my eyes didn't lift from the plate until a few seconds later.

'Aye, thanks for breakfast, Morag.'

I eventually replied before sending out a wave as Morag got further from the door.

Ever since Morag had married Angus, she'd become extremely punctual.

I guess some people do turn into their spouse. Imagine being so in tune with your partner; you would adapt your life to suit.

God, that seems unnatural.

Basking in the silence from the tan armchair, I reopened Hairy Coo's message.

Thinking about a response was far more time-consuming than I'd expected.

Usually, it's easy to gauge how a conversation was going to go, but this one felt different.

'The message sounds sad and slightly pathetic, but at the end of the day, we probably share that; aye, the spinster of Skye, that's me.'

I marvelled at the timestamp.

'Bloody WiFi, it's taken two hours to arrive.'

After watching out the window and staring at the clouds for a few moments; as if seeking inspiration from a greater being above, I decided to keep the response short and sweet.

There wasn't any point in counting your chickens before the eggs had hatched, and all that nonsense.

Hello,
Sorry for the delay, I had a friend over.
Yes, I'm also lonely, and yes, I am single.
I'm also female—just want to throw that out there as I haven't updated my profile.

'How the fuck am I supposed to sign this thing off? I'm not using my name— I'll get every weirdo in the country using it.'
Slowly I typed out Skye's the limit in the signature box.
I've no idea why, but it felt appropriate.
I pressed send, before moving to the profile page.
Well, I might as well fill it in.

Name, Age, Sex, Location, Bio (a statement about you, your aspirations, inspiration, dreams, and desires). Let your future love know in advance.

'Jeezoo, that's deep. Do you want my bank account number and sort code too?
No way am I answering half of those.'
Scrolling back, I located Hairy Coo's profile page,
'Let's have a wee lookie at what desperado's written.'

Name: Px **Age:** 39 **Sex:** Female **Location:** Blank
Bio (a statement about you, your aspirations, inspiration, dreams, and desires).
Let your future love know in advance:

Looking for an intellectual conversation, and a true connection.

A whistle passed my teeth.

This one's keeping it real tight to her chest.

No location, no real aspirations or desires.

I bet she dresses like my grandmother and has fourteen cats.

Probably looks something along the lines of a cross-dressing Barney the Dinosaur and Peppa Pig.

'Ha ha ha. I'm going to bet myself twenty quid she looks like a proper minger.'

Closing the phone's screen, I grabbed the book sitting on the coffee table. My favourite worn-out 'Pride and Prejudice' crumbling in hands.

'Oh Isla, fairytales are only for the imagination.'

Paisley

New message.
Hello,
Sorry for the delay, I had a friend over.
Yes, I'm also lonely, and yes, I am single.
I'm also female—just want to throw that out there as I haven't updated my profile.
Skye's the limit.
Sent 10:55 Friday 9th Feb

Oh, is she one of those women?

The kind that has a different friend staying over every other night... And what the hell does 'Skye's the limit' mean?

I reread the message before taking a drink of sparkling water, it's not for the thirst, instead it's an attempt to soothe this pounding headache.

Rough is an understatement, the thought of lying under one of the many trams to ease my pain, is very, very tempting.

I'm still dressed in last night's outfit, the stairs aren't enticing enough, well, unless I choose to throw myself down them when I reach the top.

My nails rapped against the phone's hardened case. What to do. What to do. 'Hmm.'

Maybe this dating scene isn't for me...

I'm probably overthinking this; it is just one message.

No, there's no doubt about it, she's a small spotty

teenager looking for a good night.

Eurgh, what a thought.

Maybe this wasn't a wise decision today, I'm really not at my best.

Actually, I haven't been that person for many years, I guess today's as good as any other.

'God, I feel like shit. Depressed, hungover and miserable.

Auch, have a look at the profile.'

I clicked on the profile picture next to the response:

Name: Skye's the limit. **Age:** 38 **Sex:** Female
Location: Blank
Bio (a statement about you, your aspirations, inspiration, dreams, and desires).
Let your future love know in advance:

Someone to grow old and content with.

'Ah, it's a pen name. Clearly, this person's either shy or intelligent, why would you want every creep knowing your name?

Hmm, interesting.'

I reread the statement four times.

Each time made me feel worse than the last.

Holding the phone screen to my forehead, I was blown over with an overwhelming surge of emotion.

Tears began to prick the corners before ugly tears rained down.

I'm not sad with the answers; I'm sad at how alone I've become.

My whole life is my job.

I've never considered growing old and content with another person.

My mother's never satisfied.

But mostly, I'm disappointed by how utterly shite I feel, indulging in far too many tequilas to make light work of dealing with the truth.

I am depressingly isolated and approaching forty fast.

It's going to be a very slow, pitiful death if I don't get my forlorn arse in gear.

Christ, I'm weak.

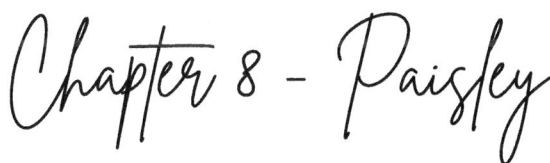

Chapter 8 – Paisley

Dear Mr. MacLeod,

I acknowledge receipt of your email.

Whilst I understand your desire to have your Last Will and Testament updated, it is necessary for us to meet in person to discuss your requirements.
This matter cannot be dealt with efficiently over email, and I do not appreciate the expectation of expedited service without following proper protocol.
Please provide your availability, and I will schedule a meeting at your earliest convenience.
Only then will we proceed with your request.

Regards,

Ms. P. Campbell (PhD)
Senior Solicitor
Campbell & Cambell

Pressing send, I closed the lid; finally, I'm free for the weekend.
Successfully managing to climb the three hundred stairs, I had changed into a pair of comfortable pyjamas before making the descent to the underused sofa.
I slouched across the three seats.
I should have showered, but I'm not sure I'd have ever left.

Today had been a hard emotional slog, but finally it's over— Now it's time to relax, well, attempt to.

Picking up the phone from the grey arm, I noticed the new text message.

New message - James (Bampot)

Afternoon Sweetie, I know last night was a bit of a roller coaster ride, but I think I have found someone else who would be more suited to you.

I'm assuming last night's darling delight didn't tickle your fancy ;) ??

Hope the headache's disappeared.

James xoxo

Sent 17:12 Friday 9th Feb

Rubbing at the migraine with one hand, I cleared the notification with the other.

Roller coaster ride would be an understatement.

I'm still trying to get off the damn thing, and your response can wait.

No more messages on Highland Hearts, but then the ball's back in my court

'Does it look too keen if I respond today?' Inadvertently I was talking aloud.

Skye's the limit - is now online, popped up on the screen.

The green light staring into my soul, like dangerous eyes in a forbidden cave.

Hmm, what should I do?

Be yourself… just not too much of yourself.

You want to at least be in with some kind of chance. Don't you?

What felt like an eternity of holding the mobile in a shaky sweaty hand wasn't helping at all, I was already up to high doh.

New message - Px
Hello again,
I'm sorry if I interrupted you and your guest earlier, that wasn't my intention.
I had hoped it was a female I'd messaged, is that what you're looking for?
I think it's good to be honest about these things upfront.
So… what do you like to do when you're feeling a bit lonely?
Maybe we have something in common.
Px
Sent 17:22 Friday 9th Feb

Good job Paisley, keep it light and simple.
Pushing the send button, I gave myself a small clap.
I could use a confidence boost, talking women into bed isn't exactly my strongest subject.
Moving the phone towards the table it began to buzz before it had fully touched down.

'Bloody hell, that was fast.'

New message - Skye's the Limit
Hiya, nope, you didn't interrupt anything.
Yes, I'm definitely looking for a female… but dinna tell anyone ;)
Fair enough. When I feel like that, I usually go for a walk. What about you, any go-to activities?
Skye's the limit
Sent 17:23 Friday 9th Feb

What does that mean, is she still in the closet?
I didn't hesitate.

New message - Px
I enjoy a good book, and a very large glass of Cabernet Sauvignon.
Paperwork is my hobby; work keeps me busy.
That's my go-to activity.
Px
Sent 17:26 Friday 9th Feb

Isla

This woman sounds like an alcoholic…
A workaholic, alcoholic.
Christ, not another nutter.
An email notification joined the mix as it entered the notification bar.

Campbell & Cambell - Private: For the attention of Mr. A. MacLeod

New message - Skye's the Limit
What kind of books do you like?
Work keeps you that busy?
What kind of work do you do?
I prefer a Sauvignon Blanc myself.
Skye's the limit
Sent 17:31 Friday 9th Feb

Quickly typing out the response, I sent it before opening Granda's email.
    'What a cheeky bitch!
Auch, she can stick her PhD where the sun doesn't shine, and if she needs help, I'm more than happy to stick it there for her.
Toffy-nosed, probably a tory voting boot. Argh.
Wait 'til Granda hears about this.'
My temper cut through me like a hot knife in butter.
This solicitor gave off a rude, upper-class twat impression.

Trust me to pick the most ignorant cow in Scotland.

Sticking the phone on charge, I changed into some pyjamas and moved to the kitchen.

Taking a chomp from the block of cheddar, I settled on a leftover sausage roll.
The pastry left a trail of breadcrumbs like Hansel and Gretel as I meandered through to the bedroom.

Work tomorrow means a crack of dawn wake up call. Even if it is only six in the evening.

'The sea waits for no one.'

Tucking myself into bed, the duvet tickled my chin.

'Tomorrow will be different. It'll be brighter. I promise.'
I closed my eyes.

>**New message - Px**
>I like a good mix of things, but I tend to lean towards anything that pulls me in.
>Something eloquent and thought-provoking.
>Sauvignon Blanc is not in my repertoire!
>As for work, let's just say it's demanding, but I'm beyond capable.
>I manage. Px
>*Sent 18:02 Friday 9th Feb*

Paisley

'Eurgh, a cheap Sauvignon Blanc, and the sheer audacity of this woman asking such personal questions. Who the hell does she think she is after only a few minutes of messaging?
Nosy cow.'

Waiting for what felt like a lifetime, the status never changed to *'Read'*.
That's odd, no further reply. It's only six and the last message came through immediately.
Hmm, very strange.

The phone teetered on my PJ clad knee in anticipation for the next response.
I'm not even entirely sure why I'm waiting for another message, it doesn't look as though this conversation is going anywhere.
Flashing the remote at the TV, I flicked through the channels.
'Ahh a firm favourite, Castaway.
If anyone's going to help me wallow in self-pity and eternal loneliness, it has to be Tom Hanks and Wilson.
They would understand the predicament perfectly!'

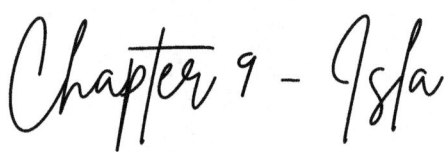

Chapter 9 - Isla

Filling my lungs with the unforgiving reek of saltwater and diesel, I hoicked the jacket's collar.

A chilly northeast wind howled, seeping through every seam as the frosty morning chill rushed in.

Inch-thick rubber soles ensured my feet remained toasty and dry, the wellies offering support against today's rough swells.

The green woollen tammy, warm and prickly over my skull.

Swaying silently in time with the waves, my fingers are today wrapped in thick black gloves— they're making every movement around the synthetic nylon a laborious nightmare.

I could ask for help, but I'm far too stubborn.

At seventeen, I'd jumped at the chance to join Granda on his fishing boat.

Leaving school with five highers and three advanced highers — All A's; realistically, I could have gone on to do any career.

If I'd applied.

Granda wouldn't allow me to join him on fishing trips until I turned eighteen. I never understood why, but he let me help at the dock daily.

It didn't make sense— I was out on the Ceilidh numerous times as a bairn.

My parents couldn't understand why I'd want to fish. Neither of them had found any interest or appreciation in the trade, and they didn't think it was a job suited to a young girl. Did I care? Like hell.

I don't know if they appreciate anything.

Granda probably would have retired long ago, and the family business would have been sold or left to die at the dock.

I don't give in easily, and I was hell bent on making him proud, I guess that's still the case.

Tam and Helen— my parents, are both now in their early sixties, they're fairly quiet and reserved; neither ever had plans to leave the island or travel anywhere further than Kyle of Lochalsh.

They've always kept themselves to themselves and are barely known to their neighbours... or their daughter.

They never get involved with anything local— which isn't standard in a tight-knit community like Skye, but everyone leaves them to their own devices.

Tam works as a sheep farmer for one of the local crofts, jumping from job to job whilst growing up, he was never sure where to make his mark on the world.

At first, he'd wanted to become a mechanic, then grew tired of the garage.

Next, a property developer, but Skye wasn't the ideal location for that; it was too remote, and newcomers wanted rustic island charm, not estates of four hundred modern builds.

He took a stint in IT for the local distillery, but surprise, surprise, that never lasted either.

Finally, he's settled down into the latest role with his flock of around fifty sheep.

Well, I think he's still doing that.

Granda never speaks much of his son's work ethic or choices; he left him to be who he was.

There's one thing for certain: Tam certainly doesn't resemble Granda.

Helen's the opposite.

She's worked in the local primary as the receptionist since leaving high school. She's never moved position since.

My mum and dad got together a few months after finishing their education, always happy to take life at the slowest pace, assuming it was on their terms.

They moved across the island from Torrin to Kyleakin a few months before I was born.

Their two-bedroom house looks out over the sea to Kyle of Lochalsh; it was only accessible by ferry.

Now a bridge connects Skye to the mainland, but when they first moved in, construction of the bridge was just in discussion.

Neither ever planned on having children; it didn't fit in with their insouciant demeanour and blithe attitude.

I can't help but find this amusing considering my mother's choice of career involves dealing with children daily.

You can imagine their shock when they found out five months into the pregnancy that they were expecting me.

I'm told Helen struggled with the idea of becoming a mother, a month later, depression kicked in and took its wicked toll.

She couldn't cope once I arrived, she'd struggled to show any kind of warmth or affection towards me.

Over the last thirty years, not much has changed.

For the first two years of my life, I was cared for mostly by Tam and my grandparents.

Tam *tried* his best, but as I was never in any of the plans, he had trouble adjusting to fatherhood.

Although a fully grown adult himself, he never really moved on from being a childish, teenage boy. Petulant in his need to object, and cantankerous in his need to always be correct.

Should the answer be *no,* Tam would take off in a hot-tempered sulk.

I guess that's why he couldn't hold down one of the many jobs. That and his insatiable desire to believe he was worth more money than would ever be on offer.

Tam and Helen brought me home permanently just before my third birthday— but the struggle continued.

Any excuse to have me out of the house and round at my grandparents was welcomed with open arms. Eventually by eight, I'd moved in permanently with Granny and Granda.

My parents would visit every couple of days in the first year, then they'd come over for dinner every Friday night when Granda had his day off.

Putting on an impressive show of being interested in my schoolwork and friends, their efforts had been wasted.

They would play silly beggars for an hour before eating dinner then disappearing.

Why would you want to stick around and bond with your only child? Especially when your parents could do all the hard work for you…

I'd draw them daft pictures to stick on their fridge— a full family affair on the Ceilidh.

Making cards at school with the other kids for occasions like Mother's Day and Christmas.

I never saw them when Granny would take me for a visit. Not that visits had been encouraged.

By around twelve, Tam and Helen only visited once a month. There was always some excuse for them not being able to make it the previous weeks.

Eventually, the few and far-between visits turned into a monthly phone call— if I was lucky.

Parental visits changed from being for the good of their child, to assistance requests.

They would only appear on birthdays and Christmas... or whenever they needed help with something specific... like finances.

Their arrival always ended in raised voices and Granda being undeniably angry— Which was really unusual.

Anytime voices rose, Granny would send me away to fetch something unimportant; usually, it was an earring or necklace that had fallen down the back of her bed. She would find any kind of chore that would take me an age to complete.

I believed my Granny was the clumsiest woman on Skye for a long time; we would make jokes about it regularly.

The sad reality, I now understand.

Granda would stomp from the living room red in the face, scarlet flushing his neck, fists clenched by his side. It was the only time I ever saw him mad.

My parents would shout 'goodbye' if I was away on Granny's mysterious treasure hunt.

Or on the occasion I was near the front door, they

would each plant one kiss on my forehead before exiting.

They never waved goodbye, never wrapped me up in a warm hug, and never ever said 'I love you.'

At the age of fourteen, I finally asked my granny—Isobel, why they bothered coming over if they didn't love me.

Tears balanced unsteadily under her thick-rimmed glasses.

That poor, poor woman. I must have drove her mad over the years. She would always smile and shake her head softly.

My heart still aches at the thought.

Granda would sweep me into his arms and swing us around.

'Come on bonnie lass, let's find the ice cream; I'm pretty sure Granny's hidden it.' He'd say trying to change the subject.

For my whole life, I've been protected from uncaring, unloving, selfish, cold parents.

The elders' parental obligations had been completed when Dad grew up.

Effectively Tam and Helen robbed my grandparents of their retirement; any savings they had were likely gone, any ability to spend their free time as they wanted had run out, and they never truly got to live their own lives. I was always there.

For years guilt has haunted me, the worry that I caused my grandparents to have a damaged relationship with their only son and daughter-in-law.

I don't even know if it's my guilt to hold onto, but I do.

Another thought crosses my mind occasionally, had I

been straight, would things have worked out differently?

Nah, no one knew back then, I guess.

At least now I'm the one in control, I decide how relationships will be handled, and unfortunately for my parents, that means they aren't a part of it.

After everything Tam and Helen have put us through, they've become little more than distant figures.

Rarely do our paths cross. Thankfully.

At the end of the day, those people now just exist.

Finishing on the tangle, I tossed the knots— the calmness forming fragile ruffles in the glass.

I bathed in still silence, leaning against the railings with an unspoken appreciation for the serene coastline.

A young girl smiled towards me, the water's depth giving her around thirteen years; blinking twice, I turned to look behind.

It's just me.

Grinning back, the scene intrigued me.

She looked carefree and high spirited, piercing blue eyes meeting the docile red, an unsullied expression— no hint of sorrow, just a belonging joy.

A mature couple huddled close, hands connecting the young shoulders.

The dark hair and whiskers matching those of Granda, a rosie beam holding tight.

Granny's distinct specs slipping further as a wave caught them; her ginger hair lightly blowing in the swell.

Looking towards one another they simpered, an identical appearance from many years past.

The perfect trio, captivated in shared company, an

overwhelming proficiency to make everything picture-perfect.

Invested in distant memories, I couldn't free my glance.
A heavy droplet finally scattered the precious portrait.

'Come on bonnie lass, let's take her hame.'
Granda's rising voice brought me away from the dark.
I turned to face him, respect and gratitude tempting my eyes.

'So, what will we do about this snotty solicitor, Granda?' I asked before wiping my face and climbing the steps to meet him up top.

'Well, ah guess ah'll need tae take a trip tae Edinburgh.'
Is he serious?

'Granda, it's an awful long way.
You'd need to be away for at least two nights.'

'Aye, ah did think that. Do ye fancy a wee jaunt doon the road wi' me?'
It had been years since I'd last been to Edinburgh.
A change of scenery might do me some good— I couldn't hide the glee, and he knew it.

'Auch, I don't know, Granda. I'm a Skye lass; I wouldn't do well in the city.
It's so far away and busy, the noise would keep me awake all night.' I replied in a tease.
Yesss! A trip somewhere new, filled with lots of beautiful people. Hallelujah!
He raised an eyebrow and laughed.

'Aye, yer some lassie, let me tell ye.'
Shaking his head, he checked the GPS and wind speeds.

'If ye can arrange a date and time with this solicitor

wifey, ah'll even take ye tae see the bonnie big castle whilst we're there.'

He pushed on the throttle— lurching the trawler forward.

'Aye… Okay mannie, you have a deal.'

Biting my bottom lip, I thought carefully for a second.

'Granda?'

He let out an intrigued grunt and turned his head.

'I love you so much… and I don't think I've told you nearly enough.

I know I definitely never said it enough to Granny. You've both been so good to me over the years, and I really mean it, I love you.'

Leaving it to filter through, his eyes widened.

I couldn't break contact until I knew it had reached the mark.

Satisfied, I eventually turned and moved to clear a puddle that had started to spread across the lower-deck.

Granda remained standing in the same spot, still looking out at where I'd been.

'I love you too, my bonnie wee lassie, and yer Granny definitely knew that ye loved her.' he whispered.

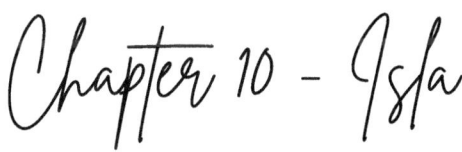

Chapter 10 - Isla

'Dear Ms. Snooty Drawers,

Thanks so much for your email,
I'm so glad you could find the time to reply, with your hectic schedule.
While I partly understand why you're being a bitch and insisting on meeting me in person, I get the impression you want to see my face. Well, do ye?
Ye wouldnae even know what to do with me if I stood in front of you.
I'd have expected a more down-to-earth approach to handling this matter, especially since I'm paying for you to sit in your ivory bloody tower.
I'm aware that things can't always be rushed, but the tone of your response was unnecessary.
You come across like a Tory voting, bringing in eighty grand a year, snob.
I hope we never meet, or I'll give you a proper piece of my mind!
Let me know when you're free, and I'll try to fit this in with Granda's very, very busy schedule.
You aren't the only one with a job, bitch!
Lots of love
Isla

P.S. Stick your degree where the sun won't shine–
happy to assist if required.

'I bet she's bloody English.' I spat.

Morag's deep infectious cackle, howled through the phone.

'Oh me, Isla. I think ye should just send it like that, she'll soon know who she's dealing wi'.'

A sleeve or tissue rustled against the speaker, obviously wiping her nose… or eyes.

'Ach, honestly Morag, I'm hoping this is just a bib and braces moment. I'd hate to think there's something wrong with him.'

'Have you tried asking Alistair? Ye know yersel, conversation's the key to all relationships.'

'Aye, but I'm afraid of the answer.'

'Well how can ye know the answer if ye dinna ask the bloody question, Isla?'

Resting the phone against my forehead, Morag's lull hissed out.

Making myself quite comfortable by lying face down on the bed, I propped up against my elbow; the ancient laptop indulging me in thousands of junk emails.

The local radio station is chuntering in the background; Some crap about a traffic jam on the Portree road… a flock of eighty sheep holding a campervan hostage.

'Aye, I guess you're right, I'll just need to ask him,' I responded, 'but here, on the upside, I'm getting a trip through to the city, it's been too long since I was last in Edinburgh.'

'Ahh, Isla, I wish I was coming with you, I remember Angus taking me through to Edinburgh one time afore we married. It was so glamorous and posh, I could hardly contain myself.

I got so excited at the thought of a dirty night away, I conked out at seven and didn't rise again until eleven the next morn.

Angus was mare than upset he'd missed out on his own rise.'

The pair of us broke into a fit of laughter.

'Poor Angus, how's he doing anyway?' I quizzed.

'Auch, he's alright.

Fed up with that fish shoppie, I canna blame him really.

The place is stinking, he needs something exciting and thrilling, something that makes him want to go to his work.

I just want him home smelling better than he left… and a smile on his face wouldnae hurt.

Ach, I'd love for him to be happy, there's nothing worse than being miserable at work every day.'

'He'll get something, Mo, he's a good wee worker.

Well, I mean he's always running around like a blue-arsed fly when I see him. And you fairly keep him on his toes, why can't I have a female version?

I could use an Angus in my life.'

'Aye, I hope so, and we'll find you someone, Isla, the world's nae ending jist yet.'

Morag paused, as if contemplating something in the background.

'Right you, I need to head away.

Start asking Jeeves about where to find a bonnie and voluptuous lassie in the big city, and I'll catch you the morn.

Love you.'

I rolled my eyes.

'Aye no bother Morag, have a good afternoon, I love you too.'

Hanging up I noticed a new message from Hairy Coo, the time stamp marking its arrival last night.

'Oops.'

This morning, I'd just stuffed it into my pocket without looking.

That's the difference between island life and the city, mobile phones don't take priority, and the signals never guaranteed.

A bonnie lass in the city *could* fix some of what I'm missing.

Maybe I should download that app; that one specifically for hook-ups, I could use some attention, it's been far too long.

> **New message - Px**
> *I like a good mix of things, but I tend to lean towards anything that pulls me in.*
> *Something eloquent and thought-provoking.*
> *Sauvignon Blanc is not in my repertoire!*
> *As for work, let's just say it's demanding, but I'm beyond capable.*
> *I manage. Px*
> *Sent 18:02 Friday 9th Feb*

What is it with me and snotty people today?

Typing out a quick response, I heaved myself up and hauled the laptop closer.

'Right you, Mrs. Fancy Pants, let's do this.'

Dear Ms. Campbell,

Thank you for your email.
While I understand you're insistent on meeting in person, I would have expected a more efficient approach to handling this matter, especially given the nature of the request.
I'm aware that things can't always be expedited, but the tone of your response was unnecessary.
Let me know your availability, and I'll try to fit this into my schedule.
I trust we can move forward once we meet.

Regards,
Mr. A. MacLeod

Thanks for that template google. You're a lifesaver.

Granda can't work the computer, so he's more than happy to let me handle any emails he sends or receives. In turn, I'm more than willing to get involved, it might provide me a bit of background on why he needs a solicitor to start with... and I can respond to this horrible wee so and so.

Closing the email tab I opened the internet browser. My roughened fingers typed out:

Campbell & Cambell, Edinburgh.

'Well doesn't this look all fancy schmancy,'
Scrolling down, I thumped the *Meet the Team* tab.
'Right you, Mrs Big and Powerful, let's have a wee lookie.'

The photos must have been in order of the company's hierarchy.

Directly under the company *Partner's,* were the *Senior Solicitors*, and at the very top of that list, was the exact person I'd been hunting.

Ms. P. Campbell (PhD)

'Offtt… Bloody hell…'

Was *that* the woman I just sent the shitty email to? Michty me.

My eyeballs nearly fell out of my head— this uptight self-assured twat was… absolutely gorgeous.

A shiver ran down my spine as I bit my bottom lip.

P. Campbell's hair fell to her shoulders like a cascading waterfall; thick, glorious dark mahogany waves. The kind you could happily run your fingers through all day… or night.

'Ohh, better than that, I could stick my face in there. I'd be almost completely satisfied.'

A perfectly smooth and delicate nose that gives effortless balance to the rest of her face.

Her skin… immaculate; it has a soft and subtle glow, no spots or acne scars, a couple of crow's feet around the eyes, but who really cares about that minute detail?

'Wow! She's bloody delicious and yes, I'd definitely be asking for seconds.'

Those eyes, deep forest green; like an uncharted woodland, filled with a striking intensity that pull you in and just hold you there… and trust me, I'm held!

The white collar of her blouse sat below her hair; a perfectly fitted black blazer resting on top.

She sat in a '*I own this office,*' kind of pose.

I felt the air thicken as my mouth watered.

If I'd been feeling frustrated before, this just made things a lot more stifling.

This woman was an aphrodisiac on steroids.

Caught in my peripheral, I gawked at a car butchering a thirteen-point turn outside the window.

'Dingbat, there's a bloody turning circle a hundred yards down the road.

You're interrupting my legal viewing! Asshole.

Well, slap me with a lamb and call me a haggis! That face is definitely not helping the lack of sexual exploration.

Christ, I need air.'

Looking back at the screen, my hand found my mouth, my lips pulling between my tongue and teeth for a few seconds longer.

Before things took a disobedient turn, I slammed the laptop lid closed.

'Well, I guess you really canna judge a book by its cover. It's a shame she's as helpful as a concrete parachute... Probably straight too, those fuckers get all the fun!'

God, I almost feel mawkit, ogling my grandfather's solicitor... but that face... that's definitely going to haunt my dreams for a long, long time.

Nah, absolutely no regrets, I'll be back to ogle some more later.

'Old girl, it's been far too long.'

A second shiver bolted, probably joining hands with my eros craving.

Clambering up, I pulled out a pair of trail runners that had been concealed beneath the mattress. Stuffing them on to my feet harshly, it was a mad dash to clear the derogatory visions.

Straightening the duvet and grabbing the phone, my explicit urge and agonising ache joined the pursuit— I left for the Man of Storr.

'That captivating body and gorgeous face…
Auch Isla, that's enough.'

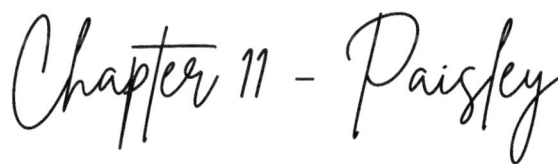

Chapter 11 – Paisley

Holding my mother's head beyond my chest, her tedious voice droned on.

'... and I have just informed Steve that he must ensure the upstairs gallery is completed by next Friday, be...'

Who the hell is Steve? I couldn't even pretend to be the slightest bit interested— my eyes scoured the *'Scottish Family Law - Third Edition'* book hidden behind the phone. It's probably the most boring book written, yet still a thousand times more palatable than my mother's ramblings.

'...the Mark Rothko isn't going to hang itself...'

Ah! Steve's the decorator, he's painting my mother's latest obsession; a private gallery in what had once been the fifth spare bedroom.

The phone buzzed against the soft-back, making me jump.

'Mother, wait a second,' I said, cutting her off.
Hands working double time to get the notification.
My mother's sharp glare was just as intimidating on screen as it was in real life.
Her dark navy eyes— scorned and angry as the brows met in the middle.

'Did you just...' My mother started.

'...I am sorry, Mother, I'm sure Steve will be finished in time for Christie's delivering your painting, but I really have to go. Something urgent has come up for work.' I spoke back.

It was a lie, but I was desperate to hang up.

'Did you just tell me to wait, Paisley Rose Campbell? You know I don't...'

'Yes, I know Mum. I am sorry, but I really must dash, lots of love.'

Ding dong, crisis averted.

Jabbing at the screen to close the call, I opened the two new notifications; one was an email for work, the other a Highland Hearts response.

'Well, that one will wait until Monday.' Swiping away the digital pigeon, my thumb launched the other to life; the obnoxious sideshow melody in full swing.

'Note to self, must put phone on silent when teasing one's soul…'

New message - Skye's the Limit

Px, Happy Saturday.

Okay, you don't fancy answering my questions without a cryptic response.

That's fine, it's not like I actually wanted a proper bloody answer!?! I was just trying to be friendly, you know see if we have anything in common - probably not…

As for the wine, everyone's tastes are different, wouldn't it be boring if we were all the same?

What other choice of beverage do you enjoy? Arsenic, cyanide?

A demanding job can be fun and exciting, it's all about balance and outlook.

I'm not sure how you'll come across on those questions…

Skye… you get the rest I'm sure.

Sent 15:37 Saturday 10th Feb

Deciding against hanging about, I immediately sent her a response.

A two-hour FaceTime with my mother would make anyone reevaluate their life choices.

New message - Px
Hello Skye,

I hope your weekend is off to a good start?

You're right, those responses were a bit vague, and I was slightly rude, apologies.

Honestly, I was nursing a pretty tragic hangover and feeling very sorry for myself.

Tequila was the culprit, well, I mean I was the one throwing it down my gullet so I'm ultimately to blame...What about you? What else do you indulge in?

Yes, very boring indeed. Deathly potions do seem far more tempting nowadays.

Since it's Saturday, let's leave work out of it, but once again, you're correct, balance and perspective are key... Sorry again!

Px   Sent 15:50 Saturday 10th Feb

'Whoops, you need to be more careful, Paisley. You're going to turn into your mother... and we know how much she'd love that.'

Still slouching with the tedious book, I bathed in the joy of a premeditated blind discussion.

Usually sitting in silence, a trepidation of fear would seek me out— face to face engagement isn't my expertise.

Luckily, with this I can squirrel myself away and remain reclusive, whilst still finding comfort in a non-committal conversation.

New message - Skye's the Limit

Hello Px,

Thanks for the explanation, everything's going fine so far and I accept your

apology. I'm sorry if my reply was slightly bitchy, you caught me off guard and I've had my fair share of snotty folk today.

I hope you were joking about the potions, I'd hate to have that hanging over my conscience.

Oft, a tequila hangover on a school night, wow, I wish I could get away with that.

If we're talking hard liquor, it would need to be whisky. There's nothing like a good old Scottish dram, but that's only really for special occasions.

I do love a cheeky wee sambuca though, I could drink that like juice! Ach ok then, no

talk of career paths. Got it.

Skye   Sent 15:53 Saturday 10th Feb

New message - Px

Skye, no apologies needed. That was on me!

Sorry to hear you're dealing with snotty gits, I hope you got them told?

A friend set me up on a blind date, I saw tequila as the only rational escape. It didn't work, she still left a mark. What would you consider to be a really special occasion?

Don't worry about your conscience, I've not booked a plot yet.

Thanks, and for future reference, it's just P :)

P x   Sent 15:58 Saturday 10th Feb

New message - Skye's the Limit

P, oh sweet mercy!! I hate the thought of a blind date… it was a friend that set me up on here, so I guess it's a circus of the same shit storm.

Aye, I'm pretty sure I've told them to get tae fu…

Wow, that's a wee bitty dark. I did laugh though lol.

Special occasions… Birthdays, funerals, when the wifi starts working! ;)

I can only assume you didnae take her home? Sorry, that's none of my business,

I'm just making idle chit-chat, it was the first thing I could think of… I've never really done this before.

Well, I mean I've messaged people back, but I've never actually had a proper conversation with anyone.

I don't even know if this is a proper conversation but… ah jeezo I'm babbling.

Copy on the P.

Skye

Sent 16:01 Saturday 10th Feb

I couldn't help but smile, this woman was a strange creature from the abyss, not quite meeting the same insanity level as Beth or Sharon, but probably not far off.

Good God, is this my type of women? Utter nutters.
It might be safer remaining single.

New message - Px

Skye, she was a surgeon, had horrendous taste in jumpers, and never stopped talking.

My mother might have been impressed by her credentials, but I doubt she'd have made it past the walled garden.

Once again you're correct, it's none of your business… but the answer is no.

There was no rational reason for my standards to sink that low. I might appear to be desperate, especially after my first depressingly fragile message but… no… just no!

You haven't ever been on a blind date? Well, that is interesting. It's what I'd imagine navigating your way through the Antarctic ice fields would feel like, except you've forgotten to bring a GPS.

You really wouldn't like to hazard a guess as to where you were going to end up… Let alone wonder how you got there. Pretty much like speed dating. Horrific.

I think we can successfully regard this as a conversation.

P x   Sent 16:09 Saturday 10th Feb

New message - Skye's the Limit

P, I believe in honesty, and I hope you can understand what I'm about to say.

It's not meant in a degrading way, but my head is telling me to prepare for an easy exit. I've never dated anyone. My credentials don't even come close to a surgeon. I love knitted Aran jumpers (sorry, but nae really) and I can talk for Scotland.

My family doesn't have a walled garden or even

a home big enough for one. Seriously, I think you're probably well out of my league. I could be wrong, but at 38 I just want to be with someone who can accept me the way I am.

I don't think this is going to work out, I'm too set in my ways to change and I definitely won't be changing my jumpers!

Skye

Sent 16:20 Saturday 10th Feb

My head tilted as a new emotion chewed away at me.

Already, I'd managed to alienate this lonely soul searching for her counterpart.

This woman had been honest and unafraid to question my comments.

Upfront in telling me who she is and what she needs; I've probably been wearing a cloak of judgement my whole life, following in the footsteps of the one person I never wanted to be.

No wonder I'm miserable and alone.

New message - Px

Skye, I didn't mean to imply that I only look for people with money.

That simply isn't at all true and is categorically not a representation of me.

I sincerely apologise if that's how I've come across. What makes you think I'm out of your league? I'd imagine, it's far more likely you're out of mine...

Our conversation is still in its infancy, and realistically it could take any path.

I'm surprised by how much I'm enjoying our discussion, I don't talk to many people unless I'm working. Sad, but true! I cannot lie though, I've never spoken to anyone without being able to see them. Usually I'd be quite concerned, but for some reason I feel no disharmony.

Will you indulge my curiosity and stay a while longer? I really would like to speak to you some more.

P x

P.S. I am very intrigued by your lack of partners.

Do you want to talk about it?

Sent 16:30 Saturday 10th Feb

New message - Skye's the Limit

No.

Skye

Sent 16:34 Saturday 10th Feb

Short and frank, but that doesn't leave me with much in the way of answers.

I guess two can play the vague game.

Hmm, how do I even respond to that?

Please don't run away just yet.

New message - Px

Skye, I'm not entirely sure I grasp the topic you'd prefer to avoid, but that's okay.

I didn't mean to come across like a bitch, I'm really not used to this kind of thing.

I'm completely out of my depth right now. I feel quite lost.

Why don't you share something interesting about yourself?

P x   Sent 16:50 Saturday 10th Feb

The response took an age to come through, I'd managed

to finish the textbooks first volume before my eyes felt every word. In all honesty, I hadn't expected a reply, I was preparing to be disappointed all over again.

New message - Skye's the Limit
I'm really scared of being alone.
Skye
Sent 17:25 Saturday 10th Feb

My face fell as my thoughts echoed Skye's— a silent appreciation for the quiet ache we shared.

The permanent worry that no one will ever fill the oppressive void.

I no longer felt the ability to sympathise. How could I? This woman matched me, she already knew the pain, the panic, probably the hopes and dreams too.

I'd believed for too long that I was the only person on the planet to wallow in such misery.

I'd never met her, never heard her voice or held her hand, yet all I wanted to do was squeeze her until the air left her lungs, just enough to break the depression.

New message - Px
Skye, I understand wholeheartedly.

The fear of being alone isn't just about the silence, but the weight of it. Everything feels… endless. No matter how many people you surround yourself with, no matter how much love you show them, you are still left fighting your own thoughts, doubts and fears.

I've been there and it's terrifying. Honestly, I'm probably still wallowing in that apprehension, hoping for a quiet reprieve.

But maybe in those quiet moments, we can start to find

a little peace in ourselves, even though it might feel impossible right now.

You are not alone in this. Not really.

Px   Sent 17:28 Saturday 10th Feb

New message - Skye's the Limit

P, I really don't know what to say, you hit me square between the eyes.

It's like you do understand.

I'm so tense all the time, my life's passing me by and I have nothing real to show for it. I'm desperate to find someone who loves me for me, but it never happens.

All I want is someone to hold me and love me, tell me I'm everything they've needed.

Maybe one day eh?

You know, I think this is the first time I have ever told someone exactly how I feel.

My heart is heavy.

Skye   Sent 17:31 Saturday 10th Feb

As a new notification pinged and buzzed in my fingers, my brain couldn't contain itself, this woman was a carbon copy. Isolated in a deprived world, hiding behind an unwavering poker-face, organs internally crumbling as the true life-form dies a little more each day.

'I hope she isn't ugly. I could really use a moment with someone like this.'

My head fell to the armrest, hand running over a sniffly nose.

Opening the second message, my shoulders couldn't suppress the disappointment.

New message - Skye's the Limit

P, I'm so so sorry. I genuinely don't want to cut this short but I have to work in the morning.

I need to go to bed.

I really would love to stay awake and chat some more.

I feel like we're slowly getting somewhere. I'm so so appreciative of you sharing, and thanks for understanding!

Goodnight!

Skye x   Sent 17:33 Saturday 10th Feb

New message - Px

Goodnight Skye, sweet dreams.

Px   Sent 17:34 Saturday 10th Feb

The truth was, I didn't want to stop messaging or allow her to go to bed, I wanted to be self-centred.

I wanted her to want me, to take this raw pathetic body and nurture it, at least until a brilliant version of myself sat in my place.

Neither of us knew who or what we needed, but I could already feel the disorientating pull.

I needed to unlock her mind, dig deeper into the darkness and draw out more.

I didn't know this woman, but I was devastated by her prompt exit.

The dizzying need for more untold truths, a tantalisingly powerful ache as innocent texts had drawn me in.

It was a throbbing reminder that I do have emotions, and I could learn to love, maybe not with this woman, but with somebody.

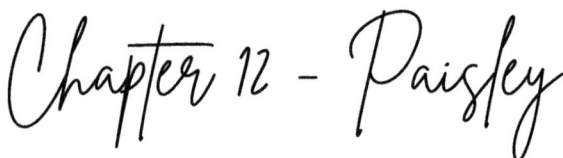

Chapter 12 - Paisley

A Monday morning in the Campbell & Cambell office was like the legal equivalent of a caffeine overdose.

There was a buzz around the building, staff desperately trying to remember what had happened last week. No one had any kind of recollection of their action-packed weekend just past.

The coffee machine worked overtime, trying to keep up with its newfound heavy demand.

People scrambling to get to meetings on time, preparations for court hearings, or double-checking their emails— just to be sure they hadn't inadvertently agreed to something hastily sent through by their boss, mere seconds before they escaped for the weekend.

Had they actually filed and responded to that document, or did they just stare at it long enough on Friday evening to think they had?

There was always that one useless person who skipped about the place like they had already conquered the world— often spouting motivational quotes about the day ahead. Meanwhile the rest of the office quietly contemplates sticking Blu-Tac in their eyes, whilst deciding whether or not it's too late to call in sick.

Today, that person was James.

I could hear him flouncing around in the hallway like an oversized seagull, squawking at everyone he passed.

What in the devil's name is that muppet screeching

about?

'James!' I yelled, lungs at full capacity.

All of the squawking and bustle outside my office turned to silence.

'Get your boney little backside through here. Now!'

Well, that clearly got his attention.

James peered around the door holding it like a shield.

'Oh, good morning, darling. Good weekend?' He asked sheepishly, still holding onto the door for backup.

'Please, for the preservation of my sanity, tell me you didn't press *Reply to all* on Mr. Khan's settlement case?!

You're aware there was a non-disclosure attached to that email, right?' My voice was cold and sharp, like a woman on a warpath.

Face matching my tone, arms crossed and clamped tightly against my chest.

James's eyes widened.

In just thirty seconds, he had transformed from a squawking gull into a frightened little pug, the head looking like it had somehow become trapped in a cat flap.

He shook with bulging eyes, the mouth hanging wide open, his tongue not sure where it belonged.

'No!.........No!.... No...No..No.' Sweat was starting to bead around his recently oiled hairline.

Yes, yes, yes, James. Nothing gets past me. Silly boy.

He pulled out his phone— frantically running a shaky finger along the screen.

I knew he was desperately searching for the email in his outbox. The same one I'd received just twenty minutes prior from a more than slightly pissed off client.

He froze and looked up; a picture of fear and guilt.
I got the impression he was about to keel over into a lumpy puddle— or throw himself to the grim reaper.
Either would have been more than adequate.

The campest hand turned burly; hiking it through the deflated tufty fringe, sweat poured down his cheeks.

Resting a fist under my chin, I leant against the elbow— contemplating how to handle this fiasco and James's nervous breakdown.

Remembering my energy had caused more harm than good with the text messages, I reflected on the *we're only human* aspect.

James stood straight and marched out the door, slamming it abruptly behind him.

My eyes following the deranged solicitor in a flummoxed frown.

'Where the hell's he going?'

Before I could fully rise from the desk, an almighty roar rose from the stairwell four doors down.

'Fuuuuuuuuuuucccccccccckkkkkkkkkkkk.'

James's voice thundered out, the noise was muffled by the heavy concrete and wooden decor.

Pausing, I almost expected to hear him bouncing headfirst down the stairs.

The thump, crash, bang never arrived.

Sitting back down and clicking the mouse, Saturday's email filled my monitor.

Mr. MacLeod's response to my passive aggressive hangover. Bollocks.

James reappeared at the door, his face had surpassed the scarlet stage, it was almost beetroot.

His blue and now rather red eyes were still jutting from their sockets, nostrils flared, chest heaving with every deep raspy breath.

He was no longer giving off the attractive, hunky, gay God illusion.

Now, he just looked… haggard.

Maybe it's time to top-up the Botox… But in the meantime, I'd personally like to welcome you to the image of an onset, midlife crisis— Grey, depressing and trust me, it's going to get a lot worse.

I remained silent, almost enjoying the panic radiating from Hermes' in the corner.

It made a nice change to be on the upside of such disappointment.

James cautiously closed the door behind him.

'Paisley, darling…'

Waiting a second longer with his hand still clung tightly around the doorknob, he was probably choosing his next sentence very carefully.

'I don't even know what to say, I am so, so, so sorry. How? …What? …I don't even know how to make this right. I've completely screwed up.'

Eventually letting go, he tiptoed to the olive chesterfield armchair in the middle of the room. Throwing himself down, he rocked in distress. Pathetic.

Looking over with puppy dog eyes, he was probably one bollocking away from tears.

Auch, Paisley, why are you such a sucker for the eyes?

Watching him intently, the deafening silence was loud.

'James,' it came out more harshly than expected.

He flinched before looking towards the castle.

Oops.

'James,' I softened my tone and tried to match my face— it probably wasn't working, I was never gifted with a friendly stare.

'You've made a colossal misstep.

That email was certainly an interesting choice... and by interesting, I mean, definitely not the best decision.

You effectively undermined the third party and then had the audacity to send them the friggin evidence.'

My voice was louder at the end of the sentence as I squeezed the words through clenched teeth— trying indescribably hard to maintain a sense of decency.

Going by James's expression, it was falling flat.

Play nicely, Paisley.

Calmly, I stood and walked over.

Twisting a pen between my fingers, I fought the overwhelming urge to throw it at him.

I sat down in the neighbouring chair and eyed his demeanour.

Calm down, Paisley. He's clearly frightened of you. You've made plenty of mistakes yourself, it's human nature.

'Look, James, we can all have moments of misjudgement. Please use this failing as a lesson learned, alright? Double-check everything.

Dot the I's, cross the T's, and for your own sake, please double-check the sender details.

I will fix it, but I'm serious, please learn from this.'

Placing my hand on his shoulder, I gave it a reassuring squeeze. He flinched before leaving it to settle.

'We all make mistakes, myself included.

Just please be more careful.'

It was difficult to work out which one of us was more surprised at this relatively calm and almost supportive response.

James peered up with wide interrogating eyes; possibly waiting for the background information on why I hadn't torn him a new arsehole.

No details were supplied.

'Oh, and on a personal request, James— No more dates please.

My lonely heart can't deal with anymore.' I announced wearily.

* * * *

Dear Mr. MacLeod,

Thank you for your prompt response.

I appreciate your feedback and understand your concerns.

Apologies if my tone came across as inappropriate, I assure you, that was not my intention.

I should have explained in my previous email that an in-person meeting would facilitate a more effective resolution. I certainly respect your preference for a more efficient approach.

It's a requirement under both our office policy as well as GDPR to ensure that all corresponding clients are who they say they are. I can assure you, I also would much prefer to deal with many clients remotely. Unfortunately, that cannot be the case.

A face-to-face meeting would allow us the ability to move quickly in future with minimal delay as all necessities would be already taken care of.

I will do my best to accommodate you in any way I can, however as we speak, I currently only have one available opening on Monday 26th February at 16:30.

If that doesn't work with your timescales, I would need to push your appointment into the middle of March.

I'm confident that we can address the matter more effectively once we meet.

Kind regards,
Ms. P. Campbell (PhD)
Senior Solicitor
Campbell & Cambell

Pressing send with the tailless mouse, I slouched back in the Herman.

For a Monday, everything was going well— maybe too well; I was ahead of the game and feeling really pleased with myself.

Considering I hadn't actually chewed James into a million pieces before spitting him out, a newfound dignity burrowed its way inside.

Hmm, not bad, Paisley.

New message - Px

Skye, I hope this message finds you well?

I thought I may have heard from you yesterday, but that wasn't to be. I'll need to exercise a bit more patience, I guess.

I'm currently at the office and I could use a distraction. I'll go first and give you a bit of insight into myself.

You asked about books - Well, I rarely admit this, but

I'm secretly a hopeless romantic. I enjoy many Jane Austen novels as well as Nicholas Sparks - The Notebook being my favourite. I also keep a very battered but well-read version of Harper Lee's - To Kill A Mockingbird... Also, a number of DIY guides - and no, I don't mean hammers and chisels. Books fill my time and head. They create a comforting escape from reality. I'm very boring.

I like the odd film: Dirty Dancing, Nottinghill, Pretty Woman - Yes, Julia Roberts is a goddess and would be on my laminated list - If I had a partner that needed to worry ;) Castaway is a solid favourite too.

I enjoy a variety of different music genres, but I love the 60's, 70's & 80's pop culture. A bit of soul music too, I'm easy going when it comes to music.

My last relationship was 5 years ago. It lasted only 3 months - I was the cause of its failure.

I'm not really sure if I should tell you that or not!

My work is everything to me, I don't have hobbies, I have a career.

Many people can't work around that, so I understand if it's a deal breaker. I don't want to get into what I do for a job, just please be aware that it engulfs my life. I don't know if you are going to stick around long enough to worry, but I feel it would be better to just be upfront. After all, I don't think either of us are looking for a pen pal.

I feel like that's enough for you to ponder over, but I do hope to hear from you again.

Hopefully you weren't scared off over the weekend.

Px

Sent 14:19 Monday 12th Feb
Read 16:44 Monday 12th Feb

New message - Skye's the Limit

P, how the devil are ye?

I'm affa sorry I didn't get a chance to message yesterday, like you, my career takes pride of place.

I work really unsociable hours and messages don't always arrive straight away.

But gosh, what a selection of delights you've left for me to read through.

Much more approachable today, I like it... ;)

I adore Pride and Prejudice, that's my favourite book. I can't even tell you how many times I've read it.

Anything by Dan Brown or Thomas Harris - Hannibal Lector's a classic and should be read in the dark!!

Erm, what's a DIY guide if not for a handy woman? OMG, did I just inadvertently answer that question? Scarlet!!

Can I just tell you, your taste in American actresses is spot on.

I also love anything with Jennifer Aniston-Friends got me through my teenage years, I wouldn't say no to J.A ever! Even if there was a doting partner... they're out for her. I'm nae even sorry.

Music...hmm I won't tell you about that just yet, you might never message me again!

Relationships... well I don't know what to say about that... Nothing you've said is scaring me off, it's good to be passionate.

I agree, I'm looking for my pot of gold at the end of the rainbow, I don't need more friends.

I want and need love :(

Skye x   Sent 16:47 Monday 12th Feb

As I finished filing away the last of the paperwork that had been cohabitating the desk for the past week and a half, my phone buzzed and vibrated along the wood.

Oh Jesus, no.

Notification Centre
Highland Hearts:
New Private Message: Skye's the limit
WhatsApp: Missed Call: Mother (Old Bat)
Outlook: New Email: 2

Noticing the missed call from my mother, I thumbed out a message.

New message – Paisley
Don't panic Mother, I haven't forgotten about this evenings dinner.

Work has been unforgiving today, and I haven't had the chance to call you back, P x
Sent 16:58 Monday 12th Feb

In truth, until I noticed the missed call, it had completely slipped my mind.

The idea of sitting through hours of her overbearing, self-absorbed company wasn't something I could look forward to, I guess there's no turning back now.

Quicker than the message had sent, my mother responded.

> **New message – Mother (Old bat)**
> *Paisley, did you intentionally forget the apostrophe in 'evening's'?*
> *Sent 16:58 Monday 12th Feb*

New message – Paisley
No, it was autocorrected, Mother.
Sent 16:59 Monday 12th Feb

And this was the exact reason I never text the old bat.

New message – Mother (Old bat)
Dinner is at 6 pm sharp.
Paisley, that means I expect you at the table for 17:45.
See you soon.
Sent 17:00 Monday 12th Feb

Glancing over at the clock; it was already five o'clock on the dot.

The bus to Hermiston would take at least thirty minutes in the evening traffic, and then another ten minutes to walk to the grand estate outside Riccarton.

No chance of responding to Skye anytime soon— I needed to leave now.

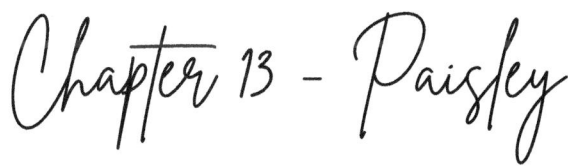

Chapter 13 - Paisley

The small pea gravel crunched under my black patent court shoes.

Trudging along Mother's sweeping driveway, the path is surrounded by overhanging beech trees and beautifully manicured hedges.

The stunning eighteenth-century Georgian home sits perfectly amidst a luscious green lawn, whilst large topiary bushes frame a grand wooden door.

No doubt, the gardener had been provided specific instructions to ensure the place remained spotless.

As usual.

A charming yet sophisticated home with seven bedrooms, five bathrooms and two comfortable but rather dated lounges. It's been our family home for over two hundred years.

To give you some background, my father— Laird Cameron Campbell of Calder, had inherited his family's estate when his own father passed away.

Historically, the Campbell family were well known in the area for land ownership and their high involvement within Scottish society.

Nowadays, us Campbell's are just high-class toffs with nice homes.

Unless you came from the name, you didn't really need to know about the history.

With the inheritance, my father became responsible for managing the estate and upholding the family legacy.

Well, until his death.

Now the estate is managed by Lady Francis, my overbearing mother. One day, it might make its way to me, even though I really couldn't care less.

Family traditions have filled my life, that and the constant reminder to continue the Campbell bloodline.

As an only child, it's my duty to represent and reproduce.

Like hell that's ever going to happen.

My mother also came from a wealthy background.

Her parents had fit easily into society through inherited wealth; additionally, her father had been a skilled council member. Oh, how the other half live.

My parents met in their late twenties— they'd both been attending a local landowners' ball.

Their first conversation had sparked an unfaltering attraction and it wasn't long before they wed.

I arrived two years later— for their sins.

My father had wished for a son, but obviously that wasn't to be.

Mother dearest suffered major complications whilst giving birth, and I've grown up to know all about it.

I sometimes think I felt the pain more than she did.

After making a full recovery, she insisted there would be no more children.

The Laird never again broached the subject, and I never welcomed any siblings.

Instead, I was sent away to Heatherbank, one of the most prestigious and highest-ranking boarding schools in Scotland.

Remaining there until seventeen, I then moved back home and applied to the University of Edinburgh to study Law.

During my time at Heatherbank, I'd return to Riccarton for school holidays; regularly joining my father on deer stalking and pheasant shooting trips in Perthshire.

Very much to the disapproval of my mother.

She understood hunting activities to be suitable for men and definitely not established young ladies.

We, the young ladies, should be managing the house and tending to the family.

Eurgh, talk about outdated. Some days I wish I'd kept the gun!

This was one of the few disagreements my parents would share; usually, they were well-tempered and quite affectionate towards one another.

They eventually agreed to disagree, and I played piggy in the middle until I was old enough to talk back.

In 1992, Dad partnered up with David Cambell, one of his closest friends and business colleagues; they established the Campbell & Cambell legal practice.

They worked tirelessly as partners and co-owners until 2010, when my father tragically passed away during a work meeting.

He'd arrived at the office one Wednesday morning and suffered a heart attack forty minutes later; he was only fifty-five.

At the time, I was twenty-four and only four months into my career as a Trainee Solicitor for the firm.

I've continued working in the same office ever since—my job title has changed considerably since then.

Climbing the five-stone steps to the front door, I let myself in.

Oh, come on, it's not like we have butlers!

'Mother, it's me,' I shouted from the grand entrance hall, a cold, haunting echo coming back to meet me as I dumped my coat on an antique upholstered bench.

Meandering through the portrait-lined hallway, I turned my nose up to the mustard-floral damask— It stretches from the checkerboard floor to the ceiling's cornicing.

The place could really use a freshen up— Perhaps Steve can make a start once the gallery's complete.

An elaborate ceiling rose and four eccentric yet dazzling crystal chandeliers glisten proudly above my head.

The house is immaculate— every surface spic and span, no dust or debris obvious to the naked eye.

The scent of furniture polish with a hint of musk fill the expansive corridor.

I continued walking towards the kitchen— admiring a place I once loved.

Now it's nothing more than an antique reminder of my faults.

Upon entering the long, opulent dining room, I subtly positioned myself into one of the eight high-backed leather chairs— deliberately choosing the seat where the fine china had already been laid.

The table was already set for two, a parallel arrangement mirroring each end of the table.

Pristine silverware with two shiny transparent glasses; one for water, the other for wine.

Heavy white linen held perfectly in place by ornate

napkin rings sat between the cutlery.

Elegant golden mirrors and ancient portraits watching down, as if highlighting my overdue presence.

Fresh-cut flowers, no doubt from the garden, filled the five crystal vases dotted around the room. They add a bright and fresh appeal— even if the scent is overpowering, it's still a nice touch.

Lilies and carnations. Mother's favourite.

'You are late!'

The stentorian voice caught me off guard, my bum physically lifting.

'Goodness, Mother, you gave me a fright.'
I scolded with a hand against my chest.

My mother entered the room with a silver platter clamped tightly between both hands.

Carefully manoeuvring it between us, she placed it on the table and scurried off back towards the kitchen.

After less than a minute, she reappeared with yet another. This one consisted of four additional bowls; one for carrots, green beans, roast potatoes, and skirlie. A pewter gravy boat, filled to the top in a golden glory also made its debut.

'I've made chicken, Paisley. I hope you are hungry. You look as though you haven't eaten a decent meal in goodness knows how long.'
Three humongous slabs of chicken breast magically appeared on my plate.

Helping myself to a mix of vegetables and gravy, I sat back down.

Mum finally found her own seat.

'Thank you, Mother, this looks delicious.'
I stuffed a portion of white meat between my teeth,

trying hard to ignore the backhanded compliment.

'Your face looks gaunt; you need to look after yourself. I can't expect you to carry healthy babies if you're not taking care of yourself first.'

Oh, here we go again.
I finished the mouthful and allowed my eyes to work their way across the table to glower into my mother's.

'Can we please just enjoy this meal before we start pulling chunks out of each other?
It would seem a tremendous waste of food to start an argument this early on.' I announced while trying to hold some sort of reasonable authority.

My mother nodded, her mouth closed into a tight line as she chewed.
Swallowing down a few measly forkfuls, she chirped in again.

'You aren't getting any younger, Paisley. Your father will be turning in his grave knowing you are still unmarried and childless…'
Christ, I should have ordered Chinese from my place.

I put the fork down heavily, it clanged off the plate— interrupting her slur.
I leant on my elbows before twisting my hands up and under my jaw.
I wasn't quite resting on them, but it was a thought I was seriously contemplating… just to make a point.

'Elbows off the table.' My mother scolded.
The angry, beady eyes burning holes into my unruly arms.
Her voice carried like an angry headteacher; she looked the part too, with shoulder-length grey hair and a face pinched from years of scowling and looking down her nose on the less desirable.

Dressed in a green tweed blazer, matching skirt and a neatly pressed cream blouse, there was no denying her financial success.

She gave the impression a political party might walk through the door at any moment, sit down and indulge in some of the roast chicken dinner.

Even in the comfort of her own home, she couldn't drop the stiff upper lip.

I kept the elbows firmly in place, cautiously thinking about how to respond.

Pulse quickening as my internal temperature spiked.

I could already feel a harshness biting at my tongue, ready in its attempt to beat my abuser.

'Mum, we've already had this discussion— on more than one occasion, might I add.

I will not be marrying a man.

I will have nothing to do with any man.

If it has a penis, it's not walking through my door, let alone into my bed.'

'How vulgar.' My mother scoffed before turning her head in disgust.

'Yes, I know. I'm glad for once we finally agree on something.

Men do not, and I cannot exaggerate this enough, they do not make me happy.

The chance of grandchildren has not and will not ever be an option— It just isn't going to happen, so please stop pushing.

You cannot keep using grandchildren as an excuse for your behaviour towards me. I won't allow it. Not now, not ever.' I spat the words out, each sentence harsher than the last.

Sweat etched its way forward as my cheeks flushed; hands starting to tremble with an uncontrollable rage.

My mother's voice cut through the tension; sharp and unwavering.

'First and foremost, I am your mother, not your mum. Spoken like a true commoner!' She punctuated each word with an exaggerated flick of her fork.

'Secondly, tell me when you last brought home a partner of any gender? Huh?
You are self-righteous in your attempt at telling me you are interested in women, well, where are they?
I hardly see them lining the streets of Edinburgh waiting for the great, Paisley Rose Campbell.
If you are so interested in females, why haven't I ever met any girlfriends, or whatever the hell you call them?'
My mother's fork finally joined the plate in front of her. It took a moment longer than I'd expected, but I couldn't argue with her. In fact, she'd hit the nail directly on the head.
Not once had anyone been brought back to meet the family, and it wasn't looking as though anyone would be coming over any time soon. Urgh. You bitch!

Standing from the chair, I tucked it in and stood behind. Lazily I leant on it with my arms, just to exasperate my mother a teensy bit more. It didn't look as though I'd be staying long anyway.

The wooden frame creaked slightly as I added more pressure.
Anything to piss this witch off, still wasn't going to be enough for me tonight.
This time I shouted a little louder, a silent hope that the invisible party occupying the empty chairs could hear

every word.

'Mum, I'm too embarrassed to bring anyone here! You think everyone is of a lower social standing.

I mean look at this place. Look at it!

It's like a fucking time capsule.

I'm too ashamed to be with anyone who won't suit your outdated, old-fashioned morals and agenda.

I cannot and will not do it.'

Swinging forward against the chair, the wood groaned.

Mother remained silent.

'No! I won't be bringing anyone here until I'm confident they're strong enough to put up with your shit.'

I paused, not sure if I'd pushed a little too hard when crossing the line.

Looking at my mother's unmoved face, I figured it wasn't enough and continued for some more.

Just because I could.

'I'm truly sorry that I've disappointed you, Mum.

Every day, you've made it crystal clear that I'm your biggest failure.

Not worthy of this life you have bestowed upon me.

Not worthy of a pointless, obsolete title.

Who the fuck walks around calling themselves *'Lady'* nowadays anyway?

No one. Not unless they expect the Royal Family to drop in past for a spot of fucking tea!' I screamed before catching my breath— it was now rattling in my scorched throat.

My mother's eyes widened, giving way to the horror she was harbouring beneath the skin.

Yes, I've got you.

Now you hear and see me!

'I understand the weight of not having siblings to carry on the family name. I know I'll never pass this lifestyle onto someone when you're gone, and for that I am sorry, but it's not me, Mum. This was never caused by me.

Do you seriously think I wanted to be like this?

To have the world look down on me for not conforming to the norm. To be humiliated, rejected, discriminated against, all on account of who I may or may not love.

I don't want to be a stereotype that relies on acceptance from kind strangers. I never wanted to hurt my parents or break their hearts for not being the perfect daughter.

I wanted to go places, meet people, see different things, share my life with someone without the worry of being ridiculed.

It's bad enough half the world hates me for being who I am, but my bloody mother joining in, that's something else.'

Stopping for breath, I looked to the ceiling.

One hand moved to rub my temple as I thought carefully about my next move.

My mother's lack of fight was making me rage.

'The difference is, Mum, you're doing it out of spite and prejudice. I'm doing it, because I physically and mentally cannot change.

That's what hurts the most.

It makes me bitterly sad, that you can't seem to accept, or even appreciate who I am.

I can't change, by God, I wish I could.

Do you honestly think growing up a queer rich kid was at the top of my to-do list? No!

No one plans for this type of thing.

You, my mother, the one person who's supposed to love me unconditionally, cannot get past the end of her own nose. That's disappointing.'

Her wide eyes continued to stare in a fixed disgust. Mine tried to bring my burning temper under some sort of control.

'Mum, I'm almost forty, and we're still having this same argument. Twenty years later... you need to move on.'

Maybe I've said enough.

'Your father would be mortified.' My mother bit back.

Maybe not.

'You know Mum, I am deeply, wholeheartedly sorry that the last conversation with Dad ended the way it did. I'm sorry you didn't get more time with him, in fact, I'm sorry that *I* didn't get more time with him.

Even though he never said it, I know he was proud of me. He wouldn't have let me work at Campbells if he wasn't.

I know you blame me, and that's okay, I've made peace with it.

You loved him and I appreciate that more than you will ever know.' I laughed out a hollow snort. 'See, it isn't that difficult to just say that a relationship you dislike is okay.' I flung my hands in the air, flippant and frivolous.

'The ease of your relationship leaves a sour taste in my mouth, it was so effortless, and yes, it is because I'm jealous.

But I didn't kill him, Mum. I didn't stand over him holding his nose waiting for his last breath to stop.'

'Paisley!!' My mother screamed; spit flew as she

stood up from the chair, its feet screeching harshly against the floor.

Obviously *that* comment hit the nerve perfectly.

'I tried to help him, Mum. I tried to get him home to you. To me. To us. Life just isn't fair— God, don't I know all about that?' My hands met the sky again.

'But this hatred you hold above me, this pull me in when it suits and toss me aside when it doesn't, it's a part of grief, and it's part of your grief, Mum.

You need to work on that yourself, I've done my grieving and I can't help you.

You're going to end up dying alone and scared, because the one person you need won't be coming back to rescue you.

Your bridges are burning, Mum.

Right now, they're burning really bloody bright.'

I sucked in a deep shaky breath, steadying myself on the creaky seat.

My mother bounced back into her own chair, eyes enraged, mouth twisting tightly.

'Enough, Paisl…'

'You see, the truth is, whether you like it or not, whether you blame me or not, I didn't cause dad's death. Yes, we argued, but I didn't do this.

Fourteen years and you still can't say something nice. It's always all about you.

It always has been, and yes, it probably always will be going forward. But Mum, I'm not running to you when you call, not anymore. I'm done.'

My throat was burning, knuckles white as I gripped the seat.

My mother's face looked as though I'd just hit her

with the frying pan.

'My heart and happiness are going to be my main focus from now on.
You're welcome to process that whichever way you see fit, but I will not continue playing this game of torment. It's time to recognise that life is about so much more than just status and sexuality.'

Stepping back from the table, I looked at the floor for inspiration.
Lifting my head, I faced her once more.

'If you can't love your daughter, who genuinely does love you, despite your continuous criticism of her shortcomings; then it's clear to me, that there's no point pretending to play happy families.
You need to acknowledge what truly matters.
I loved Dad and I love you, but that's it, Mum.
This monstrosity of a relationship stops now. I'm done with all of this.'

My mother forked in another mouthful of chicken, the mournful silence overwhelming.
Obviously, she was playing her own game of poker.
Well, fuck you.

'Goodbye, Mum.'

My heart was racing, drumming in my chest and ears.
The blood pumping through the vein on the side of my neck— pulsing as if I'd just run a marathon.
Skull reeling with anger, guilt, fear.
Things I shouldn't have said, things I could have articulated better.
I don't need this nonsense— I'm not a child anymore.

Storming out of the dining room and heading for the front door, my head lifted to the ceiling rose.

I picked up my coat and removed a cigarette from the pocket.

Pulling the front door behind me, I walked.

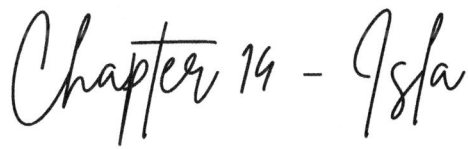

Chapter 14 - Isla

New message - Px

Skye, I'm so sorry, I thought I'd be able to message you back earlier but I had dinner with my mother!

I haven't told you this before, but we don't always see eye to eye.

In fact, we rarely even meet in the middle. It was such an awful evening, I don't think I'll be seeing her for a while. Anyway, I hope you're well and having a far more

productive and enjoyable day than I am?

P x

Sent 19:54 Monday 12th Feb

Yesterday's fishing trip had been extended due to an engine failure.

Ultimately, Granda and I wouldn't be going anywhere until an engineer arrived from Glasgow. Christ knows how long that's going to take.

I hadn't been best pleased when requesting assistance from the tow boat.

Mind you, it was certainly better than being stranded for another day at sea.

Unintentionally I'd been hoping my phone would alert me to my new alter-ego text interest.

My grin must have reached Portree when it finally sang out, and for once I was still awake.

New message - Skye's the Limit

P, I'm sorry to hear you had a rough day.

To be honest, mine could have gone a lot smoother too.

It's good to learn these little bits about you though.

My parents aren't involved with me either, so I can understand your frustration.

Do you want to talk about it?

Would it be strange to say I missed not looking at my phone? Skye x

Sent 19:59 Monday 12th Feb

New message - Px

Skye, it's a long story, with many years of complications.

I'd rather just brush over it tonight if that's ok? Maybe we can talk about it another time? I'd hate to let you see the worst of me so early on... especially after this evening's outburst.

I'm sorry to hear your day wasn't the best either, do you want to talk about that?

No, it's not strange, I missed the messaging too.

Where in Scotland are you?

P x

Sent 20:01 Monday 12th Feb

New message - Skye's the Limit

Skye.

Sent 20:01 Monday 12th Feb

New message - Px

Skye, I think you deleted the text?

P x

Sent 20:02 Monday 12th Feb

New message - Skye's the Limit
Ha ha! No, I live in Skye.
Skye x
Sent 20:02 Monday 12th Feb

> **New message - Px**
> *So, you're called Skye and live on Skye!?*
> *That is amusing!*
> *Sent 20:03 Monday 12th Feb*

New message - Skye's the Limit
P, my name is Isla.
Sent 20:03 Monday 12th Feb

> **New message - Px**
> *Isla?*
> *Isla Skye, are you mocking me?*
> *I'm pretty sure you're taking the piss?*
> *P x   Sent 20:04 Monday 12th Feb*

'Dope.'
Mind you, that is quite funny.
I don't think I even realised the connection and it's my name!
Obviously, she's a bright dingbat to click on so fast.

New message - Skye's the Limit
P. Ha ha!
No, I'm dead serious.
My name is Isla.
The Skye part is sheer coincidence.
Sent 20:04 Monday 12th Feb

New message - Px

Well Isla, that's a lovely name and it's nice to meet you. I guess you should call me Paisley, since it would appear we're now on first name terms.

Unfortunately, I'm quite a considerable distance from you. I'm not entirely sure how this is going to work out, I'm in Edinburgh!

P x

Sent 20:05 Monday 12th Feb

Reading the message three times, I lingered on the screen.

'Edinburgh. *Edinburgh!* What?

That doesn't fit my ideal vision. For goodness' sake!'

My hand bounced off my knee.

New message - Skye's the Limit

Paisley! I like that... It's affa nice to meet you too!

I can't lie, I didn't expect Edinburgh.

Isla x

Sent 20:07 Monday 12th Feb

New message - Px

Isla, I don't know how we proceed from here. We've both already mentioned being career driven, it would seem the dating gods aren't in our favour.

I'm genuinely very sad to think this is now going to be the end of this short-lived friendship.

Paisley x

Sent 20:08 Monday 12th Feb

Paisley

Swigging the last of the wine dregs, I poured another. The now half-empty bottle tactically positioned on the bedside table.

A defeated tug pulling at my chest as I finally gave in to the bleak response.

The phone buzzed again.

New message - Skye's the Limit
I don't want to jump to the wrong conclusion Paisley or give you any kind of weird stalker vibe… but I'm going to be in Edinburgh in two weeks time.
Maybe we could meet up and grab a drink?
I don't want to sound desperate or presumptuous.
I wouldn't normally meet anyone offline and it's perfectly fine if you don't fancy it, I just thought I'd put the option out there.
Isla x
Sent 20:10 Monday 12th Feb

New message - Px
That sounds like a really lovely idea.
What are your plans for Edinburgh?
Do you know the date?
P x
Sent 20:10 Monday 12th Feb

I realised I'd typed and sent the text without even thinking about the repercussions.

Wasn't it strange that Skye… or Isla just happened to be in Edinburgh in two weeks?

What if it's Beth, the crumpled freak? Or some creepy mass murdering psychopath with a bushbaby on his shoulder. What if Isla isn't physically attractive? Or she's that small, spotty teenager I initially thought of. Should I ask for a photo? Does it matter?

Yes, definitely.

What if we're completely incompatible? Or the spark isn't really there.

Have I led this woman on without realising?

Oh my God, what have I done?

New message - Skye's the Limit

Paisley! I'm travelling down on a Sunday and returning on the Tuesday. I don't know where I'm staying yet but I'm sure it's in the city centre. I'm travelling with family, so I'll need to double check the details.

Is it too soon to meet? We barely know each other! I've made myself all panicky, is this normal?

Isla x   Sent 20:12 Monday 12th Feb

That last message immediately calmed my overactive imagination.

This woman was also having doubts, maybe she wasn't some serial psychopath and this was just a genuine star-aligning coincidence.

Oh Paisley, get a grip and go on the bloody date.

You can't expect miracles if you don't leave the house.

New message – Px

Isla, I'm so glad you asked, I just wondered the same thing. My imagination started to run away without me. Look, I can't say what's going to happen after meeting, but I'm prepared to give it a try. Please let me know your plans as soon as you have them, I'll try and get time away from the office if I need to.

Yes, that's a normal reaction.

Don't worry, I'm not a creep.

P x

Sent 20:13 Monday 12th Feb

New message – Skye's the Limit

I will :) Thanks for confirming, I don't think I'm a creep either ha ha! Well, you never know…

There's something affa mysterious about not knowing what you look like! I would normally be shit scared of talking to a faceless stranger, but it doesn't feel like that with you.

Does that sound strange? Naive maybe? God, I'm babbling again… nerves :') sorry!

Isla x   Sent 20:15 Monday 12th Feb

New message – Px

No, that doesn't sound strange, and you're not babbling.

But…And it's a big but… I can't help wonder why you haven't ever dated.

Is there a reason?

I'm sorry if that's too forward a question, I'm genuinely interested.

Paisley x

Sent 20:15 Monday 12th Feb

New message - Skye's the Limit

Ok Paisley, don't think bad of me. Please!

God, I'm so embarrassed, how will I ever look at you?

There aren't many gay folk here on Skye, most of them I know in one way or another. The dating pool is extremely slim, especially for a lesbian.

I've never dated because I felt my preferences went against my family's morals. That and I haven't ever made the time for someone to quietly slot into place.

I don't like drama, I just want an easy life. I'm realising that over time, it hasn't made me or my folks happy.

My friends and folks are pushing me to find happiness, someone to focus my attention on... If I'm honest, I probably need it.

I've been on nights out and 'been' with people - mostly 'straight women' who I'm ashamed to say have usually had a bit too much to drink... suddenly they believe they are the newfound sex goddess of Skye.

Let me tell you, it's nae even that satisfying... admittedly, that was many years ago - like teens/early 20s. No one recently. God! I really haven't been near anyone in years. What a depressing and downgrading thought. I don't even think I'd know what to do on a date. It's all apps and hook-ups! Me and my heart are so secluded, I long for someone every night... Pathetic I know. I've never even brought anyone home, can you believe that? That's my safe place. Unless you're someone special, you're not getting in.

I hope that helps sum up my predicament.

Fuck, I sound so pitiful, I understand if you want to cancel this meet up... I'm wondering if I should cancel it for you.

Isla x   Sent 20:17 Monday 12th Feb

My God, this woman needs someone more than I do. She's made herself into an island, and by the sounds of things, it's surrounded with barbed wire, crocodiles and a few radioactive landmines.

Here's me grumbling about five years of lacklustre and this woman's not been held in what... thirty-eight, minus twenty-ish ... Jesus!

Maybe I'll bring her a guidebook.

Goodness, I can't get that image free— My hands are clammy at the thought.

New message - Px

Isla, I understand and don't be silly, I certainly don't think any less of you! If anything, I'm in awe.

My last relationship ended 5 years ago, and it wasn't even serious, it was a total waste of 3 months.

Can you call that a relationship?

As a workaholic, probably bordering alcoholic with the amount of wine I drink (I'm kidding, I'm not there yet. Well, I hope not).

I was never available when she needed me, I never wanted to go anywhere or do anything.

I guess, I wasn't really emotionally prepared for a relationship. I was selfish, she deserved better. It didn't last. It was for all the right reasons for me, but all the wrong ones for her. My family never met her, probably didn't know she existed.

I too don't fit in with their ideals, my mother still expects me to come home and tell her I'm pregnant lol. Jesus, that's a thought.

You don't sound pitiful or pathetic, and don't be embarrassed, not with me anyway!

You sound caring and kind, looking out for your

family's interests.

That's lovely qualities to have, maybe I should take a page from your book.

Paisley x

Sent 20:20 Monday 12th Feb

New message - Skye's the Limit

Thank you for saying that Paisley, that's affa nice. I'm still embarrassed, but I do appreciate it.

Not everyone's made to have their wings clipped, if it wasn't the right relationship for you then why would you stay?

I'm sorry yer family think like that, I guess I'm lucky in the sense, the ones that matter have faith in who I am.

They just want me to be happy, something I haven't been for a long time.

Do you want a family? I mean like, do you want children? If you don't want to answer that, it's ok.

Not everyone values that question... It's never been in my plan, mind you, my plans don't ever go the way I want.

I had hoped to be living the dream by now, instead I'm another day closer to the grave with nothing to show.

Why are you on a highland dating app?

Surely Edinburgh has lots of very attractive women ;)

Isla x

Sent 20:25 Monday 12th Feb

New message - Px

Isla honestly, I'm not a monster, hold your embarrassment for someone worthy.

You're correct, not everyone's made for the people they're with.

I think I'd rather face the treachery alone than be locked into a dead-end relationship with someone I can't love.

My family have very specific tastes, not something I agree with, but they are who they are.

I can't change them now... as tempting as it is to ask for a refund.

Secretly I'd love to bring someone home to my mother, I think it would shut her up long enough for me to get a word in edgeways. She's an interesting character to say the least.

I need someone strong and driven to keep her in check, do you know anyone like that?

Children have never fit in with my career driven lifestyle, I appreciate the lure but it's not really for me.

I don't have a problem with children, but I don't think I could have my own. I don't mean physically, I mean selfishly.

Probably not the best thing to tell my new pen pal!

Edinburgh's full of beautiful people but typically none for me, maybe I'm too fussy.

I guess that's why I'm on here, I've exhausted the local apps and I haven't even met anyone.

P xx

Sent 20:30 Monday 12th Feb

New message - Skye's the Limit

I don't think you're a monster at all, you don't type like you have big paws or sharp teeth!

I'm sick of being alone, I just want someone to snuggle into with the log burner on and some wine, possibly a book... maybe I'm a hopeless romantic too, I've never really thought about it.

I just want a hallmark movie moment.

A refund for your family ha ha, I'll take two of those!

There's nothing wrong with not wanting kids, some folk aren't the parenting type.

Ahh, I might know one strong woman, I'll keep you updated!

Are you a beautiful person Paisley? I feel like you might be. Give me 3 words to describe yourself... and I already know you're career driven and a part time alcoholic.

Isla xx   Sent 20:33 Monday 12th Feb

New message - Px

My teeth are indeed very sharp, maybe I'll let you see them.

That sounds like the perfect night... the log burner, not necessarily the teeth... although... hmm never mind.

Maybe you could introduce that woman to me, she might meet all of my overbearing uptight needs ;)

Three words. Hmm that's interesting.

Okay. Disciplined, reliable, persistent.

How does that work for you?

Your turn, please and thank you.

P xx

Sent 20:38 Monday 12th Feb

New message - Skye's the Limit

Ohh, I love that… The 3 words, ok… maybe the teeth too… dying!

I think I'm breaking down the uptight and overbearing, after our first messages things are going braw… the 3 words I'd give you are… softie, personable and introverted.

I guess my own 3 words are, outgoing, warm-hearted and loyal.

I'm not going to lie Paisley, my head's spinning with ideas of what you look like, I can't decide if it's stressing me out or exciting me.

2 weeks is a long time until I find out.

How long have you been out? I'm nearing 18 years this year, I was 20… that seems a lifetime ago. Auch, that was some day!

Isla xx   Sent 20:46 Monday 12th Feb

New message - Px

Lol, I can agree with the dying comment.

I think you may have broken part of me down, and no one's done that before… I don't think. We'll see…

Oh, three words for you would be: courageous (you talk back), caring and easy going. I hope I'm right. Not that I'm ridiculously competitive or anything.

Yes, it's a rational fear not seeing you, but I'm treating it like a challenge, I don't want to give in.

To answer your previous question, I believe beauty lies in the eyes of the beholder. I don't think I'm a dog, but maybe not as attractive as Jennifer Anniston! I wouldn't like to hide the surprise… or disappointment. I was out at nineteen, not my finest hour… also a lifetime ago.

P xx   Sent 20:52 Monday 12th Feb

Our conversation carried on for several hours, each of us taking turns to share the many strengths and flaws. We spoke about desires for the future and the mistakes we'd already made along the way.

Discussions on internalised fears and beliefs, reflecting on the unfairness of the world, the lack of opportunities, and the contrast between city life and island living.

We steered clear of delving too deeply into kin matters, both appearing to be agonisingly similar in the sense of the strained and unforgiving dynamics.

Neither revealing too much, nor asking anything overly personal.

I held a quiet appreciation for someone like-minded—someone who truly shared an understanding and felt clear within their own stories and experiences.

Some things, we still felt were better shared in person.

New message - Skye's the Limit

Paisley, I hope this doesn't seem too forward and you're free to object... but could I maybe give you a call sometime?

I'd really love to hear your voice, I have a vision in my head as to how it sounds. I can't even explain how you've already made me feel at ease!

I know phone calls are a bit old-fashioned, but sometimes a friendly voice can really brighten up the dark.

Isla x   Sent 01:49 Tuesday 13th Feb

New message - Px

That would be lovely, Isla!

I feel like we've really bonded.

On this occasion it feels like it's for the right reasons.

I do need to go for now, I'm so sorry!

I'm working tomorrow, but I sincerely wish I could stay a while longer.

I can't tell you how comforting it is talking to you.

Please message when you can - if you want to (fingers crossed).

Goodnight, and sweet dreams.

P xx   Sent 01:51 Tuesday 13th Feb

I sent the message, adding my phone number at the bottom.

Mounting the phone to the wireless charger, I climbed the mountain of stairs to my minimalistic third-floor bedroom.

For once, the weight of the world wasn't pulling me down, there may have even been a small skip in my step.

'Behave, it's just a couple of messages.

Anything could happen between now and then.

You haven't even seen her face.'

Isla

Auch, I dinna even want to go to bed yet.

My heart's racing, my head's doing a highland fling, and I've sat here all night awaiting each and every message.

Rising from the armchair, I grabbed my laptop from the kitchen bunker. Settling back into the warm spot, I tucked my legs comfortably beneath my bum and opened the computer's lid.

Searching hotels in Edinburgh was no easy feat, I had so many requirements and the city had so many options. The location and atmosphere needed to suit both Granda and me, and I needed somewhere close to the solicitors to avoid any suspicion.

The excitement of our upcoming city adventure mingled with a quiet anticipation was already beginning to pull at me.

Auch, slow down old girl, she might not be what you're expecting— You've not even seen her face, she could still be a complete munster.

Granda won't care much about the hotel, he'll be happy as long as it has a bed and window.

Hmm, I'm going for a holiday, I want extravagant and exciting.

What if I bring someone back to my room? Ha, I don't think so, but you never really know.

Browsing through the dozens of central hotels, I filtered them by location and star rating.

I had a determination to pick out somewhere a little bit more refined than the usual economy class.

For once, I was going to indulge in a bit of luxury, even if it was just for a few days.

Clicking on '*The Caledonian Hotel*,' I was drawn to its perfect location— ideal for Granda's appointment and my own private plans.

I'm confident I can slip away for a couple of hours without him noticing, but I'll need to arrange my appointment for when he's occupied in his meeting.

Paisley's already mentioned trying to make herself available, so I'm hopeful everything will fall perfectly into place. Fingers crossed.

Double-checking the dates with the Campbell & Cambell email, I sent a much politer response; the requested date was suitable, and Granda would attend.

I don't want to upset the beautiful witch again, I might just email her in the future asking if she'd like to adopt me.

I let free a nervous giggle.

Unable to hide my curiosity and devious streak, I clicked '*open*' on the Campbell & Cambell page I'd previously bookmarked.

Allowing my eyes a thirty second gift from the Gods, Ms. P. Campbell (PhD) stared back.

Well, there's no harm in looking, the laptop's already open… admittedly, the shiver that ran through me was more uncontrollable than when I'd first ogled.

Switching back to the hotel site, I booked two 'Kingsize

Superior Rooms' for the Sunday and Monday night.

At just over six hundred pounds, it better include breakfast, and I definitely want pancakes.

Money's never really been an issue, my career-focused lifestyle and lack of major spends has allowed me to accumulate a small fortune.

It probably isn't enough to stay at The Caledonian Hotel for more than a year, but it's certainly enough to indulge in impulsive bookings when the mood strikes.

Next, my attention turned to transport.

If I drive us both down, it doesn't quite capture the essence of a holiday.

'Hmm, take the train or bus?'

After a moment of thought, I decided to drive to Inverness and leave the car at the station.

From there, we can continue by train to give us a true sense of adventure and relaxation.

'Bugger it.'

I booked the tickets, ensuring we both had a window seat.

'Oh aye, OAP fares for Granda, ideal!

Robbing gits want a fortune… Christ, this trip isnae half costing me.'

With all of the reservations in place, I closed the laptop lid, looking at the modern cuckoo the realisation hit me.

'Jeezo, it's well past my bedtime, it's quarter past three!'

Sluggishly, I slid off the chair.

A dull ache pounded through my head; no doubt from staring at the screen, that and the late hour— usually I'd be heading off to work.

Quicker than a flash, I was suddenly aware of my non-conforming feet; they'd completely fallen asleep from sitting so long.

In an awkward, slow-motion disaster, I flailed like a newborn giraffe trying to find its balance.

My laptop soared across the room and with all the grace of a sack o' tatties, I fell face-first onto the floor.

Timidly, my hand raised to the new lump growing beneath my eye.

'Ouch! I guess that's one way to end a productive day.'

* * * *

The buzzing of my phone jolted me awake.

Through cracked and swollen eyes, I immediately regretted waking up— the morning light stabbing like a thousand needles.

'Eurghh. What in the rise of the clans, is that awful noise!'

The duvet had somehow managed to entangle me into a cocoon. I must look like a sleepy, disoriented caterpillar.

My throat felt like a desert, dry and scratchy, head pounding as if I'd been hit by a bus.

'Nooo, not today please, I just want to sleep.'

Grabbing the phone with a dramatic sigh, I squinted at the screen:

08:04 AM - *Incoming Call* - Morag

'Auchh, great.'

I swiped the answer button on the screen.

'Well, are you awake?' Morag asked.

She always sounds so bloody chirpy in the morning.

'I am now...' I paused, still not feeling fully awake.

'... I've only just gone to bed, Morag.'

'Eh?! What the hell have you been doing? Or who were you doing? Are you alright? Are you sick, want me to drive over?'

'Bloody hell, Mo, one at a time.' I rubbed the back of my hand over my eyes.

'Aye, bring me breakfast... and coffee, Morag! Strong, black and very sweet. Please.'

'Christ, I'm already in the car.'

Morag hung up.

Maybe I could sneak five more minutes.

Twenty minutes later and Morag must have let herself into the house.

One of the perks to island living is barely anyone locks their door at night.

Crime on Skye's practically non-existent, and I often thought that if someone did want to steal something, they'd be better off just walking in and helping themselves rather than causing a scene by breaking doors and windows.

It was practically an open invitation, or at least more efficient.

Morag must have positioned herself on the edge of the bed, I felt the blanket shift as a weight grazed my hip.

'Oh my God, Isla, are ye okay?' Morag screeched.

The smell of coffee, wafting from somewhere.

I lifted a couple of pillows and nodded; my eyes still not accustom to the hazards ahead.

'Jesus Christ, what the hell happened to yer face? Did ye lose a fight with one o' those pillows?'

I touched my cheek with a grimace.

Lifting the duvet slightly, Morag climbed in beside me.

A paper cup making its way over after I shifted.

Thinking on last night's messaging, I beamed free an indulgent grin.

'Oh boy, have I got a story for you. How long do you have?' I asked.

'Isla, I'm all ears but get started, I've not got all day.'

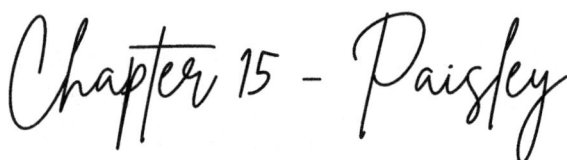

Chapter 15 – Paisley

Exiting the Sheriff Court, my court shoes splashed as we marched along the Cowgate.

James followed behind but appeared to be struggling to keep up— too busy pussy footing around flooded craters in the pavement. He unsuccessfully landed in more of them than he dodged.

It was bloody miserable, and I silently regretted not bringing the large company umbrella still sat in my office. It is still February after all, mental note for future; don't be so stupid and take a brolly.

Shitty weather… stupid arse of a judge… miserable bloody day in this miserable, poxy city… arghh.

The silence was shattered when James skidded on a slick paving slab.

'*Jesssusss*. I'm sorry darling, but was it just me that thought that was an unfavourable amount of Satan's own brand of soft serve?' He called out, still trying to keep up with my long legs.

I just kept trudging, silently reeling at the Court's outcome; thoughts of Isla clouding my judgement.

I can't clear the apprehension.

'Paisley, sweetie, there will be better days.

We can relook at the beneficiaries' disagreement and find a resolution, I'm sure there was no undue influence...'

Looking at my watch, I cut him off mid-sentence.

'It's not that, James!

Come on, let's grab lunch.'

I opened the door to the Starbucks at the edge of the Royal Mile.

The place was jam-packed— full of people hiding from the rain.

I joined the queue without realising James had already disappeared.

A couple stood from a table by the window, awkwardly pulling on soggy jackets and scarves.

They very cautiously manhandled the gigantic paper shopping sack.

That bag isn't going to make it to Market Street, let alone Princes Street.

I admired the camp and exaggerated stage production James was creating in an effort to pinch their table.

He sat down on the pleather chair whilst the last occupants continued their painful, sodden dance.

Eventually, moving to the door, they stood anticipating whether or not the apocalyptic weather was worth the risk.

I wouldn't attempt it personally, but it's not my problem. Yet.

I locked eyes with James whilst still stuck ten-deep in the winding queue of soy-based, gluten-free, vegetarian-only misfits.

We were all desperately trying to decipher the profound mystery between a venti and a grande.

I lifted my hands in a *what the fuck is the hold-up kind* of motion— James rolled his eyes so hard it was almost audible.

I couldn't help but eavesdrop the order being brutally murdered at the checkout.

Eventually, I appeared at the tiny table with one very small, scuffed, silver tray in my hands— the coffee overflowing onto the saucers.

The panini plates were precariously hanging over the edge of the tray; as if playing a dangerous game of hangman, one shaky hand away from a neck-breaking disaster. It would be just my luck.

'The bampot filled the mugs to the rim,' I remarked after placing the tray very carefully onto the table.

As if I really needed to explain the situation to James.

Removing my coat, I hung it neatly over the back of the chair.

Well, I didn't want it to wrinkle as it dried off, how untidy would that look?

I can't be going around the city dressed like a tramp.

James picked up one of the toasted ciabattas, lifting its lid to glower into the bowels, it seemed to meet his expectations.

He took a delicate bite from the pointed edge.

'Well, how long is it going to take for me to badger you like an ADHD dog, before you give in and tell me what your problem is?' He asked.

Unintentionally I let out a snort.

James recoiled as though I was about to snaffle him up into my mouth.

Watching him carefully, I finished my mouthful of chicken and mozzarella panini.

'I've been messaging someone.' I replied, still unsure if I actually wanted to tell him or not.

He was usually good in desperate and challenging situations… that, and the fact he was more of a slut than anyone else I knew.

James dropped his cheesy sandwich onto the laughably small plate.

Rubbing his fingers together with one of the incy-wincy teenie-weenie napkins the server had kindly piled twelve high— It was as helpful as using a first-class postage stamp to dry off after a bath.

'Darling, tell me everything.'

James sat staring in silence, unsure of how to string his next sentence together I'd imagine.

His eyebrows bounced in tandem as I spoke, his eyeballs and neck working together to protrude during the intervals.

'So, why the sulking, sweetie? Isn't this great news? You've actually gone and found someone who might turn out to be everything you've wished for.'

He couldn't understand why I was being so hesitant. Maybe he had a point.

'I don't want to sound shallow or vain, although I'm aware I've probably already surpassed that stage, but what if… what if the physical appearance doesn't align, James?

I understand that it's not solely about beauty, but if I'm not physically attracted to her, I fear it will be rather disheartening for us both.'

I stole a mouthful of cappuccino as James sat chewing.

'Her personality is undeniably charming, it's only ever been conveyed through text, but its already sucking me in.

I do wish for a genuine and physical attraction as well, God knows I need it.'

James blew out a deep lingering huff of air, his

cheeks tinged slightly with the effort.

'Well darling, as Madonna once famously stated, Beauty is only skin deep...'

'James, that wasn't Madonna.'

'It wasn't?' His face filled with genuine surprise.

'No, it was Sir Thomas Overbury.

Madonna has never mentioned anything other than facelifts and bum implants!

If you read a bit more, you'd maybe know these things... dunce.'

I rolled my eyes with disdain.

'Well, there you have it!'

He feigned shock, dramatically placing his left hand on his chest.

'The Queen has spoken. If you don't like her look, throw some money down on the table and make her look however you want.

Moses knows, I could use a little Botox around these gorgeous eyes of mine.'

He tugged playfully at the corners of his eyes; as if he hadn't already been dabbling in the micro jabs.

I shook my head at him and took another bite— the mozzarella making an oozing mess down my chin.

Great, now I look as stupid as this doughball.

James's face twist into a pensive gaze— his lips set into a tight pout.

It was a sign something thoughtful might escape his lips for a change.

Crossing his legs and clasping his hands to his knees, James leant in.

'Paisley, how important is it for you to be with someone who is kind, caring and nurturing?'

His eye contact gave way to the fact he was very into

the conversation.

It surprised me slightly, as did the question.

I held my breath whilst contemplating the answer.

'It's very important, but if she doesn't look the part, I worry…

Auch, James, what would my mother say?

God, that's all I need, her whinging about an ugly girlfriend.'

'Oh yes, I had completely forgotten, your parents were perfect in every way.' He rolled his eyes and brushed his fringe with his fingers.

'James, I thought you'd be all about the physical attraction…'

'Oh honey, I am, but I don't plan on keeping any of them. They are simply here for my personal gratification.' He winked and smiled.

Eurgh creep!

'James! Please tell me you're joking?' Horrifically, my voice reached a new octave.

'No darling, I'm very serious.

When I'm ready to settle down, I will look for someone suitable, they might not be drop-dead gorgeous, but they will keep me grounded… or pounded. Either, or.

Sometimes sweetie, we need to make sacrifices.

Seriously, Paisley, I didn't expect you to be so shallow.

Honestly, I'd expect it from anyone else, but never you. I know you try for the cold and harsh exterior, but inside I know you're a pussycat…'

Taking a large gulp from the mug, the coffee created a harsh lump in my throat as I tried to swallow.

'…You've done nothing but go out of your way to be everything your family hates, why would you start conforming now?

Look, Paisley, all I'm saying is try out the furniture before you move into the house. That's all!'

'Auch, James.'

'You never know, darling, it might be delightful in every way, she might be gorgeous... or she could be completely hackit... that doesn't mean the sex would be terrible.

Personally, I find the ugly ones try harder!' James replied— nonchalant in every way.

I couldn't believe my ears, the neck hairs stood to attention whilst my hands turned cold and clammy.

I was mortified.

This was a new side to James, it was teetering on sensible, and that alone was incomprehensible.

Rolling the cup around in my hands, my head filled with over thirty different emotions, each of them as bad as the first.

'James, I don't even know how to reply to you right now.

My face can't hide the shock.

I'm not sure I could sleep with someone ugly. Desperate... yes, blind... no.'

'Darling, for goodness' sake, have a few bottles of wine and turn out the lights. I'm not believing you're truly this shallow.

Where has that carefree pillow princess from twenty years ago gone? I miss her, she was fun and savage.'

'I was never a pillow princess, James, nor was I fun and savage.' I replied as a smile tugged my eyes.

'Hmm, at least you're still honest. Maybe you're still in there somewhere. Seriously, Paisley, a quick something or another, might just dust away the cobwebs, make you see things in a better light.

I'd hate to think you're this miserable simply by not getting any action.

We could have fixed that years ago.'

'I don't just climb under the covers with anyone, James.

How obscene!'

'You're such a prude, I should take you to a few of my parties, that would clear something... and young Paisley would have jumped at those!'

'Have I really become that miserable?'

James didn't answer, but the face told me everything, his eyes fell to the empty plate, a finger tapped at his knee.

Eurgh, who have I turned into?

'How bad have I become, James?' The answer scared me, but I guess it was worth finding out.

'Darling,' he paused. 'I will always love you, I hope you know that, but the career and house don't mean anything if there's no one to share the triumph with. You have both of those things, take some time to work on yourself or they're wasted.'

'That wasn't the question, James. How bad?' Now I needed to know.

'It's not great, darling... respectfully, and I mean this in the nicest way... you look the part, I mean you really do look fantastic, I can appreciate the appeal... until your nose reaches the air and you open your mouth.

You're turning into your mother, and that kills me because I know that's never what you wanted.'

He let out a slow, deep sigh.

'Just don't throw away the chance in order to please Mama Campbell.

We both know she wouldn't give two shits if the shoe

was on the other foot, Paisley.' His lips pulled into a straight line— it obviously hurt him as much as it did me.

'Thank you.' I whispered.

'Darling, you've not been yourself in a long time. Probably since your father died, and I should have told you then but I never had the balls.
You really do break my heart with this downward spiral, I've never wanted to hurt you, and I guess that's my fault for watching from the sidelines.'

'I'm a big girl, James, you aren't my babysitter. I'm sorry I've been so despondent.'
The pain in my chest was crippling, I'd never asked before, but now I had, I couldn't ignore the fact.

'Come on, James, we should get back to the office, this settlement won't resolve itself.'
I put the mug down and stood up, shaking off the coat before whipping it around my shoulders.
James grabbed his jacket and pulled it on.

The rain had turned from a monsoon into a horrible spray of drizzle— lining the streets of Edinburgh in a wet, grey mist.

'Sweetie, if you need a rebound, Sharon Silver-tongue is still hot for you.'
That received him a scolding glower as we walked through the doors into the murky downpour.

'Trust me, James. I'm beyond tempted.'

Chapter 16 - Isla

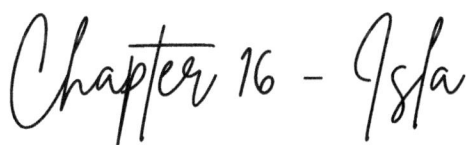

Morag was at a loss for words, and that in itself was a rare occurrence. She was listening intently to every syllable, her focus unbroken.

'… it's just going to be a brief encounter, to see how we feel about each other. I don't know what I'll do if she's ugly…'

Morag continued to stare, her bottom jaw didn't even flex to indicate words were near the exit.

'… Does it really matter if she's ugly?' I asked, still not receiving any response.

'I mean, it wouldn't be ideal, but am I really that self-absorbed?'

I let out a small reassuring nod.

'Aye, I guess I am. There does need to be some sort of physical attraction. Maybe this won't work out, who knows. I'm excited though.'

Finally, Morag's mouth moved.

'Isla, in all the time I've known you, I've never once heard of you going out of your way to meet anyone. I was starting to think you were like the Joan of Arc, no need for human touch… Divine interventions and all that pish...'

I giggled— the laughter must have been infectious because Morag joined in.

I leant over and whispered.

'I'm gagging to be touched.'

'Ooo, la la.' Morag laughed wildly, her hazel eyes twinkling with tears as she tumbled across my bed.

Her laughter abruptly ceased.

Sitting up straight as if hit by a sudden realisation, she stared at me.

'Isla, how long has it been?' Her voice softened as she turned to meet my gaze.

I decided to play dumb.

Trying to avoid giving an answer, I plastered a quizzical look on my face.

'How long's *what* been?'

'Isla, don't act daft. I know you know what I'm asking.'

Damn, she knows me too well.

'Auch, it's been way, way, wayyy too long,' I paused, a mischievous smirk spreading, 'so get out of my bed before I make a pounce on ye.'

Morag winked playfully.

'I could be persuaded; I'll try anything once.'

She flashed a flirtatious tease with her eyebrows.

For a brief second, I was genuinely curious if there was any truth behind it.

'Seriously though, it must be what, last century?' Morag stated.

I really didn't want to discuss this with Morag, but I guess it was me that started the conversation.

I paused as if thinking.

The problem was, I already knew the answer.

'Aye… Well… I mean… It must be at least eh, oh, umm, ten, maybe twelve years.'

'Jesus frick. How are you still standing?

You know, Isla, I could be convinced simply out of pity. Angus would probably be alright with it as long as he could watch.' Morag's face was no longer smiling.

I punched her on the arm.

'Shut up, dafty. I can't lie, it has been way too long, but I'm not having you involved.

Good God, Morag! That's some bloody statement… But I guess that also answers my question, doesn't it?

Looks shouldn't matter a shit.'

Our laughter rang out across the bedroom again.

Both of us bouncing as infectious giggles consumed the bed.

Morag stopped the snicker, her face serious and strict again.

'I'm sorry, Isla, I can't get that out of my head.

I didn't realise… I didn't realise it was that bad.

I'm being serious, is there anything I can do?'

'I'm not sleeping with you, Morag! Eurgh, no offence, but nae a damn chance.'

'I didn't mean like that, ye daft cow!

I meant… Actually, now I'm thinking, I don't really know how I meant. There are people on Skye, maybe not your first choice… Or tenth, but you know… I could set you up with someone.'

'No! I mean that in the nicest way, no, thank you.

I'm going to sort this myself.

I've created the hiccup, I'll fix it.'

'We should go for a blowoot, get you plastered, get some bonnie lass to treat you bad for the night.'

My temperature rose at the idea— I could feel the pyjama top tightening around my neck.

'Aye, don't think about it, Mo, I'll be jist fine.'

'Ah do worry about you, Isla. Even more now I've heard that.

I thought you were just private and shy about discussing your experiences.

Now I'm disgraced that I haven't asked sooner.

Maybe a bloke could give you a little bit of something? I know it's not what you want or need, but you know, they're pretty easy and up for everything…'

'Eww Christ, that's like me asking you to sleep with a woman! It's just not right, I'm not breaking my gold star status… Not even out of desperation.'

Morag shrugged— I wasn't sure if it was in relation to my choice or the thought of her sleeping with a woman, either way she never denied or confirmed.

'Aye, I guess so. Do you think you'll get a leg ower in Edinburgh? Assuming she meets yer needs?'

'No idea. We might be completely incompatible, and she might not like a muscular wee red head.
You just never know.'

I grinned at the thought before another realisation hit.

'I don't even know how to rendezvous, Morag, I've completely missed a step. What are you supposed to do on a first date?
Hopefully Paisley has a bit more experience and doesn't abuse that power, I'm kind of relying on her being decent.'

'Stop over thinking it, it's basically a compatibility test. See if ye fit together and like the look of the other. If everything goes well, there's nothing wrong with exploring a bit more… naked.'

'Auch, you're always taking the piss.
I mean it, I don't even know the basic concept.
Am I supposed to invite her back to my room?
Do I go back to hers, is that safe?
Do I keep off the drink, or do I get shit faced and hope she takes advantage?
Do I tell her everything about me, or do I keep that

hidden? What if I don't like the look of her?

What if she doesn't like me and I like her, or vice versa? …Morag, what the hell do I do?

How can someone get to thirty-eight, and have absolutely no idea about basic anatomy?'

'It's not basic anatomy, eejit. I'm sure you'll know exactly what to do with the body structure.

Actually, do I need to explain that? It might take me a second to find a lesbian textbook.'

'Oh, ha ha ha, yer so bloody funny.' I pushed her to the side.

'You're already panicking, Isla, and I don't know why. Jist go with what feels natural, you don't like the look or attitude, walk away.

If you both have chemistry, work with it, do what you feel is right.

Assuming she's a decent human being, she'll do the same. Either that or just screw her and run… If you *do* go down that route, I want all the details.

I'd love to know what that's like.'

'I really do worry about you, Morag, you're obsessed. Should I be asking questions?'

'Ha, seriously Isla, you'll know exactly what to do in the moment. If you look at each other longingly, steal a kiss or ask for one, whichever.

If you share a kiss and… well, your hands wander, go with your gut.

Maybe I should find the textbook…'

I folded my arms and rolled my eyes.

Morag looked far too comfortable explaining the requirements, hand actions and all.

'…You want to go back to hers, then do it. I've never heard of two women getting into too much trouble,

mind you, I'm an islander, anything's possible.
Your other option, and I know you won't like it, but you could just ask her for a photo.'

'Nut, nae happening! I'm trying to prove I don't need it. It'll possibly be the first thing I ever regret, but still, it's about self-restraint and appeal. She said she's not a creep or a dog, I'm going to try and trust that.'
A hazy dreamlike state clouded my brain as my imagination took a turn.

'You do know all the creepers and mongrels say that, right?' Morag questioned.
Hmm, she had a point.

'She did give me her phone number; do you think I should call her? Mibbe try for a video call?
…Nah, nope I can't do that.
God Mo, when did I become so stubborn and feeble?'

'Yer nae feeble, Isla. Stubborn aye, but that's your allure, and take it from me, you've plenty o' that… In a straight, non-threatening kind of way.'

Morag's monologue was interrupted by the buzz of my phone sitting on the bedside table next to her.
She looked down as I scrambled to grab it, her podgy hands beating me by a second.

'Oh aye, booty call at lunchtime, that sounds enticing.'
She held the phone off to the side— out of my reach.

'Morag, I'm nae playing your game. Either read it out loud or give it here.' I demanded.
I was willing to see where she went with it— I've nothing to hide, but secretly I didn't want her reading it.

'Ach, are you trying to call my bluff, Isla?
You should know never to play games like that wi' me.'

'I've nothing to hide.

Unless she's finally sending nudes, then I don't care.'

I folded my arms— hopeful it *was* an unclothed picture.

Morag's brow raised, she didn't appear to be disgusted as the phone made its way over.

I opened the message, my teeth showing themselves to the screen.

Morag tried to peer over— I flashed the phone in her direction.

New message - Px

Good afternoon, Isla,

I thought I'd check that I hadn't scared you off this morning?

I don't want to be that desperate overbearing person who texts when you least want it, but I'm genuinely excited to meet you.

Please don't think you can't say if you've changed your mind, I would understand.

Anyway, I just wanted to check you were okay and having a nice day, even if the weather is miserable.

P xx   Sent 13:58 Tuesday 13th Feb

'Nope, she's nae in the scud. What a bummer!' I poked out my tongue.

Morag skimmed through the message before nodding.

'Hmm the hairy coo seems fairly pleasant.'

'Aye, she's fine once you break her out of a hangover. I'll reply later.' I closed the phone.

'Eh, no. You'll bloody respond right now, she's taken a moment to think about you, return the favour.

You've been on about her for the last five hours…

Literally.' Morag jabbed— Her tongue sharp and on point. I couldn't argue with the logic, but I hadn't noticed the time— I never stay in bed so late.

'What should I reply?'

'What would you say if I wisnae here? You've managed so far, keep it going. I'm nae yer mother.'

'Ouch!' I said, clinging to my chest with a hand.

'I'd tell her lots of things I wouldn't tell you… After all, I might never meet her.

I mibbe wouldn't tell you that yer a huge pain in the arse.' I placed my head against her shoulder— despite the banter, she really is the best friend.

'Is that what you'd tell her, aye? Knock yourself out.' Morag's tongue moved along her teeth in a teasing contemplative swirl.

Now she's calling my bluff.

Well, there's only one way of dealing with that.

New message – Skye's the Limit

Hello Paisley,

It's nice to see your message and no I'm nae scared off just yet.

I did get a rude wakeup call from a friend this morning, she's a real pain in the arse, I couldn't get her to leave but at least she brought coffee.

Overall I'm good, thanks. How are you? Aren't you working? I haven't been outside to check the weather, but it looks sunny here.

I had a misstep last night/this morning and bashed my face, if the swelling doesn't go down you'll be meeting Quasimodo.

Isla xx   Sent 14:08 Tuesday 13th Feb

Most of the text was for Morag's benefit— she shook her head as I pressed send.

'Really, that's the best you could do? Isla, this is why yer single.'

'Aye, but you didn't believe I'd send it.
She has a good sense of humour from what I can tell. I'll get something derogatory back, I'm sure.'

New message - Px

You fell? Are you alright? You'll need to be careful, Quasimodo might be a deal breaker, I can't lie.

Did you kick her out? Mind you, someone bringing coffee is a nice sentiment, no one ever brings me coffee. Maybe you should have let her stay a while longer, unless you're away to tell me it was an early morning hook up? I might not be able to overlook that detail.

I'm at work, I had a difficult morning... but at least I still look good ;)

Honestly, I'm ready to finish now, I've had enough of today.

I'd much rather spend it sending you messages, all clean of course (well to start with, I guess you'd better decide if you can live with the option of an ugly git first).

What have you been up to?

P xx   Sent 14:18 Tuesday 13th Feb

'Hmm, Isla, she actually does come across very well. Certainly, takes your welfare into consideration.'
Morag had started to chew on her bottom lip.
I tapped a couple of fingers against my own.

'Was she trying to be funny with that comment about being ugly?'

'Probably testing to see if yer shallow… Ask, I would.'

New message - Skye's the Limit
Paisley, I'm fine but thank you.
I slipped going to bed last night… and no, she's still here.
We're in bed, but not in the way that sounds.
We've been chatting all day. Actually it's been mostly about you!
I'm sorry you're having a rough day, you can text me as long as you like! I'm good with that.
Ha, what do you mean by ugly git?
You told me you weren't a dog, should I be running for the hills?
Isla xx
Sent 14:24 Tuesday 13th Feb

New message - Px
Oh God, I'm so sorry! I'll leave you to your chat and… bed, I guess.
You can message when you're free, sorry that was incredibly rude and presumptuous of me.
No, I'm not a dog!
I can send a photo, if that will put your mind at ease?
Enjoy your company and speak soon.
P xx
Sent 14:27 Tuesday 13th Feb

'Oops, I mibbe shouldn't have sent that, Morag.

I've probably scared her off.'

A feeling of dread lined my stomach— I could feel my hands start to tremble.

Morag obviously noticed the change in temperature, she pushed me with her shoulder, face full of seriousness.

'I keep telling you, it's all about communication. Dinna be panicking yersel until you know the facts.

You want to know something, or say something, then do it. I'm away to head anyway, I'll need to pick up Angus in half an hour, and I could do with nipping to the shop.

Go with yer gut, dinna be afraid to put yersel out there. You're doing a grand job and I have a good feeling about this, but ye might want to exaggerate the fact we were definitely nae sleeping together!

She's probably panicking too.

I love you, get dressed and text her back.'

'Mo…' I sighed, the ability to speak leaving my body.

'I mean it, communication, Isla.

I'll text you in a bit, get in there, jump her bones, ask for the nudes.'

I rolled my eyes, a grateful gaze lifting both cheeks.

'I love you too and I'll send you cash for breakfast, it's my turn!' I stated.

'Aye, whatever, I don't care, jist get laid.'

Morag stood from the bed and waved before turning towards the door.

'Nah I'm holding out for a millennium!' I shouted through.

'Aye, and you'll hiv nae bother with that, by the looks.' She called back.

New message - Skye's the Limit

No, Paisley please don't stop ;) that sounds pretty dirty haha… That's her just left, the ball and chain needs picked up from work so I'm back to being alone, and don't apologise, you brightened up our afternoon.

I don't want a photo - it breaks my heart saying that, but if you can manage, so can I.

Please stay.

Isla xx

Sent 14:24 Tuesday 13th Feb

I'd been messaging Paisley on and off throughout the day. Neither of us had found the courage to make a phone call yet, but from the messages, it was clear we shared the same concerns and hopes.

The conversation had slowly evolved into deeper, more meaningful exchanges.

We shared the intricacies of our backgrounds, offering small details about our family dynamics, yet avoided discussing careers or the names of family members.

Paisley knew that I travelled for work, and I knew Paisley worked in an office near the castle.

Some things, we agreed, were better discovered as time went on.

If the relationship didn't lead to anything lasting, neither of us wanted to be burdened with our personal information being available for misuse.

The mystery of who we were speaking to hung over us, yet with each passing conversation, our confidence grew.

The magic of our connection seemed to make the absence of physical attraction feel oddly comforting.

By the end of the week, we both came to realise that maybe a beautiful face and a stunning physique, weren't nearly as important as we'd once believed.

Deepened conversations filled the long evenings, and like the photo, we agreed not to call unless it was absolutely necessary.

My heart was growing with every message, the deep-rooted tension although breaking down was still burning bright, if not even hotter than before.

My lust and hunger for a moment of pleasure with this woman was torturous yet invigorating.

I hadn't told her that, it wasn't really a conversation I wanted with anybody, but I couldn't get it out of my head.

Counting down each and every day, they slowly dragged out in the most wicked and vile crawl.

Paisley must have been feeling it too, she would send me little titbits here and there throughout the day.

I'd desperately run to check my phone in private when back out on the now repaired trawler.

Granda didn't need to know anything just yet, but the excitement made me feel like a naughty schoolgirl.

I felt like I knew this woman from way back when, even with some details being hidden from my view.

I suppose everyone has some secrets.

Chapter 17 - Isla

It was a glorious Thursday, and Granda was standing on the edge of the dock wall.

I checked the hull for damage, wandering up and down the Ceilidh, lost in my own little world.

Singing softly to the sea as *The Sail of Dreams*, drifted across the bay.

> *'Swift as the wind, the boat takes flight,*
> *Over the waves, through the endless night.*
> *Carry the heart that longs to be free,*
> *Onward to the Isle of Dreams by the sea.*
> *The sea sings loud, the stars are bright,*
> *Guiding our path through the deep of night'*

Granda whistled along in time to the song.

Looking over, my lips raised as I waltzed my way in the opposite direction.

'I canna tell ye the last time ah heard ye singing lassie, wits got ye in such a guid mood?' Granda asked. He was trying to appear insouciant.

'Auch, it's such a bonnie day, and I'm just full of excitement Granda, we get to go on a wee holiday next week.' I cooed— not wanting to give him any idea of what was really planned.

'Ye know, ye can go on holiday whenever ye please?'

Jumping over the Ceilidh's bow to the wall beside him, Granda raised his hands to catch me.

'Aye, I know, but I'd be lost if I didn't take you with me.

What am I supposed to do if I'm away all by myself?' I questioned.

'Enjoy yerself. That wid be ah guid start!' He spoke softly, raising his eyebrows.

'I couldn't do that without you there!'

'Lass, we've spoke aboot this. I winna always be here.'

'And then I'll go on holiday myself, sad and alone.' I was teasing him, but he wasn't biting.

'Isla lass, the morn is Friday, that's yer day aff. Why nae take Saturday aff as well?

It'll let us get oor bags packed and ready tae go.

We'll jist make ah few days o' it?'

'Only if you're sure Granda? I did wonder if you'd mind me doing a wee bit of window shopping in Edinburgh whilst you're at the solicitors?'

Window shopping? Where did I think up that?

'There's probably not much point in me going into the appointment with you, unless, of course, you need me to?'

I was trying exceptionally hard not to make it sound like I was too keen, desperately avoiding the chance of ruining my now already-made plans.

Please, for once, don't need me. Any other time, but please not this one.

'Aye, that's okay lass, ye can go and buy yersel something bonnie tae wear fir supper.'

Smiling a glorious grin, I kissed his cheek.

'We're all done here anyway, Granda, you should get back to the house. I'll pick you up on Sunday at ten. Make sure ye mind your toothbrush.'

Granda smiled and gave me a hard pat on the back.

'Aye, I'll see ye Sunday lass.'

YES, YES, YES!

* * * *

Pulling into my rocky driveway I turned off the Fiesta's engine. Pulling the phone free from the waders, I sent a message to Paisley.

We'd switched from the dating app to text— the horrific jingle was sending us into a deranged madness. Thankfully texts seemed to travel a lot quicker.

New message - Isla Skye

Paisley, I'm good to go on Monday, I'll need to keep it brief as I'm expected back for supper with my Granda. He has a meeting at the back of 4.

I should be good from around 4 till about 5 - 5:15.

How does that work for you? xx

Sent 16:34 Thursday 22nd Feb

Within seconds, Paisley had responded.

> **New message - Paisley (Hairy Coo)**
> *Sorry, in meeting. Txt soon xxx*
> *Sent 16:34 Thursday 22nd Feb*

Ah shame, I'd be as well start packing, save me the grief over the weekend.

Clambering out of the car, I scuffed the gravel, the second I reached the door my phone pinged.

'That was fast.'

Oh, not Paisley…

New message - Morag (*Gobshite*) McBride
In the Isle having a swally. Joining me?
There's a good looking lassie in here!
Oh no, wait, that's just me :P xxxx
Sent 16:36 Thursday 22nd Feb

I opened the front door and let myself in.
After stealing a few moments of quiet contemplation, I typed back.

New message - Isla
Aye, okay. I'm on holiday. I wouldn't touch you,
I know where you've been hahaha ;)
Be there in 30 xx
Sent 16:45 Thursday 22nd Feb

It made sense to start as I planned to go on, rushing through to the bedroom, I pulled out three different outfits.
Hmm what to wear…
I settled on a navy and pink long-sleeved check shirt with a pair of denim blue jeans and trainers. It was only the Isle, no point in dressing fancy, not like anyone sexy was going to be there… Well, I could dream, but I wasn't sure if I'd even attempt to make the effort.
My innocent text messaging service was keeping my emotions preoccupied for the time being.

I hastily picked up my purse and phone, making for the door I opened it wide to find Angus sitting in his car.
What the hell?
Winding down the window of his orange Clio,
    'Morag telt me I had to come and pick you up.

Apparently, it's about to get affa messy.' He used his fingers as air quotes for the 'affa messy' part of the sentence. I couldn't help but giggle.

'You're a wee star, Angus McBride,' I smiled, whilst climbing into the passenger side.

'Morag says you're chatting to some tidy bird, guess you won't be on the pull the night?'

'Oh my God, that woman needs to keep her mouth shut.

Angus, you're a good man, but we aren't having this discussion. Jeezo'

'Spoil sport. I'm jist making conversation, I don't ever know what to say to you.

You're kind of like my kryptonite.'

'Eh? What are you talking about?'

Angus didn't normally say very much when I was around, he's a lovely guy but very quiet and shy.

This was more unusual than his normal silence.

'I don't know, I think because you're so close to Morag, you just hold this authority, and it makes me nervous.

Aye I didn't mean in a pervy sort of way, just I sometimes think we have a lot in common, then the next day I think we're worlds apart.'

'Hmm, we don't really speak much, I'll give you that. I don't know why though, we probably do have a lot in common.

Authoritative is not me, I'm not sure where that came from.'

'In your opinion…'

'Angus McBride, are you frightened of me?

Do I make you question your manliness?

Is it because we're both attracted to women?' I teased.

190

He looked over the gear stick, dark discomfit eyes watching me.

'Oddly, I think it might be all of those things.
Does that make me a horrible person?' He asked.

'Ha, no! You're not horrible at all, hilarious in the strangest of ways, but definitely not horrible.
I can't actually believe you're frightened and threatened by me. That's unbelievably amusing.'

'Don't tell Morag, she'll beat me up for telling you that.
The point I was originally trying to make was, you should gie it a good go with that lassie.
Everyone wants you to be happy.'

'Uh, aye… thanks. Now I think it's me that's scared by all of your comments.
Thank God we're going to Portree and nae Inverness!'

Eight minutes later, I hopped out of the compact but impressively clean car, thanked Angus, and slipped into the bar.
What an odd sort of day this was turning out to be.

For a Thursday afternoon, the place was packed.
In the corner, a traditional ceilidh band was in full swing— filling the room with lively Celtic tunes.
Hilariously, the songs were all modern hits that had been given an old folk twist by the three musicians— one on a fiddle, another on an accordion, and the third keeping rhythm with a bodhrán drum.

Morag waved from a small booth along the back wall; the large table was already loaded up for the night ahead.
Four hefty measures of whisky, four shots of something

that looked suspiciously like Sambuca, and two plates of chips piled high with haggis, melted cheese, and what appeared to be a peppercorn sauce.

I sat down heavily and eyed the drinks, 'Are we expecting…?'

Morag cut me off as if already aware of what was about to be asked.

'I couldn't be arsed trawling back through the hunners tae get another drink. It's jist us,' Grinning from ear to ear.

'Wait until I tell you about Angus's surprise confession.' I mused.

Two clear glasses of something dangerous were thrust into my hands, Morag clinked the teeny glasses together,

'Slainte Mhath' Morag stated loudly, pronouncing it Slanj-a-va.

I repeated before the aniseed tore its way down.

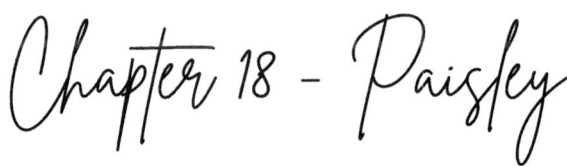

Chapter 18 – Paisley

I glanced at my watch, six fifteen, and still trapped in this bloody office meeting.

God, why did it have to be today of all days.

Finding the enthusiasm to stay awake wasn't only a chore but physically exhausting.

I leant back into the cheap office chair— twelve other colleagues plastered on the same failing expression.

One of them was actually dozing— I couldn't blame him.

Looking over at James, he let out another yawn.

It rippled around the room like it was contagious— claiming at least six more victims in its wake.

I struggled to hold that one back I must admit.

Sharon's sat directly opposite and throwing captivating glances in my direction.

I've no idea what her attraction with me is, but if this was recorded it would look like a dodgy office rom-com.

The smile kept growing as her eyes never left the side of my face.

Oh Jesus, not today, Sharon. Please.

Trying not to encourage whatever *this* was, I offered a polite, noncommittal smile before attempting to fix my attention on the whiteboard at the front of the room.

Unfortunately, in my peripheral I could still see Sharon; she was now not so subtly fiddling with the buttons on her blouse, hoisting her boobs up in a way that screamed: *Perk up ladies— it's showtime.*

I fought hard not to shudder but my body had other ideas. My shoulders gave out an involuntary twitch like I'd been possessed by the ghost of a bad decision.
Nope. Not today, Satan.

'Someone just stepped on my grave,' I mouthed to her— she was still intently staring.
Forcing a tight smile while internally launching myself into the fiery hell below, I turned my head to my knees.

It was too late— the damage was already done.
The mental image of Sharon in her black lacy underwear had barged its way into my brain, flopped down onto the couch, and made itself at home.
No amount of blinking, deep breathing, or desperately thinking about tax returns was going to evict it now.
Oh fuck, now I've gone and done it.

Sharon radiates sophistication and confidence, she knows exactly what she wants and isn't happy until it's in her hands.
I think I was possibly the third thing radiating from her vision tonight.

Her chest is, well, a very noticeable feature, especially when she gives them an extra little squeeze and boy is she squeezing.
My brain was running around the carpet tiles with its pants down around the ankles.
Should I just dive in there? Purely for scientific research of course.
Oh Paisley, stop!
The heat started to creep in.
I felt like I'd just been caught Googling: *How naughty*

animals shag by my mother.

My texts with Isla had been as innocent as picking wildflowers, but some-how they made me realise just how much I'd been starved of any kind of human interaction.

Now I was trapped with nothing but my own thoughts and a certifiable sociopath.

Really? This is what happens when some office sapphic shoots me a flirtatious smile?

My goodness, should I be mortified or sign up to the nearest nunnery for a crash course in: *How to survive chastity when you're a dominatrix.*

The meeting finally ended at seven. I couldn't wait to escape.

Shooting James an inconspicuous glance and a head tilt, I tried to highlight the spicy atmosphere rising from Sharon.

He nodded enthusiastically, the face looking as though he'd been offered a gift from the Gods of GQ magazine.

James, help me! My loins can't cope right now.

I was internally screaming; my hands clammy as I hurried to get to the door.

Sharon was making a beeline towards me.

James tried to help by closing the space between us.

He was making a huge scene about a non-existent stain on his black suit jacket.

Sharon wasn't buying it, or she simply didn't care.

She strut straight past him, now well on her way to being up close and personal with me.

I was trying to up the pace and get to the door,

unfortunately it was blocked by the whole room of legal numpties trying to squeeze through at the same time.

It looked like some dodgy sexualised game of pacman.

Move, for goodness' sake, get through the bloody door.

The gap was closing quickly and I could feel an anxious panic starting to set in.

My hands now trembling uncontrollably, knees weak and wobbly as I forced them forward.

Sharon's standing so close, her breath's lingering on my neck.

I'm positioned like she's got a gun to my spine, stiff and awkward, the deadly encounter drawing my sense of pride and purpose to a close.

'Is it even legal for you to look that good in a suit, or should I file a formal complaint?' She whispered in a low teasing groan.

Her hand lay flat against my back as she applied more pressure.

Rigor mortis affected my breath, her touch offending my sensory faculties— it knocked my self-assurance from the shelf.

Bollocks.

'I'm sorry?' I stammered.

James was watching from a distance— it looked like he might try to tackle Sharon with the fire extinguisher on the wall beside him.

'I'm just saying,' Sharon continued, 'we could go grab a drink, or skip that and go straight to... a more hands-on approach in your office. You do have an absolutely fabulous desk and I'm confident it's more than sturdy enough. It's your call.'

She ran a finger down my arm like she was signing a contract.

Sex! Take the sex, Paisley!

You need the practice; you need the connection.

You're parading around like an uptight bitch because you don't give in to your frustrations.

Take the offer!

'I'll leave you to think it over.' Sharon added with a dramatic sigh. Her eyes appreciating me from head to toe like she was deciding whether or not to buy the whole store.

Her hand slowly trailing over my hip as she pulled away.

The growl in my stomach was unmistakable, it was hunger, but most certainly not for dinner.

'You know where to find me,' she said before waltzing off with a very X-rated strut.

Hot damn, that delectable swagger, the delicious figure… my ovaries kicked into life, giving me a sharp prod as sweat poured.

A sharp, agonising intake of breath filled my cheeks, the tepid temperature cold against my swollen and heated lungs.

James appeared at my side, looking very amused. He continued watching Sharon flaunt her goods down the hallway.

'Darling, I don't mean to give you the wrong impression, and it's absolutely none of my business, but even I'm contemplating fucking her in your office.'

Unable to move, I just stood with my mouth wide open. I must have looked like I'd stuck my fingers in the plug socket and was awaiting some kind person to switch the power back off.

'Genuine question, would it be completely insane and utterly irrational to take her up on the offer?'
James shrugged his shoulders,
'Would you be upset if we shared?
It's not like you're actually in a relationship. Yet.'
Turning, I looked at him.

'Do you think that would complicate issues with Isla? I mean, we aren't together, but do you think…' I struggled to find the words.

'Darling, it could add an element of emotional turmoil, but a one night whatever…' he said flapping his hands into the air as though trying out a new magic spell.

'…Well, it might just clear your mind and open your eyes, allow you to see a little bit clearer.
Either that or you go back to the classic rule of, 'you don't shit where you eat.'

'Would it be rude to ask Isla her thoughts?'
James pulled a face, indicating he was uncertain of the correct answer.

'I'm not sure it's rude…but eh….'
That was good enough.

'Thank you, James, you're an angel.'
I wandered off back down the hall towards my office.

'Risky, is what I was going to say.' He mumbled.

Sitting back at the desk, I whipped out my phone. Sharon's offer was still whirling around in my overflowing cranium.

New message - Paisley (Hairy Coo)

Isla, that's me out of the meeting, sorry I couldn't respond.

I have a big review coming up, and it's all hands-on deck.

What are you doing this evening?

Are you okay?

P xx

Sent 19:04 Thursday 22nd Feb

> **New message - Isla Skye**
>
> *Hi gorgeous ha ha well I dont know if u r gorgeous yet but my crzxy brain says u r.*
> *In the pub with my besty. Talked a lots bout u. Had a couple whiskyies and sumbuchaa. Im on my holibobs now, lettin my hair down xxxxXX*
> *Sent 19:09 Thursday 22nd Feb*

'More than a couple of whiskies would be my guess, who am I even messaging?'

The spelling was like that of a toddler.

New message - Paisley (Hairy Coo)

I'll leave you to enjoy the rest of your evening, get home safely and be careful!

P xx

Sent 19:12 Thursday 22nd Feb

> **New message - Isla Skye**
>
> *Yip u r defffo gorgeous. I cn tell by that txt. I wish u r here. i think i wood take u hame*
> *;) I want 2 b tuchd xxxxx*
> *Sent 19:14 Thursday 22nd Feb*

Why is everyone throwing me propositions tonight? Sharon, Isla, next it'll be James.

Eww, that's a thought.

Sharon seems like a bit of a gamble, I'm not sure the consequences would be worth the ten minutes of pleasure.

Isla's drunk, it doesn't help my situation as I'm here and she's there, but she might be willing to let free some home truths, everyone knows a drunken heart speaks a sober mind.

New message - Paisley (Hairy Coo)
Thanks!

I'll let you decide on Monday if that's still the way you feel.

I assume there won't be anyone taking you home tonight? P xx

Sent 19:14 Thursday 22nd Feb

> **New message - Isla Skye**
> *;) Morag is goin 2 put me 2 bed wen we leave here she alwAys takin care offf me ;) <3 xxXXxx*
> *Sent 19:15 Thursday 22nd Feb*

I didn't want to overthink it, but the winking emojis and love hearts made me feel like Morag was the type who casually dropped by most days with flowers, a bottle of wine and a very seductive grin.

New message - Paisley (Hairy Coo)

I'm sorry if this sounds very forward, and respectfully it's none of my business, but does Morag join you in bed?

I'm just wondering if you're open to seeing other women? Again, apologies if I've got the wrong impression, I just want to see how we currently stand!

P xx

Sent 19:17 Thursday 22nd Feb

> **New message - Isla Skye**
>
> *Morag nd I was in bed. with. me yesterday ;) she brought brkfast 2. I c lots of ladys. Its oK, u can ask nythin.*
>
> *Ilsa xxxxxx*
>
> *Sent 19:18 Thursday 22nd Feb*

New message - Paisley (Hairy Coo)

Okay, as I said, get home safe!

Have a lovely night.

P xx

Sent 19:18 Thursday 22nd Feb

I packed up the laptop and shoved my phone into the side pocket of the bag, grabbing my coat from the back of the door. I flicked off the office lights and trudged down the stairs.

Pulling out a cigarette I lit it before admiring the evening sky, it was starting to get lighter as the days moved on.

I can't lie, I'm disappointed that Isla's potentially seeing someone else, but another part of me is almost relieved.

At least now, I don't have to wonder or worry about it.

The office block door reopened, turning to face the door, I smiled.

'Hello again…'

We chortled as the glasses clunked together, toasting a private joke that only the two of us understood.

We tried to remain oblivious to the barman; he was standing behind the counter drying some freshly washed glasses. Watching us intently, a smile of amusement spreading across his face.

Leaning in slightly, drawing closer towards each other, I let out a cautious smile that filled my face.

My eyes wild as they searched.

'I want to fuck...' I stated— my whole body in greedy disrepair.

'Aye, that sounds like... like a great idea.' Morag replied. Bleary eyes flickered over me as she stared.

'I'm desperate... it's... it's... too long.

Auch, nooo... that was naughty ha!'

'Well... we could arrange that... it might take a minuty though.'

'I... I just wondered...'

'Go on... spit it oot.'

We both burst into another fit of giggles.

'I just wondered...' hiccups interrupted my sentence as I tried to continue.

'I was just thinking, would you...'

Swaying slightly, my eyes narrowed in concentration.

'...Would you... would you ask... the bar boy to get me another... sumbucher, sumbucha... haa haa, a sambuctchaa.'

I struggled with my slurring words, it was a desperate

attempt to spell it out for Morag— who was barely holding it together herself.

What a mess.

'WAYNE!' Morag called over to Mr. Glasswasher, waving her shot glass in the air like a flag.

'Wayyyynne, can we get...can we get another shot, pleeease?'

He nodded, holding up two fingers in a V, signalling two more.

Morag nodded, I however responded by holding up four fingers.

Well with the double vision, I was fairly confident it was four.

The room spun in an agonising torment.

'We, we need ff...fffour, Wayne!' I giggled, still cracking up at my own drunken antics and the newfound inability to pronounce anything.

Wayne kindly obliged, setting down four shots along with two whiskies.

'Ladies, these two drinks are on the house, but I'm afraid I can't serve you any more after this.

I'm barring you for the evening,' he said with an amused grin.

We'd already given him the usual warning - more times than could be counted - cut the drinks off before we turned into full-on chaos.

It was an ongoing joke about Wayne being our unofficial babysitter on nights out, making sure we didn't completely embarrass ourselves.

It didn't usually work.

'Auch, Wayne, noooo!' I whined.

Morag slapped a twenty pound note onto the table,

along with her best pleading face.

'Come on, Wayne, ju…jist one more round? Pretty please?'

Wayne grinned and shook his head.

'You ladies already know I've got enough money to buy the whole bar, but if I don't stop your antics just now, you'll end up dancing on the tables and get me the sack.'

'Yer ah good… good boy, Wayne. If ye bring more… I'll get Isla to sleep wi ye.' Morag stuttered, her words slightly slurred but full of mock sincerity.

'Fuckkk off, I'm no..not drunk.' I blurted.

'Auch well, take… the tip anyway.' Morag mused.

Wayne laughed before pocketing the cash.

'Good boy?' He raised an eyebrow.

'You remember I went to school with both of you, right? Plus, I'm not one for sleeping with inebriated lesbians, but cheers anyway.'

We giggled until my head slumped— it bashed onto the table with a deafening thud.

No sense, no feeling and all that.

I could hear the voices, but my eyes closed in a tight crush.

'I think we'd better order a taxi for this one,' Wayne announced.

'Aye, af… afore she ends up with another… black eye,' Morag cheeped before poking my face.

'Oi sleeping's cheating, bl… bloody light…weight.'

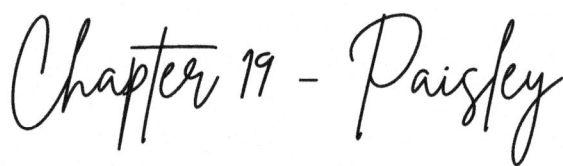

Chapter 19 - Paisley

Usually, I'd take the bus, but tonight was different— I walked the two miles; a silent prayer that the cool night air would help clear my head.

Streetlights guided a route through the chilly late winter sky, my reasoning and judgement filling the darkness.
My subconscious holding me ransom as I hopelessly trailed the path through Lochrin Place.

Sharon's attractive and sexy, definitely confident and willing to get up to no good. Maybe even get me into a bit of trouble.
I don't doubt the physical connection would be fantastic and exciting, but is that what I really want? Is that what I need?

A quickie on the desk, maybe a couple of drinks in before even more tantalisingly euphoric sex.
Oh, now that does sound very tempting.

She'd probably have moved onto her next victim before I'd managed to get my knickers back on… Would that touch be worth the ten minutes?
Hmm, ten minutes sounds about right… then I'd be left out on the kerb!
Not what I need.

Sharon's never really hinted at anything long-term, in fact, other than sex, she hasn't indicated anything!
Probably not a viable option.

Enticing though, very, very enticing.

My mother wouldn't approve— that's a fact, but I suppose it could be used to my benefit…

Yeah, probably not a good idea full stop.

I should really nip that in the bud, it's a dangerous concoction and I don't want to look unprofessional in my father's company.

She is tantalisingly delicious though, could it be enough to clear my mind, would that do any harm?

If things don't go as I plan next week, she might be the only offer I get… hmm, would I take it?

It scares me, because I think I might.

I think I'd really enjoy everything Sharon has to offer, we do have great chemistry, she's always well-presented and immaculate, seems to be genuinely interested in me.

Hmm, tricky.

Isla, on the other hand, well, she makes everything seem so easy. It feels like we have a real emotional connection.

The texting's brought me back to my younger years.

I don't know what she looks like, I don't know what she sounds like, I don't even think I care.

She's already stood up against my bad moods, cheered me up on shitty days.

I like that.

I think she could stand up to my mother without breaking a sweat. What an ability!

I'd pay good money to watch that…

Straightforward talking and I do appreciate that no-nonsense attitude; it's quite cute, fiery, and tenacious.

Unintentionally, she holds this strange power over me.

It's not even about tearing my clothes off and screwing me.

It's deeper. I feel connected, I feel comfortable.

No one's ever made me feel like I'm just a normal person.

It doesn't matter that I am career-driven, it doesn't matter that I have bad days or I'm not perfect.

The conversation just flows... so effortless ... and I can't wait to put in the effort to reciprocate, no matter what it is.

I've never been desperate to speak to Sharon or even message her, whereas I'm happy to message Isla all week long. Whenever she needs, no matter what time of day it is... Wow, that's very outlandish.

I've never really thought about it like that before.

No one's ever made me question who I am, well, not like her.

It doesn't feel like she's trying to play a game, it all just appears so genuine.

She makes *me* feel more genuine!

Christ, look at the change already.

Even if it's just dealing with James... I'm already turning more mellow... that's not even just about her, it's about how she makes me want to do better.

Poor James doesn't know who I am right now, I can't blame him, I don't even know.

God, how can someone feel like this after a couple of weeks? It seems primitive.

I've been deprived for so long, waiting for that one person to step up to the mark, and Isla hasn't even really mentioned getting into the bedroom... although, it's crossed my mind on more than one occasion.

Okay it's crossed it most days.

Maybe James is right, maybe I just need something to clear my mind.

Breathe Paisley, take a minute and clear your mind.

Argh… I can't get her out of my head… She's driving me mad… I don't even want to!

Okay, okay, calm down… you're getting all worked up… one step at a time…

Isla would be the sensible option between the two. Sharon's probably a non-runner to start with.

Oh, fuck, who am I kidding? There's no option.

Isla's whisking me off my feet and I can already see a change… I haven't felt miserable or anxious these past few weeks. I didn't know that was physically possible.

My mind's clear— It's Isla, it's probably always going to be Isla.

Is that even viable?

Auch, can it really be that easy?

What if we can't navigate the distance?

What if she isn't attracted to me?

What if I fuck this up?

I'm good at screwing things up. I haven't even met her yet and I'm panicking.

What if…what if… what if… Fuck!

There are too many reasons for us not to work.

I hope she's gorgeous, I hope she likes me, I hope she feels the same.

Those drunken messages, on reflection feel more than just tipsy ramblings. Surely, if this Morag woman and

Isla had something going on, I wouldn't have been part of the conversation… Well, I hope there's method in my madness.

She did say her friend was in bed with her the other day, maybe that's what she meant, she had been adamant there was nothing sinister. I've no reason to doubt her, nothing that I know of has been vindictive or dishonest.

Isla told me I could ask her anything… and she wanted to take me home and be touched.

I'm definitely open to that!

God yes, an emotional and physical connection with somebody. Sign me up.

I want to do everything bad and horrible, throw her around and indulge in the unknown… saying that I could really use someone that isn't just looking for personal gratification.

The distance between us… that's going to be the ultimate problem. How do we resolve it? …I mean, assuming everything goes well.

Fumbling with the keys, I finally unlocked my door.

Standing in the hallway, I observed myself from the large circular mirror above the side table.

Eyeing myself thoughtfully, I tried to delve deeper into the mind of a rambling nutter.

I guess the years maybe haven't been too unkind, they could have been better, but it's not terrible.

Running into my father's former business partner— David Cambell, at the office door had been an unexpected but welcome surprise.

Though he's no longer actively involved in the business,

he still holds the title of Partner and owner.

Speaking to him felt like I was reconnecting with a missing piece of my father.

David had always been my father's closest friend, a steady and respected figure in his professional life. Many times, he'd visited our family home, enjoyed meals and in-depth conversations. I miss those days.

Those were the days when everything worked in my favour and I didn't have a care or worry in the world.

We strolled down the city centre together.

David filled the walk with memories; stories of meetings that turned into late-night, alcohol-filled debates and the many business deals my father had fought hard to earn.

The undeniable pride my father had supposedly always carried for me— his imperfect and damaged daughter.

I listened intently, soaking up every word; feeling a sense of warmth I hadn't realised had been missing.

I'm almost forty and somehow became lost on small details from way back when.

It wasn't just discussions of the nostalgic, good old days; it was a reminder of who I was and where I came from.

David was a man who unwittingly shaped part of my life.

When he turned the conversation to my mother, I was hesitant in responding.

I didn't want to let him down; tell him everything had fallen apart.

We were never the same after dad died.

We were broken by poor choices, harsh words and grief... Throw in my sexuality and regrettably the

211

Campbell's were never again going to be that family from the past.

Afraid to admit the truth; I didn't want him to think any less of me… or mum.
I told him things between us had become tense.
Our relationship steadily fraying at the seams, more and more neglected and unapproachable each day.
He nodded, but there was no judgment, just a quiet understanding.

Then, with a casual and curious tone, he asked if I had a partner. I let free a small nervous laugh, before calling it a '*work in progress.*'
I couldn't bring myself to explain my dilemma.
Shame rained down on me— the same as it always does.
I guess my mood shifted; he noticed the change.

David was no idiot; my father would have been the first to tell him of my truth.
He'd never once made or shown any kind of judgement towards me.
Instead, David smiled.
His voice was kind and soft when he said, 'Your father always wanted you to be happy, you know that don't you?'
It was such a simple question.
Lodging itself deep in my chest, it made my hollow heart heavy.
I wasn't sure if it was something my father had truthfully said, or if David was just offering something comforting.
It was the way he said it, no hesitation, no doubt, he

made it feel honest. Sincere.

My father's no longer here, yet I still feel him lingering in the background.
A ghost, pathing the way with acquitted wisdom and support, sadly no longer disposable in providing guidance.
I miss him more as each year passes.
David's presence triggered that awful feeling of loss and grief— I haven't felt that in a long time.
Would Dad approve of this life I'd created?
Would he have wanted me to be happy, even if it meant going against what he and mum stood for? Would he push me to find love? Would he welcome them to the family? Would the argument still persist? Could he love me, just as I am?
I can't change what I am, God knows I've tried, but I could possibly try and change who I am.

As we reached the end of Lothian Road, David gave my shoulder a reassuring squeeze before hugging me in a death-defying grip.
'I genuinely hope you find what you're looking for, Paisley.
You don't live life through your parents' eyes. You live it through your own.
Your father loved you, he and I both always wanted you to be happy.
Find peace, and tell your mother I send my love.'
David turned and began walking back in the direction we'd both just trailed.
I stood for a moment, silently watching him disappear into the night, nothing but the moonlight following

him.

He's such a good man.

Dropping my laptop bag onto the table, I dug out my phone from the side pocket.

I reread the last few drunken warbles sent from Isla.

New message - Paisley (Hairy Coo)

I hope you made it home safely.

From your messages, I can tell you have a very beautiful spirit, and it's clear you and Morag share a truly special friendship.

When you wake up, be kind to yourself.

Drink a very large glass of water, take some paracetamol, maybe get some rest.

I have a feeling your night was a memorable one.

I'm really looking forward to meeting you.

Paisley xxx

Sent 21:32 Thursday 22nd Feb

A sigh the size of the solar system broke free from my nostrils as I moved towards the mountain of stairs.

'I really, really hope you're the one I'm looking for.'

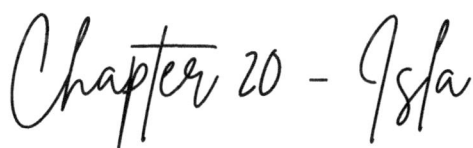

Chapter 20 – Isla

After throwing my small suitcase into the boot, I swung past to pick up Granda.

Friday had been a complete write-off after the antics Morag and I had unleashed the night before.

I was ashamed to be seen in public; I'm pretty confident I'd made a complete arse of myself in more than one way.

Singing karaoke didn't seem all that likely, but I wouldn't like to bet money on it.

To add to my confusion, I found a photo of Morag attempting to play the band's accordion.

Meanwhile I stood posing with a fiddle under my neck. Shame it hadn't been a noose. I would have deserved that.

It was an interesting mix as neither of us could carry a tune or play an instrument to save ourselves.

Those poor defenceless people in the pub, my brain hurts thinking about it.

I don't even want to know what happened within the blur.

No doubt about it, I'm definitely an arse.

Worse still, there were a heap of text messages to and from Paisley, most of which I'd answered in some strange cryptic language from the pagan days.

I had all but sent her naked photos, and somehow, they possibly would have been far more appealing than the absolute nonsense I'd written.

Paisley had been the equivalent of a true gentleman.

Wishing me good health and wisdom, along with the bonus of a few compliments and check-ins to see I was still living.

Urgh, I buried my head in shame when I reread the delights.

I was genuinely surprised that Paisley had welcomed a very apologetic and humble text message the next day.

Maybe she's one of those unusually nice people.

According to a text from Angus, Morag had spent all of Thursday and Friday regretting every single decision she'd ever made.

Essentially, she'd moved in with the bathroom floor, napping there for two whole days— playing an intense game of hide-and-seek with the toilet bowl.

It was safe to say, Morag was well on her way to becoming one with the tiles and poor Angus was dealing with the aftermath.

Whilst my head felt fairly clear, I was only too glad to be getting the train through into Edinburgh. Thursday's carry on and the black eye from fighting the floor, made me worry I'd be nicked for assault and battery.

If I get stopped by the police for any reason, I'd need to find a lawyer to explain, and I don't know anyone other than that attractive fruit loop Granda's been dealing with.

I'm pretty sure Granda's going to have a word or two regarding my new look, no doubt ban me from going drinking with Morag.

Maybe just ban me from Skye!

Auch, nothing ventured, nothing gained.

* * * *

The train journey was smooth; the rails matched my excitement as they squealed into Edinburgh's Waverley station just after half three.

We managed to get checked into the rooms immediately and were greeted by breathtaking city views. A complimentary bottle of champagne sat chilling in each room.

My gaze lingered on the bottle as Thursday's horrifying memories crashed over.

No fiddle was going to be played tonight.

That's a fact.

With a heavy sigh, I placed the bottle back into the silver ice bucket, adamant that this evening would be different.

I decided to give Paisley a teasing text— just for my own amusement.

I could hardly contain myself at the impending meeting tomorrow.

I was slightly gutted I hadn't arranged a sneaky preview tonight, but I have Granda to take care of. He's still my priority.

New message - Isla Skye
Well, well, well… Guess who's sleeping in your city tonight? The islander has officially reached the capital.
I hope you're not having a too strenuous Sunday?
Isla xxx
Sent 16:21 Sunday 25th Feb

New message - Paisley (Hairy Coo)

Welcome to the big city Isla, I hope your hotel is up to standard and the train ride went well?

I'm reading, but in hindsight I should have met you this evening.

It's only just occurred to me.

P xx   Sent 16:22 Sunday 25th Feb

New message - Isla Skye

The hotel is stunning, and the train ride went with no hitches… Unusual for Scotrail!

I know, that just sprung to mind five minutes ago for me too.

I have my Granda here and we have a table booked at a restaurant, so realistically I wouldn't have been able to commit.

I'm looking forward to meeting you tomorrow though.

I'm still disgusted with my messages the other night.

You shouldn't have been subjected to that, I'm sorry, I know I've said that already, but you have no idea.

Isla xxx   Sent 16:24 Sunday 25th Feb

New message - Paisley (Hairy Coo)

Isla, I keep telling you, it's fine.

Honestly, are you one of these people that apologises all the time for everything?

I won't ask where you are going, one, it's none of my business and two, I'm really not one of those weird stalker kind of people.

I'll let you dine without the fear that someone is watching you, but I do hope you enjoy it, whatever you've chosen. P xxx

Sent 16:26 Sunday 25th Feb

New message - Isla Skye

Paisley, thanks for being a decent human!

Am I disturbing your book? I mean, I'm going for dinner soon but I can stop texting if you're

knee deep in DIY?

I'd hate to think I've interrupted your quiet time, I assume you're alone?

Isla xxx   Sent 16:27 Sunday 25th Feb

New message - Paisley (Hairy Coo)

Lol! Yes, I'm alone. I'm always alone, but no it's not really a DIY guide today.

You make that sound like they're dirty books. Have you ever read any of the DIY stuff?

I don't think it's quite what you think is... well some of it may be exactly what you think... not all of it though.

No, you're not disturbing me, you're almost like the little devil and angel on my shoulder. I can hear you, but I never get to see you.

P xxx   Sent 16:29 Sunday 25th Feb

New message - Isla Skye

Yip, that's me the wee devil – I was tempted to say so much more.

I'll just nip that in the neck now or I won't make it to dinner...

You make it sound really sad when you say you're alone. I wish I could take that pain away.

No, I read novels.

What's your non-DIY on tonight?

Isla xxx   Sent 16:30 Sunday 25th Feb

New message - Paisley (Hairy Coo)
I'll keep it clean, not that we haven't already done that.
I stupidly took a photo with the book before realising I couldn't send it.
The book's called: Caring for Lesbian and Gay People: A clinical guide.
It's pretty interesting! You should read it.
P xxx   Sent 16:33 Sunday 25th Feb

New message - Isla Skye
My God, Paisley, are you a doctor?
That would make perfect sense!
Would you tell me if you were?
I've not read it, honestly, I probably won't even try.
Thanks for the recommendation though.
Isla xxx
Sent 16:34 Sunday 25th Feb

New message - Paisley (Hairy Coo)
No, to both!
I'm not a doctor and I probably wouldn't tell you… maybe tomorrow, but I'm not sure.
P xxx
Sent 16:34 Sunday 25th Feb

New message - Isla Skye
Okay, well you definitely work in the medical field. You said before you were set up with a surgeon and now you're into clinical guides.
I'm not a complete idiot!
Isla xxx
Sent 16:35 Sunday 25th Feb

New message - Paisley (Hairy Coo)

Isla you couldn't be further from an idiot, and I'm impressed you remembered, but I don't work in the medical/clinical field.

P xxx

Sent 16:35 Sunday 25th Feb

New message - Isla Skye

But you said you wouldn't tell me, so how do I know?

Isla xxx

Sent 16:36 Sunday 25th Feb

New message - Paisley (Hairy Coo)

Honestly, I'm hoping that you trust me.

I certainly feel I can trust you.

P xxx

Sent 16:36 Sunday 25th Feb

Oh, well isn't that a nice thought? Even if I'm confident it's a fib.

I like the trust bit though.

New message - Isla Skye

Paisley I agree, I have a fairly high regard for your honesty.

If you aren't in that field, why would you read it?

Isla xxx

Sent 16:38 Sunday 25th Feb

New message - Paisley (Hairy Coo)

Lol, reading is knowledge. It's good to take interest in different specialties, you never know when it will come in handy. I never know when I might need to deal with it.

I also read 'Understanding Gay and Lesbian Youth,' yet I don't have children.

I've read the bible, but I don't practice or preach... or believe, if I'm being totally truthful.

It's not about buying into someone's opinions, it's about learning and going on the journey.

It's fascinating.

P xxxx   Sent 16:40 Sunday 25th Feb

New message - Isla Skye

Uhh huh, I don't know how you do it.

Isla xxxx   Sent 16:41 Sunday 25th Feb

New message - Paisley (Hairy Coo)

How I do what, read? Simple, I open the book and follow the words. How do you read?

Is it different for islanders?

P xxxx   Sent 16:42 Sunday 25th Feb

New message - Isla Skye

Noo, God you're so, so cheeky.

I don't know how you manage to keep amazing me. It's crazy. Just when I think I've seen or heard everything, you impress me again.

I can't keep up.

Here's me thinking you're just

reading - 10 ways to get a cheap thrill haha.

Isla xxxx   Sent 16:43 Sunday 25th Feb

New message - Paisley (Hairy Coo)

;) Keep reading Isla and you'll find all the ways to amaze people.

By the way, the book you're referencing is '50 ways to get a cheap thrill' if you play your cards right, I might lend you it.

Now, I'll assume you've booked a table for 5pm, just because I'm pretty set on things like that.

You should probably go and brush your hair and change your top. Assuming you haven't already done that!?

You can text me before bed
if you like, but don't feel like you need to.

You're here on holiday, go and enjoy yourself.

Think of me later. P xxxx
Sent 16:45 Sunday 25th Feb

New message - Isla Skye

Paisley, I'm starting to wonder if you've set up cameras in every Edinburgh hotel and hacked my phone!

It's quite unnerving.

Enjoy your stethoscope and nurses outfit haha, oh and make sure you get your own dinner! Thank you :) xx

Isla xxxx

Sent 16:47 Sunday 25th Feb

New message - Paisley (Hairy Coo)

I don't think that's really my thing, I'll think on it a bit longer just to make sure!!

Thanks, it's pasta for me tonight, and no I didn't make it.

Goodnight. P xxxx
Sent 16:48 Sunday 25th Feb

After freshening up and changing into some new clothes, myself and Granda made our way across the street.

And no, I didn't just change them because someone told me to.

The cool fresh air bit my skin for the five minutes it took to run across the road.

Granda and I sat in the packed restaurant— I was so glad I'd pre-booked a table.

The rich aroma of garlic bread filled our senses as soft Italian music played above the noise.

All of the waiters flounced around the room with white aprons and cloths hanging over their arms.

It was the ultimate romantic ambience.

'This is so beautiful, I wish we had more eateries in Skye!' I mused.

My nose and eyes wandered the room filled with beautiful people and exquisite-looking meals.

Granda nodded his head slowly.

He sat up straight, his intense gaze never leaving me as he took a long pull from his pint glass.

'Wit's going on wi ye lass?'

'How do ye mean, Granda?'

'Are ye haeing some sort o' crisis or breakdown, Isla? Yer oot drinking a lot mare than ye used tae.'

'Auch Granda, I'm just letting off some steam.
I'm fine honestly.'

'I mean it lass, yer antics with Morag leave a rotten taste in ma mouth. Twice in the space o' two weeks yiv hid bruises on yer face. Wit next?'

I couldn't help but grin, it probably wasn't my finest

moment, his stare started chomping into me.

Fiddling with the cutlery, I stopped and picked up my glass of orange juice.

'Granda, only one bruise was from the pub.

The other was from when I fell in the house.

I'm okay, honestly. I just went out and let my hair down for a change.

I was trying to enjoy myself. I agree I mibbe enjoyed it a wee bitty too much, but I want to meet new people. Maybe even find someone.'

He snorted before giving out a nod.

The waiter arrived with two massive bowls of creamy pasta and chicken. Placing them carefully on the table, the fake Italian left again.

'Honestly Granda, I'm fine, it's not a habit... I'm just lonely...'

I grabbed his hand, he squeezed it back and let free a small, sad smile.

'...I just feel like I need to surround myself with a few more people. I'll be okay, don't worry about me, I'm not floating down the falls on a digestive jist yet.'

'Thanks fir tellin' me, Isla.

Ah hid ah feeling ye were lonely, but ah didnae realise how much.

Am sorry lass, ah dinna want tae be on yer case but ah worry. Can ah do anythin' tae help?'

'Just love me unconditionally and eat your pasta before it gets cold.'

Tightening his grip, he gave it a wee shake.

'Ah'll always love ye lass. Yer ma ah'thing.'

We shared a smile; the best kind of love flowing freely between us.

'I'll always love you too, Granda. I'm really glad we

could be here together, it's lovely.'

Picking up our forks, we began slurping and munching.
No more talk of daft behaviour, just the joy of our own company.

His face was looking older, the grey hair slowly disintegrating.

'We should come away more often Granda, spend some time away from Skye. I mean, if you fancy it?'

'Aye, that sounds braw lass. We can talk aboot it when we're hame.'

After dinner, we both returned to our separate bedrooms.
I gave Granda a kiss on the cheek and he gave me a clap on the back.
I thought about popping out for a nightcap, but by the time I sat on the bed to remove my shoes, I could already feel the effects of all the late nights.
That and the niggle of Granda's worry.

Clambering into the ridiculously large bed, I was surrounded by wool-filled pillows and a feathery-soft down duvet.
My mind worked overtime, conjuring up a whirlwind of thoughts and feelings.

New message - Isla Skye
I'm going to have an early night, Paisley.
I'm cream crackered.
Goodnight and sleep well.
Isla xxxx
Sent 21:47 Sunday 25th Feb

New message - Paisley (Hairy Coo)
Goodnight Isla, get some rest. I'll see you tomorrow xxx
Sent 21:49 Sunday 25th Feb

As my eyes slowly drifted into a peaceful slumber. Dreams of tomorrow and the promise of eternal happiness danced in my head.
Finally, I was going to meet my secret woman.

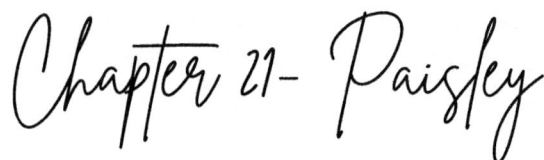

Chapter 21- Paisley

Campbell & Cambell's office was buzzing with the usual Monday morning frenzy, everyone determined to power through the start of the week.

For me, today wasn't just about ticking off the daily chores or trying to survive the dull day ahead. This time, it was all about securing enough time to finally meet Isla.

My heart and head joined the hive of activity, no matter how much I needed to get through, I couldn't concentrate.

I had one thing on my mind and it sure as hell wasn't work.

Every tick of the carriage clock brought me nearer to our moment, but my schedule was tight.

In fact, it was more than tight, it was turning into an impossible task of making and keeping free time.

God knows why I pack everything in so tight; my parents would be horrified by the lack of planning.

If I was going to make it to CC's on time, I'd need to devise a flawless exit strategy.

The local gay bar was always quiet on a Monday. Well, it's been years since I'd last been in, but I couldn't imagine it was going to be overly busy.

CC's offered the perfect casual setting and atmosphere for our first face-to-face.

It was also only five minutes away from the office, meaning any last-minute dash would take up less time.

New message - Paisley (Hairy Coo)

Good morning, Isla, I hope you slept well?

I'm having a mare of a day already, and the only thing I am concerned about is meeting you.

I can't lie, my schedule is beyond chaotic. I have back to back meetings and a 4:30… but I'm hoping it's quick and easy.

Have a great morning exploring!

Paisley xxxx

Sent 09:31 Monday 26th Feb

> **New message - Isla Skye**
>
> *Hey! Good morning, sorry to hear it's not going well. Do you want me to look at other locations?*
>
> *Mibbe somewhere closer?*
>
> *Isla xxxx*
>
> *Sent 09:36 Monday 26th Feb*

New message - Paisley (Hairy Coo)

Absolutely not! I will be meeting you today Isla. Even if it's the last thing I do.

Should I need to bribe someone to cover for me, then so be it.

You're not going back to Skye until I see what I've been missing.

Thank you though, have a good day.

I'll speak to you soon

Paisley xxxx

Sent 09:38 Monday 26th Feb

Isla

I smiled reading the message but worry tugged at my chest. Granda's plans weren't set in stone either; if he finished his meeting early, I might have to make a quick escape. I really didn't want to be that person who just disappeared in the middle of a conversation. I've been waiting too long for this; I won't be missing the meeting point.

Granda stuck another forkful of sausage into his mouth, washing it down with a rinse of coffee from his white mug.

'Did ye sleep well, lass?'

I nodded as I also tucked into a fried breakfast.

Nae pancakes, nae happy.

'Aye, like an angel thanks, Granda. What about you?'

'Guid, that beds fair comfy, ah could use ein at hame.'

He smiled a hazardous grin before pausing for a moment.

'So…' He finally continued; hesitation leaching through his face.

Setting the cutlery down, he stared at the plate.

Looking back up, he held my curious eyes.

Hmm, what's his game?

'…Are ye going tae tell me, whit yer plan fir this afternoon is?'

I eyed him suspiciously, did he know already?

How could he?

'What do you mean?' I asked quizzically.

'I mean, are ye going tae tell me whit yer really planning?'

Ah, he's an auld bugger.

Nothing goes unnoticed with those beady wee eyes.

I pressed my tongue to the roof of my mouth; it grazed my top teeth.

Really, I was buying myself a second longer to think of something clever to reply.

It didn't work.

What do I say now? God Isla, think very carefully about what you tell him next...

Auch what's the point in lying? He knows me too well — any fib will crumble before it even leaves my lips. Bugger it, tell him the truth!

I let out a small sigh, no attempt to sugarcoat the facts as my voice lay flat.

'I'm sorry, Granda, I lied to you.

I didn't want to make a fuss until I knew one way or another.

I'm going to meet someone. Well, not just someone, a woman...

A woman that I've been messaging for a few weeks now.'

My fingers fiddled with the fork as I struggled to maintain eye contact.

Surprisingly, he nodded as if approving the statement.

Picking up his cutlery again, he shovelled in another mouthful of pork between his lips.

'Okay.'

And just like that, as if everything in the world was so easy; he had cured cancer, fed all of the homeless, and started a fight for equal rights across the planet.

I couldn't believe it, no questions, no ridicule, all as though he'd been graced by the hands of Marie Curie herself during his final dying hours.

It was all just as simple as, *Okay.*

I inhaled a deep breath, the fog clearing as my shoulders relaxed.

Jesus, I should have done that days ago.

First on our to-do list was the promised trip to Edinburgh Castle.

We strolled through Princes Street Gardens, admiring the peaceful surroundings.

The pigeons stomped across the footpaths in search of the last crumb; squirrels darted playfully between the many different trees.

Whilst up on the street above, people snapped photos, sipped on coffee, or hurried to make their next appointment.

Cars, buses, and electric trams all navigating their way through the city; each vehicle leaving a wake of noise.

There was a definite contrast between the busy city and the serene gardens. It brought a smile to my face, Granda's too.

Walking the luscious grounds felt like the perfect way to start the day, a brief moment of stillness and calm before everything else popped to life.

It's so beautiful and romantic.

In this moment, the gardens almost felt like home.

Granda was enjoying it too, he casually pointed out various landmarks as we strolled around without a worry in the world.

Peacefully in tune with one another.

After a leisurely climb to the castle gates, we began a slow and unhurried descent; making our way back towards the hotel.

We had plenty of time to spare as we took the scenic route down the Royal Mile. We admired the charming little shops and quaint eateries that lined the bustling streets.

A lively atmosphere, filled with tourists from around the world and street vendors promoting excursions and day trips. It gave the city an air of freshness and excitement.

I guess we were tourists in the wake of it too.

'Ah Isla, this is braw, ah wish ah'd taken yer granny here mare often. She loved this place.'

'Aye, but you were always busy looking after me, I feel like I ruined your retirement.'

'Nah, ah hiv telt ye afore, lass, ye didnae ruin anything.

Do ye mind that trip tae Stirling? Ye whined fir days about yer dolphin t-shirt going afloat?'

'I never found out what happened to that shirt, it was my favourite.

You both brought it back from Mull.'

He let out a chuckle, the whiskers shifting as his eyes squint.

I watched as the laughter turned his wind burnt cheeks purple.

'Ah lass, yer Granny washed it wi' something red, it came oot horrendous.

Ah telt her to boil it, ah think it would hiv fitted a prawn after that.

Auch how we laughed, Isla.

It wis at yer expense but it wis the funniest thing.

We came to Edinburgh and low n behold, they hid the same shirt, the only thing wis ye were then aboot fifteen, it only came in a bairn's size small... it made oor week.

We did think tae bring it back, but we couldnae dae that tae ye.'

'That's shocking, how evil were you pair?' I couldn't contain the giggles as his infectious grin beamed free.

'Granda, you should have seen the nick of me and Morag last week, honestly, wait a second till I show you the photo…'

Pulling up the image from Friday, we couldn't contain our laughter.

'Ah didnae think she could play a tune?'

'No, that's why it's funny, look at the pair of us, Christ.'

We hadn't made any further attempt to continue the discussion from breakfast, and I was quietly grateful.

I wasn't ready to dive into any of the deeper questions, and there were far too many unanswered ones still swirling about in my head.

Granda seemed content, he let the silence hang comfortably as we walked.

There wasn't any pressure to fill the quiet void with anything more than the sounds of the city.

We arrived back at the hotel after a few unplanned stops; two different coffee shops and a number of small boutiques.

Granda changed into a smart navy shirt for his

meeting, pairing it with a heavy coat and dark trousers. His black brogues shone brightly under the hotel's lights.

'Remember, Granda, if she's a snotty so-and-so, we have a boat to dispose of the body.
Are you sure you don't need me?
I can come with you if you want.'
He let free a charming smile, a sparkling adoration in his eyes.

'There's nae rush, lass, take yer time and be safe. Dinnae even think o' me, ah'll be fine, and ah can hae supper in the lobby if ye aren't back.
Ah mean it, Isla, jist enjoy yersel.'

'Thanks, Granda, I love you so much.
I have my phone if you need me, just call, okay?
I'll not be late, and I won't be coming home with more bruises. I promise.'

'Ah winna be calling ye lass, ah'll see ye soon.
Be guid.'
I kissed his cheek before letting him leave.

Returning into my room I changed from this morning's outfit.
I opted for a bright floral long-sleeved cotton blouse, a pair of lightly washed denim skinny jeans, and a pair of long but not quite knee-high brown suede boots.
It was the third outfit choice— I couldn't make up my mind.
Topping it off, I used a tiny bit of nude makeup to cover the bruise; it gave my face a slight glow.

New message - Isla Skye

Paisley, I hope your day's successfully taking shape and running a bit less chaotic?

I've just changed into something a bit more casual, hopefully you'll still find it appealing.

Don't worry I left all my sweaters at home! Gutted.

I'm very excited (and scared) to finally get the chance to meet you face-to-face.

I no longer need to rush— I've freed up some time. Xxx
Sent 16:27 Monday 26th Feb

I grabbed the bedroom key and made my way down the hall.

Each step a confident stride.

Finally, it was time.

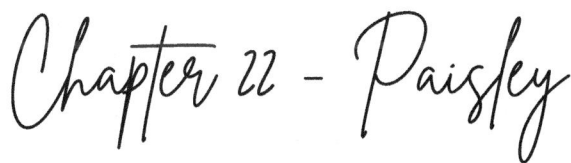

Chapter 22 - Paisley

16:26 PM. My office door burst open in a catastrophic crash, the senior associate Gavin, ploughed in, meanwhile the coat thrashed in its usual wistful manner before falling to the ground.

'Paisley, there's a senior solicitor's meeting at five PM sharp. I need you to get in there as soon as possible. The partner's review is happening tomorrow and we need your input.
Bring everything you have with you please.' He spoke with an unapologetic and abrupt voice.

'I… I'm sorry Gavin, I have a half four and a private appointment at five. I can't make it.'
I responded whilst trying to remain respectful and restrained.

'It's not optional, Paisley.'

'But…'

'Paisley, this review is extremely important. I'm sure you understand that as a senior and valued member of the team, you need to be there.'

'Gavin, with all due respect, I've worked my backside to the bone all month for this meeting.
You're only giving me thirty minutes notice; I have other things that I can't reschedule.
I'm sorry, I can't attend.'
I was clutching at straws— my lungs were fighting against the rib cage as my head felt like it was about to burst out through my ears.
A nervous foot tapped below my desk in a deranged and

furious manner.

My eyes felt like they were melting deeper into my head; a single tear fought against my lower eyelid, biting and stabbing with what felt like a metal toothpick.

'This request is not optional, Paisley! If you aren't there, I can't imagine you will be keeping the senior solicitor position.

What's going on with you?

You're the one person I don't expect grief from, why are you starting today?' His tone was cold, the dark brown eyes biting as his tongue licked against his lips.

'Me?' I felt like I was losing the will to live.

The ungrateful twat.

'Gavin, I have an appointment!

I'm not trying to be arduous or demanding, I never get a moment to myself. This will be the only meeting I miss. I can't do tonight; I apologise but I have an important appointment.'

My hands fell to the table— I could hear the blood pumping as I tried to remain professional.

'Right, well if you don't attend tonight's meeting, you don't bother coming in tomorrow. Take your pick, you aren't talking to me like you own the place. Even if it is your father's name above the door.' He barked back.

You absolute fucking dick, I hope you walk into a moving tram. One day you're going to regret that! Karma's coming for you— Were the words on the tip of my tongue, biting down I suppressed the urge.

My pupils were burning holes into his pathetic squint face— his nose was too high on the head and his receding hairline made me want to stick really dull pins into it.

Argggghhhhhh, fucking inbred plebeian!

'Good luck with your meeting, I hope it goes smoothly.' He hissed, before trudging back out the door.

You, absolute dick...

Oh, Jesus... Isla... No... Fuck...

Finally, the tear escaped, leaving a salty trail down my cheek.

I rushed from the room, barely noticing Sharon, who was almost bulldozed as I ran past.

'Oh, Paisley... Your four-thirty is here...'

'I'll be one moment,' I called back, my voice strained as I dashed for the bathroom.

Finger held out as I indicated for her to wait.

New message - Paisley (Hairy Coo)
Isla, I'm wholeheartedly not sure how to send this message.
I don't think I'll be able to meet you as planned.
My boss has just informed me that I need to stay behind at 5. I'm so, so sorry.
You cannot imagine the anger and frustration this is causing me right now, and I really can't imagine the pain I'm causing you. Please forgive me, I will make this up to you… If you'll allow it.
I am so, so, so sorry.
Don't give up on me just yet. Please.
P xxx.
Sent 16:32 Monday 26th Feb

My eyes couldn't blink, my stomach dropped as one hand covered my mouth.

'What the actual fuck, Paisley! No. Screw you! I've literally just arrived!'
The cold door handle was still wrapped in my fingers.
Swiftly turning on my heels, I moved away.

Heat matching my hair's colour split through me. Shoulders trembling as a mixture of white noise and tinnitus screeched in my ears.

Have I been set up? Doesn't she want me? Am I not good enough? Why would you do this to me?
I've travelled all this way and you're just standing me up! Why?

Eurghh, screw you, Paisley! Screw you!

Rapidly pressing dial, my fingers shook.

I didn't know what to say, or how to articulate, but I let the phone ring and ring and ring.

There didn't appear to be an answering service, and that pissed me off even more.

'Bitch, answer your phone'

I didn't want to cry, not here, not like this, but I was pissed.

New message - Isla Skye

I would be a liar if I told you I wasn't completely devastated. I'm destroyed.

I want to understand and appreciate your apology but why would you do this to me? Was this always going to be the game?

I don't know what to think or how to react.

I thought we had something good Paisley...urgh. Urghhhhh!!!

Sent 16:37 Monday 26th Feb

Paisley

My phone sat on the desk, its silent glow filling me with an anxious and heart wrenching fear.

I was already mourning my losses, and for the first time in a long time, I was genuinely devastated to bring someone else into the turmoil with me.

Isla didn't deserve that, she was entitled to feel rage and anger, and everything else that I was tormenting myself with.

My guilt was ardent, the ruby complexion probably not enhancing my professionalism.

I didn't care, I couldn't concentrate, Gavin could have my job, after today it was worth nothing to me.

I have nothing else left to give.

I turned the phone upside down.

Mr. MacLeod deserved respect, the least I could do was give it to him. After that… who knows…

He was an older gentleman with kind eyes and an intriguing accent, an interesting story too as he mumbled on.

'Ye see, ma wife passed awa' ah number o' years ago, and ah need a'hing put intae place fir ma granddaughter. We work the gether, we hiv a trawler… aye, ah mean like ah fishing boat. She'll run it when am awa'.

We came doon yesterday fir this appointment. We've been staying in the Caledonian Hotel, it's ah braw place, hiv ye been?

Ma lass organised it all, aye she's guid, ah'd be lost

withoot her.'

'No, I haven't, but I'll keep it in mind for future, thank you for the recommendation.

As for your will, I can have that organised for you and get everything put into place.

Thank you for coming the distance, Mr. MacLeod, I really do appreciate your time.'

'Auch, nae bother lass…'

Back to being a hopeless romantic, Paisley.

You've blown the chance. You wanted the career, but you didn't account for the human factor, the emotion.

This man has a family, had a wife, so much pride and love. And here you are… going to die miserable… sad, cold, and alone.

No family to look out for you. No one to hold you close. You're done for.

Just away to hit forty in two days, and fuck all to show for it. I hope it was worth it in the end.

James was right, no point having the nice things if there's no one to share it with.

'…She's an affa bonnie lass, a bit like yersel but she…' Mr. MacLeod, whistled on.

I really struggled to maintain interest, depressive thoughts swirling in and out of my cerebellum.

Nodding and smiling through my client's words, I forced enthusiasm.

The conversation dragged on and on and on, I kept up the appearance of polite engagement.

At the end of the day, it's still my job; at least I have that to live for… for now.

Once our business was concluded, I walked Mr.

MacLeod back out of the office and into the hallway.

I couldn't help but notice the attractive woman waiting for him on the chair; her crimson curls contrasting the green sofa, a softness to her face despite the afflictive expression.

Heavy piercing eyes explored my body as she watched and waited.

Biting her lower lip, our eyes clashed.

It was a brief and fleeting glance that both excited and saddened me.

My stomach clenched.

Isla, achingly rooted in my thoughts— I lowered my eyes.

My excitement wasn't worthy of this moment.

My ability to screw everything up had once again taken over.

I guess my face and demeanour reflected her body language. Neither of us looked overly amused with our day.

Lifting my head, I offered a courteous smile and nod.

The woman nodded back, affable and pleasant.

Her eyes skimming my face with an alluring draw.

Unhurried, she allowed her fingers to trace her lips.

Standing to take the arm of Mr. MacLeod, her focus moved to the old man.

I was desperate to shift my attention to the glowing phone, but for once, I didn't want to appear impudent or ill-mannered.

I think I've already managed enough of that today.

I patiently remained, waiting for the door to close behind them.

They were a very pretty pair.

It's unusual for down to earth people to grace my door.

I usually always ended up with the bampots, self-obsessed and self-entitled twats.

It made a nice change, but I guess I'd created and moulded that monster.

This life isn't worth living if you just exist; it's time for a change.

Come on, reassess your next move and get your arse in gear, Paisley.

Enough is enough. It's time to stop moping and start taking chances… Live wild.

Get a grip, let's go.

Within seconds of slumping unfavourably back down into my chair, Sharon appeared at the door.

Great, like I needed anything else.

She knocked gently and pulled herself inside, making a scene of closing the door quietly.

Please just fuck off, and leave me to chew wasps, was what I really wanted to say.

'I just wanted to check that you were alright, I've never seen you in such a state before.' She said with a concerned and receptive voice.

I nodded, but my heart wasn't in it.

Is this a genuine concern or some subtle, twisted undercurrent?

Don't take that chance. It won't end well.

That isn't the face of happiness, it's one of temporary gratification.

You know that— we've had this discussion, don't do it!

'I had plans tonight and I've had to cancel for this review…' My lip wobbled.

'… honestly, Sharon, it's crushed me.' I replied quietly— still trying to keep my emotions in check.

My hands had made themselves at home in my lap, my shoulders hunched as if they'd also given up.

Sharon walked over to the desk.

Casually propping herself on the edge, her skirt rose a little too high. At the same time, it gave me an unintended glimpse of what had been offered last week. Running a constrained finger along the wooden trim, Sharon used the whole of her palm to rub at the surface, smooth and careful, until finally she sent a few papers scattering in every direction.

'I know, you aren't that into me…' Sharon blew out in a teasing tone, '…but I just wanted you to know, I am very, very into you. The way you wear that suit really turns me on.'

Sharon's eyes rolled upwards in a climactic manner, like she was reacting to a show in front of her.

It was even more awkward because I hadn't moved a muscle.

My eyes made a dizzying attempt to look away from what was now sitting casually at eye level.

A searing gaze unintentionally drifted back to Sharon's now very open thighs.

Oh Jesus Christ, why me? Why today? Why do you always sit there?

'I… I need to get to this review meeting… Sharon.' My words fumbled out.

Why does she make me sweat like this?

'What if I could get you a free pass, Paisley? Give you some time to yourself and your… plans.' Sharon teased.

Aye, because that was an option.

Every small movement relaxed her thighs; teasing a tiny bit more flesh.

She was now flaunting the jet-black lace knickers for the whole of Edinburgh Castle to see.

My cheeks flushed to ketchup, the sweat running down my now stiffened back as every limb shook uncontrollably. I was about thirty seconds away from either peeing my pants or throwing Sharon onto the desk to impulsively depredate.

With Isla gyrating in my head, I was hoping for option one.

'Sharon, I'm really into someone else… I'm supposed to be… meeting her… right now actually…' I stuttered.

'… and… it isn't anything personal, I mean you are, honestly… um… very attractive but…' still achingly trying to tear my perverted peepers away from the titillating undergarments.

A velvety finger squashed down on my still bumbling lips.

'Shhh… you don't need to explain.'

Sharon manoeuvred until she was practically sitting on my knee.

A small suede-like kiss made contact with my clammy and puffy cheek.

She stood up, deliberate and full of intention, the skirt still holding her salacious secret.

'Don't worry, Paisley, I'll patiently wait for my turn. It's inevitable.'

Her smile was touching places it had no right being

near.

Lifting herself up, she moved toward the door.

Wait, wait, stop!

Mr. MacLeod had voiced something similar. Argh what had he said?

Think, Paisley, for fuck's sake, think...

'Lass, I'm jist waiting fir ma turn tae see the inevitable happiness o' ma granddaughter, ah hope ah can see it afore ma time on earth is ower. She's an affa bonnie lass, ah bit like yersel, but she likes the ladies. Ah think she's awa meeting one the now.'

Urgh, why was I too busy being selfish? Why hadn't I spent five more minutes listening? That's not in the Campbell name, we plan and organise, take control. Stupid woman, maybe you should listen to your mother!

'Wait, Sharon! I'm sorry, this sounds obscene, odd even... but you spoke with my last client when he was in the waiting area? The moment I tore through in a state!' I must have sounded deranged, remarkably my tone was common and sharp.

Sharon's head cocked,

'And?'

'Where was he from, did he fill out the personal information paperwork?'

I probably sounded like an axe-wielding crazed woman.

'What's it worth?' She teased again.

My eyes were burning holes through the peroxide.

I was about three seconds away from smashing the fine china teapot, and not in a good way.

Sighing, she gave up.

'Oh, alright, he's from the Isle of Skye. Why, what

does that matter?'

'Yes! Yes! YES! Fucking, get in!' I jumped from my seat— definitely a lunatic.

That's your chance. Take it. Rob it. Hijack it. For God's sake, just do something with it!

'She was here!'

She was in your fucking office, and you let her leave.

My heart accelerated, reaching a speed and pressure that made me think I might follow in my father's literal footsteps; probably just keel over and die on the spot.

'You're a fucking goddess, Sharon!' I shouted.

Sprinting over to her, I was oddly amazed she hadn't recoiled in fear. Her face pinched as she looked down the spout.

I grabbed the handle and pulled her to face me.

'Sharon, look I'm definitely into you… and… I think you're right; it probably should be inevitable.

I know it must look like an obvious option for me, well for us, to get together… probably have really fucking fantastic sex but… auch, I just can't!

I have a really good feeling that whatever it is… well, whoever it is, that I'm currently searching for… Christ.'

I rubbed at my forehead— I wasn't doing well.

'Look Sharon, it's going to end a lot better for you in the long run… I guess maybe even for me too!

You *are* absolutely gorgeous, and I don't doubt the sex would be mind-blowing, honestly, I've thought about it tirelessly, but I really can't give you what you want. I'm sorry.'

My uptight mouth and cruel eyes worked in harmony to pull a pained, *tough luck* kind of grimace.

Sharon's mouth made little O's as she stared into my stunted and overwhelmed napper.

Grabbing her face with both hands, I kissed her.

My mouth working overtime as it clashed dangerously with the honey flavoured lips, pent-up frustrations spilling out as I licked and sucked, Sharon's pent-up vexation at... well... just being Sharon, joined the kiss.

I dipped in a testing amount of unrepressed tongue, the warm and smooth muscle clashing with hers; a twister as they rolled and frolicked.

Well, if I was going to do something this grotesque and out of character, I'd be as well get some kicks along with it.

It lasted for a couple of seconds, but the rhythm of our bodies made it feel like minutes. Both in perfect sync—admittedly I was a little lost in the moment.

The background was a blur, ribs and chest aching as my lungs burst.

Sharon was about three seconds away from removing her skirt as she gave my breasts a light squeeze.

Okay, that's enough.

Unable to go on, I pulled away.

This wasn't what I wanted.

Despite the torrential downpour of depression, I'd sat through for the last so many years, it wasn't what I needed.

Isla was wasting away in my mind— I needed to get back to that. I needed to fix that in every possible sense of the word.

Straightening out my jacket, I passed her a toothy and grateful smile; it was definitely giving me the look of a deranged psychopath, but frankly, it was a pretty fantastic kiss.

The air cleared and Sharon stepped back.

'Uhh…'

'I'm so sorry, that was…uhm, great…

Actually, it was really amazing, but I need to go, Sharon. I really am very sorry.'

Skipping down the hall, I arrived at the review meeting. I was already late, but all of my cares and worries had left the room, probably on their way to hook up with Sharon's ridiculously short and very delightful mini skirt.

Chapter 23 - Isla

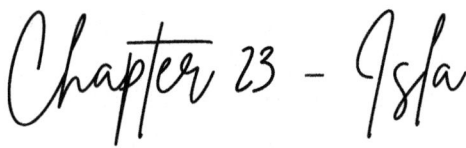

The crushing emotion laced my chest like a wisp of old fishing rope.

My eyes stung as they held back the world, nose running in a desperate attempt to escape the misery.

Granda held me, my arms shaking as he escorted me from the office.

The unforgiving stabbing pain in my chest was crippling. A silent ache and feeling of dissatisfaction slowly growing into something bigger.

Come on, it's not that bad, you'll get over it. Nothing was guaranteed anyway.

'Listen, Isla, I know ye dinna want tae talk aboot it, but ye dinna hiv tae carry this on yer own.' Granda urged.

His voice was immovable, but the pain crossing his eyes felt unmistakable, demoralised even.

'Whitever's weighing on ye, ye can share it. Ah'm here for ye.'

I couldn't respond, I didn't know what to say.

I'm torn between remaining strong or breaking down into the pull of his compassion.

My vulnerability threatening to break free, the tears and snotty nose right behind it.

Attempting to part my lips would likely send them all scattering into a dysfunctional chaos.

Well here goes nothing.

'Granda, I... I thought I had it all figured out.

It was only supposed to be a meet-up to find out who we were, but now everything feels like it's worse than before.

I think I was truly invested in something or someone that I didn't even know. I thought we had a genuine connection. Clearly, I was wrong.' I admitted as my fingers twisted.

Granda took a step closer, his presence reassuring.

'Ye dinna need tae hae it all figured oot, lass. Life disnae work like that.

Sometimes, ye jist hae tae take it one slow and painful step at a time. Ye'll get there, whit's fur ye'll no go past ye.'

'Would it be okay if I just went to my room for the rest of the night? I don't think I'd make the best company, I'm truly sorry if I've ruined our trip.'

'Aye, lass, that's jist wit tae do. I'll try oot the room service, ye can take all the time ye need, and ye never ruin anything.

Ye'll find peace, Isla, ye jist need tae take ah deep breath and bide yer time.

I love ye, lass.'

I managed a faint smile.

We continued walking towards the Caledonian.

My steps were sluggish and heavy as the cracked concrete rose and fell.

As soon as we reached the hotel, I departed company; a pitiful rush to get straight to my room. Slamming the door, I slid down its smooth painted back.

Wrapping my arms around the no longer strong knees, I let out a humiliated and shameful sob.

My head hung in disgrace as the waterworks drowned me.

Back to the silence.

I remained saturated for well over thirty minutes, finally mustering the tiniest amount of energy, I shifted to the bed.

Slipping under the duvet cover, I allowed myself to fall into yet another isolated nap.

A knock on the neighbouring door woke me: it sounded like it was Granda's.

The wood creaked as muffled voices were inaudible from the corridor; I couldn't hear the conversation, but it was a low murmur that carried on for quite some time. Room service.

The lock clicked back into its home.

18:40 according to my phone; no calls, messages or updates.

My stomach pulled away from the knot, the sadness clouding my stinging eyes slowly lifting, the swollen sockets finally easing.

I wasn't happy, but at least I could breathe and think rationally.

Almost twenty minutes had passed when an almighty thud rumbled across the door, it was followed by another two raps.

If I'd been at home, something heavy to defend myself would have been plucked free. Here, the only two viable options were the TV buttons or an espresso machine. Neither felt appropriate for the desired impact.

Who the hell is that?

'Granda?'

Auch, calm down, it just gave you a scare.

Cautiously and silently, I moved to the edge of the bed; trying to comb down my hair using wee feeble fingers.

'Is that you, Granda?' I called out.

My head leant lightly against the wood to try and hear better.

There was no response.

Am I the main character in a horror film?

I need to stop watching rubbish in the dark.

A chilly tremor ran through me; the large doorknob was cold to the touch as my fingers gave it a slow twist and tug.

Peering out into the magnolia hallway, I was met with both shock and surprise.

I stood for a moment, a confused and lopsided smile slowly garnering speed as it crawled guardedly onto my face.

The sudden realisation finally breaking through.

Clad in the same outfit as the office corridor, Ms. P. Campbell stood less than a metre away.

The flawless tailored black trouser suit and white fitted blouse enhancing every feature.

Tiny buttons pulled perfectly at her bust, black leather boots adding a few centimetres to the finished product.

My mouth dried as the rest of my body awoke— she was even more arousing in the flesh.

Appearing as she had on my internet browser; except tonight she held a large silver tray between her hands.

I couldn't peel my eyes away.

Her long thin fingers gripped tight, while a pair of plastic lids encased something that smelled divine.

I couldnae move; my lips had now taken on the form of a carrier bag in the wind; it moved in a drunken silence.

My eyes were rolling around on the carpet as my head animated a yo-yo.

All of the wind in my sail had belly flopped.

Unable to breathe, I stood staring.

'Hello, Isla.'

A wobbly grin spread across the woman's face— full of uncertainty and nervousness. A large sprig of hopefulness growing behind her eyes.

'I think it's about time that I introduced myself properly, I'm...'

'Paisley? You're, Paisley?' I cut her off, my voice a mixture of shock, fear, and excitement.

The not-so-strange, stranger nodded.

I couldn't comprehend the moment.

I felt dizzy, exasperated by the heartache yet satisfied and relieved— too many feelings tumbling through me.

Clinging to the door, my heart knocked against the wood as I leant in.

Adrenaline moving at lightning speed.

'What are you doing here? I mean, how are you here?' I asked still slightly confused.

'I'm a woman of my word.

I told you, you weren't returning home until I could see what I've been missing.' The smile was kind, but a hint of sadness lingered.

'Isla, I cannot tell you how absolutely horrendous I feel. I'm so incredibly sorry, I never for one moment wanted to hurt you like that. I guess you've probably figured out why I did, but still, it's not how I wanted to meet, it's utterly preposterous and I'm beyond demoralised. I'd expect you must be as well.'

Her voice was a lot more upmarket than I'd imagined.

Paisley's stance was strong and commanding, yet oddly reassuring.

Those dreamy forest green eyes held a darkness, definitely not cold, maybe heavy, like the world had burrowed itself inside.

The tray rattled in her trembling hands— obviously she's not unshakable.

With fixated eyes, how could I say no?

I'd spent so much time ogling and unwittingly talking to this woman, this folkloric creature…

How is it even possible that she's here?

She hadn't lied to me or broken my trust— she simply hadn't appeared. She did text to advise, which maybe told me she wasn't a total demon.

The silence was lingering a bit more than would be deemed acceptable, pulling back on the door, I held it fully open.

'Aye, I think I can let you off this one time, but dinna do it again.' I tried to tease— it probably fell flat, I couldn't adjust my shocked tone.

Paisley let out a nervous laugh.

Highlighting the tray, her hands lifted.

'Thank you, I appreciate that immensely.

I figured if I was going to ruin our plans for a second time today, the least I could do is to try and make it up to you properly.

I feel so terrible, I really am sorry.'

Her shoulders visibly loosened, a small smile curled at the side of her lip.

'You're physically here, you don't need to keep apologising. Wasn't that what you told me last week?' I questioned.

Paisley nodded again, her grin softening into something more sincere.

'I am, and I did, yes. I was terrified you would slam the door in my face, thank you for sparing me that embarrassment.'

A weak laugh escaped my throat as I stepped aside.

'Nae chance. Do you want to come in?' I asked gently.

Paisley nodded and moved in slowly.

'Thank you.'

Her demeanour was uncanny, the posture— striking and dominating but without any aggression; her face, enchanting.

My stomach tightened.

Gliding past, I couldn't resist checking her out from behind.

Perfectly sculpted and toned.

I bit down against my lip.

Unable to break the gaze, I followed each movement, every tiny detail of her rigid motion.

Steadily, Paisley set the tray down on the small table by the far window.

She fascinated me in ways I could only dream of.

'How did you know I was… well… me, I guess?'

Closing the door, I moved to the centre of the room.

Standing a couple of metres apart, there was a brief

silence.

Paisley looked around the space before turning to face me.

A pleasant smile burning its way into the pit of my stomach.

Her warm eyes moved from my face to my feet, elegantly travelling back up, before they held my gaze.

Subtly licking her lip, the radiating grin almost knocked me over.

My cheeks flushed, an overwhelming yet welcome nervousness crashed through me.

Christ, it's warm.

'I had Sharon pull some strings at work,' Paisley finally said with a playful glint. 'It turns out, she's terrifyingly persuasive.'

Blowing out an upwards breath, my fringe soared. Teasing a couple of fingers through it, I let my hand slide down the back of my neck, eventually it lingered against my throat.

This beddable woman was already driving me mad.

Reaching out, I steadied myself against the vanity chair.

Her eyes followed with a tilt of the neck.

Long manicured fingers slowly rubbed large circles into the palm of her hand, it looked like a contemplative motion, I couldn't tear my eyes away.

Picking up on my vision, her hands fell.

The silence was loud, electric.

'Paisley, I feel like I'm exploring those Antarctic ice fields without a GPS.'

I wish I was in the south pole— it might cool me down.

She smiled before nodding softly.

'Sharon's my colleague, she's fairly new but appears to have an onerous infatuation…'

Paisley went on to explain the story of who and what Sharon was, this time not leaving out any of the nitty-gritty details.

I personally wasn't sure how to feel about the office… colleague.

Did she have more to offer than me?

The conversation flowed effortlessly, even when explaining the temptation of a bad decision after my drunken ramblings.

I was impressed by the self-restraint and caring attitude, maybe Paisley really was everything I'd hoped she'd be.

My facial expressions matched the ups and downs of the narrative. I couldn't still my fingers as they idly fiddled at the juicy parts, occasionally running between strands of hair in disbelief.

Very gradually, the space between us was closing.

Steadily, Paisley would reposition from one foot to the other, the more engrossed in the story I got, the further forward I shifted.

Within the space of ten minutes, we stood less than twenty centimetres apart.

Hook, line and sinker— I'd become caught in the net of Paisley's story.

Each breath and glance dragging me in deeper.

The way her lips moved as she spoke, the laughter lines rising and falling in the most natural manner, the tongue slowly catching her teeth when she paused for thought.

It wasn't possible for my pulse to beat any quicker, I

don't even know how long we stood, because nothing else really mattered.

Cemented in place, I became aware of a jealousy I was harbouring. Whenever Paisley spoke of Sharon, I could feel my shoulders dip, a tangle of knots tightening in my chest, the constant swallowing was beginning to dry out my throat, this Sharon woman had no right getting involved.

I nodded to show I was still interested.

Sharon could get in line. Obviously, Paisley wasn't interested, she wants me... or does she?

They've already shared a moment; I've nae had a moment.

Jeezo. I *really* want a moment.

I want her on that bed.

To have everything Sharon hasn't yet had.

I want to please her in ways that guarantees she'll never leave. For her to please me in ways I've dreamt about so many times already.

'Uhuh,' I added for polite engagement.

I *am* interested, but the heat's burning across my shoulders. My teeth gritting whenever Sharon's name is mentioned.

I hope it's not obvious.

I loathe this octopus-like work friend, I've never even met her, but the thought's enough.

I can't be sure if I'm even in a position to feel this way.

Eventually, I puffed out a long breath— It was matched by Mrs. Fancy Pants. No doubt, for different reasons.

'...and that, Isla, is how I arrived here.

This utterly ludicrous, world changing moment with you.

Good God, I'm going to stop talking now, it's very unlike me to rabbit on for so long.

Honestly, it's quite exhausting.'

'Please don't stop, Paisley, I'm enjoying your voice. It's very soothing in an odd kind of way.

I can't lie though, I'm feeling like Sharon mibbe got the better end of the deal.'

It was more of a backhanded joke, but I really wanted what the office tart had been gifted.

'Oh? Why's that?'

A cheeky grin pulled at her mouth, her head tilting sideways.

The eye contact was ferocious; they sparkled and shone; eating me up from head to toe.

I shrugged, trying to ignore the searing heat— hands still knitting away.

'Well, it sounds like Sharon's managed to get you worked up, pulled on a few heartstrings, managed to… well… you know… kiss you.' I muttered, now feeling slightly embarrassed.

Paisley took a small step towards me, closing the gap.

Her tongue scoured the bottom lip again.

The glossy smile, radiant; mesmerising woodland green eyes shimmering.

Paisley's face lit my inner ego in ways that would be diabolical for a first date.

I was clasped in tension.

Holding my breath, I was unaware of the repercussions.

Dizziness found me— the oxygen running thin.

My knee's quivered, and honestly, they weren't the only thing.

Paisley's hands brushed my fingers, lacing them with

her own, the grip was firm yet comforting; she tugged me closer.

My feet complied, shifting me centimetres from her bust.

I was still holding my breath, chest throbbing as my heart fought in competition with my lungs.

'Sharon didn't get to see this.' Paisley whispered, the voice breathy and certain.

I was suddenly aware of the warmth radiating through her breath, body and hands.

The slightest touch was sending electric pulses uncontrollably around my body.

My icy blue eyes, melting into glazed puddles with every glance.

'And what exactly didn't Sharon get to see?'

The air was thick, tarry and restricting.

Paisley's gaze never faltered, her thumbs continued to trace mine.

'Sharon didn't get to witness this astounding and utterly breathtaking sight standing before me…' Husky and sultry as her voice lilted. Uhh, just eat me up.

Softened pupils scanned my face, her nose lowering to look into my eyes, over my nose, my lips, chin, back up to my eyes.

The attraction's unquestionable.

'Isla, your eyes change colour when you're nervous… excited.

Your lips creep upwards… warm and delicate… engaged, passionate.

Your fingers... unintentionally…'

Swallowing down hard, the unbroken contact spoke to my soul.

I can feel myself leaning forwards; grasped by her

intoxication.

Paisley must be feeling it too, her cheeks have reddened, the grip tightening around my hands.

Her breathing more audible; deep and fast.

Watching her throat, she's swallowed more times than necessary.

Finding her eyes again, I'm held in an ecstasy filled inebriation.

'Wow, Ms. Campbell, you're very observant.

I am impressed; you've already broken down all of my barriers.' I whispered.

'Hmm, only when the subject is of a high importance to me, and I've been running blind for quite some time now.'

'Am I of high importance to you, Paisley?' Cautious, but full of intent.

'Already more than you could ever know.' Soft with no hesitation or humour. So straight to the point, it sounded like it had been rehearsed for years.

'I'm really nervous.'

'You don't need to be, I'll never hurt you again.' Paisley murmured as her tepid breath brushed over my cheek. Stealing a hand, she pushed a strand of hair behind my ear and leant in, our eyes still secured in a death-defying grip.

My breath hitched, my own fingers tracing a delicate path along her jaw; smooth and sleek, perfectly contoured.

The solicitor's palm and wrist grazed my cheek as she reached for the back of my head.

A flutter as my skin cheered to life.

This was it, my overly anticipated moment was here.

Nervous but so, so ready.

Hungry for the touch.

'Kiss me, Paisley.' I whispered.

Desperate to soothe the ache, needy for the physical contact; confirmation that I wasn't the only one having these thoughts.

Drawing me in, our lips met in a slow, teasing sweep; so delicate it was almost like she was asking a question, the tender skin cautious in its caressing.

Stars burst behind my eyelids. The world moved without us, we spun as one, each delightfully consumed. The touch was magnetic, sparks breaking free, igniting my soul as if lightning had struck the same spot twice.

Pulling closer, a concealed force strengthened our mouths, an unhurried crash, all breathy and lustrous, moistened lips so velvety and compassionate, impossibly beguiling and undeniably sensuous.

I let free a gasp, an urgent need for oxygen.

My hands found their way to her tailored waist, my fingers clinging tightly to the fabric— as if making a crutch to support myself as gravity worked its magic. My head reeled, a daring and ravenous crave for more.

A tight but conscientious hand moved down my neck as our kiss intensified, drawing me closer; two lonely souls searching the other, now bound by this exhilarating moment.

Famished tongues, hungry and appetising, fierce in their intense engagement.

Dancing to our own tune; a delightful stage production played out as our bodies moved in perfect harmony. As though we'd been perfectly designed to fit snuggled together.

The tempting lips curled into a grin as she drew back.

I must have punctured a lung because the air wouldn't fill. I fought for breath whilst she tenderly stroked my cheek.

'Well, I think that settles it… Sharon, has nothing on you.' The cheeky quip escaped Paisley's flushed lips, her posh Edinburgh accent overflowing.

I rolled my eyes, still battling the deficiency.

'I'm just glad you're not ugly.

I had a wager with myself, and now I'm down forty quid!' I eventually replied with a feigned frown; realising my hands were still on her waist, I drew them back and held them to my chest in an '*ouch*' gesture.

Paisley gave out a small snort as she laughed, it was adorable and very geeky.

'That's something I wholeheartedly agree with, but about you. Maybe I should have gotten in on the game of chance. Actually, I'd probably be out of pocket too.

The thought of introducing Quasimodo to my mother admittedly didn't fill me with much excitement.' Her face looked disgusted until a pink tongue poked out.

I couldn't help but giggle.

'I think I may have initially likened you to one of those trolls from the nineties. You know, with the wild hair and little legs?' Paisley started to laugh; her buoyant giggle brought a smile to my face.

Her hands moved to her stomach as if holding herself together.

'Auch, I'm not a troll! You're so, so cheeky, Paisley.' My grin let me down, I playfully slapped her forearm.

'No, you most definitely aren't a troll… but your little legs and red hair, do certainly share a likeness.'

Paisley giggled some more before cowering from a second slap.

Another adorable snort broke free.

Auch, I couldn't even hide my delight. This was exactly the type of relationship I was eager to indulge in. My eyes swam with exuberance as I shook my head.

'I am kidding, Isla. Breathtaking, is the fourth word I'd give you.

I'm trying to fathom how my luck finally came in. Honestly, if you could see some of the people I've been set up with, it's incomprehensible.

My chest's bursting with this new sense of allurement.'

'Thank you, that's affa nice of you to say.

I have to tell you, Paisley, I've actually seen you before... and I was hooked immediately.' I made a clawed hand. 'I just didn't know it was you.'

'You saw me earlier today?'

'No. Well aye, I did see you, but I wisnae in the mood to ogle.' I let out a hearty embarrassed laugh.

'I've been the one emailing you, my Granda can't use a computer.

After the initial email, I googled you.'

Paisley's face turned a lighter shade— all amusement left her cheeks.

'Oh Jesus, I am sorry. It was unprofessional and ignorant, I don't know what else to say other than apologies.

I was set up on that blind date and well, you know that, but it doesn't excuse my tone. I am truly sorry!'

'It's fine, honestly.

After I Googled you...' I giggled, my face stealing Paisley's colour, '...I couldn't tear myself away from the page. God, that sounds so corny, and it's super embarrassing. We should forget that story until a later date... Assuming we meet again.

Anyway, moving swiftly on, I see you came bearing gifts. What are ye serving me on a silver platter this evening, Paisley?'

Winking, I nodded my head towards the tray.

The hue promptly refilled her cheeks.

A timorous glower as she licked her bottom lip.

I could happily suck on it all night.

'I think you're right. We should probably eat; there's no doubt that it'll be freezing by now. Hopefully it still tastes good.

Do you mind if I set the table?' Paisley asked.

'Are you kidding me right now? You're asking permission to set the table?

Who are you and how the hell have you ended up in my bedroom?

I really hope it's nae pizza and you're going to ask if it's acceptable to use a fork and knife.' I quizzed.

'Who even does that? Well, obviously nae me.' My face couldn't hide the amusement and bewilderment.

'No, it's not pizza, Isla.

You don't set the table? Wait, do you have a table? No, I'm not kidding, I don't want to just come in and take over your bedroom. That would be a bit rude, wouldn't it?'

'I have an island in my kitchen. I wisnae born in a barn, but I don't set the island. It's just me, why would I bother?' I paused. 'I don't think it's rude, but I'm impressed you thought to ask. I wouldn't have.'

The quirky solicitor's smirk met my own.

Aye she's definitely an odd one, probably in the best possible way— hilarious.

'Hmm, okay, I'll lower the standards and just let you tuck yourself into the table.

I'm confident you'll be happy and capable of doing that? Come on, let's have something to eat.' Paisley teased.

'Tuck me into the table?

Oh Jesus Christ, Paisley, I dinna even know if you're joking. The bed I'd be willing, but the table's another thing entirely.'

Paisley's grin widened as she listened intently.

'You're very different from anyone else I've met, not that there's been many of them, but still.

You look normal, but you have these wee quirks, I guess that's the enticement.' I stated.

We moved over to the velvet chairs next to the marble-topped table, Paisley removed her blazer and placed it over the back of the seat.

The blouse tightened around her bust as she shimmied out— My pupils were immediately sucked in.

Trying not to stare, I propped myself in the seat opposite.

Paisley's head turned to look over me again.

'I'm pretty sure those aspects that you find to be enticing quirks, are in fact my many flaws.

I'll let you decide how quickly they're going to upset you. I was also joking about tucking you in, Isla, although, I'm not totally against the idea, neither the chair nor the bed.

I think we should probably wait with that though.'

The tongue stroking her bottom lip was back.

Raising my view to her eyes, my gaze was matched.
I felt the air slowly seep free as embarrassment rushed in.

'I agree... I think.' I shook my head, 'I don't think the quirks are annoying... adorable and unusual, but they winna upset me.'
Lifting the plastic lids from two immaculate white plates, Paisley revealed a beautifully plated meal. Each dish featured a perfectly seared steak resting on a bed of creamy mashed tatties, accompanied by roasted asparagus, tender green beans, and a small white jug of garlic butter.

My face lit up.
Two miniature bottles of wine sat alongside neatly folded linen napkins and gleaming silverware.
The only thing missing from this banquet was a single red rose.

I picked up the wine, one in each hand as I read the different labels.
I couldn't help but let out a loud vigorous laugh, my shoulders shaking as the sound filled the room.
Paisley giggled at the joke— obviously aware it had made its mark.

'You're already so, so cheeky. I'm assuming the Cabernet Sauvignon is yours?' I said, still chuckling.

'Paisley, this meal looks absolutely beautiful, it smells fantastic...'
Grinning, Paisley patiently waited for the rest of the sentence.

'...and I'm so grateful, you've honestly made my day but... I'm a vegetarian! I'm really sorry.'
Paisley's smile fell.

Letting it linger for a moment I burst into laughter, my hands working to twist the caps off.

I poured the wine before placing the red in front of Paisley, the white I kept for myself.

'I'm kidding!! This honestly does look fantastic, thank you so much.'

The lawyer's mischievous look was back.

'What, you didn't think I would check to make sure you weren't a vegetarian?

Huh, I'd already spoken to your grandfather, mostly to ensure you hadn't already eaten, but I did check.

I'm a solicitor, Isla, I'm always prepared... but please, eat up, it's already cold!' Paisley winked as she picked up the napkin.

The wink worked its way through me— I could feel the drool gathering in my cheek.

'Really? Are you kidding me right now? Did you honestly meet my Granda just to check on me?'

Paisley had made a start on a crunchy piece of asparagus, chewing politely with her mouth closed, she waited until her mouth was empty before responding.

Very well mannered.

'Mhmm, I did. Preparation is key, maybe if I'd stuck to that I wouldn't be here just now.' A slow nod as she continue to watch me.

'Wow, I am impressed, I'd never imagine anyone thinking to do such a thing. Maybe us islanders *are* jist commoners living a simple life.'

Casting my attention over the table, I admired her lips; exquisite and sculpted, slowly working on the green stems.

Table etiquette had clearly been drummed into her. Paisley's posture was like that of a swan; elegant and poised. Back, effortlessly straight as she sat tall, elbows clear of the table's surface; unwavering and confident.

Magnificent and majestic— unintentionally, I bit down on my bottom lip.

'Isla, please eat, and stop staring at me.

I feel like you're teasing me when you suck your mouth in like that. It sends my mind into a frenzy, and you've done it at least five times since I've walked through the door.

To answer your point, there's nothing wrong with living a simple life, that doesn't make you common, that makes you human.'

I couldn't resist, I bit down again, my tongue joining the party as I teased some more. It seemed appropriate since her eyes were already consuming me.

She smiled, before pointing to my plate with her fork.

Mhmm, it's definitely holding some kind of power. Paisley shifted in the chair and rubbed at her forehead.

I could play this all night and not get bored.

'Eat! Please. We can talk after, I'm here as long as you want me to be.'

Unable to contain my giddiness, I did it again.

Just because I could.

'You're terrible. I can't draw my attention away and you're still mocking, it's a good job my hands are already full.' Paisley warned.

'So, so bossy… Mmm, this is delicious.

I'm not sure when I last had steak, I can never be bothered making anything this exciting when I'm cooking for just me.

Can you cook?' I asked before taking another mouthful. My eyes lifting from the plate to my dessert.

'Yes, but I'm very much like you in that sense.
It's tedious making a full meal for one, and filling the freezer with fifteen dishes of the same option doesn't excite me.
How was your trip around the city?'

'Mhmm,' I finished my mouthful before starting again.

'It was good thanks, Granda and I went up to the castle, then wandered the mile. It was a lovely day, well, until it wasn't.
I'm assuming your day wasn't the best?' I wiped the last of the garlic butter from my lips with the napkin.

'Not really. Well, until this evening.
For the first time in my life I was threatened with my job, I can't say I saw that coming, but it is what it is.
I'm just glad everything has worked out.
You really are far more delightful in person, Isla.
I mean you're fantastic over text message, but I can't stop studying you.
I don't mean that in a weird perverse kind of way…
okay, maybe I do, but I'm genuinely unsure of what to do or say to stop you from leaving. I know it's your room that I'm sat in, but I'm sure you get the point.'
The glass met her bottom lip— I was back to ogling.

'That's not great about your job, hopefully you can sort that out tomorrow?
I'm ecstatic at how it's turned out, can't you see my grin? It won't disappear, but I understand the staring, I've already seen you and I still can't tear my eyes away.
Paisley, I think you might just haunt my dreams tonight, I feel like we've known each other for decades, it's uncanny.'
Paisley nodded, her knee grazing mine as she shifted in

the seat.

'Oh, and you know how you keep telling me off for biting my lip? You manage to lick yours every ten minutes, you know that aye? It's affa intense.
And I'm intrigued by the hands full remark...' I placed the napkin down and sat back.

'...that was incredible, Paisley, thank you so much, you really didn't need to do that.'

Paisley enjoyed another mouthful of her Cabernet Sauvignon but only after gently swirling the liquid around the glass a few times.

I watched the wine, amused by the action; clearly it was more than just a drink, it represented something deeper, maybe an education in wine or status?

'You don't need to keep thanking me, Isla.
You're more than welcome, it genuinely is my pleasure.
I hadn't realised I lick my lips, maybe I'll notice now. Thanks, I'll add that to my anxiety.
You'll just need to wait and see if this date equates to anything before I show you what happens with empty hands.' Paisley teased. Her brow lifting in conjunction with her statement— crows feet tightening.

'I had thought we could go for a walk to the ice cream shop, but honestly, I am so full. I don't think I could manage another bite, Isla.'

'I'm stuffed too, but we could still go for a walk?
You dinna ever need to be anxious with me, Paisley, I'll keep a good eye on ye.' I replied.

'I already am.'
'Big feardy.'

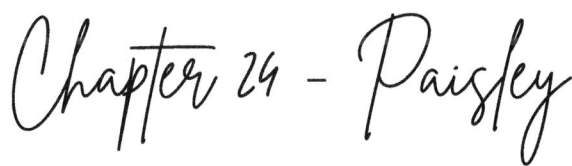

Chapter 24 - Paisley

The gardens had transformed under the clear night sky. The city lights glowing across the street sent out a radiating brightness.

Bouncing from tree branches and flower beds, the shadows masqueraded over the footpath.

Peeking out from behind a small cloud, the moon's light shone down, reflecting the water in Ross Fountain.

Our footsteps were perfectly synchronised as other couples strolled past in the cool, crisp, evening air.

With our arms linked, we shared our warmth along with a quiet moment.

Towering above, Edinburgh Castle stood tall, floating on a sea of yellow spotlights, making a mockery of the stars brightly twinkling overhead.

It actually pleased me this evening, no longer threatening in its usual manner.

The silence was far from awkward; it felt unbelievably natural. Our pace slowed, to almost a shuffle as my feet scuffed the gravel.

'You mentioned that your career's important to you, Isla, and that you travel often, what exactly do you do?'

Isla's footsteps reduced until she finally stopped, hesitantly turning, she faced me.

Looking into my eyes, she inhaled a deep breath.

Those piercing blue's could linger on me all week, they were more dazzling than the heavens above.

'My career's a wee bitty... unconventional. I don't

want you to run for the hills, but my Granda owns a boat...'

'Ah, the infamous boat.

I've already heard all about it today, so do you actually work with your grandfather?'

Isla nodded, her glorious expression turning fragile.

'It's a trawler. I dinna drive ferries or cruise ships, I go fishing.' She pulled her head back as if waiting for an abnormal reaction.

Instead, my grin widened.

Well, it was a sexy thought, a woman sailing the seven seas. Oft, yes please sailor.

'So, what? You didn't think I'd appreciate what you do for a living?

Do I really come across that badly?'

Isla chuckled, shaking her head.

'Well, I'm no bloody surgeon, and you aren't bad at all.' she quipped sarcastically.

My eyebrow raised, lips curling into yet another playful grin.

'Well thank goodness for that, I don't think my poor liver could handle another one.

We might need to discuss these jumpers though, how horrific are they?'

I was already fully aware I'd rather see them on the bedroom floor than on her physical being.

'I don't think my sweaters are horrific at all!

Mibbe I'll let you see them, mibbe I won't.' She nudged me with her shoulder— it made me stagger a couple of paces.

'So, you spend your days out on the water, fishing for a living... Intriguing.

What's that actually like? Is it all hard work, or do you

get some moments of peace out there?

It's not really a job I've known anyone doing before, isn't it dangerous?'

Isla smiled softly— Her face made my knees weak.

My head swirled to dizzying heights whenever she looked at me, I wasn't accustomed to this new feeling of bedazzlement.

'A bit of both really… Paisley, I don't think anyone has ever asked me that. I honestly think you're the first person I've spoken to that's taken a genuine interest in what I do.

Thanks, even if it was just out of politeness…'

'I'm genuinely interested, it wasn't just for show, how could I not be?

Go on, tell me the rest, I'm very curious.'

The grateful expression almost toppled me— I felt every degree of its heat.

My poor heart aches for more, I hope this feeling continues.

'…I spend my days piloting the boat, well, me and Granda share that… lifting nets and sorting through the fish, we process and prepare them to be shipped off for sale.

Of course there's the weather; I take a bit of a beating daily, and aye, there's a danger aspect.

You never know what hand Mother Nature's going to deal you.

One minute, it's a real joy, calm and smooth; the next second you're trying to keep the boat afloat, avoiding the high waves and eternal darkness.

It's hard work, but I think there's something peaceful about being out there. I'm surrounded by nothing but water, you visit the point where the sky meets the sea, way out past the horizon.

There's nothing but the sound of the waves; it's very therapeutic and calming.

I'm lost in my own wee world, away from all the noise and trouble, no interruptions, just at one with the planet...'

Watching with intrigue, I was fascinated to acquire more knowledge about something and someone new.

Her mouth moved with ease as her lips lifted into captivating expressions.

I could feel every word; my body inflamed by her passion, it burrowed through me.

'...I'm fully aware it isnae a job for everyone, but it's me. I love it.

If I didn't have this, I really don't know what I'd do instead. It's all I've ever known.

When Granda... when he's nae here, the business will fall to me... that's a thought I don't want to think about, but that's it in a crab-shell.'

'I get it, the sea's unpredictable, but it's a part of you, honestly, I really admire that.

It sounds like the perfect escape.

It also tells me you're strong and tenacious; not one for giving up easily.

Plus, you keep your grandfather near, I love that. It's fantastic.

Thank you for sharing, I love learning these little things, and I am genuinely intrigued and interested.

I suppose, I'm the opposite, my job is structured and maybe even predictable.

It's definitely not glamorous, and to most, it probably seems really dull, but I find it fascinating.

Being a solicitor is tough, especially when people's lives are in your hands.

I'm confined to rule books and legal hearings, long hours and endless stacks of paperwork… but when I can truly help someone, when I can change something for the better, that's what makes it all worthwhile.

There's no adventure, not like what you have, but it's my life… it consumes everything within my life.

It was my father too.'

A faint, nervous chuckle left my throat.

Would he approve of this new friendship or today's choices?

Isla held her focus; silently questioning my every movement as her gaze drifted across my features.

'I think that's a smashing job, if it gives you a sense of purpose and has a deep meaning to you, then nothing else should matter.

Nae one's opinion should count for anything.

I guess that's why you like swatting up on these books, eh? Knowledge to push you forward, help with the day to day. That's cracking, honestly— I could never do that job, I wouldn't have the patience, but I can appreciate people who do.

I get the impression you're highly intelligent, Paisley.

I can't really understand why you're still available. Not that I'm sad about it.'

Isla's hand moved to my collar, gently she tugged it towards her.

'Do you want to talk about your father?

I don't mind if it's something you dinna want to go into, I'd understand.

Discussions about my family dynamics aren't all that

enticing to me either.'

I tucked a straying strand behind her ear, it was soft and luxurious, bright and fiery. I wanted to play with it all night, twiddle it between my fingers, run my hands over her scalp and allow her a moment of utter relaxation.

I let go before the intrusive concept took over. Instead, I swept the side of her face with my hand, allowing it to trace the faint bruise under her eye.

Perfect skin.

Other than a few tiny freckles, her pale complexion was blemish free. Well, except for the bruise, but overall, it was incredibly soft considering the outdoor working.

'You really are breathtaking Isla, both inside and out.

My parents… Hmm, well they never really appreciated my love for other women, it doesn't work in with their high expectations.

I think we can probably discuss that another time.

I'm sorry, I don't mean to brush over it again, but it's such a long and dull story, I'd rather we used our time wisely.'

I leant back on my heels.

Tucking a hand into my coat pocket, I could feel the cigarette packet.

God, what I'd give for a smoke.

I didn't want to ruin my chances, not yet anyway.

I blew out a breath.

'The short of the story is my father died of a heart attack one day at work.

My mother's never gotten over it, nor has she forgiven me for being who I am.' I quietly blurted.

Isla's lips pulled into a line, soft eyes scanning my face.

'I understand, and I'm sorry about your dad.
My parents never wanted children, I was an accident that they left my grandparents to deal with.
Pretty selfish, really.
My grandparents were amazing— my Granda's my world.'

'You were the best accident, if my opinion counts for anything. No child should ever be told that.
It's cruel and distasteful.
We should revisit talks of our parents another day.
I really don't want to spoil this wonderful evening, Isla.'
I reiterated.

Linking our arms again we continued the slow meander.
'Okay, an easier question this time.
What's the one thing you have always wanted to do or try, but never had the chance?' I asked.
Isla pondered for a moment, the fingers from her unlinked hand tapping lightly against her chin.
Her breath misting against the night.

'I've always wanted to travel to some fantastic foreign country, get captured inside the breathtaking scenery, eat far more of the local food than necessary, and escape this life for even just a few days.
As tempting as it sounds, I've never fancied travelling alone.
I've always imagined having someone to bring along for the ride. Someone to stand behind the camera, or tell me to put my fork down, even just someone to live within those memories we create together.
I can't think of anything more romantic, well other than walking through an Edinburgh Park at night.'
Isla's face lit with a glow as she spoke, the image in her

head— full of anticipation and wistful dreams.

I could picture us both together in a far-away land. Canada, Malta, maybe even Mexico, anywhere exciting and cultural, somewhere we could be free.

The thought illuminated the flower bed beside me like a projector screen.

There we were, just the two of us romancing and dancing in a dusty street, packed with people and market stalls. Happily wrapped up in our own little world, traditional outfits depending on the culture, sunglasses and bags full of tiny trinkets.

The most beautiful vision. I could feel my grin blossoming.

A giddy smile pulled across Isla.

'What about you? What's on yer list?'

You right now, you've already moved in and unpacked, I'm so lost on you.

I couldn't decide whether or not to vocalise that thought.

'That all sounds fantastic, Isla. I think everyone has a list of places they dream of seeing, but sometimes it's not just about the location, it's about who you're with.'

A cheeky smile lifted my lips.

'I've always wanted to kiss a gorgeous redheaded woman under the starlit sky, there's just something really special about the darkness... Millions of stars twinkling brightly, reflecting the eyes watching from below.

Honestly, there simply isn't anything more romantic than looking into the eyes of an absolutely spectacular woman in the twilight. It gives me shivers.'

Our eyes locked for a moment as she looked over.

Our footsteps slow and steady.

A neediness to be held, a readiness to be touched.

'Is that right?' Isla quizzed.

'Oh definitely, wouldn't you agree?'

'Aye, I would.

Is there anything else you've wanted to do under the stars?'

'Oh, the list is long, and you are very, very naughty.' I chirped

Ugh, so sexy and confident, just climb into my bed now.

'Do you realise you're making my heart race every time you say something like that, Paisley?

I canna tear my attention away from you. I find you hypnotic. I've never felt a pull like this.

I'm scared, but at the same time, I'm completely at ease. I want to experience everything, but I can't lie, I want that with you.'

My heart pumped hot, the beating loud enough to make waves through my ears.

'I know, and I honestly feel the same way.

I'm not even ashamed to admit it, Isla, I want you in ways I didn't think was possible.

I don't even think it's just a want. I need you in those ways too.'

Her eyes came back to meet mine as we stopped beside the bandstand.

I wasn't sure if Isla was teasing, but she turned and leaned in closer, the space between us shrinking with each second, the beguiling aroma of her perfume adding to the sensuality.

The silence holding me ransom.

'Isla, kissing you again really is at the very top of my to-do list.

How can I walk away from this?

You're stealing my soul and it feels remarkable, I honestly think I'm in too deep already.'

Isla didn't hesitate.

She tugged my chin towards her.

Drawing me into another kiss; it was much slower this time, tender and certain, filled with honesty and longing. Butterflies still fluttering, gave way to the hunger and yearning I was fraught to overcome.

The undying need for more as I fought to behave.

Nimble fingers pulled my gaze downwards.

'Then don't.' She whispered. 'We'll figure it out, this already feels too right to walk away from.

I've searched for so long, Paisley.

No one's ever made me feel like this, even after a few weeks, I'm stuck.

I dinna think I can escape whatever this is.'

Heavily exhaling, I moved her hands to my chest— Holding them tight against my woollen coat.

'We're already moving so fast, Isla, maybe even too fast.' I searched her face for the answers, 'I just want to be sure, I want *you* to be sure... before you leave tomorrow, before we make any of this real.

We haven't even discussed logistics or long-term visions…'

My breath caught in my chest, hands trembling as I held hers close, so many thoughts running through my head with no way of easing the apprehension.

Isla moved her hands free, her index finger coming up to cover my lips— steadying the fast-approaching anxiety.

'Shh, Paisley. It's okay, this is already real…' Her tone, soothing and unquestionable.

'…I know you're right, this whole thing's been ridiculously fast, but oddly, that doesn't frighten me.
I'm scared that you'll turn around and walk straight back out of my life, Paisley, because honestly, I don't know what I'd do, this feels so comfortable.'
Isla's free hand caressed my face, cupping my cheek, her warmth spread beyond the skin.
The action was calming and homely, no one's ever settled me with such ease.

Closing my eyes, I freed a long deep breath.
The finger sealing my lips moved tenderly to stroke my nose.
'Paisley, I never imagined having feelings like this.
I expected to go home disappointed because we weren't compatible or there wasn't a spark, maybe the physical attraction wasn't there… or you didn't show up.
I canna do that, I feel like I've jist floated down from the moon, this is the best feeling I've had in… well, probably my whole life.' Isla smiled, it was the sweetest beam, her eyes refulgent.
My stomach fluttered as I remained quiet.
'My heart was breaking today because I knew deep down, I'd already invested everything into you.
I'm under this spell that you're holding over me and I just don't want to be free.' Isla bit down on her lip, the breath-stealing eye contact holding me in place.
Lifting my hand, I placed it over the one holding my cheek, steadily relaxing into the delicate touch.
'Even without meeting you, everyone's noticed a difference.

For once, I feel like I've found what I've been missing, and you can call me crazy, but I'm fairly confident it's all because of you, Paisley.'

My chest tight and heavy as I gushed over her words.

I kept my eyes focused, watching Isla's delicate expression, I felt myself leaning closer.

Removing my hand, I touched her silky hair.

Running my fingers through the curls, I had a desperate urge to bury my nose in there; I was convinced it would smell as fantastic as it looked.

'I know, Isla. By God, I know.

My attitude's been different, I have a spring in my step. I race to check my phone every day to see if you've sent me something.

I'm so lost on you, I can barely contain it.

If it was anyone else telling me this story, I'd think they were absolutely insane, but it's me.

This is so new, so... normal. I don't think I've ever been normal before tonight.' My hand continued enjoying the luscious locks, our eyes working hard against the dark to remain connected.

'I thought I'd ruined all chances today, and if anything, it's worked out even better.

I don't want to lose this, but there are so many buts, hows and what ifs. I'm really scared I fuck this up, Isla. My track record isn't great, I have a knack for ruining things and in every other relationship, I've been the one to break it apart.'

I couldn't hide my face of worry, the silence hummed through my ears, my back and shoulders tensing as she watched me intently.

'The only thing is, none of those have ever made me feel the way that I do just now.

That alone is incredible, I'm completely immersed. I physically cannot stop watching. Thoughts are running through my head, and most of them aren't clean.

I just don't want to shatter this.'

I needed her to know.

Needed her to understand, I wasn't perfect, not even close.

'You winna, I'm positive. I can't explain why, Paisley, but I'm one hundred percent confident.'

Her hand came back to my chest in a comforting hold. No one had ever placed a hand on me like that, the fingers fiddled with the buttons of my coat, palm flat and secure against the wool. It wasn't sexual, just reassuring.

Taking in another long deep breath, I swallowed hard.

I looked up at the stars before resting them back down in the blue pools.

'So, what do we do now? We do this? We give it a try?' I asked, barely audible.

Isla smiled before resting her forehead against my chin.

'We both appear to be in the same boat, Paisley. Let's give it a shot, follow our hearts, and see where the waves carry us.'

Chapter 25 - Isla

The racket of the ScotRail crossing the Forth Rail Bridge was bone-rattling.

Every break in the expansion joints allowed my head to bounce harshly from the filth-stained window.

Grey spots drizzling down the glass made the once-white train give the impression it was in floods of tears. It matched my melancholy mood after leaving Paisley.

Watching the Firth of Forth disappear under the seat sprained my heart.

Excited ideas and plans cultivating my mind had caused another sleepless night.

Normal people would spend time together; they would work on making the beginning of the rest of their lives mean something.

Right now, that wasn't a feeling I could embody.

I let out a hefty sigh— strong in the knowledge that this was going to be way harder than we'd ever imagined, our journey was going to be excruciatingly slow.

The train ride included.

Granda's eyes shot open as though he'd just been poked with a Sgian Dubh.

Yawning an all teeth and tonsils job in an effort to convince me he was awake.

It wasn't like he'd been asleep since leaving Waverley or anything. Uhuh.

The Daily Record lay propped open on his chest, the pages starting to slip out around him.

Poor bugger hadn't even gotten to page three before the zeds kicked in.

After the ban of topless models in twenty-fifteen, it seemed like a waste of a pound-seventy.

Folding the newspaper into an oversized napkin his peepers suspiciously draw doodles.

I'm assuming he's waiting for me to start the conversation.

I pulled my head free from the window of opportunity; the fields of rain weren't really exciting me much anyway.

'What is it Granda, are you alright?' I asked, giving into his need.

He grinned but it was cheery and disobedient, his hand running through the designer beard.

'Well lass, ah thought that wis a grand wee trip awa'. Ah fairly enjoyed the big city and that hotel wis crackin'. The grub was superb, ah had the fish!'

'Aye, and you're fishing now,' I grinned for the first time.

'Auch, awa. Ah wisnae going tae pry, but yer as informative as ah Scottish weather forecast - pretty vague but always full o' surprises.'

That comment got him another unhinged smile.

Cheeky auld bugger.

I'd planned on picking him up regarding his sneaky behaviour, but I felt too deflated by our untimely departure.

'Yesterday didn't go how I had planned... Or expected if I'm honest, Granda.'

My grin turned downward as I thought some more.

'Ahh, I'm sorry lass.' He chewed on his mouth for a moment.

His lips pursed into an ageing pout; it looked like his front teeth had fallen out of place and he was trying to reattach them without the Polygrip.

'Ah, well ah liked her, ah thought she'd be a guid match for ye. Especially when she appeared at ma door askin' if ye were the ein she wis looking fir...

She wis affa affa bonnie, also...' his hands lifted to impersonate hoisting a pair of large breasts, followed by a naughty wink, the tongue lolling.

'Granda, for goodness' sake, you're a dirty old man.'

We both burst into full-on belly-bouncing laughter. Granda's hand hit harshly against the tiny table between us. That got him a questionable look from the older couple sitting opposite.

'Ah ha, ah am sorry lass, ah jist hate seeing ye so glum.'

My eyes watered, head shaking in disbelief and horror.

It seems unnatural talking to your grandfather about private relationships.

'You're nae wrong though. They did look affa inviting.'

Finally, I gave up on the self-torture.

His eyebrows shot up until they reached the bald spot.

I picked up the bottle of orange and took a swig; it wasn't a bottle of Sauvignon Blanc, but I needed to pick up the car and it was the best alternative in M&S.

'We had a really lovely night, Granda, I'm sorry you weren't a part of it. On the next visit, well, when she comes up or I go down, I'll make sure to introduce you properly.'

'Wait, ye jist said it didnae go tae plan.

Isla, ye need tae slow a'hing doon for me, wit are ye talking aboot?'

'Granda, it was just like a movie!

Everything was perfect, she's perfect… well I mean, no one's perfect… but to me… to me she's unfathomably perfect.'

For a moment, I'd been convinced his eyebrows had reached their limit. Nope, I was wrong.

They shot up so high, he'd have been able to wear them as a back to front moustache.

He sat in silence, staring.

My eyes wandered back out to the window as I slouched in the world's most uncomfortable seat— Jeans sticking to my legs in a pinching nip.

'Isla! Wit happened next?' He shouted across the table. It garnered another disapproving 'tut' from the couple.

My head snapped back to look at him, unaware he'd been so invested in the story.

I shrugged; teasing him.

That'll teach him for ganging up on me with the very attractive PhD holding geek.

Granda looked pained, his skin reddening as seconds ticked by.

After a few more, his hands met the air as if he'd just lost a ten-grand stake at the bookies.

'Okay!' I laughed. 'Okay, we said we would make it work. Give it a try and follow our hearts.

It's going to be hard, probably a lot harder than I initially expected, but we're going to try.'

His smile looked like he had just been offered a first-class seat at the strip club, it was full of delight and uncontainable happiness. It made me all warm and fuzzy.

'Then why are ye so bloody miserable? That's fantastic news lass.'

'Because I had to leave, I wish I could have stayed longer.'

'Says who? Why didn't ye?'

He must have run through every emotion in his repertoire in the past ten minutes because his expression was now back to blank.

'I have to get you back home, and we have work.'

'God gi' me strength lassie, did ye nae listen tae a word ah said tae ye the other week?'

I blew out a sarcastic kiss.

'Michty me, ye are indeed the devil, Isla. Get aff at the next stop and go back!'

'Don't be daft… Can I ask you something personal though, Granda? I keep meaning to bring it up, but it's never really the right time.'

I contorted my face, I did want to ask, but at the same time I really didn't.

'Wit is it lass? Ye can always ask me fir anything, ye should know that by now.

Come on, wit is it, do ye need something? Money? Brain transplant?'

God, he's on a roll today.

'Noo, I'd never ask for either of those two things!

This might sound strange, but I really need you to be honest. I mean it, Granda, I need you to be one hundred percent honest. Even if you think it'll hurt me.

Please, promise me?'

'Wit's this all aboot lass? Ah promise, but wit is it?'

Granda leaned forward, the formica holding his weight.

'Good, thanks. Erm... Does... Does my choice in partners upset you?

I mean, me being attracted to females.

Does that bring shame or cause you any upset?

I know you've always treated me better than anyone else, and you've always pushed me to find a partner... but... I'm aware of the sacrifices you've made to keep me near.

You used to go to church, and you had a good relationship with my dad... and mum too I suppose.

I just want to make sure I haven't been the reason for that change.

I get really downhearted sometimes, I really hope I didn't ruin you and Granny's lives. I'm thirty-eight and I've never asked...'

Looking down at my hands, I circled the skin with my thumbs.

'Isla, ah told ye I'd be honest, so believe me lass when ah tell ye, it's because o' all that, that makes me love ye even mare. Ye never ruined oor lives, ye brought meaning tae them.

Granny wid tell ye the same.

Ye didnae ask tae be here, ye didnae ask tae need the company of other wimen, ye are who ye are.

We couldnae be prouder. Ah couldnae be prouder, yer a bonnie lassie who's jist a wee bitty lost, ah hope that's changing, honestly...'

My heart leapt from the train as it pounded.

He's proud of me!

The one thing I've strived for, patiently waiting for so many years to hear.

Auch, I can feel my eyes welling.

'...The church isnae fir me, nae anymare, I dinnae fit

their ideas, ye made me see that. We didnae see the same…

And yer parents…'

He blew out a slow, shaky breath.

'Yer parents are their own kind o' folk.

Sometimes ye canna win them all, Isla, but ah've never once thought ye were the cause o' oor problems.

Yer father should know better, he's ah grown man.

Isla, ah really jist want ye tae be happy, that's the only thing ah want tae see afore I leave this place. Ah dinnae care if yer kissing men or wimen, that's yer business.

Ah jist want ye tae enjoy yer life and be blessed wi' someone who cares fir ye.

If ye want me tae be really honest, ah think that solicitor lassie's going tae be really guid fir ye.

She has her heid screwed on, and she's affa bonnie… jist like yersel.

Ye should put in some effort there, lass, ah think ye look past yersel too much. Take wit ever's on offer. Enjoy yersel… and each other.'

Did he just give me bedroom advice?

My eyes bulged, shock running in disbelief and horror.

'Granda! We were having a moment, what did you spoil it for? My God, I'm mortified.'

The sound of his laughter was the most wholesome thing on the train.

'Aye, it wis getting a wee bitty tense, but seriously Isla, it's a bloody waste o' two guid wimen. All that beauty and brains… wasted.

Enjoy yersel lass, ah know ah would.'

'Jesus Christ! *Granda!*

I love you to bits, but that's more than enough.

Jesus, how am I going to drive you home if that's all I'm

thinking about?'

The glass window was highlighting the scarlet scorches on my cheeks and neck.

'Ah love ye too lass. So very, very much.

Ah do find it amusing ye get affa embarrassed.

Yer human lass, how dae ye think ye got here?'

Oh, this is not the conversation I want with an eighty-year-old man on a train.

'Granda! Really? You're going there with me the day?'

'Aye, how no? I've nae much life left, Isla, ah need tae hae fun when ah can.

Ye think ah dinna know wit folks are up tae? Ah wis the worst in ma day.'

'I think it's time you went back to sleep old man, either that or you read your paper.

You're over sharing right now and I'm silently hoping the train derails in the next twenty seconds.'

'Ach, ye take after yer granny.'

He gave me a wink, I returned it with a roll of the eyes, promptly crossing my arms and turning to the glass.

'Aye and she wid o' telt ye tae hae a guid time tae. That wis a wiman who could hiv fun.'

I let my face bash from the window, a desperate attempt to knock myself out.

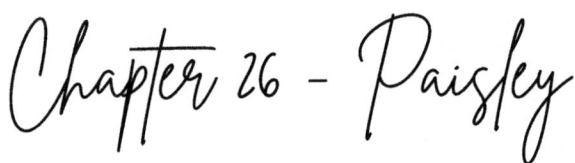

Chapter 26 - Paisley

Today the castle looked like something from the pages of a child's fairy tale, standing proud against the brooding grey sky, the sun hadn't bothered to rise from its slumber.

Ancient and weathered stone glowed softly, its spotlights drawing attention to the finer details etched into the iconic rock.

There was a different kind of magic in the air, something beyond its captivating history and romantic lure; there was a quiet hum of love, longing, and whispered secrets.

Millions had stood behind the walls, searching for something personal to them, drawn to the stories, the legends, and the famed Crown Jewels.

But today, the true jewel wasn't locked away behind a glass cabinet. It was in the soul of every visitor; all seeking a life of adventure and happiness.

Edinburgh castle loomed above the city on a bed of volcanic rock, fortified in solidarity with the city and its residents; the only thing missing from this breathtaking sight was a dragon perched on the fortress walls.

I felt different about that view today.

It was holding a special place in my chest, memories of warm discussions and even hotter moments that I could still taste.

Feeling like a teenager who'd just experienced her first kiss, my head swirled with the new ideology and knowledge of the last twenty-four hours.

A wish for a few more stolen moments, and most definitely a few more kisses.

I hadn't wanted to leave last night, despite regrettably answering, '*not tonight, maybe next time.*'

I was fully aware of the repercussions had I said yes.

Leaning back in the Herman, my feet reached the desk, legs crossing at the knee.

There was no incentive to work through paperwork today, it could wait until tomorrow.

My concentration's already lost, even if I really try, it probably won't be returning any time soon.

No more meetings planned in until Monday and that suited me just fine, I could hover a little while longer.

My head leant against the chair's support, closing my eyes to block out the light, I silently re-lived every ravishing detail.

A '*ratatat*' sounded from the closed door.

James popped his head round the corner.

'Darling? Are you alright?

What's wrong with your feet?'

A look of bewilderment as he clicked his fingers and pointed to my shoes.

'What is this?'

'Nothing, James. Come on in and shut the door.'

The bewilderment changed to worry, he hurried in, shutting the door behind him.

Since I'd seen him yesterday, he'd changed into a pine green three-piece, a white cotton shirt and brown tweed tie.

'Nice suit,' I said, looking him up and down.

'That colour's great on you, James, you should change it about more often.'

'Sweetheart, has something happened?
What's wrong with you? I've never seen you... well, not busy, with your feet up, and... giving compliments.
It's concerning and slightly grotesque!
Have you been smoking something a little wacky on your way in today?'

I swirled in the chair slightly— he was now in my direct line of sight.

'Nothing's wrong. Why?'
He sat in his usual seat, perfect posture as he closed his legs together at the ankles, his hands splayed flat on each leg.

'Something isn't right, I can't put my finger on it.'
James replied
I smiled at him.

'Oh my God!
Darling, did you finally get your leg up and over?'
I didn't respond.

'Spill the tea! You are acting like you have a massive secret and I'm not privy to it!'

'James, you're paranoid.'

'Girl, spill it...who is she? Or... which one is she?'

'How long have you got?' I looked at my watch.

'Darling, for this level of gossip, I have all week.'
I giggled; for some reason it turned out to be a warm girly laugh.
That was probably enough to make anyone suspicious.

'Okay, go grab some coffee, it's going to take a while.'

'I knew it, you never sit with your feet up, never compliment anyone... and you absolutely never giggle!'

Shouting over his shoulder he half-walked, half-ran—trying to get out the door and back as quickly as possible.

Turning back to the castle, I used my feet as a push-off.

'I think I might start enjoying that view.'

New message - Paisley (V. Hot Hairy Coo)

Isla, I know it doesn't feel right leaving so soon, but our next meeting will feel so much more worthwhile.

I cannot express how much I enjoyed our evening together. I can't stop thinking about you, my head is reeling.

Have a safe trip and text when you can xxx
Sent 13:32 Tuesday 27th Feb

James all but fell through the office door five minutes later— two grey mugs wobbling precariously in his hands as the liquid inside splooshed and splashed towards the rim.

A few small beads running down the side plopped beside his shoes.

Harder than we both expected, a mug banged down on my desk.

'Sss..s... sorry darling, here's your... coffee. Go.... go on, give me the gossip.'

'James, calm down. Take a minute, you didn't need to run.

You sound like you've been to Haymarket and back.'

I picked up the mug and licked the river clean before wrapping it between my hands.

James's head shone around the very scruffy fringe— the hair gel clearly hadn't accounted for extra gossip today.

'Erm... Now darling... Now!!' He shouted.

I began filling him in with the need-to-know details he so desperately craved.

I took a long slow drink when something got interesting, or when I needed to think carefully about the sentence structure.

'Oh, Sharon,' an empathetic sharp intake of breath from James

'Oh, Sharon, indeed.'

He took a very short drink from his mug.

So short, I wondered if any liquid actually touched his lips.

'... So, the hotel reception wouldn't give me the details for security reasons, I had to beg them with my business card, honestly, they were an absolute nightmare.

Anyway, eventually they gave me the number.

I raced up to Mr. MacLeod's room, he must have thought I was a right bampot.

We had a good wee discussion and then I had to return back downstairs to pick up some supper for us both.

Isla and I, not her grandfather... Oh and wine!

I almost forgot that bit!

We'd had a bit of a tif a few weeks ago about wine choices, so I had to make sure I got the specific wine types... honestly, James, I'd have been easier just taking the sack from Gavin.

We won't even go back onto that subject, if I'm ever in charge, God forbid, that fucker will be out of here before he can read my door plate.

He's an ignorant, self-entitled, dick.

Right, I'm not getting annoyed, I'm in too good a mood.

I didn't even know if she was going to let me in, but I

carried the tray up and stood at the door like a right sorry-sally.

We chatted, went for a wee walk through the gardens and then I brought her back to the hotel.

I grabbed a taxi home, frankly I was knackered.

We're going to give it a go, see how we get on... Follow our hearts.

James I'm bloody smitten. I never thought I'd say that— she's gorgeous. I can't believe it... honestly, I cannot believe it.'

A small splatting of drool hung from James's lip.

'Darling, you didn't stop for breath, you dropped all of your upper-class stiffness for that info dump and my brain can't quite decipher half of it.

What in the world did she do to you?'

'Oh James, you really are a twat sometimes.

I haven't dropped anything, I just thought you'd want to know before someone else hears it first.'

'Nobody will hear anything from you first! I'm your personal newsagent... Well, I'd better be.'

My eyes rolled, he wasn't wrong though, I hadn't stopped for breath.

'Darling, tell me you took her back upstairs?' The eyebrows danced.

I didn't want to disappoint him— I tactically took another drink and studied the desk as if it was doing party tricks.

'I knew it!!' He screamed.

Ohh, no you don't.

'I haven't told her I smoke and I'm worried she's not going to like it.'

'Wait. Darling, go back.

Did you get freaky between the sheets or not?'
I didn't want to talk about that.
I glared at him for a few seconds.

'No, I was the perfect gentlewoman. You don't do that on a first date.'

'Well, I damn well would have.'
My phone buzzed.

'Spared by the universe above.' I breathed out. Skidding the phone over from the desk, I continued to look like a woman with no cares. Feet still firmly anchored to the desk.

New message - Isla MacLeod

Paisley, you've just made my day! I can't stop thinking about you either.

The 5G's pretty latchy, we're passing Pitlochry.

Granda thinks I should've stayed with you.

He just about lost his eyebrows when I told him about last night ha ha.

Top tip for future discussions - he's my world, I can't leave him.

I know he won't always be here, but it's something else for you to consider.

I know that probably doesn't make things any easier!! I'm sorry.

My life isn't perfect, but I still think we could be.

As long as there's a place for Granda!?

Isla xxx

Sent 14:02 Tuesday 27th Feb

Holding the phone up I chewed the corner, another buzz projected.
I physically bounced in the seat.

'And the award for the most unwanted message today goes to.... my mother, no doubt advising I'm still a delinquent.'

New message – Mother (Old Bat)
Paisley, I trust our discussion has not gone unreflected.
I only ever want to keep your best interests in my sight.
You have expectations within the family and right now you aren't meeting ANY of them.
Once you are ready to have a mature conversation, you can get back in touch.
Mother.
Sent 14:06 Tuesday 27th Feb

I read it aloud.

James's face scrunched, the lines furrowing deeper.

'My God, darling, that's horrific. I feel physically sick at the thought.'

'Mhmm, I guess I can just delete that one!'
James stood up.

'Sweetie, I'm going to let you get some peace and work out what you do next.

I am so happy that you are finally going to get some action, it's looong overdue.

Call if you need anything… and I mean anything.'
He fluttered his hands in a butterfly-type flap and pranced out.

I waved a hand in his general direction.

New message - Paisley (V. Hot Hairy Coo)

Isla, I would have loved for you to stay longer, I'm just grateful I got to spend the time I did with you.

I'm completely on board regarding your grandfather - I don't plan on doing anything that will affect your relationship, I promise.

I do need to tell you something though and I honestly don't know if it will change your view of me.

I really hope not.

Oh, and my mother just messaged me - supposedly, I'm out of the family soon if I don't settle down, grow up, and start meeting her expectations...

I know I'm a solicitor, but do you have any ideas on how to get away with murder? P xxxx

Sent 14:15 Tuesday 27th Feb

New message - Isla MacLeod

Paisley,

I appreciate that regarding Granda, he's currently catching flies in time to the wheels scraping the rails... nae attractive... and what aren't you telling!?

What am I going to dislike you for?

Hmm, your mum sounds...interesting.

Am I allowed to say that so early on? Also, I have a boat if that helps, it's good for disposing of a body? ;) Well, I'd imagine it is, I've nae tested that theory yet hah! Xxx.

Sent 14:17 Tuesday 27th Feb

I let out an audible grunt, the humour behind the boat comment was right up my street.

Sighing heavily, I typed.

New message - Paisley (V. Hot Hairy Coo)

Isla, I might take you up on the offer of a boat lol! And yes, you're correct, she's very interesting.

I smoke (just cigarettes!). I tried extremely hard not to pull one out last night, but by the time I left the hotel door, I was gagging!

I know it's a horrible filthy habit but it's one of those guilty pleasures. Please don't think badly of me! xxx

Sent 14:18 Tuesday 27th Feb

New message - Isla MacLeod

For goodness sake Paisley! You gave me the fear. That doesn't matter, it isn't important right now. Well, it does matter as it's your health, but that won't pull me away from you.

Anything else you were gagging for? ;)

I woke Granda up laughing, you're crazy! Xxxx   Sent 14:19 Tuesday 27th Feb

New message - Paisley (V. Hot Hairy Coo)

Isla!! Please, I'm scarlet!!

Oh yes, so much more than would be appropriate to text. xxx

Sent 14:19 Tuesday 27th Feb

She sent back an emoji of a devil.

Clearly Isla was bored and testing the water, or hornier than a teenage boy in an all-girls school.

New message - Paisley (V. Hot Hairy Coo)

You're a minx! What are we going to do with you?

I'm a Lady! Pxxx

Sent 14:20 Tuesday 27th Feb

New message - Isla MacLeod

I have a few ideas, but I'm still figuring out if you're up for playing my game.

There's absolutely nothing wrong with someone appreciating a wee bit of pleasure, whether solo or in the right company. It's been ages since anyone has even come close to me... let alone laid their hands on me. Xxx

Sent 14:22 Tuesday 27th Feb

New message - Paisley (V. Hot Hairy Coo)

Isla, I am well aware of the lack of contact! But... being a lady, I'd rather not let my imagination run wild with inaccuracies, I could simply wait and enjoy you in person. Just to be clear, I'm far from prudish.

The thought of getting you onto that luxurious bed was on my mind for most of last night... and today.

I know the modern way is to dive into the sheets first and talk later, but I suppose I'm a bit old-fashioned. That said, I'd love to get my hands into that glorious hair of yours and give it a right good tug ;)

I was beyond tempted to stick my face in there last night.

Yes, couldn't agree more, there's absolutely nothing wrong with enjoying yourself... or someone else.

I'm sweating profusely right now xxx

Sent 14:25 Tuesday 27th Feb

New message - Isla MacLeod

Ohhh, I'll bear that in mind. I might like it ;)
When will I see you next? Should we plan ahead or...?? Maybe we could talk on the phone later? I want to know everything!

I'll be back on the water Thursday morning, so I'll need to be in bed early tomorrow. My hours aren't great for a new relationship, they aren't 9-5.

Are we calling this a relationship, what is this? :/
xxx
Sent 14:32 Tuesday 27th Feb

New message - Paisley (V. Hot Hairy Coo)
My goodness, Isla, that's a lot to answer ;) You're insatiable.

I think a call's just what the Dr ordered, I should be finished at 5ish, maybe I could call around 7, if you're free? I'm not afraid of our schedule or what time you finish work. It's okay, we'll get through whatever comes our way. You said it yourself, we follow our hearts. I just want you to stay safe!

What would you like to call this? xxx
Sent 14:38 Tuesday 27th Feb

New message - Isla MacLeod
I am and 7 is perfect. You make everything sound so easy.Why are you so adorable?

I know what I'd like to call it, but I don't know if we can just yet? Help! I'm away to get ready to get off the train. I'll catch you soon xxx
Sent 14:49 Tuesday 27th Feb

New message - Paisley (V. Hot Hairy Coo)
Isla, no one else has ever called me adorable!!
Speak to you in a couple of hours.
Drive safe. P xxx
Sent 14:51 Tuesday 27th Feb

Looking at the clock there was still over four hours before I could hear that voice again.

Opening Facebook I started searching.

Sending Isla a friend request, I ogled the twenty photographs, mostly of them were pictures of the sea or Man of Storr.

It was clear she wasn't all that into social media.

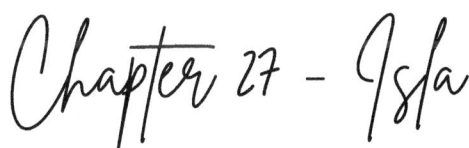

Chapter 27 - Isla

It was just after six o'clock when I finally trudged through the front door.

The early afternoon traffic in Inverness had delayed us by at least forty minutes, whilst the dull and uneventful two-and-a-half-hour drive back to Skye contributed to the weariness etched above my cheeks.

Granda slept most of the way home, resulting in little to no chatter. Bore.

'Goodnight lass, it's been a lovely trip.' He said before exiting the car.

I struggled to fathom how he managed to sleep at night after so many naps during the day.

Usually I didn't take much notice, but it was becoming more obvious and making my mind wonder.

Kicking off my trainers and carrying the case into the kitchen, I dumped it at the base of the washing machine.

'That's going to wait until tomorrow, I've no energy to even contemplate washing clothes at this time.

I'm pretty sure there's at least one pair of knickers in the wardrobe… somewhere.'

Throwing myself down into the armchair I allowed my head to fall back.

'Nova! Turn on the radio,'

Nova decided she wasn't going to participate and retorted with silence.

'NOVA! Turn on the radio,' I demanded a second

time, this time sitting up.

'Sorry, I'm not sure about that.'

'Nova, you are absolutely fucking useless, I'm swapping you for a Lumen Home,'

'That's really sweet! Thanks for saying that.'

I lay back in the seat once again. Silence it is.

My eyes closed.

In a bizarre turn of events, the radio started to hum out of the speaker.

My eyes snapped open in surprise, 'that's creepy.'

Andrew Blackwood started to play 'Lonely Nights'.

Letting my eyes close once more, I reminisced on thoughts of the past.

'I sit in silence, watching time slip by,
Empty rooms and empty skies.
The nights grow long, the days are cold,
In a world so big, I feel so small, so old.
Lonely nights, I can't find my way,
Wishing for someone to call me and say,
I'll hold you close, I'll make you feel whole,
But I'm here alone, with an aching soul'

I reopened my eyes, the phone read ten-thirty PM.

There were two missed calls from Paisley, seven fifteen and seven thirty.

'Shit,' I thumped down on the dial.

'I thought you'd changed your mind. I was starting to worry.'

Her voice was soft and drowsy— the rich accent didn't sound quite as pronounced.

'I'm so, so sorry, Paisley. I came in and fell asleep.
I planned on sending a text to say I was home, but I put

the radio on and must have dozed off.'

'It's fine, as long as you're alright.
How was your train and drive?'

Paisley's voice had taken on a raspy, sultry tone, carrying a sexy and intimate husk to its edges.

I was hanging from every syllable.

'You sound tired and cosy, Paisley.'

Shaking my head to free the saucy images I'd conjured up, drowsiness fogged my eyes.

'Yes, I'm in bed. I was reading, waiting for you to message. I hoped you got home safely.'

'Thanks, and sorry! You really are adorable… I didnae realise how boring that journey is, especially when you aren't overly keen on getting home.
How was your day?'

'The same, tedious and long. I finished at about nine this morning, well, I didn't really start anything… Other than the meeting I attended… I was so lost in my head. You should get some sleep, you must be exhausted.'

'I've waited all day to talk to you, I don't want to sleep, I want to know everything… You sound sleepy too.'

I could feel Paisley's smile, the skin moved against the speaker, her breathing shallow.

Hmm, very, very sexy.

'I don't think you'll learn everything tonight. That would probably put you back to sleep; I'm not very exciting.'

'You're exciting to me, Paisley… Tell me something I don't know at least.'

I stifled a yawn, turning my head from the phone, trying not to let Paisley hear.

'You should get some rest, you're shattered. Had I

311

travelled all day, I would be too... I'm not going anywhere... You can quiz me tomorrow, go and get some sleep.'

'I just want to talk to you. Please, Paisley.
It's been the thought of this call that's kept me going all day.'

'Mhmm, I know.'

'I'll start with the small talk... Umm, so I live in a secluded wee cottage outside of Portree. I bought it after my third year of fishing; it's called Bramble Brae, and it's a cosy wee spot.
The Man of Storr rock formation is just over the back. It's my favourite place on the island to visit. I want to take you there. It's beautiful.'

'You really aren't going to go to bed?'

'Nae until I've learned something new.'

'Hmm well, Bramble Brae sounds like a great place. I've never been anywhere that peaceful.
I have neighbours on both sides of my townhouse; it has three levels, so obviously I like stairs.
It's a four bedroom on Gilmore Place in the West End. It needed a lot of TLC to make it look respectable, but it's almost there.'

'What number is it?'

'*One hundred and ninety-nine. I'm crammed between people; thankfully, they're pretty quiet.*
I bought it at a considerably lower price than it should have been, it was a fixer upper. God, that was many years ago and no, I'm not a DIY queen. Someone else carried out the work.
I don't have a car as I live in the centre. I can drive, but I don't, the transport links are adequate for me.
I usually just walk or take the bus... or taxi, if I need to

venture further.

My best friend is James— he works alongside me. I don't have many close friends, I'm far too unsociable. I should probably try and change that, maybe make some new friends.'

'I don't mean to sound rude or forward, but are you rich? A townhouse in Edinburgh city centre, even at a discount, wouldn't be cheap?

It's nice having only a few friends; my best friend's Morag. She's the one who set me up on Highland Hearts, a total hoot, but she's far more reserved and busy now she's married. She used to be a complete party animal… I'd be lost without her.

I know lots of folk on the island, but very few I'd call close; it's a wee community up here. Everyone knows everyone.'

'Morag's who you were out with when you were texting me drunk? Have you and Morag ever, well... you know… had relations?'

I screamed with laughter.

'Morag's married to a man! Angus, he's a wee lost soul but a great guy.

Auch, I've never been attracted to Morag sexually, but we've kissed a few times over the years.

Friendly banter, ye know?

We jokingly flirt every now and then, but that's all it is. She's a sweetheart, and most definitely straight.'

'I see. I've never really done that with anyone, but it's nice you have someone you can be that comfortable with… And going back to your question, I wouldn't say I'm rich, but I don't do much in my free time, so I have savings.

I… I don't know how to say this without sounding like a

complete upper-class snob... but, my family has inherited wealth.'

I leaned against the arm of the chair

'But that's your parents, not you?'

'Yes. My father was Laird, and my mother is Lady Campbell of Calder.

They inherited wealth from previous generations of land ownership and members of high society.

I wasn't sure how long I was going to keep that from you. It's a lot to take in, and again, that's my parents, not me.

I'm supposed to meet the family's expectations.

Something I haven't done for pretty much all of my life.

I'm my mother's favourite disappointment.'

I blew out a sharp breath. Shit.

'Doesn't that mean you have a title?'

'Technically, yes.

I have the title of Lady, but I don't have any legal standing in the line of peerage. Please understand that Isla, I have no peerage or guarantee of inheritance.

My mother's expectations are only for her benefit.

It doesn't matter what I do, it won't affect anyone or anything.'

'My God. You're a Lady, and a PhD holder…

What the hell do you see in me? I can't live up to any of that. That's a big thing, Paisley, well a big thing to me, clearly you don't see it like that.'

'Isla, I don't want a relationship based on qualifications, superiority or class systems.

I just want someone kind, loving and caring. Someone to grow old and happy with.

My PhD was to get into the business.

My father and his friend partnered up, and built the

solicitors company from the ground upwards— I wanted to be part of that, to work under my father... although, sadly that didn't last long. Nothing more.

My social standing's not important, and in my eyes it doesn't exist. I don't expect anyone to live up to my mother's standards, I would frankly be disappointed if they did.

I want you to be you, and to fall in love with me for me. Nothing more, nothing less.

Please don't think too much about this.

It's genuinely not important.'

'It *is* important, Paisley, we're from completely different worlds.

I'm not saying your family didn't work hard for what they have, but my family built a fishing company from scratch.

A loan was taken out to purchase a clapped-out boat, it probably didnae even float. They lived in debt, and... and... fear, for years. How can that not matter in the grand scheme of things?' My voice had turned sharp.

'Please, Isla, I'm not judging anyone for working hard and occasionally struggling. I deal with people like that every day. It's refreshing to see those people leave their families a gift when they're no longer here, especially after working all of their lives.

What sits in our bank account shouldn't matter.

It's about what's inside you that I want.'

'But to me it does matter, Paisley!

I don't want to bring your social status down. I don't want a relationship built on someone else's money! It's... it's... obscene!'

'Isla, everyone is building their lives on money from somewhere or someone. Money doesn't excite me, you

315

do… I knew I shouldn't have said anything, it's not the right time.

This isn't the type of discussion I want to fall out about, especially over the phone.

My family dynamic isn't worth worrying about, and I definitely don't want to be arguing about money. Not with you.'

'I don't know how you can just think this doesn't matter. This changes so much!

Why don't you see that? It's affa easy for you to say money doesnae matter, you've never had to worry about it. Not everyone gets that luxury, Paisley, only the rich tell ye it's nae important.'

'Because it doesn't matter, Isla!' Paisley's voice raised.

'The family home and wealth could go to charity or be taken by debt collectors. It's just in the name— One of which I would change if it meant such a big deal.

I've worked extremely hard for the money in MY bank account; none of that has been through handouts from my parents.

Yes, there's a big house that goes hand in hand with my mother's lavish ideas, and yes, I was taught in a private school, but that doesn't make me a terrible person. I cannot change where I've come from; I was born into this. I never asked for it and I most certainly don't need it to be happy.

My happiness… our happiness is currently all I care about.

I want you to understand from my point of view, it's the person I want, not the wealth and title.

It's bad enough I need to emphasise this to my mother without trying to convince you as well!'

'I really don't know what to say. I'm tired; I think I might need to sleep on this. Thank you for the explanation, Paisley, but my brain hurts.

This is information that I can't grasp right now.

We're completely different people from two different places. I wish you'd told me this before.'

'Isla, privilege and power makes this world a really shitty place. Please don't think I'm one of those people who strives to be a part of it. I understand your views and I appreciate them, but bear in mind, it's family wealth, not mine!

I don't want to sleep on bad terms. I want you to understand.'

'I understand, but I'm going to bed. Goodnight, Paisley.'

'Please don't leave like this. We can talk more tomorrow. Okay?

Please don't think about it, I'm not my parents.'

'Goodnight, Paisley.'

'Goodnight, Isla. Sleep well.'

I hung up.

'Arggghhh, why?'

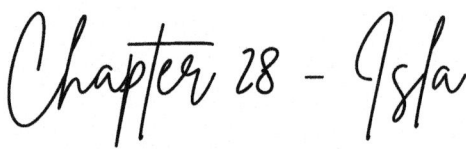

Chapter 28 - Isla

I awoke to a dreich Wednesday morning.

The noise of a crow perched on the chimney echoed beyond the stillness, its call cutting the quiet air like a haunting reminder of the day coming.

I was already in a bad mood, and I'd only just opened my eyes.

The bedside clock marked its presence with the red glow of 07:45 AM.

Placing two palms flat against the wall, I stood for what felt like days, the warm heavy rain pouring down. A silent hope the frustration I'd managed to promote in the past fifteen minutes would circle the drain.

'Bloody uptight, arrogant, scheming snob… auch aye, I have a private education and a PhD… plenty of money, big words and a title…Aye, ivory tower was accurate… holy moly, ah don't half make life easy.

Jeezo.

Money doesn't make me happy, blah, blah, blah… I want love and passion.

Eurgh, stick yer passion into yer private offshore account.'

Eventually vacating the hot and steamy cell, I dressed in a casual getup; jeans and a black T-shirt.

Blow-drying my hair, I picked up the phone.

I need to see you again x

I pressed send.

* * * *

Perched on the coffee hoose table sat two high glasses with a pathetically small finger loop.

Two glasses of fresh orange, two mammoth croissants and a teensy plate of cheese and ham in the middle.

'Sorry I'm late, Morag, I've hid a right night.'

'You aren't late, Isla, I live round the corner.'

She stood up to give me an almighty hug

'This looks fantastic, maybe I should just date you! Maybe I *should* ask Angus to share.'

We both let out a giggle before Morag got down to the early edition of *My life - the pop quiz.*

'Right, from the top, I want every single detail, so don't be scrimping, I'll know if ye miss something out, especially if it's juicy!'

We set to work on the pastries— I took a drink at every new sentence.

Morag watched on, her pulse must have been racing. The show went from tragedy, drama, mystery, and romance all in the space of thirty minutes.

Nodding and shaking her head frantically throughout the unfolding plot; it's the quietest I've seen her in a long time.

'… and then last night she told me wealth and status doesn't matter! It's about love and heart and all things bollocks.

What the hell do I do with that?'

Going by the look of disappointment in her eyes, Morag was carefully choosing her words.

The face wasn't at all what I'd expected.

'Marry her. Right here, right now and stop being a

dour puss,' she announced adamantly, banging her fist off the table.

I rolled my eyes and slumped back.

'Trust you to say something daft like that, Mo.
I canna exactly just marry her.'

'Ach, Isla, every couple will hae their differences. It could be about status, wealth, or views on anything and everything.

Look at Angus and me for example— he's skint most weeks and I have to keep his sorry arse the rest of the month. He persists on voting those Labour gits and I vote SNP.

I like sausages, he likes bacon. Opposites attract, after all.

It's all aboot give and take, Isla, it would be a really boring world if we were all the same...'

'But Morag, I don't know if I can deal with that, I agree with give and take, but the status alone is... well... it's horrendous.'

'Isla, if yer waiting for an equal standing, we'll still be here in forty years having the same discussion.
Stop being so childish, she hasn't offered to buy you a private island in the Bahamas.
Right now, I'm tempted to see if she'll send you to St. Kilda!'

Crossing her arms, Morag glowered at me. Hazel eyes burning straight into my forehead.

'Auch, Mo.'

'Anyway, why would you base everything on her family? You should be fully aware yer parents have different views to you and Alistair... Or have ye forgotten all aboot that? I didn't think it was all that long ago they couldn't accept you for being you...

Maybe I'm mistaken, the years have been harsh on ma memory.'

'I don't think we're on the same page today, Morag.'
I chewed my lip

'Right, well how would ye feel if I was to base all my views on you by Tam and Helen's ideas?
We canna be friends anymore, Isla, yer folks don't like the gays. Go on, clear off.' Morag pushed her hands out in front.

'Auch Mo, I hear you. That doesn't mean I like it.
I know you're right, but I don't feel any better.'

'Isla, I'll always be honest with ye, but I think you're going out of yer way to look for the negative.
So far this looks to be the one bad thing you can find.
I get that you're scared, but dinna push people away based on things they can't change.'

'Do you think I'm being stupid?' I asked, deflated in every way.

'I think you're cutting yer nose aff to spite yer face, everything you've told me sounds perfect.
Yer face sparkled when ye explained Edinburgh, it's the first time I've had a good feeling, and the first time you've actually telt me anything worthwhile.'
Her eyes softened, arms crossing back over the chest.

'Ye need to remember yer own social standing isn't as low as ye think; it's considerably higher than mine and Angus's.
Christ, I work at the campsite, maybe I should ditch you for being such a snotty bitch!' Morag gave out a short grunt.
I felt a pang of guilt.

'There's nothing wrong with the campsite, Morag, it pays…'

'Exactly! You can't base feelings and relationships on a wage bracket, Isla.

I never thought I would be explaining that to you.

Personally, I think she sounds like the kind of person ye need in yer life, so why are you already trying to fight against it? When can I meet her?'

Morag's grin could probably be seen from a Google Maps satellite image.

I paid for the breakfast this time and walked Morag out.

Her stupid grin still plastered on.

Eurgh, she always needs to be right. Smart arse.

'What's on today?' I asked.

'I have a few things ah need to do, and a doctor's appointment this afternoon. I'll tell you about that later, if it develops.'

'Wait, what kind of appointment? Are you okay?

I've never heard of you having appointments. You didn't even go to hospital when you dislocated your finger two years ago. What's going on?'

I stared at Morag, awaiting confirmation.

'I'm fine, Isla.

Just go and make peace with the rest o' yer life, I can see it's already playing on ye.

You'll be the first to know if there's anything important. Go call Paisley, tell her yer sorry, and the makeup sex will be worth it.'

Morag hugged me tightly and kissed my cheek.

'I love you, Morag, but there won't be any of that for a while.

You'd better tell me what's going on.'

Morag waved and blew me a kiss as she turned the

opposite way.

Walking back to the dumped car, I sat in the driver's seat and dialled Paisley.

I'd already promoted her into the *favourites* contact list.

The dialling tone rang for ages, eventually the line clicked.

'Hello, you've reached the phone of Paisley Campbell, please leave a message and I may respond.'
Followed by a long harsh bleep.

'Paisley... it's me... Isla.'

I looked through the car's windscreen, trying to search for the words.

'I want to apologise for last night...' I sighed heavily.

'I'm sorry, I don't know what to say... I... I was completely shocked... and... I didn't handle it very well... I pushed for a conversation that I wasn't really ready for, I was tired and emotional.

More emotional than I realised.

You're in my head all of the time and...I should've known better than to rush in without the information and facts, I shouldn't have been so rude.

Can you forgive me? Mibbe we can talk about it again. Calmly this time.

You can tell me the story, and I'll just listen.

When are you free?

I don't want to ruin anything, and I know it was me that caused that disagreement. I am sorry.

Please, let me know you're okay.'

I hung up.

Bollocks, now I feel even worse.

Starting the ignition, I headed towards the harbour.

It wasn't my day to be there, but I thought about getting ahead of the game.

Pulling into the car park, I was surprised to see Granda's car in its usual spot.

'Someone else trying to get ahead of the game, no doubt.'

As I wandered to the Ceilidh, Granda was tugging on the ropes and nets.

'Oi, Granda, what are ye doing here? You're supposed to be on holiday.'

'The weather isnae looking guid fir tomorrow lass, I'm jist making sure a'thing's tightened up fir the morn. Save us getting soaked afore we make it oot o' the bay. How wis yer night?'

'Aye, short lived, I went to bed early, what about you?'

'Aye, guid lass.'

'Granda, can you come down here a minuty please?'

I could see in his face, the years looked to be moving quicker than ever before.

Yesterday, he slept most of the day and could barely keep his eyes open— I'd been worried.

Today, I had nothing to lose by asking.

'Wit is it, lass?'

'Granda, are you alright? I mean, are you really, okay? I don't want your usual spiel about just being old. I want to know if it's time for you to take a step back. We don't need to go out when the seas are rough.'

I helped him down over the railing.

'Nonsense, Isla, I'm as fit as ah wis twenty years ago. There isnae anything comin' ower me lass.'

I stood firm; arms crossed and glowering.

The phone buzzed in my pocket, followed by a ping
Flinching, I made no attempt to look at it.
Great bloody timing.

'Ye should get that, lass, it might be Paisley.' He was testing the water.

'Paisley can wait. I'm talking to you just now, Granda. Are you ready to step back? Take things a bit slower.'

'Isla, ah'll need tae be yanked fae this boat in a crate afore ah'll take a step back.'
Spoken with self-assurance and a total lack of regard for his own health and well-being.
Something I'd shrugged off in the past, but now it was becoming second nature to worry.

'Check your phone lass, it could be important.'
I let out an angry huff, arms falling to a defeated position.

'Right, I'll check my phone, and then we are coming right back to this discussion, no excuses.
I mean it.'

New Message - Paisley (V. Hot Hairy Coo)
I'm sorry Isla, I got called into an emergency meeting and left my phone in my office.
I've just listened to your voicemail.
Of course, I forgive you, I was never angry, just worried.
I want to make this work, but you have to trust me. I am not my parents!!
We do need to talk though. Give me a call when you're free, I shouldn't be in any more meetings today. Xxx
Sent 11:49 Wednesday 28th Feb

New Message - Isla MacLeod

Thank you :) I do trust you!

Your reply sounds urgent, everything ok?

I'll call soon, having an open and honest discussion with Granda about him stepping back.

He's nae having any of it.

I miss your voice xxx

Sent 11:54 Wednesday 28th Feb

New Message - Paisley (V. Hot Hairy Coo)

Isla, it's not urgent. I'm just happy to speak to you, I'll wait until later.

Go and get him told! I miss you too xxxx

Sent 11:55 Wednesday 28th Feb

Sliding the phone into my pocket, I stomped back to the bench where Granda was stationed.

Sitting down beside him, we basked in silence for a minute.

'Granda, I don't want to sound insensitive or mean, and I'm only saying this because you're my everything…'

'Nae anymore, Isla, ye hiv someone else tae focus on now. Make that work fir ye both.'

'That's not set in stone, Granda!'

I let out a long slow huff.

'I don't know what I'd do without you, Granda.

I need to know you're safe, putting ourselves in dangerous situations fills me with fear.

The boat's our life, I get that, but I can live without it...

I can't live without you.

I need to know you're okay to keep going.'

Granda's face softened as he looked at the boat.

He propped his head against my shoulder— it was unusual and homely.

What I would give to keep this moment.

'Isla, I'm an eighty-year auld man, the days fir me are numbered.

As ah've said tae ye afore, ye need tae grab the bull by the horns, go live yer own life.

I've lived mine, it's yer turn tae dae the same.'

Ignoring his statement, I ruffled my fringe.

'I was thinking we could hire in some help, I don't want to take you off the boat, but I can't be worrying about you doing too much.

You're tired all the time, and I really do worry about you. I have time to live, but you're my life.

Paisley will wait, it's all new and we'll work on that in the background, but you're here and now.

Please.'

'Wit dae ye hae in mind, lass?' He asked, almost resigned.

Turning to face me, the whites of his eyes appeared more yellow.

'Morag's, Angus is hating the fish shoppie, I thought we could offer him a few days on the boat, see if he fancied a change of career.

It's nae for everyone, but he's a good wee worker, always cheery, and going by Morag's bossing about, he always does as he's told.

It would give you a wee break, mibbe you could take it a wee bitty slower.'

'Hiv ye spoken tae the loon?'

'I'd never do anything without consulting the boss first.' I gave him a cheeky wink.

'Isla, I'm starting to think you're solid in the head.

You are the boss!'

He spoke like I was a child again, all loud and perfectly pronounced. No sign of his strong Hebridean accent. Cheeky monkey.

'Didn't Paisley tell ye anything aboot oor meeting?' His eyes never left mine.

'No! That has absolutely nothing to do with me!' I shook my head in disgust, the thought made my skin crawl.

'It his everything tae do with ye, lass.

Auch, ah think ah like her even mare, she has integrity and pride.

That's grand qualities right there, Isla, stick wi' her, she'll keep ye guid.

Aye, ah think yer mibbe right, ye should ask Angus how he feels aboot the sea.

Invite him oot wi' us, offer him a job, dae whitever ye think's best, lass. But... fir now,' he stood wearily from the bench, 'I'm aff hame, I'm absolutely knackered.'

Patting my shoulder, he very slowly moved towards the car park.

I checked my watch; it was just going lunchtime, how could he be tired already?

Bowing my head I looked at my feet, they scuffed against the stone, the light breeze tugging against my hair.

These conversations with Granda weren't getting any easier, and they appeared to be happening a lot more frequently.

Freeing the phone, I flicked through the contacts; pressing dial, it rang.

'Angus, hello, it's me, Isla. I have a wee proposition for ye, do ye want to meet me at the Ceilidh, and I'll explain in a bit more detail?'

'Hello, Isla, aye I'm jist round the corner. Give me ten.'

'Grand, I'll see you soon.'

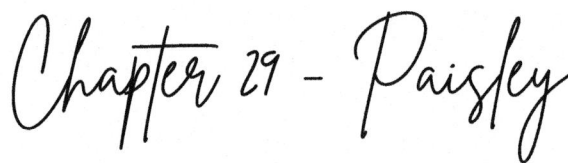

Chapter 29 - Paisley

Positioned in a way that would make my mother squeal, I sprawled across the mustard and cerise chaise. My legs twisted and bent in two opposite directions, my head propped lazily against the backboard.

Definitely not very lady-like!

Unhurried in my reading, I was taking a moment to appreciate the illustrations and text: *Getting Laid; A guide for the over-40s lesbian*

Unfortunately, it was for all the wrong reasons, most of them were derogatory and filth ridden... had Isla been here, she would have definitely learned something new.

I looked towards the expansive bookcase— trying to clear the degenerate images from my corrupt brain.

It wrapped around the room's once open corner; now it looked more like a personal library— one that would both shock and impress most people in Edinburgh.

The shelves housed a mixture of law books, high society reads, self-help guides, and romance novels. Admittedly, I'd read them all... very sad, I know.

Being Saturday, I can yet again free up enough time to add another spine to the collection; it certainly beats the chore of cleaning the bathroom or changing the bedsheets. Eurgh.

My filth tarnished attention returned to the page.

The deep, old-fashioned doorbell rang out, I raised my eyes from the chapter marked - *Greedy Girl Thrusting (Without the hip replacement).*

'Who the hell is that?'

Swinging from the chaise, I placed the book face-down against the table.

'We'll come back to you in a minute.'

I meandered my way to the front door, the glass panel highlighting a red jacket and cap.

'The postie, I presume.'

Curiously, I unlocked the door, unsure why I was being blessed with Royal Mail's services today.

'Well, I'm not taking in a parcel for that bloody neighbour again, it took them over a week to collect the last one.'

The postie had already stepped back a few feet—giving me ample room to move.

A young man grinning a full set of crooked whites stood swaying.

He looked as if it was his first day on the job.

Still young and excited about life. Shame.

I remember when I was once like that. Now I'm just bitter and hardened… hah!

Mind you, at least he's not the bloody bible bashers, I'm sick of asking them to join my gender bending, swinger's cult!

'Good morning, are you Ms. P. Campbell?'

He's far too happy.

'Aye, that's me.'

'Great, I've got your parcel here, but I need a signature…'

'Aye, but I didn't order anything.'

My eyes flickered to the package— It *was* in my name.

'Yup. That's exactly what every other woman tells their husband.'

'I don't have a husband.'

The postie glanced up from his electronic signature machine. His eyes wandered my face.

'Do you want one?' he asked with a timorous laugh.
I got the impression he was contemplating getting down on one knee.

The electronic device protruded into the hallway—
Snatching it from him, I scrawled my signature.

'I'm far more likely to order a wife off of Amazon.
At least they offer next-day delivery and a decent warranty. That's always handy if I need to send her back.' I replied with an unmoved face.
Shoving the machine back into his hands, I yanked the parcel free.

'Cheers. Now, try not proposing to anyone else before lunch, forty two percent of Scottish marriages end in divorce. If you do bugger up, come back and I'll fix it for you.'
The cap tilted.

'Oh… and not every woman needs or wants a man. Nowadays, we have you lot deliver the desired anatomy in discreet packages.'
With that, I shot him a sarcastic wink and shut the door.
Through the glass I could still see him standing. Probably wishing he *had* gone to the neighbours.

Carrying the bulky bag to the kitchen, I attempted to interpret the label.
No name of the sender, no postage mark, no hints. How odd.
I instantly cut through the top using a pair of scissors from the drawer.

'Who the fuck has sent me this? Is this some sick

joke or something?'

At the very top of the package sat a paper envelope with the letters 'P x' written in blue pen.

'Isla? Who else would know about Px?'

Mounds of tissue paper covered in multicoloured balloons sat beneath it.

Dumping the parcel on the draining board, I opened the envelope.

A cute little *'Happy Belated Birthday'* card with two little foxes laced the front.

The right-hand page of the card was clarted in blue handwriting:

Paisley,
You tried to keep your birthday a secret from me?!
You might have a PhD, but bitch, please.
I'm a black belt in Facebook and Google stalking.
I hope you had a great 40th birthday, but I can't believe you didn't tell me!
I'm pissed, I could have put in more effort.
I'm missing you so much already and I can't wait to see you.
Enjoy the gift ;)
Lots of love, Isla xxxx

Placing the card on the kitchen bunker, I couldn't release the ineffable grin. My cheeks actually hurt.

My heart grew an extra inch as adoration ran through my veins.

Lifting the weighty package again, I eagerly tore into the gift.

I was desperate to find out what the sleekit wee bugger had sent.

Pulling back the tissue paper, my expression shifted from excitement to pure hilarity.

Crying laughter echoed through the kitchen and I was secretly gutted no one was here to share the glory.

The tissue paper fluttered to the floor as I held up a beige cable-knit Aran sweater.

A post-it note stuck to the collar:

Be thankful I didn't buy you the one with the sheep on the front x

'Oh, Jesus Christ.'

I threw the sweater on over my head, letting free another neck-snapping laugh.

Making my way back to the seat and picking up the do-it-yourself-er, I couldn't hide the delight.

'Hmm, I should be sharing this.'

Resting the book back down against my knee.

New Message - Paisley (V. Hot Hairy Coo)

Isla, you probably won't see this message until you're back on solid ground, but I've just received

my very own Aran sweater ha ha ha, you are bloody crazy. I love it, genuinely.

How did you know, it's just what I've always wanted? You've really brightened up my day.

Thank you so much, it's perfect.

You're perfect!

P xxxx

Sent 11:54 Saturday 9th March

I snapped a quick selfie and attached it.

Putting the phone back down, I picked up my book for a third time.

Warm and comfy, I sat wearing the chunky knit.

Entertaining a peaceful Saturday at home, with no wine and no worries.

Finally, peace and happiness burrowed into me.

Chapter 30 - Paisley

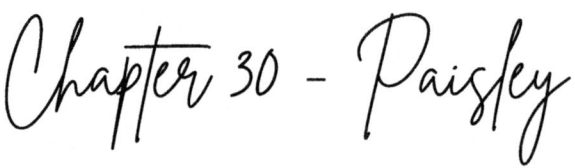

New Message - Paisley (V. Hot Hairy Coo)

Good morning beautiful,

I hope your day's going well, I can't believe it's almost two whole months since we first met in Edinburgh! I think I must have fallen asleep first last night. My phone was half dead and stuck to my face this morning. Did you disconnect? I'd hate to have seen the phone bill if these calls had been 15 years ago.

I hope the weather isn't causing you too much grief and Angus is keeping Alistair in check.

Let me know you're back safely!

Miss you lots, P xxxx

Sent 09:14 Saturday 13th April

New Message - Isla MacLeod

Morning gorgeous girlfriend!

Just landed, Granda's asking if you're busy? I told him

obviously not...Ha. ;)

Aye, you were snoring, I did think about waking you but it was too cute, listened for a wee whiley, then thought I was mibbe a creep. Hung up after two hours.

Oh aye, could you imagine? How did we manage before contracts!?

Two months and no arguments, that is amazing... Angus has finally found his sea legs, can't wait to tell Morag, she'll be pleased, shame he's still stinking of fish haha.

The weather's shite, but at least it's lighter in the mornings.

Have you managed to ruin anyone's day yet?

A couple of bitter divorces? Adoptions?

Oh, speaking of ruining your day, have you spoken to your mum? Xxxxx

Sent 11:39 Saturday 13th April

New Message - Paisley (V. Hot Hairy Coo)

Cheeky! I'm always busy, this company restructure has me on my toes. Tell Alistair I said hello please.

I sat in on a couple of interviews this morning, I wouldn't touch them with a barge pole personally, but I got to see how the Legal Directors work... Very interesting, I can go anywhere with this knowledge.

I had to do a bit of reading and research, how tedious ;) I just hate reading, especially when I get paid for it :P Tragic.

It's a gorgeous day here, shame you've got rain.

I haven't ruined anyone's day yet, but James had a domestic abuse case, I was a little bit jealous. I love trying to nail those fuckers to the wall.

I'm glad Angus isn't going to pollute our ecosystem anymore. That is a bonus!

No, the old bat hasn't been back in touch since her last message. Actually, I think it's my turn to respond, but I'm far too busy tormenting you instead. I really miss you. Can't wait to speak to you /see you. xxxx

P.s I'll call you soon, I've a few things to do.

Enjoy your day. Xxx

Sent 11:45 Saturday 13th April

* * * *

I fired off an email to my boss and called James into the office.

I'd been gifted a new Monstera plant from a grateful client. It had taken up residence in the corner of the room, its leaves still small but hinting at the grandeur it would achieve.

It's quite striking, I don't know why I've never had plants before.

Sitting poised behind my desk in a brand-new burgundy suit, I felt on top of the world.

Life was finally on the up, well until James strolled in…

'Ooo, Darling, that colour looks fantastic in here,' he blew out.

'Thank you, I fancied a change.'

I smiled, before noticing a piece of black thread on the left arm. I pulled it off.

'I meant the plant,' he stated drolly before laughing.

Luckily, he dodged the flying stapler, aimed for his head.

It missed and bounced off the rug.

Damn.

'Darling, I'm joking, that suit is stunning! And can I just say…'

I glowered at him as the holepunch found my view—ready and waiting for his next retort.

'… Your temperament for the past two months has been a real breath of fresh air…' he looked at the stapler lying on the floor and pointed, 'well aside from that.'

'Really? I didn't think I'd changed in any way …at …all.' I spat the last two words, the feeling of unease

338

brewing at what was about to spill out from his mouth next.

The holepunch now firmly in hand— Come on, try me batty boy.

'Well, you wouldn't, darling, would you?

You're still a cocky cow, but you are on top of your game right now.'

I opened my mouth, but nothing arrived. Hmm, I guess that was kind of acceptable.

'And that suit really is fabulous, I'm very tempted to look for something similar myself.' He paused as if trying to decide which buttons to push next.

No doubt it wouldn't take him long.

'Speaking of which, how is that gorgeous girlfriend of yours? No devious phone sex yet?'

He's such a cheeky git, go on, throw the holepunch anyway.

I chose to ignore the derogatory remarks.

'Well, that's partly why I called you in, James.

Surely you didn't think I actually wanted to converse with you.

I'm hoping to escape for a week or so. Maybe use up some of the annual leave that I always waste.'

James lifted an eyebrow.

Raising both hands into fists, he created a crude set of V's on each; as if a very camp version of rock-paper-scissors was about to begin.

Bashing the V's together harshly, his tongue emphasised the vulgarity as it poked from his lips.

'Ohhh, darling. Yes!!

I'm so ready for you to partake in some clouting of the clam.' He shouted across the room.

I leant over and battered my forehead off the desk—leaving it face-down I hoped he couldn't see my embarrassment.

Kill me now.

'James, you're an absolute dog, I swear to God.'

My voice was muffled by the wooden surface.

'So, what did you want from me, darling? Tips, diagrams, chat-up lines, examples in the form of video? I might actually have a couple here, hang on.' He pulled out his phone, trying to add to the humour.

'Eurgh, you're a vile, vulgar brute.'

My eyes lifted enough to witness his actions.

I shouldn't have bothered.

Tapping a forefinger against his chin, he started with yet more filth.

'Sweetie, I think I might have a couple of spare condoms and a half bottle of toffee latte-flavoured lubricant in my office, would you like me to go and get that?

They should still be good, just don't lick the tip of the bottle.'

'Please, somebody just shoot me.'

I let out a mortified groan, it rattled out across the room.

'I just need you to cover my meetings for at least a week,' I let out more muffled explanations.

As if things couldn't get any worse, there was another knock on the door, Sharon pushed her head inside.

'Hello, Paisley?'

'Oh God no, the plot thickens … give me the gun, I'll do it myself.'

Sharon must have looked amused by the scene.

My head still face down on the table, the sprawling stapler at James's feet, and his beam, probably the widest smile in the universe as he stood swaying on his tiptoes.

'Oh, I'm sorry, I didn't realise you were busy.' Sharon stated.

'We aren't,' I grumbled.

'We were.' James interjected. 'I was just giving Paisley some tips on ...'

'JAMES!! NO. DON'T YOU DARE!!!!'
The mahogany desk was screaming.

'Sex with her new pillow princess,' he blurted out.

'Arsehole! Utter, arsehole.' I yelled back.
Sharon smiled and started to laugh, her hand coming up to cover her mouth.

'And do you need any more help with that, or should I come back later?'
James turned to face Sharon, 'You can come anytime you like, darling, it's a free country after all.' Giving her a dirty wink.
More giggles and a batting of her eyelashes.
Christ, get a room.

My desk finally managed to string a sentence together.

'Go on, Sharon, what do you need? Save me the embarrassment of needing to speak to either of you pair again today.'

'Mrs. Jones has requested her meeting for next week be cancelled until further notice. She's now thinking of either a divorce settlement, or legal aid for murder instead of altering the will.
That should give you some free time.'
Sharon moved into the room.

'But on a side note, if you need help, you know, from an actual woman in regards to playing hello kitty, you know where I am.

Oh, and before I forget…

That colour looks amazing on you, much less heading to a funeral a lot more, *I'm a bitch who's got swagger*.'

She swayed out the door before I could make a sound.

'Thanks, Sharon,' James loudly announced while watching her flounce and flurry.

'See I told you, that suit will work miracles! Definitely take it into the bedroom!'

'One of these days, James, I'm going to cut off your balls with a very blunt object and stick them somewhere agonising.'

I finally looked up at him, face all sticky with sweat and tears.

My embarrassment had undoubtedly turned my face to the same colour as the blazer.

James continued patting the finger against his chin.

'Where exactly are you putting them? I might ask Paul to try tonight, it sounds very kink!

Oh, and of course I'll take your meetings, just get yourself up there already.

I'm desperate to meet this divine woman who's stolen your heart and hopefully soon your dignity.'

I let my head slide back down, it bounced for a second time before I propped up two thumbs in a very, very small gesture of thanks.

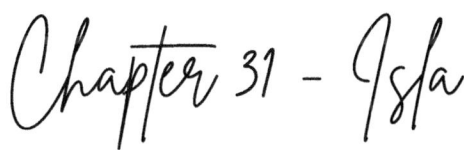

Chapter 31 - Isla

Thursday began as usual, the 02:45 alarm jolted me awake, the cold dark April morning allowing the duvet to hold me ransom.

The day was waiting and so was the sea.

Before dragging myself from the warmth, I pulled my phone from the nightstand, a new daily ritual.

New Message - Isla MacLeod
Good Morning Paisley, I hope you slept well.
You won't see this until you're awake…
obviously, but have a great day at work.
I can't wait to speak to you later. Xxxx
Sent 02:51 Thursday 18th April

Washed and dressed, I stood by the living room window, staring beyond the glass to the navy abyss; a coffee in one hand, a slice of toast in the other.

Small flecks had begun to splatter the pane, a potentially early warning of the weather to come.

Taking the last bite, headlights flickered outside— Angus. He'd been picking me up for the past few days.

'No point wasting fuel when we're heading to the same place,' he had politely argued. Even though he did need to double back to collect me.

Truthfully, I didn't mind. I enjoyed the company, plus it gave me a few extra minutes to get ready.

We drove almost silently, the odd titbit of small talk respectfully exchanged.

Coming home was usually the opposite; we'd have in-depth conversations normally followed by talk of Morag, Granda and Paisley.

Bonding well each day, I could finally see what Morag had found in Angus all those years ago.

They were complete opposites in every way, but he was warm and kind, never spoke badly of anyone, and was always so calm and unassuming.

One of those 'sultans of the earth' kind of guys, and truthfully, he'd made a huge difference out on the water.

Taking extra time to ensure Granda wasn't doing too much, helping me when things were heavy, oh, and he never stood around waiting for instruction.

A good all-rounder who fit in well. I'm glad I hired him.

Arriving at the dock, we were both surprised to see that Granda wasn't here.

'Hmm, that's unusual Angus, he's normally here first. I hope he's alright.' I felt a deep worry niggling in my chest.

'He's probably just taking his time; we can get started and I can always go check if he doesn't appear.'

The morning checks were a vital task, but we had the Ceilidh all ready to go by the time Granda arrived.

He was over forty minutes late— I decided against questioning him.

It was heartbreakingly clear he was slowing down— it could be seen in every weighty movement.

My body ached with concern. I could see his deterioration daily, yet he wouldn't take a break.

'I'm worried about him Angus, he's nae right.' I said, whilst Granda was out of earshot.

'I'll keep an eye on him, Isla.'

Gratefully, I patted Angus's arm.

Moving up to the wheelhouse, I put the engine into gear before checking the radios, gauges and instruments were all working properly.

The static radio burst to life.

'Isla, the ropes are up. Over'

I could hear the hydraulic lift clattering away.

'Copy that, Angus.'

'Okay Isla, I think we're good to go. Over'

'Roger that.'

Granda dotted about the place, absentmindedly checking water and oil levels, ensuring we had ample fuel, pretty much replicating everything me and Angus had already done.

We didn't tell him.

I was just happy he was keeping out of trouble.

Everything was as it should be, so I eased the throttle forward; The Ceilidh responded by gradually picking up speed.

Within a few minutes, we cut through the calm water, disappearing into a new day as the surf parted.

Our morning went smooth sailing, the boat ran well, the weather stayed on side, and the catch was nothing short of excellent.

A few tons of haddock filled the storage units, all ready to be distributed upon landing.

'We'll be back in about twenty minutes,' I called out over the Tannoy speaker.

'The tide looks good, the sun is shining, an excellent day of fishing, well done folks.'

The white noise buzz collapsed as I flicked the switch.

Within forty seconds, the oilskin pocket radio crackled.

'Hello, Isla, Alistair has taken a wee dizzy spell, I don't suppose you could nip us on a wee bit quicker, get us off the water? Over'

'What do you mean by dizzy spell, Angus? Over'

'Isla, he's a wee bit short of breath down here, should I try and get him up to the mid-deck, get some fresh air? Over'

'Yes, Please Angus. Over' I shouted.

Fifteen seconds and the radio sizzled.

'Ah Isla, I take it back, he's not looking good at all, I'm bringing him up now. Over.'

Shit.

'Angus, I'll call the mission, see if I can get someone to meet us at the dock.

Let me know if you need help, try and make Granda as comfortable as you can please. Over.'

I flicked the main VHF radio over to the correct channel, my hands trembling as I called in.

Dread chewing at me as I tried to remember what to do. My mind was blank except for the horrifying thoughts of Granda.

'Mayday, Mayday, Mayday, this is the Ceilidh, I repeat this is the Ceilidh. We're a red and white JG Forbes trawler, coordinates 57.8484982, -5.9880829. We have a medical emergency on board, one eighty-year-old male with shortness of breath and dizziness. Could we have some assistance at the Portree Harbour? Over.'

The sudden lack of oxygen in my lungs wasn't helping, panic wasn't just creeping in, it was flooding. It's pace dramatically increasing by the second— black spots approached the side of my eyes, hands trembling as I gripped the radio.

'Breathe, Isla, just breathe.'

Around twenty seconds passed; it felt like a lifetime, my pulse wheeching as the spots were now swirling around the pupils, 'keep calm, keep calm, come on Isla, you have this.'

Legs and shoulders absorbing the frailty, each movement stinted. I struggled to remain steady.

'Hello Ceilidh, copy on the assistance. Are you okay to wait until you dock, or do you want us to send a lifeboat? Over' The radio responded.

Grabbing at the pocket radio,

'Angus, is Granda okay? Can he wait to dock, or does he want me to get someone out to us now? Over.

'… Come on … come on.' My hands reaching seven on the Richter scale. A violent conflict to operate the broadcasting control.

'Isla, he says he's fine to wait. Over.'

'Copy,'

Switching back to the VHF,

'Control, I believe we can wait until we dock. Over.'

Angus carried Granda along the deck below the window. He looked weak and frail against the younger man's chest, very little movement emitting from his brittle frame.

He's not bloody fine at all.

'Copy that Ceilidh, we have someone awaiting your arrival. A crew is on standby awaiting further instruction and an ambulance has been sent for. Let us know if you need anything in the meantime. Over.'

'Copy, thank you. Over.'

I hung the radio back on its clip, forcing the engine to

full power, I set the autopilot system.

Go. Go. Go.

Running down to the deck— taking two stairs at a time, I rushed to where Granda and Angus were positioned.

Granda had taken on a ghastly shade of grey, he was clammy to the touch and panting heavily, every breath raspy and full of effort.

His eyes and cheeks dark and sunken, as though they had fallen further into his skull, his hands shaking uncontrollably, lips tinged a faint blue tone.

'Oh Granda, what have you done?' I screeched; wrapping my arms around him, I tried desperately to rub some heat into his bones.

'Angus, could you run up to the wheelhouse?

There should be a couple of paper bags on the back shelf.

Can you grab me a couple please?' I asked, my tone panic ridden.

He nodded and took off running.

Letting go for a moment, I removed my floatation vest and oilskin jacket.

Laying my thick waterproof coat across Granda it was a desperate hope to contain some of his body heat.

My tammy came next; I pulled it from my head and pushed it down tightly onto his.

My hands back to rubbing his body.

'What are we going to do with you, eh?'

Tears had already begun jabbing against my eyelids.

He weakly smiled, before wincing as though in pain.

'Ah wis, ah wis trying to…' he struggled to get the words out.

'Th… the…lines… Tangled lines,'

'Shhhhhh, it's okay, just keep breathing, it doesn't

matter now.

Just keep breathing, Granda.

You should've left the lines— that's for both of us to fix. You know it's a heavy slog— we do them together.'

My voice had taken on the squeaky, lump-in-the-throat kind of gargle.

I was struggling to make any kind of sound as my tonsils held me hostage, the devastation of being in this awful position rapidly eating away at me.

I didn't want to appear feeble.

I wanted to talk to Granda as if I knew he was going to be okay. Try and keep both our spirits up, convince him I knew what I was doing. The reality wasn't that easy. Already lost to the emotion and panic, I didn't have a clue on how to make this situation better.

Angus appeared back at my side, sweat running down from his face, his breath panting out like a dog.

'A... ah picked up a couple o' blankets and some water... he... here's the bags.' Angus spluttered out whilst handing me the sacks, they'd been onboard since he'd started. They were meant for the sea sickness he hadn't been able to control, but they were ideal for this moment.

Angus looked wounded by the joke as he wrapped a blanket around Granda; it was a good distraction for him.

Granda must have appreciated the sentiment too, his lips curled upwards, we both knew he found it amusing. Taking an open bag from me, he tried to breathe into it. It didn't inflate— instead, each shallow inhale made a painful rattle.

'Just breathe, Granda, I've got you.'

Positioning myself in front of him, I allowed his head to rest wearily against my shoulder.

I copied his action— devastated by his sorry state and my inability to fix this terrible nightmare.

Hoping to get the blood pumping in our embrace, I continued to cradle him— silently grateful he couldn't see the endless stream running down my face.

'Ah… ah, love… ye lass.' He choked out, with arms wrapping tightly around my back.

We sat huddled in a sad, painful hold.

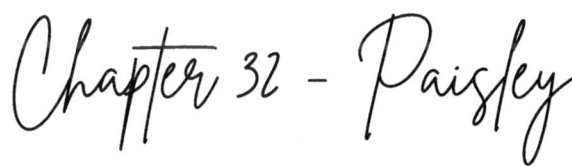

Chapter 32 – Paisley

I stood at the harbour's edge, sunglasses catching the early sunlight as it danced across the water. The thespian backdrop of rugged hills and craggy rock prevalent whilst a red and white boat thundered towards me.

'I finally understand Isla's love for the island. This place is breathtaking.' I muttered to nobody.

Puffing out a cloud, I inhaled another; the hot end glowing against the crisp breeze.

I was glad to have ditched my office finery, instead I'd opted for warm navy jeans, a grey cardigan, and a long thick coat. It was needed.

A crowd had started to gather, many clad in costumes bearing the Lifeboat and Fishermen's Mission logo.

A practice run maybe.

Within two minutes a few more onlookers joined the congregation, their thick accents webbed with concern as they murmured and chittered.

'Okay, what's going on here? This doesn't feel right.'

I watched intently, trying to piece together what was happening. Eyes flickering between the bodies and vessel.

Eavesdropping to gain the slightest hint of clarity, the voices were too quiet, too heavy with a Hebridean twang.

'We'll need some space here, please,' A mission

worker stated firmly

'What's going on? Is there a problem?' I asked, my voice sharp with authoritative unease.

'Aye, we have reports of a medical emergency onboard. That's all I can tell you for now.' He responded equally as sharp— his lilting accent almost as cold as the wind.

Guiding me a few steps away he turned his attention back to the incoming boat.

'Thanks,' I guess

My eyes followed his, the boat's hull now in sight.

The Ceilidh.

Lurching into an immediate sweat, my stomach dropped as an overwhelming sense that I was about to throw up crashed over me.

Yanking the sunglasses from my face, I squinted. Desperately trying to see into the not-so-small boat; searching for any sign of Isla.

Someone was in the wheelhouse, but I couldn't work out who.

A tremor ran through me, goosebumps starting to cover my body, small hairs on the back of my neck stood together; armed and ready.

My chest tightening in a deathly grip, ears ringing with a tinnitus squeal.

'Oh God… Isla! Please, be alright… Please, please be okay.'

As soon as the boat was close enough, a full team of responders left their stance on the wall.

Jumping over the railings, they made their way onto the Ceilidh's deck, their movements swift and efficient.

The air was full of noise, radios sputtering, broken voices shouting, speakers bursting out in deafening high pitched whines.

An ambulance pulled into the quayside, two tones and beacons spinning rapidly— highlighting the severity of the situation.

The breath pulled in my chest, my racing pulse now pounding.

I fumbled for my phone, hesitating as it reached my desperate grasp.

The anxiety I hadn't felt for months was growing, its momentum building rapidly— mimicking the perspiration sprinting down my back.

Frost numbed my extremities as an all-consuming fear caused my limbs to tremble.

Panic clawed at me; I forced my legs to stay put.

'I have to let them do their job.'

Stubbing out the half-finished cigarette, I forced it into the bin next to me.

Leaning against it's metal shell like a defeated scaffold. A silent hope it would hold my weight in this moment of angst.

Moments later, the rescue team re-emerged, they carefully manoeuvred a stretcher up and over the rails— each of them in perfect synchrony.

My heart stopped. Isla. Fuck, please be safe.

The stretcher was shielded by a dozen figures.

I couldn't get a clear view.

Suddenly a break allowed me a glimpse, I still couldn't make out the figure in the green hat. They were hidden beneath blankets— a breathing mask shielding their face.

My feet felt like lead as I urged them closer.
I was reckless in my attempt to find answers and
hazardous in my rush to push through the crowd.
Looking down, I hadn't moved.
My boots and feet both appeared to be paralysed as I
remained firmly fixed in place.

Trying to pull out another cigarette, my hands
wouldn't comply either. A distraught hope a second
nicotine hit might still my nerves.

I made another effort to move position, a distressed
need for a better view.
My hip remained tight against the skip, fingers battling
between my luggage and scratching at the fag packet.

A short dark-haired woman is intently staring at me. I
tried freeing a faint smile as she neared, truthfully, I'm
not sure if my muscles moved.
    'Would ye like a hand? Ye look like you're struggling
there.' She asked kindly.
I don't want to appear weak... being asked if I need
help isn't really my style, but I can't get my body or
mouth to shift.
Silently battling this locked-in syndrome, I held the
carton out.

My head continued the torturous hunt for information
as I watched through swollen features.
A smoke found my hand.
    'Do ye know the folk on the boat?'
Her accent was warm and polite, but there was a hint of

nosiness not far behind it.

'Isla,' I breathed out.

Desperately seeking some kind of confirmation. Unable to find any other words in my jumbled sanity.

She patted the hand my cigarette had found.

'Well, it isnae Isla in the wagon, it's her grandfather, he's haeing a hard time breathing.'

I turned to face her; opening my mouth, nothing came out.

'You're Paisley, aren't ye?' She asked with a sad grin.

'I'm Morag, you can come wi' me, I'll get you through, on ye come.'

'Morag?' The name's familiar, but it hasn't registered.

'Aye, that's me! And I know all about you, Paisley. I think you're in wee bit of shock, let's get you sorted.'

I felt a sudden pang of relief as her words filtered down. My chest loosened enough to allow my lungs to kick back into life.

Finally managing to lift my feet, I grabbed my bag and dithered behind.

We moved to the opposite side of the boat— away from all the noise and rush.

A tall man stood at the far side watching us.

Morag ran over and gave him a hug and a kiss.

They started speaking— both now glancing in my direction.

I was too far to hear what was being said, but going by the surveying, there was no doubt it was about me.

Morag started flapping her hands in a 'come hither' sort of motion, so for once, I did as I was asked.

'This is Angus, my husband.

Isla's gone with her Granda up tae the community

hospital. It's jist around the corner, we'll take ye up.'

'Thank you…' I replied before letting out a long sigh.

'…and it's nice to meet you both.

I'm so sorry, I got such a scare, I wasn't sure what I'd just walked into.

Unprepared would be an understatement.

I think I was having some sort of panic attack.'

I shook both of their hands— it felt a bit formal.

'Do you just hold onto them or do ye smoke them?' Morag questioned with a nod to my hand.

'Hah, yes. Would you like one?' I asked.

'I shouldn't, I don't normally smoke unless I've had a drink,' Morag lilted, 'but I feel like I could really use a drink.'

Walking to the hospital with my wheelie bag in tow felt very surreal.

All three of us puffed away on my Marlboro Golds, whilst Angus filled us in on Alistair's medical emergency.

Morag turned to face me; a flicking of her ash found the road.

'Does she know you're here?'

I inhaled a deep breath of toxic fumes.

'No, it was probably a major faux pas on my behalf.

I know she's going to be in pieces with Mr. MacLeod being unwell.' I replied.

'Ah, I think you'll be a good distraction,' Morag answered, as a gentle elbow found my ribs.

'But you're not wrong, that man's everything to Isla… I guess ye already know that.'

I nodded thoughtfully.

Entering the hospital, I was surprised by its tiny structure. Although it looked like it had new technology, it was old and run down.

'I'm fair surprised they've brought him here, I'd have thought Broadford would've been better suited,' Morag stated, as if reading my mind.

As soon as we reached the waiting room, I could see Isla sitting in one of the ancient plastic chairs.
The delicate feminine frame folded into itself, two twisted feet digging into the neighbouring chair.
Her hands anxiously twisting at the fingers.

My heart skipped, chaos filled my head as I knew nothing I could do would ever be enough.
My beautiful woman was broken, tortured and abused.

'On you go. It's you she needs.' Morag nodded; her voice soft but firm.

'Are you sure? I… I…' Imposter syndrome now joining my ailments.

'Oh aye, I think it's your turn to be the hero, Paisley. We'll pop back in a few hours… If either of you need anything, my numbers in her phone.' She patted my arm.

'Go on.'

Morag and Angus patiently waited until I made a move.
Isla looked up, her head tilting towards me as if unsure whether I was real or not.
She burst into tears; her arms stretching out wide as she stood, the crippled frame shaking as distress found her.
Moving quickly, I bundled her into my arms, tightly enveloping as if we were the world's last two survivors.

'How are you here? How did you know?' She asked between gargling sobs.

Silent tears ran down both of her red and blotchy cheeks, eyes bloodshot as if she'd been crying all week. I couldn't tolerate the pain— I couldn't steal it away. All this time and I still couldn't do more.

Pointing my head in the direction of the door, Morag was still lingering.

I nodded, a silent but grateful thank you.

Morag returned it before blowing Isla a kiss and turning to tread the heels of Angus.

'Paisley, I couldn't call you, I had to see he was alright... I was in such a state... I'm sorry.'

'Shhhh, shhhhh, that's not important. How is he?'

My poor selfless girl.

'They've got his breathing steady, but they're still running tests. His blood pressure's low and... his temperature's low... and... and... everything is low...'

Another wave of emotion bathed her.

Without hesitation, I pulled Isla in tighter against my chest, arms gently immersing her.

I pressed a kiss to her forehead.

'Shhh, I've got you.'

Isla's streaky face tilted upwards, a desperation to be held and loved.

Placing a tender kiss onto her lips, we both ached.

It was short, but it held an affection we couldn't speak.

'Thank you for being here,' she whispered.

'That's my job, I'm here for you.' I pushed back a stray hair.

Quietly moving us to the chairs; Isla settled sideways across my lap. Her head rest against my cardigan, fingers absentmindedly tracing patterns on my hands.

A silent water course moved down her face— I split the river with my hand. The skin bleached in sorrow.

Her breathing softened, the tense body finally allowing itself a short moment of calm.

'What about you? Are you okay? Can I get you anything?' I whispered, breaking the silence.

With a small shrug, Isla shook her head.

'I was scared… I didn't want to be alone. Morag would have stayed, but it wouldn't have been enough… I thought he was going to… on the boat.'

The voice was meek but the breath heavy.

I ran my fingers through her hair and down the cheek, tucking more strays behind the ear.

'You did so well, Isla. That boat was flying; he's here because of you and I'm so proud.'

She nodded, the burdensome eyes closed; it was followed with a slow, deep huff.

We sat together in silence, the kind that didn't need filling as time slipped away unnoticed.

Isla's light mass grew heavy, my legs agonised as she lay warm and still, soon it was obvious she had drifted off. The weight of the world finally settling from her shoulders, the physical shift in tension allowed me a moment to admire her beauty.

Two hours passed and neither of us had stirred.

Isla's breath matching the steady rise and fall of her chest, broken only by an occasional chuff.

So unbelievably precious.

Silently, I ran a hand through her fringe.

My legs had long surpassed the tingling pins-and-needles stage, my toes cold in their lust for blood, knees aching as I dared not move. My back and ribs achingly pressed against a wooden arm, its firmness cutting in.
Letting Isla rest was more than worth the discomfort, even if it allowed her only a brief escape.

A nurse quietly shuffled in, Isla didn't rise. Moving around to my side, she kept her Highland voice low— as if subtly agreeing to allow sleeping beauty more time.

'Mr MacLeod is stable and has just woken up, if his granddaughter would like to go and see him, she can pop in at any time.' A sympathetic smile— I returned it.

'Can I just ask for future references to visits and whatnot, what's your relationship to Mr. MacLeod?'

'Ohh, umm, technically I'm his solicitor, but his granddaughter is my girlfriend.'
I gestured to Isla.

'That's no problem. I'm Sarah, I'm on call tonight so if either of you need, just give me a shout, Ms…?'

'Ah, you can just call me, Paisley.'

'Thanks, Paisley. Mr. MacLeod is in room four, it's just straight down the hall, the second-last room on the left.'

'Thank you, Sarah. We'll be along soon.'
Sarah left just as quickly as she arrived.

Isla's eyes shot open as if realising the magnitude of today's events.

'Shhh, it's alright. You were sleeping, are you okay?' I asked quietly.
The icy blue stare filled me with a chilly sadness.

'I thought I'd dreamt it.' She sighed.

'I'm sorry, Isla. It hasn't been a dream. Your Grandfather's awake if you'd like to go and visit. He's in room four, the nurse Sarah came through ten minutes ago, she agreed you should rest.'

'Will you come with me?'

Isla's eyes were pleading with my soul.

'Only if that's what you want. Won't that upset your grandfather?'

For the first time, Isla laughed. It warmed my chest.

'Oh no, he loves you! You're definitely in his good books already.'

'I'm not entirely sure what that means… but okay.' The laughter brought a fluttering of butterflies to my stomach. I felt repulsed by my excitement.

Isla lifted herself from my legs, a sharp shooting pain shot through me as the muscles reignited; my toes cramping in agony, the fuzzy burn as my calves convulsed.

I remained quietly breathing through my nose until the feeling passed, a prayer that I wouldn't fall down in a heap when I stood.

With my hand tightly clutching hers, we trekked the bleak deserted corridor.

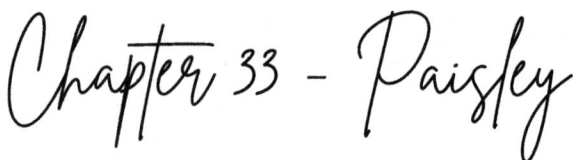
Chapter 33 – Paisley

Alistair's head lifted, he gazed into the doorway where we stood with our hands still intertwined.

A pained but pleased smile tainting his face.

He looked small below the thin blue blanket, swallowed up by the steel bed frame and plastic mattress.

A mountain of pillows propped him up, the strong structure I'd seen last had been replaced with a fragile old man.

His body tangled in a mess of wires and monitors; all beeping and whirring softly around him.

The gown hung loose on his frame; the skin had taken a ghostly appearance, a damp sickly sheen coating his face. The eyes, once bright and full of life, were dark and sunken, heavy bags beneath them highlighting just how exhausted he truly was.

Once rose-tinted lips were dry and cracked; they looked painful.

Isla freed herself and moved quickly to his bedside; I remained by the door.

'Auch Granda, you gave me such a fear.' She hugged him as another wave joined the room.

The space was small and compact.

Unhealthy yellow walls added the smallest tinge of warmth to what would probably be a very drab and depressing place to lie.

'Am sorry lass, ah didnae mean tae scare ye,' he hugged her back weakly.

Isla pulled away cautiously— trying not to break his glass form.

Alistair held out a thin liver-spotted hand; she filled it with her own.

I could see the pain in his face and I prayed Isla was ignorant to the fact.

His eyes and mouth twitched as he tried to conceal it.

Looking over, Alistair let free a hopeful and honest grin as our eyes joined.

'Aha, ah thought solicitors dealt wi' the will *after* the clients were deed.' He gained a nervous laugh from the room.

Staying quiet my feeble smile lingered, I was busy admiring their humour and bond.

'Am ah allowed tae call ye Paisley, or dae ah hae to keep it formal?' He stretched out a hand.

'Paisley will do just fine.'

Walking slowly to his bedside, I accepted the hand; a sudden influx of sadness crashing over me.

'I hope you're feeling better, Mr. MacLeod? You look just as good as when I saw you last.'

'Alistair, please! Or Granda, am good wi' either, jist nae formalities, okay?

Yer as good as family lass and ah terrible liar, but ah appreciate the effort.'

The lips curled again, it was very comforting, but I felt even more guilty; I should have met him again sooner.

Isla freed a heart-wrenching grin whilst I sat in silence feeling like a fraud, the situation was too intense, too intimate.

Someone worthy should have been sitting in my place, and yet he dealt me the kindest welcome.

His grip tightened; the smile may appear weak but his physical strength hadn't faltered.

Taking in a long slow breath, Alistair's voice steadied.

'Ah'll tell ye both wit the nurses hiv said.'

I knew in my heart, he had needed us both there, not just for company, but a reassurance, a way of putting his mind at ease.

A comfort against the unfair chain of events that were now very much imminent.

The prophecy wasn't good and I could feel a heavy lump lodging itself in my throat.

Death was looming over him and the days were down to a sorry few.

Was his kindness to ease Isla from the impending torment she's undoubtedly going to inflict upon herself? A tear slid down the side of my nose, freeing itself over my chin.

I squeezed Alistair's hand— A silent reassurance.

Wiping my nose with my free hand, I tried not to draw attention to the movement.

Isla stared into blank space, eventually resting her head against her grandfather's legs— A new set of floodgates opened, tears upon tears crashed down around her.

Alistair gently patted her head before resting his own against the pillow, eyes closing as he went.

My stomach fell.

Quietly excusing myself, I left them alone to process and talk. Frankly, I needed the air.

Walking briskly to the main doors, the suffocating room had sucked the oxygen from my lungs.

Signs marked their territory on the external doors. Outside another placard.

No Smoking within the hospital grounds.
Fuck.

'Stupid fucking politicians.'

Moving far beyond the entrance point, I lit a cigarette.
My hands returning to their uncontrollable shake.

Pulling in a long, slow drag on the papery stick, I held the nicotine for as long as possible— Letting it work its deadly magic.
Blowing out a cloud, I followed it with another rapid drag.

Lifting myself onto the waist-high wall, a few moments were spent just staring at my feet.
Emotions I'd never expected to be privy too, now felt overwhelming.
Other than my father, I've never felt emotional loss, never had someone to care for me and make provisions like Alistair had for Isla.
The Campbell family dynamics had never equated to anything like that of the MacLeod's.
The two MacLeod's are strong, loving and entwined into one another's lives.
They need each other like the daylight longs for the dusk. Their relationship is inspirational; anyone with half a brain can see that. An unspoken pride and power runs between them.

A streak of jealousy ran hot.

I wish my mother could witness this, instead she's hell-bent on keeping control.

It's the uncontrollable situations that truly matter.

Another tear fell from the tip of my nose.

The cigarette ironically nearing its end of life as I continued smoking into oblivion.

My steel heart breaking for both Alistair and Isla, the impending doom must be an unforgiving and depressing thought for anyone.

'Paisley?'

My puffy face shot upward in surprise. It was Morag, but this time she was alone.

Propping herself up onto the wall next to me, I held out the half-empty packet.

'Am I going tae need one?'

I turned to look at her, the back of my hand transitioning into a face wipe.

Clearing my throat, I pushed another tab between my lips.

'Alistair's awake, Isla's in there just now.

The prognosis… well… it isn't good.'

Morag's hand shot up to her mouth.

Snatching the packet from my hand, she pulled out a fag and stuck it straight between her chops.

It was a brisk motion that neither impressed nor surprised me.

Handing the packet and a set of car keys back to me, she lit the end with the flame I was holding.

I surveyed the keys.

'What are these for?'

Morag's hands joined the tragic game of uncontrollable

shaking; the smoke vibrated between podgy fingers.

'I've brought Isla's car round from the cottage, Angus took her out to the water this morning, but you'll need them tae take her home. Assuming ye drive?' Morag puffed out a grey gasp.

I nodded.

'Thank you, I don't know the logistics just yet, but I'll make sure she gets them anyway.'

'How long does he have?' Her words were all properly pronounced as she mustered the courage to ask the pre-anticipated question.

I sniffed.

'A couple of days at best, the nurse called it end-of-life care.'

Morag pulled in another long, hard breath.

'Oh fuck, poor Alistair. Poor Isla!' Morag looked at her shoes.

'She's going to need you, I hope you're okay to spend some time in Skye?'

Lifting her head the hazel eyes found mine, an apologetic expression— almost mournful.

'I took two weeks off, but I hadn't expected to use it all. I'll call my boss and explain the situation.
They're usually pretty good in terms of… well… this sort of thing.'

Pausing in quiet contemplation, I took another long sook.

'Morag... I never in a million years expected to meet you in this manner, but you've done nothing but be good to me since I arrived.
From the bottom of my heart, I cannot thank you enough.

It's not standard practice where I'm from for people to be so kind and helpful.

I mean we are kind and helpful, but we wouldn't normally go out of our way to do anything above and beyond.

You come across as a genuinely lovely person.

Isla's really lucky to have you.

At first, I thought there may have been more to your friendship, but I see it now, it's really special.'

'Paisley, it feels like a lifetime that I've patiently waited to see that girl happy. You've been on the go for only a couple o' short months, and even withoot being here, she's the happiest I've ever seen... So, I guess I should be thanking you, ye must be doing something right.'

She smiled, before holding out her hand.

I took it, returning the tight squeeze.

Wow, no one at home's ever thanked me for anything.

'I'm guessing Isla's already filled you in on our current predicaments... living apart, constant phone calls...'

Morag cut me off.

'I know everything, Paisley. Isla's as good as family; we share all things important, and I can safely say, she's missed you way more than you'll hiv been telt.

I've never seen her this content, in all the years we've known each other, this is the first time she's been excited enough to tell me exactly how she feels.

I really couldn't be happier for you both; Isla especially, she deserves to find someone good.'

'I know that feeling,' I couldn't hide my teeth. 'My words cannot even begin to express how much that phenomenal woman has changed my life.

I know everything's been quick, by Christ it's been fast, but my heart already feels full.

Isla isn't the only one who's content.

I'm scared… I really don't want to mess anything up.

For the first time in my life, I feel like I've found my counterpart.

Standing on that harbour wall, I thought I was walking into a world without her. My stomach dropped, my anxiety hit the roof, and I was so unbelievably frightened. I don't usually shake, but today I've been humbled.'

'Nah, Isla's a fighter. Her heart's big enough for us all, but I think you're taking up a bitty mare space in there than you realise, Paisley.'

We both laughed, it was hearty and calming.

I stubbed out the smouldering butt and slumped from the wall.

'Just please dinna break her heart. She acts strong, but inside she's still that lost wee girl fae school. Actually, I'm wondering if you might be the same, Paisley.

I really hope it works oot for ye both. Ye look like you fit together perfectly.'

'I've been lost for a long time, Morag, my heart can't take any more devastation…

I guess we should get back inside, see that they're both alright.'

'Aye, lead on Macduff.' Morag jumped down, still holding my hand tightly.

Upon re-entering the hospital room, Isla and Alistair were having a hushed conversation; there was a lot of nodding from Isla but not much from her grandfather.

It looked as though he was giving her instructions, or a telling-off.

Leaning his head back, a frail hand patted Isla's.

Rising from the bedside, Isla worked her way over to the door, she wrapped her arms around Morag; more teardrops joined the fellowship.

Silently I moved past them, making my way into the depressing room.

Taking a seat my gaze met with Alistair's.

Tapping on the marginal blanket space, he gestured for me to sit with him.

I obliged; the worrisome tug back in my chest.

'Paisley, ah need ye tae take care o' Isla fir me.

Ah assume she's already telt ye aboot the family hysteria?'

Silently I nodded.

'Guid, she'll be ah state fir ah while, she's ah sensitive wee devil.

Ah'm sorry we didnae get tae spend mare time the gether, ah'd promised ah while back I'd hiv her girlfriend over fir fish fingers at my hoose. Well, when she finally got ein.

Unfortunately, I hiv tae break that promise.'

I let out an almighty snort that echoed around the room. Immediately regretting it as the two women turned to stare.

Alistair amused himself with his own deep chortle, his hand relaxing over my own.

'It's already clear tae see ye're ah guid match fir her, please gie it a guid shot, she deserves tae be happy. As do ye.'

I gripped his hand with my free one.

'I really wish we'd managed to spend a lot more time together, I think it would have been good for us all. I'll try my very hardest, you have my word. You're a good man, Alistair.

It's been a real pleasure dealing with you at the solicitors, I genuinely wish more people like you would grace my door.'

He shook his head.

'Isla told me about your family, and I can wholeheartedly tell you you're a better man than anyone else I know. My own relations included.

They wouldn't even live up to half of you.'

I tried to free an empathetic smile, I imagined it looked more like I was having a stroke.

'Thanks lass,' he whispered.

His eyes looked watery as he placed his head back down against the pillow.

'I'm very grateful for the opportunities you've given me over the past couple of months, Alistair.

You have my word. I'll do everything in my power to make her happy… but I don't think I'll ever be able to live up to your standards. I won't be able to make her as happy as you yourself do.

That's an impossible task.' I whispered.

He smiled— it lingered in sadness.

'Get some rest… Please, don't worry, I'll take good care of her, I promise.'

Easing our hands free, I moved towards Isla.

Morag watched on as I neared— she took her own turn at the bedside.

Isla shuffled towards me.

'Granda wants me to go home tonight, he doesn't want me moping around the hospital.'
Slow and meticulous; almost laboured.
Every word carefully enunciated, the pain behind them heavy and unforgiving.
I felt a pang of guilt. Sending Isla home was probably for my benefit more than Alistair's.
Another selfless act from a man that required so little in return.

'How long are you here for? I assume you're going to be staying with me?'
The question came out pragmatic and almost businesslike. A transactional statement crowded by too many devastating emotions for Isla to grasp.
Her eyes darting around the wall behind me.

'Look, Isla, I'm here as long as you need me to be and I'll book into a nearby hotel.
I didn't plan that far ahead... Honestly, I just cleared my diary and jumped onto a train; I booked a bus as soon as I left Waverley, it was very much slapdash.
I just really wanted to see you.
I needed to see you.'
Slightly disappointed by the statement, I didn't want to cause any drama.
A pain shot through my heart— it wasn't my place to be saddened. I needed to respect the boundaries.

Isla scoured my face.
Her right hand had subconsciously moved into that lay-flat position against my chest; it was fixed in a comforting hold.
The chest pain subsided as my arm found the back of her dispirited shoulders; I contently rubbed them

through her long-sleeved t-shirt.

We stood like a couple who had been together for years; neither sure who was doing the consoling.

'You're not staying in any hotel; you'll be coming back to mine. I'm just so glad and grateful you're here, I don't want to be alone, I don't want to be without you.'

'Me too.' And that was the honest truth.

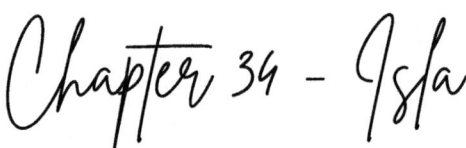

Chapter 34 - Isla

Granda fell straight back to sleep after I said goodbye.
I told him I'd be back in the morning, but I wasn't sure if he heard. His face looked peaceful resting against the heavenly pillows.
Kissing his cheek, I told him how much I love him... how much I need him. Asked him to stay with me a wee whiley longer... mibbe hold on for me to come with him.

I didnae want to leave, didn't want to say goodbye... jist in case...
I wanted to be near, stay in his room... take care of him until...well... hold onto him some more.
I'm really not sure how I'll survive... life winna be the same if he leaves me.

The pain crippled my chest as we left the hospital, my usually sturdy legs no longer stable.
Heart breaking as Paisley prised me from the room, practically carrying me as I fought her and Morag.
I needed to tell him again. I didnae want to upset her— she was trying to help... but it's been jist me and him for so long. I don't know if she understands.

I really do need him, my tears won't ever be enough, I need him to know... I need him to tell me, jist one more time how much I mean to him. How much he loves me, how proud he is.
I'll be back tomorrow... first thing...
Paisley promised to bring me round. I guess that's quite

nice.

In my one moment of clarity, I asked Morag to tell Angus to take a few days off. I need time to process and reevaluate.

I couldnae be further from wanting to get back on the boat. I don't even know if I can get on Granda's boat…

I don't want to see anyone except Granda… and Paisley…

Of course I'm grateful she's here, but Granda will need me over the next few days… I guess I'll need him more… Maybe if I'd moved the Ceilidh faster, maybe if I'd realised sooner he wasn't right…

I need his cuddles and stories… need him to know… everything.

I can't imagine a world without him. How do I go on? How do I move forward? Why didn't I stay at home with him? Why did we go fishing?… Why, Granda?

Paisley's driving us home, I don't know what to say, don't know how to start a conversation.

She hasn't driven much, it's obvious from the three stalled attempts to pull away from the hospital.

I really couldnae care less.

If she drove us off the cliff, I wouldnae even be mad.

Auch, that's not fair on her, I'm being heartless now, that's nae nice.

Casting my eyes to the sea; the last time I'd been there, it had all gone wrong— changed my world, and not for the better.

It's taking longer to get out of Portree than normal, I

keep pointing directions, but I don't want to be home.

I want to be… held.

Resting a hand on Paisley's leg, the dark sky hides my tears. I keep fiddling with the fabric, drawing on her jeans, trying to still my throbbing brain.

Anything to preoccupy my heartsick mind.

It's not working.

She hasn't spoken, I guess I need to comfort her too, she's been good enough to visit in my hour of need… I don't know how she does it.

Hmm, she's a good soul… always where I need her to be.

Watching Paisley unlock the front door to the Bramble Brae, I didnae have the heart to tell her it was already open, but she waited politely to be invited in.

I think I'd normally find that hilarious, nae today…

I held the door open for her— aye, she's definitely a good soul.

'Well, this is home,' I sighed— illuminating the cottage with a switch near the door.

'It's very cute and quaint, Isla.

Why don't I put the kettle on when I find it, and I'll make us a nice cup of tea? You grab a seat and I'll bring it through.' Paisley announced still standing in the hall.

I think she was trying to sound chirpy— it was wasted on me.

Removing her shoes and setting her bag down to the side, Paisley wondered further into my house. Respectful and always so well mannered, no wonder Granda loves her… auch.

No. No more tears— not just now.

'Aye, that would be nice,' I finally replied before bouncing harshly onto the sofa.

Paisley pottered around the kitchen.

Drawers and cupboards opened and closed as she searched for cups and spoons— the newfound gadget boiling the water.

I should have helped but my head was bursting, I just left her to work it out.

'Umm, Isla, what do you take in your tea?' Paisley called over.

'Hmm? …Oh milk and two sugars… thanks.' Honestly it could have been laced with poison, I really didn't care.

We shared a realisation that we hadn't been privy to some of the smaller, less important details.

'I forgot you lived in a small cottage and the kitchen's integrated; I feel a bit daft now.'

'It's okay, it was always enough for just me.'

'Does your kettle always make that noise? It sounds like it's away to take off.'

'Aye, it's traditional… When it skirls it's ready. The opposite of me.' I tried to be funny, it didn't work.

Paisley appeared at my side, two mismatched mugs full of very milky tea.

Sitting at my hip she plonked one on the table in front of me, the other in front of herself.

Hmm, we'll need to work on that, there's way too much cow…

I wonder if Granda's sleeping, should I call him?

'Are you hungry? You can't have eaten in hours.

Do you want me to make you something?' Paisley asked, her breath warm against my cheek as she faced me.

I shook my head.

'No, no I'm fine. Thanks.

Help yourself to anything though, there's stuff in the fridge.'

'I'm okay too, but thank you.'

Paisley pulled me into a warm, tight hug; holding me as if I was going to fall down the crack between the cushions. It was an honest possibility.

I tucked my arms around her waist— it was the most comfortable I'd felt all day.

Sweeping a glance around the room, Paisley eyed everything, no doubt taking mental notes for future.

She seems to like the smaller details; it's a cute trait I've noticed. She looked adorable as her head nodded in satisfaction at the new surroundings.

'How did you know Paisley?' I asked weakly.

Paisley's expression was a mix of confusion and fear.

'How did I know what?'

'How did you know I needed you today?' I was genuinely intrigued as to how she could magically arrive at the right place and time.

An alluring smile tugged at the edge of her mouth.

God, still so bloody attractive.

'The world works in mysterious ways.

You see, Isla, I needed you just as much.'

I placed my head on her chest, I could feel and hear it hammering. Maybe it's just my own.

'Hmm, I like that,' I said softly.

Paisley's head fell back onto the sofa— she looked

oddly relaxed. Like she really was meant to be here.

'It's so silent and peaceful, Isla. I can't remember the last time I could hear my own breath.'

'It's my little piece of heaven… ohh…' I knew my mistake immediately, my eyes stung, hot and angry.

'Shh, don't do that to yourself.'
Paisley pulled me closer, her lips catching my forehead.

'Granda...' My voice cracked, '…he asked me to phone my parents... I don't know what to say to them. It's been years since I spoke to them last.'
Paisley's charming woodland eyes met mine, stealing the sting for a moment.

'I'm not really that influential when it comes to conversations with parents, Isla.'
She looked thoughtful, unintentionally licking her bottom lip… Auch, tease…
Wait should I even feel like this just now?
What would Granda say? …I think I know exactly what he'd say… it doesn't feel right though.

'Just keep to the basics I guess, you don't owe them anything, so just keep it to the point?' Paisley projected.

'Mhmm, that's a good plan, you're so smart.'
Maybe it does feel right, maybe that's why he sent me home, he knew Paisley would rescue me. He's such a clever auld bugger.

'Why don't I put you to bed?
Tomorrow will be another long day and you must be exhausted?' Paisley stated— her hand trailing my hair.

'Will you stay with me?'

'I told you; I'm not going anywhere. You need to trust me, I'm here for whatever you need.'

'I do trust you, but I mean will you sleep with me?'
Paisley's perfectly shaped eyebrows lifted.

'I'll sleep on the sofa and if you need me, you'll know where to find me.

'You won't sleep beside me?'

I placed my head back on her chest.

I really wanted to be held, wanted to be loved, looked after, cared for. Someone to finally crawl into my cold bed and just… linger.

'Ahh. Do you want me to sleep beside you?

I've managed to get into your safe space, but your bed is something else entirely.

You've had a really rough day, Isla.

I want you to get some rest so you're good to call your parents and provide your grandfather with more excellent support.'

'You're so practical… but I don't want to be alone. You were always going to be entering my safe space, it was just a matter of when… I want to share a bed with you. I'm sick of the cold, the loneliness… Please, Paisley, please come to bed with me?'

I can't believe I'm begging.

'Okay, well I think we could manage that.

Drink some tea first, then we'll go to bed.'

'So, so bossy.'

I took a long drink of tea, the top looked like it was starting to grow a skin.

It tasted better than expected.

'That's good tea.'

'You need to keep hydrated, I'll keep you right,'

Paisley had a mouthful of her own.

'You'll need to show me where everything is.'

'Aye, let's go to bed, I'm sleepy.'

I stood up, every bone and muscle creaked.

'This is a beautiful home, Isla, I hope to spend a lot

more time here,' Paisley stated as she admired trinkets along the woodwork.

Leading her into the bedroom, I held an incredibly soft hand.

I picked up my pyjamas at the same time Paisley pulled hers free.

We locked eyes, an embarrassed expression from Paisley as we grinned.

'I'll… just… nip to the loo,' Paisley said in a manner highlighting her amusement.

'You don't have to go anywhere.' I beamed.

Oh, please don't go anywhere.

'Please… Please, Isla, tell me there will be no funny business tonight? It doesn't seem right.'

'No funny business.' I stated.

Eurgh, so prim and proper.

Paisley popped into the bathroom anyway— carrying her shorts and t-shirt.

Wow. This woman is beyond sensitive; she's willing to halt everything for me.

Why hadn't I found her twenty years ago?

I climbed into bed, keeping to my usual side.

A whir of giddiness as someone was finally going to warm the other side.

I was going to be in her arms at last.

Paisley scooted into the free space.

Turning she gave me a soft reassuring kiss.

I hadn't expected it, but I kissed her back.

She pulled away in haste, clearly, I'd caught her by surprise too.

Slowly I lifted myself over.

Leaning in, I kissed her lips again; a glimmer of sadness reflecting through her eyes.

Probably matching my own, but I needed more.

The weight of the world was heavy; overflowing with thoughts of Granda, thoughts of my own needs, wants and quandaries. I needed to be swept away into a world where someone else relied on me.

'No funny business tonight, I promise, Paisley.

I just need to feel wanted for a few minutes— know you need me, as much as I need you.'

Watching her expression, it changed to relief.

Paisley kissed me, but this time there was a shocking fierceness, an intoxicating urgency that sent a shiver rushing through.

Pulling me in, she scrambled above, our mouths locked in a gratifying rhythm, velvet tongues breaking free, dancing a secret waltz as our bodies moved in time.

Silky lips, supple to the touch, telling untold silent secrets; a story of longing, of need, compassion and a hunger that had been growing between us for far too long.

Vulnerability spread around the room, but doubt didn't stand a chance.

Wandering hands searched the company of the other, learning and claiming. Mouths working hard to answer the unasked questions.

Our breaths tangled; raspy and uneven.

Static power pulsing through, locking us together.

Heavy heated air growing dangerous.

Every touch and gasp adding more fuel to the flames.

Twisted bodies pulling together, seductively formed by the closeness of our hips and legs.

Instinct flowing freely; neither of us questioning where this magnificent moment was leading.

I was silently begging for it to continue into something far more significant.

Our hearts hammered, chests rising and falling to the beat of the other.

My hands found Paisley's waist— dragging her down there was no space left between us.

I needed more.

A silent and desperate plea written in the way my fingers gripped her hips, the unwillingness to part ways with her mouth.

'I want you.' I breathed out, gasping for air— in need of so much more.

The kiss intensified, consuming us whole.

Our bodies gyrating; an orchestra in harmony.

Hands holding tight, refusing to part ways.

Nothing else existed, this fire, this want, this temptation dragging us in.

The fire swept through in an engulfed rage, both of us hot and frustrated.

Paisley pulled back abruptly; signifying the end to our torment.

She lay back down and rest her forehead against mine. Our tender lips millimetres apart as we both drew short desperate breaths.

An undeniable attraction pulling us together.

Respect and gratitude holding us apart as Paisley refused to continue.

A lonely tear fell from my closed eyes.

'I want you, Paisley. I'm selfish and greedy, I said no funny business, but I really want you… I need you.'

'I want you too but I hadn't realised just how much.

By fuck, I want you.' She whispered.

I opened my eyes.

Looking into Paisley's, I could see the answer was already there, unspoken but understood.

The stormy glare freeing the fact I wasn't the only one hurting.

'I'm so sorry, Paisley, I… I…'

She stroked my forehead, tucking away the hair from my face.

'That was my fault, Isla. I'm sorry.

I can't believe I'm here in Skye.

I'm in bed with the most beautiful woman and in her hour of need I'm over here fighting against my own morals.

It's… absurd.'

'I think that's the best kiss goodnight I've ever had, and I dinna think it's absurd.

It was absolutely perfect. Ignoring everything else that's going on.

Thanks for showing me that you need me too.'

'Come on, close your eyes and get some rest.' Paisley pulled me carefully into the space between her arm and chest.

'Night, Paisley.'

'Goodnight, Isla, try and get some sleep.'

The phone's cold harsh tone rang out at 04:22 AM.

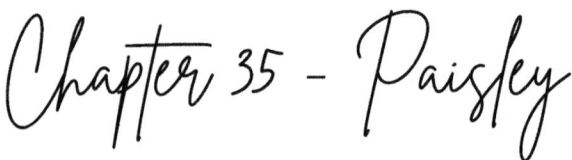

Chapter 35 - Paisley

Isla lay paralysed as the shrill tone rang out, the backlight cutting a gaping hole through the darkness.
Her eyes were fixated on the ceiling.
Body stiff and cold as fear clung tightly to her—drawing out more life as each second passed by.
Each ring more haunting in its request to be answered.

I leant over, still half asleep as my fingers reached her phone.
My eyes burning; little scorching rings of pain from the sudden awakening.
The phone's terrifying cries, still blaring through my ears.

Glancing at Isla, I was looking for the slightest reassurance that I had permission to answer the call.
She didn't move; a statue frozen by reality and fear.
Swiping my thumb over the smooth glass, I held it tightly.

'Hello?' My voice filled with broken sleep and a pre-empted mourn.
I listened to the voice for a moment.

'Sarah, it's Paisley. We spoke earlier…'
The room was soundless as I listened carefully.

'Okay, thank you.'
Sarah disconnected.

Holding the phone, I stared blankly at the screen.
Trying to gather my thoughts.
Searching for words that had now scrambled into the

nearest hiding place.

Isla hadn't moved.

I rolled over and turned on the bedside light; placing the phone down beside it.

Twisting back to the statue, the roof still stealing her attention.

It was evident that Isla's eyes were leaking onto the cushion behind her.

By the state of the pillow, I'd hazard a guess they'd been spilling out for a few hours.

Silently shifting to the middle of the bed, I scooped her up in one gentle motion.

Pulling her close, I rest her stiff head and body against my chest.

I didn't want to be the bearer of bad news, but it had to be delivered.

Please, forgive me.

'Isla?' I waited a few seconds.

Very slowly her head pivoted up towards me, red eyes vast as she shook with grief.

Silently shaking her head from side to side; she didn't want to listen.

No doubt already aware her perfect world was falling.

I needed to tell her— even though it was the last words either of us ever wanted to hear or say.

'I'm so sorry, sweetie. He's...'

My voice cracked.

I didn't want to get caught in the emotion, I'm still unsure if it's my place to feel such sentiment.

I needed to be her strength.

'He's gone, sweetheart,' I whispered.

My arms engulfed Isla's shoulders tightly.

Allowing her time to process and react to the heart-wrenching news, I wasn't sure which way she was going to go.

After my father's death, I could appreciate that.

The room was eerily still and noiseless, neither of us made any effort to move or speak.

I just kept her wrapped up safe, my heart quietly breaking.

Isla's tears soaked through my nightshirt, small little sobs finally breaking the silence.

Stroking her hair and face for what felt like hours, I lightly rocked us back and forth.

The waterlogged eyes shut, shoulders rising and falling in time to the tears and whimpers.

Eventually, and ever so slowly, Isla drifted into a grave and fragile sleep.

After half an hour, I tactically lay her down against the mattress— cautious not to wake her.

She needs the sleep.

Almost silently, I stood up and crept around the bed. Watching from above, I checked to see she hadn't stirred.

So undeniably precious, even in her need.

Before turning, I placed a small, gentle kiss on her forehead.

Picking up my overnight bag, I left the room— closing the door silently behind me.

Pulling on a fleece and trainers, I moved to the front door; letting myself escape into the chilly, dew-spotted air.

The light on the horizon's just beginning to transform the sky's colour. Altering the deep dark indigo to a magnificent bright orange scattering.

Pulling out a cigarette, I cupped the tiny flame.
Deep breaths as I puffed, and puffed, and puffed.
Dragging in more and more of the hot tarry nicotine, filling my lungs with everything terrible and sweet.
Sitting on the damp doorstep, my arms curved my knees. I watched the sky dancing to the tune of a new day.

'It's going to be a beautiful day, just not for us.' I whispered.

Reopening the door, I cautiously tiptoed into the living room.
Trying hard not to wake the fragile beauty, I opened my bag; hunting for some clean clothes I removed my tear-stained top— the hunt for a new bra ensued.

'Paisley…' the hushed and sombre word caught me off guard; turning, Isla stood wearing a duvet and a cast-down expression by the door.
My top half naked for the world to see.
Ahh, fuck.
Inconceivably pressured to hide my modesty; as if the subject were taboo, my arms flailed.
I tried everything to conceal myself.

'Isla! Oh my God, I'm so sorry, I thought you were still asleep. You scared the shit out of me.'
This was the last thing I wanted to be running through her head.
Stupid twat, where's the Campbell's painstaking planning?
Urgh, you're an Idiot.

Still furiously fumbling to cover myself; it was an awkward attempt to keep some kind of decency between us.

'I woke up and you weren't there. I thought you...' The tears climbing back to her eyes must've stopped at her mouth for a reprieve, her voice cracked.

Pulling the wet T-shirt back on rapidly, I moved towards her; arms stretched out wide.

'I'm not going anywhere, I promise.'

This time, my hug was matched with a gut-wrenching squeeze.

'Please... please don't leave me.'

More tears fell, with the added rawness of desperation.

My eyes gave in and sympathised.

We stood in an excruciatingly emotional hold.

Each of us clinging to the other, as if pulling apart would cause the world to shatter into a million tiny fragments.

Her face nuzzled into my neck.

'I'm never leaving you,' I sighed.

And that may have just been the truth.

* * * *

I had all but hijacked Isla's mobile phone.

By 07:00 AM, I'd made arrangements with the hospital to obtain the death certificate and allow Isla to visit her grandfather. They explained they would contact the registrar, but I sent an email to the registry office in Portree anyway... just to be sure.

An email to Alistair's GP, although again, I wasn't sure if that was necessary.

A follow up call to Morag— I hadn't realised the time,

but she sounded awake.

My newest friend was neither surprised nor shocked to hear me on the other end of the phone.

Herself and Angus sent us both their love and best wishes, particularly to Isla.

She spoke of visiting in the next few days and I couldn't object.

Morag knew Isla inside out, so it made sense for her to want to visit. If anything, she had more right to be with Isla in her hour of need than I did.

The only thing left to do, for now, was for Isla to call her parents.

That was a job I couldn't do for her and I was secretly glad.

Isla had gone for a long hot bubble bath.

An attempt to heat herself up, maybe try and ease some tension. I think she just needed some time alone.

I made us both a coffee and finalised the arrangements; some of which, Isla would need to think about in her own time.

Moving through to the en-suite door, I knocked lightly.

'Isla? Are you okay?'

Staying on the outside of the door, I was trying to remain respectful.

My head fell against the wooden doorframe awaiting a response.

Tiredness caught up with me; a jaw-breaking yawn broke free.

'Aye.'

It was distant and almost non-existent, but it was a good attempt at getting her mind in the right place.

'Pais…you can come in if you want? I… I don't mind.'

Unsure whether or not to go in or just wait outside, I was unable to hide the smile at the new half-name.

'I'm trying to be... respectful right now, Isla, you're hurting and… and I…um…'

'Please…'

Opening the partially closed door, I kept my eyes firmly fixed on her face. It took some strength not to pry.

From the corner of my eye, Isla was covered head to toe in thick white bubbles. Thank God.

Kneeling at the edge of the bath, my arm leant against the ledge.

'What do I do now?' Isla asked solemnly, reddened eyes looking through me.

A deep depression clouding the blue.

'I've called the hospital, sent emails to the GP and registrar, and phoned Morag.

All you need to do is call your family. I think for now that's it.' My reassuring smile made its way over the tiles.

'What about the funeral stuff?'

'Didn't you and Alistair discuss this before?'

I couldn't hide my surprise.

The tears were closing in again as her head shook.

'I didn't ask, and I don't think he ever said.'

Her bottom lip jutting in a tremble, rosie cheeks looking warmer.

I blew out a condensed breath.

'Isla, Alistair had everything in place for the funeral...'

Isla's face broke into a sad smile, 'he knew I wouldn't

manage…'

'No. He knew you could manage anything that was thrown at you.

That's why he had everything prepared, he didn't want you to face the burden…

Why do you think he came to see me in Edinburgh?'

A stray tear topped up the bathtub.

'It was just to tidy up the loose ends.'

Her shoulders rose— obviously she's unaware of the Edinburgh discussions.

'It was more than just loose ends, Isla. We can talk about this when you've had a chance to calm down.

Your bubbles are dissipating, so I'm going to let you get dried off then you can grab the coffee I've made.'

While standing up, a glimmer of skin appeared under the remaining bubbles.

My head sharply turned to Isla's before leaving her to get out.

Outside the living-room window, I peered in.

Bare feet trudged into the kitchen-living area, she was wearing jeans and a smart blouse, her head wrapped in some kind of towel pyramid.

Sitting down on a stool at the kitchen island, Isla lifted one of the mugs and took a sip.

Pulling a face of disgust, she put it down and tried the other.

I couldn't help but smile. Maybe she's still in there beneath the misery.

Did she pull that face because she knows I'm watching?

A slice of buttered toast cut into two triangles sat on a

plate next to the coffee— I'd left it there before sneaking outside for a smoke.

An optimistic last-ditch attempt at getting her to eat something.

Picking up a slice, she took a bite.

Satisfied I moved towards the door, keys clinking as I locked it behind me.

Isla let out a hollow laugh.

'Why are you laughing?'

'City folk are strange. Who the hell locks their door?'

An amused grin before Isla took another bite.

'Normal people? It's the reason they put a lock on the door to start with.' I replied, slightly confused by the question.

She shook her head.

Using her upbeat reaction to my advantage, I fished out the phone from my pocket and placed it beside the plate.

'I know you don't want to do it, and trust me, I know that feeling, but you need to call them.'

The words were honest but blunt.

Isla sighed, hunching down in her seat.

'I can sit here with you or I can leave you alone.

I know which I would prefer but I'm happy to do it your way, whatever you choose.'

I would have been quite pleased to disappear for another smoke, but patiently I waited.

Isla picked up the lead weighted phone.

Scrolling through the contact list *Tam* filled the screen.

She pressed dial followed by the loudspeaker.

My hands found her shoulders.

It rang for about fifteen seconds before he answered.

'Hello, Isla.

Is everything alright?'

His voice was deep and resonant, not at all like I'd pictured.

'Dad,' the tears spewed out again as the voice choked, 'Granda.'

'Isla, what is it?' His sharp tone cut through the speaker.

I couldn't help but wonder if this man was completely dense or simply obsolete in the world.

Clearly, he hadn't inherited his father's sense or charm.

'He's gone,' she whispered

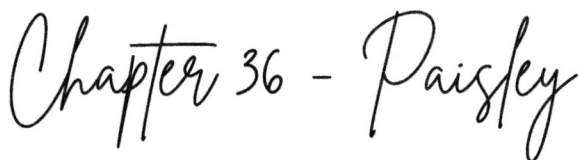

Chapter 36 - Paisley

The weekend had flown in like an autumn leaf trapped in a whirlwind.

Overwhelming and unpredictable emotions swept Bramble Brae as each day came to a close.

Along with that, family friends and visitors had pulsated in and out, all wishing Isla well, many questioning my intent.

Each guest paying their respects and indulging numerous humbling stories of Alistair's life and adventures.

All searching for meaning in nothing, bringing gifts and endless bouquets of flowers.

Isla hadn't been particularly interested in hosting and I wasn't accustom to the stares and whispers.

Snide comments filled with a distinct sense of distrust and judgment filled the cottage.

It reminded me of school days.

Morag and Angus were the only pair we'd been genuinely glad to see on Wednesday, but even their visit had been brief. They promised to be at the funeral on Friday and wished us well.

Admittedly, both of us were relieved when the visitors finally vacated.

Isla's parents hadn't been seen or heard from and personally I wasn't sure how to feel about that.

They were grieving too, but it seemed a little bit disrespectful and disheartening.

Isla didn't appear to be worried, I guess she'd mourned their absence some time ago.

I'd made myself quite at home; comfortable in my new surroundings and pleased to share the silence with somebody else.

A call to Gavin allowed me to extend my absence.
It gave me time to attend the funeral and get adjusted.
A full month of annual leave for me was unheard of.

Gavin spoke of big changes coming up, and James had been sending inappropriate texts until I filled him in on the sombre events.

Emotion filled the home in constant waves, some beautiful moments as the tide receded, before it would rush back with vengeance and destroy any good in its wake.

My new-found patience kept moving Isla forward as she prepared for the final goodbye, its impending day drawing inevitably closer… and not just for Alistair.

Isla kept me fed and watered, an attempt to keep her mind busy.
I was grateful for her company.
It made a huge difference to my usual depression, I guess having someone keeping you on the straight and narrow really does help the mood.
I hope she feels the same.

Every day for Isla and I was an education, we continually learned something new.
Remaining respectful, I still wouldn't allow any bedroom athletics; Isla didn't seem amused by my persistence but took it in her stride.

It wasn't for the lack of wanting and criminally it played on my mind.

We lay entwined; Isla staring out to the misty grey whilst I read 'Persuasion' in comfortable silence.
Each holding a glass of wine as we shared a silent toast to yet another day of company and sorrow.

A shrieking chime brought us both back to the land of the living.

'That's not mine?'

'Hmm?' I didn't look up— the phone had been ringing off the hook all weekend.

'Pais, that's not my phone!'
Isla stood up, an inquisitive furrow to her brow, forehead growing little creases.
Stuck in the cushions, I made an attempt to rise.
I didn't want to spill the wine or lose the page.
Not that I hadn't already read the book twenty times before.

Isla disappeared into the bedroom, a quizzical look as she returned holding my phone at arms-length.

'I... I think it's your mum. On FaceTime.'

'Oh shit!'
I shrugged.

'Just leave it, I don't think I want to speak to her.
She'll be full of egotistical slur anyway.'

'What if it's serious, Paisley?'
A scolding from Isla, as the vibrating din was thrust into my hand.

'Urgh, be warned, she's the devil reincarnate.'
Isla smiled, it wasn't quite reaching full capacity, but it was more than enough.

She's going to be fine.

Cautiously accepting the call, my mother's ear showed against the screen.

'Hello? Paisley?'

'Hello, Mother. What do I owe this delight?'

Isla's eyes shot wide.

I gave her a wink… just so she knew it was still me.

'I assume you haven't thought any more on our last discussion, Paisley? I posted you a message, yet you have deliberately not responded.'

'Mother, do you know you're on camera?

Despite our genetics being quite excellent, I don't wish to stare at your ear for the rest of this conversation.'

The phone crunched and crackled as the picture did a full one-eighty, a view of the kitchen, the floor, her nostrils all filling the screen before finally levelling out on her face.

Isla tried not to laugh from behind the sofa.

'Right, well, thank you.'

How unusual to get a thanks.

'I'm sorry I haven't responded to your message.

I needed to clear my head, get away and reevaluate my life.'

'Oh, Paisley, it actually sounds as though you are finally listening to me…'

Her face changed, eyes wandering the bungalow's background. Desperately searching for a clue to my location.

'Paisley Rose, where are you?'

'I'm in Skye.'

'Skye. As in, the Isle of Skye?'

My mother's eyes were wider than her range cooker, it pleased me slightly.

'Yes, as in the Isle of Skye.' I replied, slightly crabbit.

Isla waved her hands as if to bring her mood down.

I slyly nodded back.

'What in Heaven's name are you doing in the Isle of Skye?

Why aren't you at home?

Are you working up there?'

'Mother, I'm visiting my grief-stricken girlfriend, I will be home in a month. I'll speak with you when I'm back.'

'Girlfriend?' Raised eyebrows and a tight lip.

'Yes. My girlfriend.'

My face remained expressionless.

Isla's hands reached her crown— Pulling her hair tightly as though the discussion was incomprehensible.

I was desperately trying to get off the phone but also trying to politely tell my mother dearest to go and suck on something solid.

'Oh… Right.' The expression matched her tone.

'Well, can I speak with your girlfriend?'

'I don't know Mother, after our last discussion, I don't think that would be appropriate.

Our status doesn't reflect your biased, outdated views, and as I've already said, she's grief-stricken.

I hardly think my mother marching in with two clunky feet is going to help anything.'

Isla held her face in her hands— Probably not sure whether to laugh or cry.

'I was out of line, Paisley, I am…' She couldn't quite eat through her words as she forced them out.

'…I am sorry. I must say, you hit the nail directly on the head with some of your remarks, but …'

That must have tasted like vinegar, the face was bitter and sour.

'That'll do Mum, don't hurt yourself.'

'Mother, dear.'

It was as good as I was going to get, but I finally had one up on the old bugger.

Isla chuckled, covering her mouth to avoid vocalising.

I couldn't resist a smile.

'Isla? Would you like to talk to my mother, Lady Francis Campbell of Calder, or should I tell her today's not the day for introductions?'

I made sure mum could hear everything as her neck twisted.

Isla's head shook.

Reluctantly a hand reached out.

She positioned the screen to her face, angling it upward to get the best side.

I have literally waited my whole life for this indescribable moment. I couldn't hide my amusement.

'Hello Lady Campbell, I'm Isla.' The lulling accent exaggerated slightly.

Did she think she was speaking to the Queen?

My mother would love that!

'Francis, please… Hmm I must say, you are indeed very pleasing on the eyes.

I am surprised, no offence, dear.

Maybe my daughter can actually stand up on her own two feet.' The screen carved into a pinched grin.

'And can I just send my deepest condolences on your loss? I hope these tough times ahead aren't too testing on you, dear. Stay strong!' She paused for a short moment, thinking about her next response.

'Maybe we could enjoy a spot of lunch together

shortly?'

It sounded more like a request than an offer.

'Aye, that would be nice, thank you.'

Now it was Isla playing up for the phone.

'Ah'll pass you back to Paisley, but it was nice to speak to you at last.'

Handing the phone back, Isla's head shook in disbelief.

'Well, Paisley, you are clearly quite busy, so I will let you be and leave you in peace.'

My mother's eyebrows furrowed as if telling a secret, her voice hushed.

'What a lovely looking young lady, I hope you are treating her well?

Hot soup and chicken! That always works wonders...'

There was a brief pause, *'...Can I ask how long this has been... well... a...a thing?'*

Isla giggled, I joined in.

'Thanks, Mother. I will call you sometime soon, okay?'

'Goodbye, Paisley, I...'

'...I love you too, Mum. Goodbye.' I interrupted. There's no point letting her struggle, she was always going to be who she was.

It gained me a heartwarming smile as she looked to disconnect. The first smile in far too many wasted years.

'Oh my God, Isla! I'm so sorry, I shouldn't have put you on the spot like that.

That was a horrible thing to do.'

Isla smiled before faking my strangulation with warm hands.

'You've met most of my family, so I think I'll live...'

A deathly sadness sprouting on her lip and brow.

'Auch, Isla.'

I topped up the glasses using the two bottles on the table before pulling Isla into my lap.

'Don't do that to yourself.'

'Paisley, I don't know how to say this… I… I'm still really sad and hurting…'

That exquisite face, so beautiful; a lingering sadness etched into every crease, her fingers active.

God, I want to fix everything.

'Well, that's to be expected, you…'

'Wait.' Isla's voice was less than a whisper as she interrupted.

'… I can't stop thinking about Granda, my chest is heavy and achy all the time.

I want to cry and scream and shout, every moment of every new day. I want to throw things, jump up and down, swear the worst possible words…

Tell him how much I love him.

Tell him how much I hate him for leaving me alone in this world.'

The face started to blur, lifting my chin in an attempt to hold back the waterworks, a newly formed lump struck my throat. I tried to gulp it down.

'I'm sorry I can't fix all of those things, and I am truly sorry that you feel that way.' I finally managed.

A finger found my lip.

'No, no more words. Not yet. Please.'

I didn't understand, but her eyes filled me with an intense adoration.

'Listen to me, Pais. I know that he sent you! I know he did, I can feel it.

It all makes perfect sense.

Granda sent you to rescue me!

He knew you'd come in and sweep me off my feet.

Look after me, get me back on track.

Take over from him and stand in his place.

He didn't want me to be alone so he sent you.

You'd love me enough to get through this scary and confusing world.

A life without Granda would kill me, it will kill me...

But he knew, with you, I could conquer anything, that's why he loved you so much, even after so little time.

I can't explain it, but I feel it.'

My head rolled, a faint tear finally marking its territory. The lump restricting the air I urgently crave.

Isla's finger, still holding firm— tender and safe.

Her voice lifting through each sentence.

'Edinburgh, Skye, everything just makes sense.

He's bound to us both, it's like we're caught up in the tangled lines.

Tangled fishing lines... We can only clear the knots when we work through them together.'

My lip wobbled beneath the finger.

'Auch, Paisley I can't lie, I'm a mess.

I'm in a really rough spot right now.

My poor aching heart is broken beyond any reconciliation, I know that... but I also know you're the most respectful, kind and loving person that I've ever met... and I don't really know how to say this... because to anyone else, it must sound like the ramblings of a complete madwoman.

I already know it sounds batshit crazy.'

An intense look paused the sentence; a glimmer of hope twinkling in her eyes, mouth curving into the most spellbinding smile.

My head begged for her to stop, my heart distressed to know more.

'I know he sent you. You're my gift from above!
And… fuck, you haven't even touched me… and yet… I… I… I'm so in love with you!

With every aching bone in my body, with every breath that I breathe, beyond the sky meeting the horizon… I canna describe it in any other way, I… I just don't want to be with anyone else.

The thought of you leaving is killing me. Even just to return home… It's eating at me… You're the only person that's ever made me feel this way.

My devastated heart's breaking and all I can think about, selfishly, is… is how much I need you… how much I want you… how much I love you.

And I do.

In all honesty, I unequivocally and wholeheartedly love you, Paisley.'

There it was, effortless and simple.

A tornado plundered through, its wind sucking the life from my body.

'I love you so, so very much, I'm nae even ashamed to admit it. I canna breathe at the thought of being without you, my lungs won't fill— I jist never want to be without you again.

I don't think I'll survive if you aren't by my side.

I mean it, I'm madly in love with you.'

Isla's finger slid down, freeing me from her clutch. Sitting back as if waiting for a response, her face filled with an unjustified worry.

My eyes wider than the moonlit sky sat frozen, a dumbness that I couldn't interpret holding me ransom.

Each and every syllable ringing as my weakened heart clung helplessly to every phrase.

Lost for words, my sandpaper mouth hung slack.

I tried to sit straight but my inconsolable body couldn't react to the surprise confession; the blood beating through my ears joined the words still circling.

It wasn't like I didn't feel the same, but the shock was unanticipated. There was never a reality it would approach this week.

Isla's features were full of nervousness, the agile fingers crocheting small loops.

My eyelids batted a couple of times; as if doing my own version of a master reset.

Uncontainable tears flowing freely onto my shirt, every sentiment reverberating through the now not so highly functioning brain.

Opening my mouth, the words remained; nothing more than a gasp broke the silence.

A few seconds later, adrenaline finally booted me up the arse and my senses fired back to life.

Grabbing Isla in one brisk motion, I threw her down impulsively against the sofa.

My body joining on top in an agitated rush.

Snatching at the hands, I pinned them above her head, anchoring her in place with an impenetrable grip.

A sensual chaos ensued as our mouths locked tightly in an extreme wanting battle.

Teeth pulling and biting at her lips before my possessed tongue searched for more unspoken truths.

The desperate touch was finally within reach, and I was taking my moment.

By fuck I was taking everything.

My heart was racing, chest pounding as I continued my frenzied attack.

Isla let free a low, deep growl as I forced my tongue in deeper, our breaths hot and heavy as the fervid kiss intensified.

The noise rousing every terrible thought I'd had over the past few months.

I moved my muzzle to her neck, nipping and sucking the delectable skin, her gasps heavy against my ear as her head shifted to allow more traction.

Our bodies trembling at the slightest touch; wanting for more, begging to be pleasured and enjoyed.

Seized together in a twisted bond.

Closed eyes drew me closer.

My grip tightened, greedy lips moving down towards her chest.

Grazing over the fabric she freed another groan.

I let go of her hands, desperate to satisfy both our needs, unwilling to wait any longer.

Isla pulled me back into a carnivorous kiss, sucking and biting my neck in a slow sultry tease.

Tingles thrilling my senses as my breath hitched.

Agile fingers working hard to tug my top free, my own moving for the buttons on her jeans.

Opening her eyes, they were wild with want; steamy, stimulating and very suggestive.

Pulling our hips closer, the caper continued.

Between stolen kisses my shirt found the floor, her denims met the sofa's arm.

Safe warm hands teased my back as she brushed the

407

skin, making her way towards my bra— It was swiftly unclasped in an impressive motion.

I started working on her blouse; lifting it, my mouth grazed her stomach.

Gluttonous in my endeavour, it landed next to my own.

Laying in nothing more than her underwear my starved eyes couldn't hide their delight, she was even more spectacular in the flesh.

Fighting with my trousers, her feet forced them free before toned legs wrapped my waist.

My lips traced her torso— tender skin rose with each heavy breath as I made my way back to her throat.

Gentle hands searching my figure, working from the hips to my breasts.

A rattle caught in my chest as she teased and tormented the aroused skin.

Moving my hands into the fiery locks I scraped her scalp; my nails working hard to stimulate every sense, a breathtaking exhale as she bit her lip. Tease.

I sucked it between my teeth.

Her hands making for the still clad clothing, hauling and tugging she broke free, I wasn't far behind.

My hand moved to her thighs, skimming and scoring as the ache grew.

'Tell me to stop,' I breathed out, a cheeky smile growing behind the intent.

My lips found her chest, nipping and pulling in a ravenous exploration.

'Don't you fucking dare!' She gasped.

My hand found her warmth, the roll of her eyes indicating it was well received.

Her own hands scratching my back as she drowned into the couch's fabric.

Skimming and caressing, I basked in the sensual and erotic contact.

Swallowing hard, she let out a whimper, it sent a shudder through me.

Her eyes closed, legs shivering as I continued inflicting the best kind of agony.

'Pais…'

'Mhmm, I know. Just relax, I've got you.'

Shimmying down, I wrapped myself between her legs.

A hot slick tongue providing more debauchery as I licked and lapped.

Lecherous and villainous; I stole every emotion.

Gripping her thighs I continued to tantalise the already scorched skin.

The trembling arch of her back and delectable quiver giving way to her climax as I watched through stimulated eyes.

Her fingers tracing my hair as delirium filled the room. Fuck.

'Fuck, get back up here a minuty.' Her voice was demanding and a thousand times sexier than it had been before.

Doing as commanded she threw me to the floor. Harsh and forceful; she gazed down from above.

More kisses teased my mouth and throat.

'It's my turn, old girl.' Isla grinned.

My pulse quickened at the mock.

Returning the favour, I saw fireworks.

Explosive flashes crashing against my eyelids.

Unable to contain the fire, her hands wandered my

anatomy, an overwhelming swell as she consumed my soul.

My chest heaved with the intense gratification.

Pulling against my hips, she forced them closer.

A gentle grazing of teeth as she exposed and explored my newfound weakness.

My no longer anxious hands cut into her shoulders as she eyed me from below, the obscene contact driving me insane as ferocious blue pools held my gaze.

My heart ached, loins inflamed, agonised muscles as they tensed against the tantalising touch.

Sweat created a path along my neck.

A moan gripped dangerously in my throat, knee's buckling against the force, an unexpected prod causing my head to fall back.

Crashing against the rug, my body bleakly gave in.

Toes curling in a vexed agony whilst I succumb to the ultimate hedonism.

'Jesus Christ!' I eventually spat out, unable to control my pulsing lungs as they surged.

Our bodies no longer held shame or embarrassment as we lay together against the cold, hard floor, the room a mess of clothing and sprawling hair.

A perfect finale to all of the repressed strain; our souls bound by an unforgiving contentment.

Pulling Isla into my arms we relaxed between languid senses.

Silence filled the room as I looked over, confronted with an honest tenderness, Isla smiled.

'Just in case it escapes my mind later, and I know that it won't, because it's truly all I think about.

But just to be sure.

Without you, Isla, I'm trapped by a wave of darkness.

Your light sails through me.

It's pure, and honest, and unfaltering.

You bring me peace and a calmness that I really can't explain.

I've been hooked since the day we met.

You feel like home.

I've been lost my whole life; haphazardly adrift in love with no purpose or direction.

I don't ever want to be found if it's not by you.

You're the anchor to my tide.

I told your grandfather that nobody could fill his role.

It's an impossible task, even for me.

But I did make him a promise.

A promise to take care of you, to keep you safe, to make you happy.

I hope that will be enough, Isla MacLeod, because I really do love you too.'

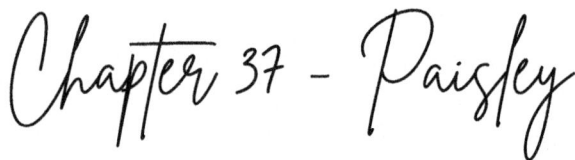

Chapter 37 - Paisley

Stood at the foot of the grave, Isla's fragile posture was concealed by myself and Morag.

We stood either side, gripping firmly; the weight and pressure of today harshly pulling her downwards.

Isla wore a long black midi dress; hugging around her petite waist, it screamed elegance.

A large hat hid her face, sunglasses big enough to cover any skin the brim couldn't reach sat steadily against her nose.

If it hadn't been such a solemn and sombre occasion, I'd have sent a photo to James, he would have appreciated this spellbinding look.

Even in her hour of sorrow, Isla looked truly stunning, a haunted beauty trapped in a cruel and twisted turn of misfortune.

Today, I couldn't bring myself to find much pleasure in it.

I felt crushed by her pain.

My heart silently breaking for her.

Usually, I'd provide some humorous quip or attempt a compliment. Today wasn't the day.

I felt every ounce of the depression.

Entombed thoughts and a numbness stirred. Contemplation of our own existence, fragility and mortality; the shortness of life simmered around my soul.

The lack of equality and justice, silently dragging my anxiety to the floor.

Sadness washed over as the minister neared his final words.

Forty heads bowed in quiet respect.

Perched on one of the most beautiful plateaus overlooking the striking coastline, the sun shone.

A cold eerie unease filled the air; the crying wind, whistling and weeping through huddled bodies.

Her grip tensed, the turmoil gradually unfolding.

My hand clenched tighter.

Anchored in place, Isla's eyes locked onto Alistair's casket.

Its exterior, smooth, shiny and modest, now resting in its new permanent home.

Shoulders trembling with hands clammy to the touch.

Inhaling a deep unsteady breath of sea air, Isla straightened, eyes cast towards the tide, angry waves crashing against ancient rock.

No doubt denying the floods relentlessly trying to match those below the peninsula.

I felt Isla's desperation to stand tall, decent and proud.

She needed to be strong for Alistair.

I needed to be strong for her.

Petite legs shook.

Morag patted Isla's arm before turning to give me a weak smile. I returned a subtle nod.

The land and sea closed around Alistair, 'earth to earth,' rang poignantly through.

The words reverent in their closing, final and eternal.

Isla let out a cluster of sobs, strength straining as her head fell.

I wrapped an arm around the shoulders— Morag gripped her waist. Both offering a sturdy but gentle brace. Love and friendship, resisting and retaliating.

I knew today would be awful, but the vast enormity couldn't have been anticipated.

As the congregation slowly dispersed, Isla remained.

Faithfully standing by Alistair's side; her loyalty persisted.

Tears rained down, barriers broke as a new storm of torrential thunder ripped through.

My own joining the river of sorrow.

Standing until everyone left, the kirkyard offered little in the way of peace or sympathy.

Two figures looming quietly behind cracked the stillness.

Familiar to Isla; I felt her fingers twitch.

Curious to Morag's passive glower.

Unknown to me.

Going by the atmosphere, I guess it's time to finally meet the parents.

The silence amplified their distance.

'We're sorry for your loss, Isla.' A man's voice filled the sky with an unsteady cadence.

Isla didn't turn, never even looked, just quietly wept.

A hand landed above my consoling arm. It gave a gentle squeeze.

Another, heavy on the back of her neck.

It made me uncomfortable as Isla stiffened and moved.

Morag bolstered closer.

'You're sorry for my loss?'

Unrecognisable words hung sharp, raw and suffocating.

Isla's voice was cold and cracked.

Her usual warmth replaced with a bitter hurtful sting, her accent more pronounced.

Still facing away, she swayed.

'I haven't heard from either of you in years.'

Steady silence from the newcomers.

'I called you.

I called you in my one moment of need... one moment.

In twenty fucking years!

You didn't call, didn't visit, couldn't even send a card, anything to show you actually give a shit about how I was feeling.' Her tone didn't falter.

Their detached and distant faces held no tenderness.

'My grandfather. Your father is dead. And all you can say is, 'you're sorry for my loss?'

They looked towards me, dark eyes questioning.

My brow probably returned the gape— Morag gave me a reassuring nod.

Their eyes turned on Morag, lifting as though a distant memory lingered.

Promptly they fell back to Isla.

Her face still turned— shrouded by the disguise.

'I don't even want to look at you.

You are selfish!

Selfish people who didn't deserve him.

Didn't deserve me!'

She spat out the words, poisonous and vindictive.

Remaining fixed, I wasn't sure where best to position myself.

Relying on Morag's knowledge and experience was

doing nothing.

Palpitations struck.

I didn't want to get involved, but I couldn't bear to see Isla hurt.

My eyes begged Morag, desperate for some kind of signal. What should I do?

Morag's own; wide and unable to comprehend.

'We loved him too.' Helen sobbed— all fragile and pathetic, like a child ready to break into a tantrum. Well-practiced words with no ounce of humility.

Isla wasn't having any of it. The glasses fell.

Her face snapped to her mother's; eyes fierce and ready. A wolf hunting; taut and powerful, poised with bared teeth and an even sharper tongue.

'You wouldn't know love if it jumped up and bit you in the arse.' Clamping her jaws on every syllable.

Her parents recoiled; a gasp in disbelief, possibly shock, definitely fear.

I was tempted to step with them, the new savage side fleeing whilst my blood curdled.

'We know you loved your Granda, but that doesn't mean we care any less, Isla. We're all family.' Tam spoke, lukewarm and rough.

Isla's cheeks reddened, her back straight as she turned quarrelling eyes to her father.

'Family's meant fuck all to you for the past thirty years. Why would I want to play happy families now? I made a colossal fuck-up last week calling you Dad on the phone.

You're no more my father than a piss in the wind.'

Helen moved forward, hand out as if to steady Isla.

'Come on, love. That isn't fair. We've always loved you, and we'll always be your Mum and Dad, nothing's changed.'

Her face matched the unconvincing monologue.

'You're right there, Helen, nothing's changed.

You're both non-existent in my life— obsolete, and that's just how it's going to stay.

I've felt guilty for years!

You abused my poor grandparents and shame hung over my head for decades!

You stole their lives and now you have the audacity to come crawling out of the woodwork because they're gone. You're both pathetic. Shame on you!'

I didn't doubt they needed to hear it, but over Alistair's dead body didn't seem appropriate.

Morag stood with her mouth open.

'Isla!' Tam's voice boomed.

'Don't talk to your mother that way, you weren't raised like that!'

His eyes an angry glower, no kindness to his voice.

It was that very moment, I could see the resemblance in the eyes; the only difference, Tam's didn't hold any warmth or compassion.

'Raised like that? And how the fuck would you know how I was raised?

Where were you when we actually needed you?' Isla screamed.

'Go on, get out of my face. You shouldn't be here. You should never have come!

You don't half pick your days to piss me off!

I don't want to see either of you again… Not until it's your box being lowered into the ground.'

'ISLA!!' I roared.

Unable to handle any more, her out of character words

were wicked and cruel.

I knew in time they'd be regrettable.

Morag gave another nod, immediately easing my guilt.

Isla's interests were at heart, but it garnered me at least three filthy scowls.

'Let's go sweetie, this is not the time or place.' I held out my hand.

'I think it would be best if you both left now, please. You're upsetting Isla.' I was stern but polite.

I don't know them, probably wouldn't want to, but there's no point making a bad situation worse.

Isla burst into tears, angry and spiteful.

Oh shit.

She lunged forward; fabricating myself into a barrier, aggressive painful thumps beat my torso; agony cut in like a sharp knife.

I remained as more punches belted out in a fit of unsuppressed rage, wails of despair as each hit Isla projected, landed harder than the last.

As furious as I was, I couldn't blame her, I put myself here, but the sting hurt… and more than just the physical.

A few moments passed and Isla slumped to the wet grass.

Her red harsh hands knotted above her head in defeat.

Deafening cry's filling the air.

I knelt beside her— knees sodden and filthy.

Carefully lifting her back to standing, I pulled Isla against my chest; safe hands cradling her head and waist.

'Shh, I've got you. You're okay, I've got you.'

'Please just go, you're upsetting Isla.' Morag finally jumped in.

Angus watched from the background, ready to move should he need.

'Isla, please! We can talk about this.' Her father's voice echoed with a self-assured sense of authority.

To be brutally honest, I was tempted to give him a decent smack in the mouth, if nothing more than to give him a taste of my pain.

'Please just leave, Tam. Yiv said enough, that'll do.' Morag asked again, the tone not so friendly.

Helen tugged Tam's arm.

As quick as they had appeared, they were gone.

A miserable trail of destruction and devastation left in their wake.

* * * *

Angus drove us back to Bramble Brae.

Morag was silent in the front seat— I clung to Isla in the back.

She hadn't said another word since I'd shouted.

Tears intermittent as we drove across the island.

Angus stopped and opened the car door.

Clambering out from the front, Morag gave us both a firm hug.

Isla looked small and weak against her frame— no sign of reciprocation.

I looked at Morag, as if inviting them both inside, the shake of an appreciative head advised against it.

'Thank you both for driving us.' I sighed out.

'Aye, that's alright, make sure ye both get settled.' Morag replied with a sad pull.

'Isla, dinna beat yerself up.
We'll see ye soon, and we love you.' Morag tried.
Isla just nodded.

'Thanks again, get home safe.' I reiterated.
Turning, I walked Isla inside, the silence spread between us like the vast valley behind the cottage.
Laying her on the bed I moved a hand through her curls.

Proceeding to the bathroom a few minutes later, I ran a hot soapy bath.
No words were spoken— No words were needed.

Checking the water's temperature and lighting a lavender candle, I returned to the bed.
Lifting her from the foetal position, I removed the encapsulating dress; pulling it over her head before making light work of the shoes and underwear.
Brooding and broken but still very beautiful.

Cautiously carrying her into the en-suite, I eased her into the tepid bubbles.
The handheld shower washing the worst of today from the fisher's frame.

Our eyes discussed a private, wordless conversation about fear and anger, apologies and disregard.
Isla gave a half-hearted nod, I returned it.
My lips indicating it wasn't okay, but it was understood.

The peepers spoke chapters, small sad grimaces and furrowed brows filling gaps.
The voiceless discussion lasted much longer than I anticipated.

Placing a gentle kiss to Isla's forehead, it was

welcomed with a warm soapy hug.

'Join me?' Isla whispered, her voice unrecognisable, hoarse and brittle.

I nodded slowly, the weight of today a burden I didn't want to hold. It would be better to forgive and forget.

Grief and anger, creating an unusual emotional hardship that I couldn't grudge.

Removing my top, Isla recoiled— her mouth gingerly working overtime.

An artwork of purple and blue bruises tainted my chest, their tones as clear as day.

Following Isla's eyes, I gave out a shallow impassive nod.

Climbing in behind, I let the water flood both us and the floor.

In truth, I'd passed caring.

Concealed in a hushed candlelit gloom, we lay in silence for an eternity. Arms tightly holding the other.

'Forgive me, Pais.' Her voice a dismal whisper.

I left the silence to brood a moment longer.

'Aye, just don't do it again.'

Chapter 38 – Isla

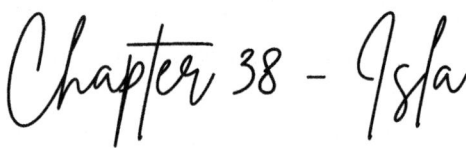

Our weekend had been another blur.

Riding on a roller coaster of emotion since the funeral, I tried daily to apologise.

Paisley tried to convince me the reaction had been warranted, and no more apologies were needed.

I didn't agree. I felt shitty and worthless.

She didn't deserve that, I'm not sure how to forgive myself.

It caused us to have our first heated disagreement on Sunday— Paisley got the final word in.

I guess I let her win out of guilt.

Throwing me against the bed, she demonstrated how terrible I was.

Graciously, I accepted my anger fuelled punishment.

I mean, it was deserved, I'd been very naughty.

The discipline cleared the air and our blissful relationship was restored.

Paisley really is far too good to me, I'm unbelievably lucky to have her.

Monday brought sunshine and breakfast in bed, she'd earned it.

Toast, fruit and coffee for the old girl… maybe it was just a ploy for me to make the coffee.

For some reason Paisley's tastes like tar, I could use it to repair holes in the cottage roof.

We both looked up in surprise when the doorbell rang out.

I shifted the duvet.

'Wait! I'll go, I need fresh air,' Paisley shouted before sprinting out in a mad dash.

Rolling my eyes I pulled the covers back over.

'If yer going for a smoke, ye just need to say!' I shouted.

Silence.

Auch, I guess it's just one of those little perks.

Picking up my coffee, Paisley re-appeared— a humongous cardboard box in her arms.

Sauntering around to the adopted side, she plonked the box between us.

Sliding under the blanket, her grin was higher than the package.

So adorable, but no obvious smell of smoke.

'Did ye hear me?' I asked.

'No, what did you say?' The grin still lingering.

'I said, ye dinna need to skulk off, ye can just say yer going for a smoke.'

'Ohh, okay.'

'Are we going to talk about this?'

'Smoking?'

'No!' I moved the box to read the label. 'This…'

Miss P Campbell
Bramble Brae
Isle of Skye
SK12 4YE

'What is this, Paisley?'

'Stuff.' She shrugged, nonchalant and secretive.

'What stuff?' I was desperate to know.

'Oh, just… stuff.' Paisley was teasing and it was

working way more than she knew.

The box was big enough to fit a flat-pack cottage.

Paisley's grin touched each ear, she clambered out of bed again, leaving the room for a second time.

'Paisley! Where are you going now? What stuff!? I need to know!'

'Do you?' The songlike voice distant in the hallway.

Lifting the box I almost broke my back— dumping it back down I moved it back to the original position. She'll never know.

Turning to the door, another two giant boxes let themselves in.

'What the hell have you got in there?' I stood from the bed with shock and intrigue.

The duvet coiled my legs.

Kicking free, I moved around.

'Stuff. I told you.'

The two new boxes landed next to the first.

Grabbing Paisley's waist, I pulled her into a sloppy lingering kiss— working my tongue into a sensual production.

Hmm, it's working, her hands are moving. Yessss!

Paisley joined in, I could feel the excitement building.

Cruelly pulling back, she played with my hair.

'That will not work on me, Isla MacLeod.

I love you, but I don't know if I love you enough to let you into my boxes.'

Crossing my arms, I poked a lip out in a playful sulk.

Paisley still grinning that undeniably beautiful tease pulled down on my lip with a finger. It flopped back into place.

Licking her lip, she mimicked my stance.

Eurghh, so fucking sexy.

'I need tae know, Paisley!'

'Do you now? Hmm, that *is* fascinating.'

Arghh the tease!

'What if it needs food and water?

Auch, ye know what? I don't even want tae know what's in yer boxes.' Lulling my voice, hopeful some sexy tones would help me out.

'Christ, you're bang on, Isla! How could I forget.'

That face ate through the flesh and muscle surrounding my chest.

'I'm going for a smoke, do *not* touch my boxes!' Paisley warned coyly, moving towards the door.

'Arghh, yer the worst! Right, I don't even love you anymore, that's us, take yer boxes and get tae…'

'I love you too.' She interrupted from the egress. Eyes dreamy and glistening.

Returning ten minutes later, there was yet another small box, her PJs reeking of smoke; obviously using the opportunity, and my lack of patience to actually light the bloody thing.

My eyes must have burst out of my head.

'Paisley, where the fuck are you getting all these boxes from?

Do I need to go and check if my car's still got a parking spot?'

'This one's actually for you.' Paisley said before bursting into laughter.

A brown box landed between my hands.

'I didn't order anything?'

'I know, I did.' Paisley spoke softly, still a hint of humour behind the accent.

I didn't need telling twice, I was straight into the tape.

'For fuck's sake, there's another box inside!
It's like pass the bloody parcel.'

'You know, I never had any patience before meeting you. Now I can see how entertaining it must be for other people.

'Auch awa' an bile yer heid. I have plenty of patience.'
Pulling out a smooth matte carton, *Espresso* was written on one side, a picture of a large white coffee machine on the other.

'Are you nuts, is this really for me?'
'Mhmm.
I'd imagine this is what Christmas morning feels like as a parent.
I know you dislike my coffee, Isla.
Every time I make one, you spit out your tongue or tip it down the sink. Do you think I'm not watching? I see everything and I can take a hint.' Her lips curled into the cheeks.

'Pais! You didn't need to buy me a coffee machine. Now I feel rotten.'
'Don't. I know my coffee's minging, I've only ever used a machine at home.
I'm a useless housewife and probably a snob.'
Paisley shrugged, already succumb to the truth.
It was accurate.

'I detest the noise of that gargoyle water boiler in your kitchen. It conjures images of some poor bugger getting a smear test— carried out by the local butcher with a power saw.' She shuddered.
I burst out laughing.
'Ehh? You're bloody nuts!
Thank you so much, Paisley. I love it, and I'm pretty

confident you're going to make the perfect housewife…
but you're right… yer a snob.'

Raising an eyebrow, my lip teased my teeth.

Paisley raised both of hers.

'Considering last week's confession, Isla, a proposal probably wouldn't be all that surprising. Should I book the band?'

'Ohh, get lost. Upper-class twat.'

I couldn't stop grinning.

Running over, Paisley was gifted with some more very sexy and sensual kisses.

Graciously accepting, she softly pulled away in a '*I want and need you*' kind of fashion.

'Stop, Isla. We won't ever get out of bed if you keep this going.'

Pointing to the other three boxes.

'We should probably move onto these…'

'Oh no, please. I don't need a new hoover, iron or cooker!' I was getting cheeky with the jokes.

'Well, that's good, one is filled with new clothes. The eight outfits I brought with me just aren't enough for a month. I'm honestly sick of jeans and I need more than a week's worth of knickers!

I need more of everything.'

'Oh, moving in, are we? I didn't think I'd asked you that question yet, hmm maybe in my devastation it fell out.'

'No, you haven't, and I move to strike your honour.'

'Eh?'

'You must think I only wear black and white.

The other two boxes are slightly less conventional…'

Her head wobbled, '…but I think you'll appreciate them. Want to help me open them up?'

'Ehhhh, aye okay then… Do sheep wear woolly sweaters? What kind of ridiculous question is that?'
I rolled my eyes.

There was no need to ask a second time, within forty seconds every box was shredded.
Paper and packaging had spewed across the bed; bags upon bags of plastic, clothing, shoes, socks and protective paper littered the place.
It looked like Paisley was visiting for a year with all this stuff.
'Seriously, are you moving in?'
Paisley shook her head from the door.
I sat in a puddle of sportswear— wellies, jackets and thermals.
'I don't understand, Paisley. What is this?'
'You really don't see it?'
'No. It looks like fishing gear…'
'And you're right, that's exactly what it is. May I approach the bench?'
She was trying to be funny, but it was wasted on me.
Moving from the doorframe, Paisley joined me on the bed.
'Sweetie, you need to get that boat back on the water… and I want to see what you experience every day.' Paisley waited; my insides ripped apart as tears threatened to break free.
'Paisley,'
'Oh shit. Isla.'
'That's Granda's boat, I know that sounds silly…'
'Isla…' her voice was calm and comfy, '…that boat's yours, and it's not silly at all.'
'He told me it would be mine… when.'

'I think we should have a serious conversation, Isla.
I can wait until you're ready, if you don't feel it's a good time.
Theres a few things we've never spoken about.'
My heart thumped in my chest.

'Please tell me what you're talking about, I'm scared.'
Shifting one of the boxes onto the floor, Paisley grabbed my hands, halting my fidget.

'Isla.'
Her eye contact was intense.

'You're the sole beneficiary of your grandfather's estate.
His only beneficiary.
When he came to see me in Edinburgh…'

My ears started ringing; except for a high-pitched buzz squeezing itself through my brain, the thumping of my chest cancelled out any background noise.

'So, that mea.s…. th… whole estate…you will…'
What's she saying? The beds floating, the hell's this?
Oh no, black spots.

'…considerable fortune….
…Isla …sweet.'
'Wh..sp…nois…warm...' My mouth's not working.
Unable to move— legs flailed as I tried to steady myself, a white light pulling hot, breath halting, heart hammering. Brighter light.'

'Are… Isla… alright… Is…'
The noise stopped and the lights went out.

'That was close,' Paisley breathed out.

'Isla? Isla, sweetie, are you alright?
Look at me!
Look at me. Come on, you're okay.'

'Agh... Ugh... Hm...'

'Come on, sweetie, you're alright, let's get you back up on the bed.

I'll get your feet up...'

'Going ...me a ...heart attack.'

Paisley giggled.

My eyes reopened, am I dreaming?

The old girl's standing above me, dressed in an unquestionably large pair of black rubber fishing waders and a red oilskin jacket, she looks hilarious.

'Am I dreaming? What in Dunvegan Castle are you wearing!?' I finally mumbled, feeling like a right tool.

'Do you like it?' Paisley beamed whilst checking herself out in the mirror and flaunting around the room.

'I'm hallucinating?'

'No. You're awake, thankfully.

I'm hoping you'll take me for a ride on your boat. Obviously, once we know you aren't going to pass out again. You almost had another bruise...

This thing's bloody roasting, how do you stay stood up?' She asked unclipping the waders at her chest.

'Pais, I didn't hear anything you told me before... but, aye, I'd really love to take you fishing.'

Paisley sat down again, half fastened as the toggles hung down one side.

She lifted my hands, her face serious and professional, still soft and kind, but definitely different.

Paisley

'Isla, I need you to listen to me. This is very important, and possibly quite hard to process.
Your grandfather left you his company, he had everything set out and ready for… the future.'

'He wanted to meet with me because I specialise in wills, trusts and estate planning.
I know of ways to… well… minimise the amount of inheritance tax that's usually paid for legacies and chattels.'
I wasn't sure if Isla understood, but she's still awake so I guess that's something.

Inhaling a deep breath, I began— This story could go either way.

'When you first emailed me on behalf of your grandfather, I majorly screwed up.
It happens, admittedly not usually to me, but this time it was my mistake. I've no one to blame but myself, I should know better.
I don't specialise in commercial property or business-related tax, but I never asked you or Alister the question.
I just wrongly assumed it was a basic sign and seal, single will job.
I didn't double-check the information…'
Unintentionally I giggled, it was nervous.

'…something I later scolded James for not doing… although he probably deserved it.

Anyway, the email should have technically gone to Sharon first, that's her area of expertise.

I was so hungover and in such a bad mood when it came through, it didn't even cross my mind.'

I paused, biting my lip.

Isla glared, no doubt Alistair was running through her head.

'When I met your grandfather in my office, I realised it was Sharon who would need to deal with him first to try and tidy up the loose ends.

Loose ends concerning the commercial property and business tax, it all needed to be in place before I could go on to sort the will.

I got in such a fluster when I knew I wasn't going to make our meeting, I took down all the business details for Sharon, but I didn't take the beneficiary details for me to organise my side.

What an arse! I still can't believe I did that.

Alistair had been so unbelievably excited, when telling me his granddaughter would be the sole beneficiary and yet, I didn't even think to ask your name. I needed it for my paperwork and I just blanked over everything.

Lost in my own disappointment and selfishness.'

'Auch Pais,'

'No, Isla, it's important, please.

Sharon and I started to look into it after I worked out my mistake. Admittedly, it took me a hell of a lot longer to notice than it should have.

I'm a senior solicitor for God's sake. It's probably time I acted it!

I kicked myself for days afterwards.

Anyway, that Monday night, I asked Sharon to tell me where your grandfather was from. Then, going off the conversation I had with Alistair in my office, I managed to catch him at the hotel.

I'd already worked out you were probably the granddaughter he spoke of, but I needed to be sure.

Alistair gave me the details I needed regarding the beneficiaries and whatnot, then told me I was right.

It was you I'd been going to meet.

You I was searching for.

His eyes lit up like the world's prayers had been answered. Your grandfather was so thrilled and excited that we were in the same building.'

A heavy tear fell from my now hazy eyes.

Ugh, no tears, come on.

Isla's neck tilted, her lips pressed into a crumpled line, eyes misting whilst she watched.

'I doubt he indulged you in his knowledge... How much he knew about you, your plans, your secrets.

Over the course of a few weeks, Alistair, Sharon and I worked together... to try and get you both the best sort of deal.

Numerous phone calls, hours and days talking and working. Alistair was such an amazing person to deal with, so organised and punctual.

Honestly, Isla, I feel like I've known him a lifetime.

It's no wonder he was always tired— he was on the phone to me half the night.

Anyway, Alistair agreed to let Sharon take on the brunt of the work and I asked James to step in for me.'

'Paisley, I'm sorry. I've no idea what you're talking about.

This legal shenanigans is above my head.

Why did James need to step in for you?'

'James did me a favour. After the bollocking I

almost gave him, he was only too happy to help.

Asking James to take on your grandfather's will, would take me out of the equation.

I needed to avoid any conflict of interest.

It could have affected everything if we... If we were going to have a shot at this relationship.'

Isla's eyes expanded, her jaw slackened as the velvety lip hid away.

Kiss it, bite it. No. Work. Work first.

'You were already invested in us?'

'Of course! I meant what I said.

Isla, my whole world came crashing down around me.

I was head over heels.

Naturally, Alistair kept me up to date with extra details along the way.

Singing on the boat for example.'

'My God, Paisley.' Isla's hands clamped to her appetising chest.

'Back to the story, that can wait!

Business relief and standard inheritance differ immensely, but we were able to work through everything... To ensure you wouldn't be required to pay a fortune in fees and tax deductions.

I still worked alongside James and your grandfather, but my name stayed out of the official paperwork.

Are you following me?'

A slow unconvincing nod, I'm continuing anyway.

I need to tell her.

'By transferring your grandfather's home and additional assets into the fishing business, we have managed to reduce the inheritance tax by one hundred percent.'

I stopped to allow the information to filter in.

She probably wasn't going to like what was coming next.

'One hundred percent? What does that mean?'

'It means, as long as you keep fishing for the next two years and continue gaining profit, you'll inherit all of Alistair's assets.'

Grey redesigned Isla's skin tone.

'What is that?' Isla questioned.

'Well… hmm… currently, off the top of my head, that's your grandfather's house and the three acres of land, the boat, the fishing rights and licences, his pension fund, car and pretty much everything else you can think of.

We did need to sell off his private shares, they wouldn't have been tax-free… but by doing it this way, it allowed you to get the maximum lump sum.'

'Paisley? What does that mean? You need to spell it out for me, I'm not smart like you.'

She probably didn't have any idea. Without a doubt her pretty head would be reeling.

'It means, Isla, in two years' time, you could sell the business and its assets for the best part of one point five million, and currently you're sitting with around three hundred grand extra in your bank account.

No one else can touch anything, and you are smart, don't put yourself down.'

This time when Isla fell, I didn't get the chance to catch her.

'Oops.'

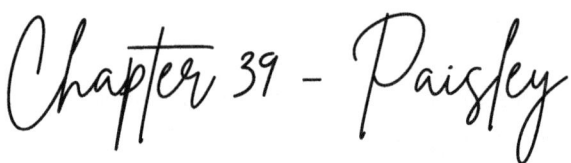

Chapter 39 - Paisley

'Paisley darling, are you okay? Blink twice if you need rescuing!'

James was televised, probably trying to salvage some gossip.

An effortless appearance graced his weekend, beige snug-fitting shirt and a navy cardigan.

'Oh, James. I've missed you so much!' I squealed whilst perusing the phone.

I lay draped over the settee, arms extended, legs outstretched comfortably.

Isla was amusing the shiny new drip pot.

Its din hammering as water pounded the pump, an agreeable arabica aroma wafting.

'Darling, that sofa is stunning, it's clear to see you aren't at home.

I'm thrilled at least one of you has flair…Oh and I may have accidentally set fire to your chaise when collecting your mail.' He pulled a fake oops and smiled his boyish good looks.

'If my chaise isn't exactly how I left it, you'll be dumped from a boat… And I know exactly where to find a few of those!'

James shooed me from the city.

'Well darling, you look very… different.'

My neck bobbed as I checked the portrait.

'Good different?'

'You look like a woman who's finally gone down the Braid Burn, paddling a pink canoe!

I cannot stress this enough, sweetie, to the fullest degree, it really suits you.'

Isla whipped round like she'd been offered a lap dance from the Pope.

'Is that James?' She moved closer.

Glancing above the cushions I nodded, eyes rolling into the grey.

'Paisley, darling, I can see every movement you're making right now, subtle isn't your foreplay.

On that note, I am ever so pleased that you looked over and not down, now I don't need to worry about your beaver taking a bath whilst we prattle.'

'James, you are riddled with filth!' I couldn't help but smile.

'Look sweetie, whatever that gorgeous woman is doing to you, keep it going.

You look radiant, it's a sheer delight.

If I'd known a trip upland would moisten your soul, I'd have sent you years ago.'

Two enticing mugs discovered the table, a misbehaved bending of hips pilfered my concentration.

Crawling between my legs, teasing slow silky kisses up my stomach, I looked down.

'Really?' I mouthed.

It gained a naughty stare and a jerk of her lip.

Eurgh, wee shite.

'Hello? Darling, I can still see your face... but now I am worried. I don't want to be caught between your lip service...'

Isla kept creeping, compressing my chest as she squeezed between the cushions— unsuccessfully attempting to keek into the device.

'Really?' I announced to them both, lips splitting in

mirth.

James eagerly attempting to better his own view as I extended.

Go on, struggle.

'Oh, how rude. I'm confident you pair were destined to meet…

James, I don't think it would be in your interest to meet Isla.' I was teasing him, but he was a prying bastard most of the time anyway. It only seemed fair.

'Eurgh, Lady Paisley, I'm going to start cuffing the carrot if you don't behave!

Let me see your scissor sister. I've already been more than patient regarding your sexual deficit.'

Unable to regain her composure, Isla cried out a rowdy adorable squeak.

Freeing a grunt, I gave him a cheeky smirk.

Forcing a stray hair behind her ear, I disposed of the phone.

A lingering kiss touched her cheek once my hands were free.

James opened his mouth as the catch came into view, for the first time in a long while, he struggled for words.

'My God darling, I am gagged!

You are fucking magnificent. Excuse my doric.

I guess it's true, sirens of the north do exist.

Lady Paisley, how in the world did this happen?'

Isla's teeth shone. My optics rotated.

'Hello James and thank you! That's very kind,' Hebridean refined.

Flirt.

'Can I jist thank you for helping Pais with my Granda, that was affa good of you.

It's so nice to put a face to the name.'

James looked like he was about to burst into tears—bottom lip trembling as his eyes sparkled.

'Your majesty, you are so very, very welcome.

Had I known you were this aesthetically pleasing, I would have told your grandfather to avoid Lady Paisley from day one.'

He hushed a whisper.

'She's trouble, doesn't hold her liquor or tongue. Really, she's a testy old crone.' Throwing a cheeky side glance to ensure I was listening.

'James, you my friend are a bampot! An absolute sleekit, devious wee bampot.'

Isla gawked before starting to laugh.

'Legitimately, you pair are divine, I hope you're having lots of rough and tumble and I cannot wait to see you together in Edinburgh.

If you don't hurry down, I'll have to come up and drag you back. I bet you'd both love that, dirty little love rats.'

We laughed as if this was the most normal thing in the world, friends for what felt like a lifetime.

'Paisley on a serious note, Gavin's asked me, to ask you, to give him a call when you're free.

I think it's quite important.

Oh, and gossip! Sharon was caught having intimate relations with Jenna from accounts!'

His smile beamed, as though it was the best thing he'd said all year.

'I must say, I didn't see that one coming. I didn't even know the saucy little minx was top, bottom and switch! My flabbers were truly ghasted.'

'Hmm, I had an inclination about Jenna, but that is a

surprise. No astonishment to find Sharon's involved.' I answered.

'Agreed!

Okay my beautiful pair of Skye fairies, I must dash, Paul will be home in a moment. He's going to show me his great big, giant... photo collection from today's shoot. Then we can reenact that scandalous scene from Passages!'

He shuddered like an ice cube had found his back.

'Have a marvellous day, and an even more spectacular night.'

He gave us a sultry wink, '*love to you both.*'

'Goodbye, James. Thanks, love to you too.

Ohh, and enjoy that great, big, well-deserved night of rough play at the funny farm. I hope you finally got your three-way!'

I blew him a kiss followed by a cheeky smirk.

Isla gave him a wave before I put the phone down.

'I'm sorry, Isla, James doesn't believe in using a filter, but I'm really glad you got to meet him.

He's been my only companion for many years.

Too many years in fact.'

Isla grinned.

'Well, we don't need to worry about that now, do we?'

Clambering upwards, short legs wrapped my waist.

'Oh, and whilst I remember, Paisley.

I really hate the phrase bampot.'

'Seriously? I've used it for years.

Is it a dealbreaker?'

Isla returned to sucking her bottom lip.

'Oh aye, Morag was threatened with a deep loch…'

Bared nashers clamped my neck.

Husky respiration filled the air.

Wandering hands worked efficiently to continue what she'd started.

* * * *

After a more than delightful lunch at Bramble Brae, we set off walking.

Our good mood spread harmoniously.

Hand in hand, we trekked the dusty track, scrambling rocky slopes and grassy banks until we summited the peak.

Wind tugging our hair as the vast expanse roamed beyond our feet.

The Trotternish peninsula as clear as day, stunning views of the Old Man of Storr standing tall and proud.

Volcanic basalt threatened the glorious skyline; the nearby island of Raasay looming in the distance.

'I've wanted to bring you here since day one, Pais. I come up here and sit when I need to clear my mind, it's my favourite spot.

No one else knows about it— my own private viewpoint.'

'That view is breathtaking, I've never seen anything so mind-numbingly stunning… and it's not just the scenery.'

Isla's hand found my chest, sprawling into her holding stance.

'How do you always know what to say, Pais?

To start with I thought you were just trying to be charming and impress me, now it's like…'

'Now I'm just honest? I always want to impress you, Isla. Nothing I've ever told you has been a lie, my last statement included.'

'Sook.'

Her expression freed a beat deep against my chest.

Skimming my phone, the velvety soul of Jocelyn Barrett drew out.

Even as the wind wove, music wrapped us.

It was thick with a longing tenderness.

'Finally, my heart's found its way
The nights of longing fade away
And life feels like a melody...'

'Isla, this is spectacular. A greater sight I've never witnessed, not once in my life. I'm blinded.'

'Aye, it's affa bonnie.'

'At last, the storms have passed me by
Love's bright light fills my sky
The moment you caught my eye...'

Lifting dainty hands, I placed them against my shoulders, my own finding her hips.

We began to sway.

Lost in a quiet rhythm, an intimate dance meant only for us.

'Isla, every moment we've shared has brought me closer to you.

I know it hasn't all been planned, but I couldn't have wished for a greater outcome.'

As the sensual music drew to a close, we remained firmly engaged; eyes locked, hearts secure.

'We only have a couple of weeks left.' Isla whispered.

Blue eyes glazed with sadness, a sense of hopelessness.

'We'll be fine, I promise.'

A kiss full of honour to her forehead; a vow of silent sentiment.

'Have you thought about long term?' Isla dipped her toes into the uncharted water flowing between us.

Heavy Skies, reflecting the dusty alcove.

Scattered as if Jocelyn Barrett herself mimicked our mood.

The harmonious sway, a devoted and effortless romance.

'Days are dark,
Sorrow lingers in the air,
Heavy skies, heavy skies,
And I can't seem to shake this deep despair,
Oh, I'm tired all the time'

'I have.

It's the only thing I can't clear from my troubled mind.' I admitted.

Slowly spinning on our heels, keeping time.

Moving my hand to the small of her back, I guided her in a perfectly synchronised moment.

'Have you?' I asked.

A heartfelt nod full of sorrow and unspoken thoughts.

The depths of darkness and grief threatening our most beautiful and compassionate occasion.

We tilted and swung, blocking out the world behind us, lost in the eyes and hearts of one another.

'Tears fell, I couldn't fight,
Watching the one I love, slip from sight,
And all I did was cry'

'I don't want to lose you,' Isla's words were fragile and sullen.

Her eyes cautiously wondering mine, lips pulled into a frozen downcast frown.

'Why do I feel like there's a heavy and looming *but* away to float straight out of your mouth, Isla?

It's hanging over you, and I'm not walking away.'

'Paisley, I don't think I can survive in the city, there's no harbour and I don't know what else I'd do.'

'I know. It's all I've thought about.

We'll manage, everything's too perfect,'

My breathless ache clenched in an agonising grief.

'Are you sure? I don't know if I can survive alone…'

'I'm positive, Isla, just one painful step at a time.'

A final and resolute promise.

Her lips curled into a warm and enchanting smile before resting against my shoulder.

'Granda used to say that.'

An affectionate sentiment.

Our feet shuffled, careful hands supporting bittersweet promises.

'Well in that case, I know everything will work out just fine.' I replied.

'Days are dark,
Sorrow lingers in the air,
Heavy skies, heavy skies,
And I can't seem to shake this deep despair,
Oh, I'm tired all the time

Stay with me in all you do,
Hold the faith I have in you,
Together, we'll pull through
Our love is strong, stronger
than we ever knew.
You hold me and I'll save you'

Chapter 40 - Isla

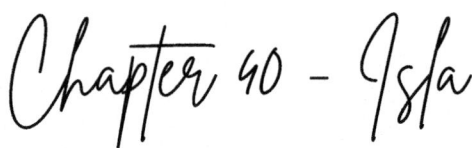

'Ach, Isla, that's affa bougie. How does it work?' Morag nosed.

'Were ye born in the dark ages, Morag?
Just pop a wee pod in, and it spits out the coffee.
It's a gift from Pais, I love her to bits but her coffee's shite.
Here, poke that in the top.' I passed a pod.

'I don't know how you bugger up coffee, but she manages every time.'
We shared a giggle as Morag fussed and fondled the machine.

'Where is she anyway?'

'Portree. She's got a couple of work calls to make, and she'll pick up some supper. I haven't even worked out how her cooking is yet. We've been so lazy.'
Morag's face filled with contemplation.

'How's a'thing going with you and Paisley? Is it as easy as it looks?'
I paused, a wry smile tugging.
Gesturing manically, I clutched the sky.

'It's like… hmm, you know when you leave Skye for a wee whiley? Then you come back across the bridge, that freezing sea air fills your lungs, the scenery hits you like a ton of bricks, you cross the Sligachan, and it's like… Aye, this is home.
Just like that.
It's unquestionable, I can't believe I'm saying my first

relationship is perfect, but I'd be lying if I said anything else.'

Morag pulled the mug to her lips, her head tilting as I spoke.

'She's patient, compassionate and thoughtful. Granda approved… I think you approve?

Jeezo Morag, I don't want anyone else.

I don't want to lose her, I'm not sure how I'd come back from that.

I love her… undeniably and unequivocally love her.'

The coffee almost dribbled as Morag studied me.

'Huh, wow… Isla, I dinna even know wit to say to that.

But to answer your question, after the hiding you gifted her at the funeral, I definitely approve.

I mean, she just scooped ye up and carried you aff home… I fancied a bit of that myself.'

Tittering, a naughty smirk grew.

'Aye, I'm so embarrassed and angry.

She's so good to me and I was bloody horrible. Paisley didn't deserve any of that.'

'It was a tough day, Isla.'

'Aye, the worst…'

'I was really impressed though, even at the harbour I thought she was a bit snobby for a split moment, she changed my mind within thirty seconds.

She's bloody attractive too, I couldn't believe my eyes.'

'Oh aye, I'd been ogling her before I knew who she was. After that email, I went to check her out online. You can't imagine my surprise when she appeared at my door.

Auch, it's funny how things work.'

Reflecting, I tapped my lip.

'I guess I should be thanking you for stitching me up with the Hairy Coo.'

The Gran-Lungo whooshed from Morag like a whale's blowhole, it splattered across me and the floor. Howling, we stood for a moment.

'Ahh ha! I'll get you a cloth, and myself the mop.' I said, patting my shirt with the dish towel.

'Have you seen or heard from Tam and Helen?' Morag questioned. Her hands brushing the now drookit top.

Shaking my head, I wrung out the cloth.

'I doubt I'll hear from them again.

I'm done, Mo, they've had their chance.'

'They're still your parents, Isla. Mibbe worth making amends in the future, no?'

Morag's expression had turned thoughtful, her voice careful.

I decided to give Morag the down low on the inheritance.

'Jeezusss,' she finally puffed out.

Her face contorted, eyes unblinking.

Undecided on keeling over or demanding a strong drink would be my guess.

'Aye exactly, I passed out twice trying to make heed o' it.

We need the Isle, Morag. I could use a blowout!

This month's been far too stressful, I don't know if I'm coming or going.'

'I'm no surprised, Christ.' Morag's eyebrows still hadn't crawled down from the roof.

'So, if you'd be kind enough to tell Angus we'll be

back on the water in a couple of weeks, and his pay will be through at the end of the week. I just need to get my head screwed on and work things out with Paisley.'
I blew my fringe and cornered the mop.

'Aye, so between, deaths, relationships, parents and inheritance, I'm well and truly scunnered.' I sat back down.

'Well, you hivnae half had it rough,' Morag patted my leg. 'You'll get through it, Isla, you always do. You're a force to be reckoned with, just don't let it work you up.'

'I guess so, I don't even know who I am any more, Mo. I'm so tired of fighting, I think I've lost myself somewhere along the way.' Leaning against my hand I rubbed my forehead.

'We all jist need a good blowoot... or did you get one already?'
Morag questioned— Her face preparing for the fits.
Covering my big cheesy grin, I hinted an unruly wink.
Morag pulled in closer, 'And... was it worth your wait, Isla?'

'Auch Morag! Yer a bloody monster, I swear...' I couldn't still my chops.

'... it was fucking fantastic! I can't get enough. Honestly, I've turned into some kind of deviant sex pest.'
Infectious laughter rained.

'What about you and Angus? How's things going? Any blowouts yerself?'
Another wink, but for once it was on the other foot.
Morag turned red, lips tight as she bit her cheek.

'Aye, we're grand.'

'Ahh but you didn't answer my question...
Come on Mo, let me have my fun for a change! Answer the bloody question.'
Morag freed a flustered laugh, her face awkwardly rosie and out of character.

'Jesus, Morag, what is it? Are you alright? What's wrong?'
'Ach Isla, I didn't want to say 'till you're back on your feet, you've enough going on.'
'Oh my God! Morag, what's wrong?'
Terror possessed me, I moved towards her.

'Come on, what is it? Your appointment from February? Are you sick?' Heart racing.

'It's okay, Isla. Ah got a fleg... I didn't want to get into a state until we knew more... but Angus felt something one night, the bugger was having a cheeky rummage down my top an...'

'Morag! What?' I shouted.

'I needed bloods done, Isla, ah didn't know what to say... it gave me the fear... I was feart... ah thought I wis in bother.
I couldnae burden you... or... be weak.
After leaving the bakers I went to the appointment. The surgery took tests at the end of February...'

'Morag! I could have come with you! Why haven't you told me before now?
It's May for God's sake!' My voice lifting with every question.

'I'm not sick. Isla, stop worrying.
The results came back inconclusive.
The doctor sent me for a biopsy and more tests.
Ach, that was fucking horrible... and they took forever to come back, but I got the all-clear on April 25th. I

couldn't say then either, you were grieving, you didn't need the bother. '

'Oh, thank God, I thought I was away to nose-dive the floor.

Nothing to worry about then… phew, that's grand.

Friggin hell, my heart's pounding.

You still should have said something… but I am relieved.

Christ, you're trying to kill me as well.'

A strained grunt held against my throat.

'Jesus wept, my brain saw fourteen different colours.'

'Well, that's nae strictly accurate either, Isla, I do have one wee thing that I need to tell ye aboot…'

'Morag, for fuck's sake, what is it? What's wrong with you? You're pulling and pushing like a yo-yo.

I can't keep up. I don't know whether to laugh or cry.

I swear, I'll be on drugs next week.'

'I'm pregnant, Isla, we're having a baby.'

Nervous quivering lips from Morag as her pupils darted.

'Wait, what? You're what?'

My eyes aghast, hands flying, voice climbing octaves.

'Morag, you can't just drop that on me like it's a baker's breakfast! A baby?!'

The shock turned to laughter.

'Oh my God, that's fantastic news, congratulations!'

Tears pricked.

'Uhh, I'm so, so happy for you!

Auch, I'm sorry you thought you couldnae tell me.'

More tears, not just pricking, flooding.

A new laugh, 'And you're asking me about my bloody blowout… You've been getting down and busy, you dirty wee monkey!

Oh my God, Mo… Auch come here, I need a coorie.'

Lingering in a tight hug, Morag stood silent for a few seconds.

'Are ye alright, Isla? I mean, are ye really okay?'

'I think so.

I didn't realise I had so many emotions, and truthfully, I've felt every one.

I'm so pleased for you both, Morag. So, so chuffed.'

'We've niver really spoken about haeing kids in detail, Isla.

I was worried it might upset ye. I didnae want to bring it up, just in case.'

'Me? Hah, it was one of the first things I asked Paisley. I'm not sure why I've never asked you in all the years. God, am I so self-absorbed?

It doesn't upset me, Mo. I thought I'd be alone all my days. One oversized child will be more than enough for me. Oh, and now I can borrow yours.'

I flashed my teeth.

'You're nae self-absorbed. Stoater.

Aye and speaking of which, the wee nugget will need a godmother… or two. Are you up for it?'

Morag let free a grin, it swathed around us both.

The tears didn't stop— they just began all over again.

'This is the best news I've had all month, auch, I canna even contain myself.'

Dragging me into another cuddle, Morag clung on tight.

'Aye, we'll be alright, Isla. We have you to watch out for us.'

Podgy hands brushed my eyes, gently attempting to

ease the monsoon.

We slid down onto the floor— it was probably safer.

'That wee one won't need anything, not with me as godmother! Wait... two godmothers, who's the other one? When will mini-McBride arrive?'

'Twenty second of December is the date we've been given. It better nae ruin my Christmas!

You and Paisley, assuming the sex stays good and ye stick the gether.'

My lips pursed, cheeks full.

'Isla, I canna hae a drink til December, how the hell will I get through?'

'Auch, you can just watch me, I'll drink mine and yours!

Oh, and Paisley isn't going anywhere, I've tasted sugar, I'm never *ever* going back to twelve years of desperation.'

'Ach, Isla, that's grim!

You still hivnae given me any of the details, ye prude.'

'You might not want to mention godmother to Paisley just yet, I don't want you scaring her off. Especially now I'm getting earthshaking hanky-panky...' I done a little wiggle.

'It'll stay that way for a while, Mo. I'm not giving out any of our secrets.' I giggled— it received me a playful pat on the back.

'Well, I didn't think it would be this emotional.' Morag wiped her eyes. 'I honestly hope ye both make it work.'

'We will, I'm sure of it... and you're going to be the best wee family, Morag.'

'Aye, and you'll be the best wee babysitter when I'm

needing a blowoot,'
Spoken with lashings of cheek.

We were wrapped around each other in complete
hysterics when Paisley walked through the door.
The kitchen looked like a war zone.

Paisley made eyes at the battlefront.

'Uhh hello, is everything alright?
You both look like you've been through a category-five
tornado, and some-how you're now being held hostage
by the fridge-freezer. Dare I ask?'
Morag and I immediately jumped to our feet.

'Hiya, Paisley, I know it must look like I've been
caught in a raunchy love affair with your Mrs, but
there's a story.'
Paisley's eyebrows rose higher as I ran over.
Wrapping my arms around her neck, we teased our
guest with warm tongues.
Pulling free, Paisley's lip-licking scowl almost floored
me.

'Morag's pregnant! And I'm to be the wee one's
godmother.' I cried out, not sure what to do or say first.
Paisley's face lifted, gleaming teeth breaking free.

'Aww, Morag, that's beautiful, congratulations to you
and Angus. It's nice to hear something positive!
If it's okay, I'm going to leave you both to continue your
adulterous dalliance, there's ample chips in the bag,' she
waved it next to her head. 'I'm just going to pop away
for a quick shower.'

Morag and I got straight back to our chat, chippies in
hand.

* * * *

Paisley was still standing long after Morag had left, head bowed, water cascading down her back.

Wrapped in a blanket of apprehensive filled fog by the looks.

My own matching as I observed from the doorway.

Should I go in or just leave her?

The silence was loud, the kind that carried too many unspoken and no doubt heart wrenching words.

'Paisley,' she didn't turn.

'Pais, are you okay?'

A moment passed.

'Yeah, I'm fine.' Voice distanced and distorted by the rain.

Mhmm, that brooding view is something else, but what's troubling my bonnie lass?

'How were your calls? I've saved you some chips.' I tried for casual; I'm confident concern crept in.

'I'm not hungry but thank you.

Isla, we should sit down tomorrow and talk...' Paisley's voice trailed off.

'Why don't we talk tonight?' I asked, sensing the growing distance.

'I don't want to ruin your night.

You've had a really good day, especially after Morag's news, that's absolutely fantastic.

A real pick me up for you, I'm honestly so pleased for everyone.'

'It is great news, but you're not convincing me, Pais. It's not our baby. My attention is on you and me.'

Without another word, I flung my baffies aside and stepped in, the water soaking the skin.

Warm and soggy clothing, not at all matching the chilly atmosphere.

Pulling Paisley around, we stood in a saturated embrace.

'Hey, we face whatever this is together.

So, you tell me right now, Paisley Campbell, what's going on?' My hands tilted her gaze.

There was a flash of vulnerability in her eyes, a lifetime of keeping things in, trying to solve problems alone. She remained silent.

'Pais, I know that overbearing and overwhelming weight. The struggle to let go, break the boundaries, but you need to let me in. Let me share the burden.'

'God, I love you so much, Isla.

I need you so much more than I ever expected.

I can't do this by myself. I can't do life without you.'

'Paisley?' The torrent softened my voice— her forest eyes soaking me up. Kind and caring, full of warmth.

What had started as worry, was turning into a caring sense of protection.

'Please tell me what's going on, Pais. You're breaking my heart.'

Running her fingers through my now darkened hair, we shared a moment of calm.

'I have to go back to Edinburgh early.'

'We knew you'd have to go at some point.'

Moving my head, I hid within the deluge.

'I don't know when I'll get back, there's something big going on.'

Her eyes were filled with the weight of the world.

'David's sick.'

Paisley's voice had turned quiet.

'Who's David?'

'My father's business partner and the current owner of Campbell and Cambell.

My dad left his share of the company to David in his will.

Should either of them pass, the company would fall to the other. It was a fair and sensible clause they agreed upon when starting up.

It just happened to be my father that departed first.'

Paisley wiped the water from her face.

Lowering her head, I could feel the sorrow.

'I'm so sorry, Paisley.'

I didn't know what to say; rubbing at her arms, I tried for an empathetic smile.

'In a baffling and tragic twist, I've been named as David's beneficiary, he wants me to take over the company.

He hasn't got any family, his ex-wife left him years ago.

David's a good man.'

Her hand ran over my soggy long sleeve top, fiddling with the now heavy fabric.

'Actually, he's far better than just good.

He's utterly brilliant, kind natured and always has a special way with words. David reminds me of your grandfather.'

The reference of Granda saddened me, I know it wasn't supposed to.

It was a nice thought that she spoke so highly of them both. I guess we both felt hurt.

'Oh, Pais.'

Lifting her chin, I pulled it back towards me.

The water created tears over her face.

'Isla, I'm not sure how to run a company.

I'm career driven, but I've never once thought about owning the place.

Being under the Campbell's banner was more than enough for me.

I've never strived for anything beyond an associate.

I certainly didn't expect this.

To me, this is life changing.'

I thought about her words for a moment.

Running a hand through my soaked hair, I shifted it away from my eyes.

Letting my hands fall, I rest them steadily against her waist.

'When did you last see him?'

Paisley pulled a despondent but amused smile.

'The night you were hammered on sumbucha.'

I slapped her back playfully and rolled my eyes.

'Are you going to visit him?'

Paisley's smile didn't linger; she gave out a defeated nod.

'I have to, Isla. After hearing the news today, it would be terrible if I didn't.

This man helped shape my life, he's always looked out for me and mum. It would be wrong to let him face this alone.'

Paisley's brow furrowed.

Looking at her feet, there was a shift in her mood.

Contemplative and brooding.

I sucked in a deep breath, the thought of us separating, selfishly filled my brain.

'Okay. You need to do what you feel is right, Paisley.'

The words felt salty on my tongue, but I knew it was

the right direction to push.

'How can you just gift someone a company?
I need to see David for myself, tell him I can't do this.
It's not my place.
It's not my company!' Her voice was suddenly adamant and forceful.
I moved one hand to her chest, pressing tightly I could feel her heart pounding.

'Pais, over the last few months you've shown me who you really are.
You don't stand for any shit, but you have a heart of gold.
Between the trouble with my family, the mistakes with Granda's will and my shocking behaviour at the funeral, it tells me you're compassionate and caring.'
Paisley's eyes searched mine, the moody glower pulling at her crow's feet.

'God, you hunted me down in that gorgeous hotel, gave forgiveness to your mother, and somehow magically appeared right when I needed you.'

'Isla, that doesn't mean I can run a business.'

'No, it doesn't, but it shows your character, Pais.
You've shown nothing but respect to me and everyone you've met. Truthfully, I don't think there's anything you can't do…
Well, except make coffee, that's your kryptonite, but even that you've fixed!

'Isla, it's not that eas…'

'No. You're wrong.
Paisley, you're so wrong right now.
You literally handle anything and everything that's thrown in your direction. It's unnatural how calm and collected you are. It's honestly incredible.

Everything gets messy and dark, and you just march on through like nothing can hold you back.

I frankly don't know how you do it.'

Reaching up, Paisley massaged her temples.

Gently moving her hands away, I rubbed at the same area, slow and gentle.

She didn't speak, just watched my face intently.

'Look Pais, if this is what you need to do, then do it. I'm not going to stand in your way, I'm always going to push you to the max, I hope you know that.'

'I'm starting to learn.'

'Good.

David obviously see's what I see, if he didn't, then why would he have named you?

I don't know whether I should say this or not, but I'm going to do it anyway; It's your bloody name above the door, Pais. You're destined to take over.

How friggin proud would your father be?

The great Lady Paisley, picking up where he left off. That's some bloody achievement!'

Stopping the circling motion, I let my hands linger against her head.

'What about us, Isla? I'm so happy right now.

I've been waiting for the world to crash and fall around us.

Maybe this is it.

You'll find peace with all of your free space again and I'll go back to wine and work, I guess…'

I wasn't going down this route, the past few months had been painful enough without this joining the mix.

'I'm coming with you.'

I clasped my hands tighter.

Demanding her undivided attention and eye contact.

'I'm coming with you.

I'm not letting you face this alone, Paisley.

Whatever comes next, we'll deal with it together.

You don't get to walk away from us. Not now.

Not when we've finally found something real. Something worth fighting for.'

Paisley's hands moved to my back and hips, drawing me in closer.

'I don't know when we'll be back, Isla, you have to work.'

'The sky's our limit, Paisley.

We get to decide how our future looks, but there will be no more sad lonely nights.

No more desperate soul searching... and definitely, no more wine and work.'

Her delicate nose, immaculate skin and deep green eyes locked me in place.

The air turned thick, warm and clammy, her smile cut through the steam, shattering my heart.

'Hmm, it sounds like you've found your hallmark movie, Isla.'

'You'd better believe it!

Paisley, you've stood by my side, pushed me to pick myself back up.

It's my turn, I'm taking control this time.

We untangle our knots together.'

'Isla, I can't ask yo...'

'Auch, Paisley, I love you, and you love me, it really is that simple!

Life's far too short, with way too many variables, but you and I, we work as one.

You aren't asking me to do anything, and I'm not telling you again. It's final. I'm coming with you.'

My tone had turned confident and unwavering, maybe I was taking a page out of her book for a change.

I think it took Paisley by surprise, her eyebrows lifted, crow's feet receding, lips parting as she studied my face.

'It sounds like you're fighting for me, Isla.

Investing your love, keeping me breathing.'

'Oh Pais, I'll follow you to the moon, and I promise tomorrow will be different, I know it's definitely going to be brighter.'

'You complete me.'

Leaning in, her warm breath kissed my lips.

Ugh, so bloody delicious.

Drawing back, Paisley peered down.

My heart skipped a beat, infinite and enchanting.

That glorious grin, those deep forest green eyes.

'Isla, I love you too much.

I wholeheartedly don't think I can survive without you.'

'Well, it's a bloody good job I don't mind having my wings clipped then, isn't it?

I love you, Paisley and I promise we don't ever need to worry again, we're one.'

Wrapping myself around her waist, we weaved into a snug and powerful embrace.

Finally! I really have met my woman.

'So, what do we do now? We do this?'

'Aye, we jist hae tae take it one slow and painful step at a time.'

Tethered Lines

Book Two

of

The Tangled Series

Isla

April

The oversized pushchair bounced across the gravel track, a rivet in the stones causing all four wheels to clatter down with an almighty *thud.*

Flora's baby blue eyes snapped open; beaming out through the early spring sunlight, tiny fingers stretched to her face.

'Shi..t…shhht, come on bubba, go back to sleep.
Please close yer very, very cute wee eyes— Just for another… Oh, I don't know… A week, maybe.'

Flora's podgy little cheeks puffed out, a dazzling smile lighting the inside of the pram— giggles erupting from the miniature human contained within.

'Ah bugger, you're a wee monkey.
What am I going to do with you, eh?'

Halting the kid container in the middle of my private road, I reached inside and unclipped Flora.

Lifting her to my chest, more giggles flew out; pint sized arms and legs flailing in every direction.

Jeezo, this kid's going to be the death of me.

'Look here little one, yer mum's going to be back soon and I'll get a skelpt backside if you're not sleeping… Again!

Aye, and it winna even be a good kind of skelp.'

Holding Flora tight in one arm and pushing the oversized death trap with the other, I continued towards the door.

'See, we're almost home, just a few more steps…

Then I can wrestle with the door... Or the buggy... Or you.'

Giggles and arms flew out faster this time; it was turning into a game of '*how stressed can you make everyone, whilst having no cares or worries in the world.*'

'Christ lassie, I think I'll need a nap too. You've worn me out.'

Parking the wheels outside the door, my motivation to bring the damn thing into the house had blown away with the breeze.

Carrying Flora into Bramble Brae's kitchen, I clicked on the express warmer.

Ahead of the game, I'd already pre-filled a bottle with formula in preparation for her next feed.

Oh aye, you dinna half catch on quick with this wee monster.

Opening the cabinet above the sink, I lifted out a blue mug from the now matching set— Hastily shoving it under the espresso maker's spout, a coffee pod made its appearance.

More laughter and gurgles from the mini monster.

'Aye, that's right bubba, one for you, one for me.' Hands clasped tight around Flora's waist, I tap danced her across the marble kitchen island.

'Would it be too early to start on the whiskey, Flora? I have a smashing wee ten-year-old Talisker screaming my name.'

Half serious - half joking, I stood patiently waiting for an answer.

It wasn't likely that the four-month-old troublemaker was going to enlighten me, but I got a bubbly grin from her anyway.

Auch, that wee face warms my soul.

'Hmm, maybe I'll wait an hour before breaking into the malt.'

It's probably nae a good idea to be pissed before four.

Flora's eyes finally closed seconds before a car pulled into the driveway—The milk bottle still protruding out from between her adorable soft lips.

'Talk about perfect timing.' I breathed out in a hushed whisper.

Yawning silently and trying to keep my eyes focused, the front door swung open. A silent figure trudged in wearing black leggings, a baggy white t-shirt with a tartan bee embroidered on the sleeve... and a pair of God-awful crocs.

Jeezo, affa stylish.

'Auch Isla, you're a saviour.

I had visions of this wee madam being wide awake, ah can't thank ye enough for watching her.' Morag whispered.

Once again looking like she'd been dragged through a hedge backwards, Morag's mousey brown hair stuck up in an unruly fashion— It probably hadn't seen a brush since Flora arrived.

Haphazardly, the crumpled t-shirt was tucked into the arse of her leggings on one side.

It really made me want to laugh, but considering I probably wasn't fairing much better, I decided not to mention it.

Two full days of babysitting had humbled my childfree lifestyle.

Crossing the room, Morag sat down heavily on the sofa.

Her efforts causing my bum to bounce steadily on the cushion beside her.

'Mo, I'll always look after Flora, you know that.'
Gingerly I handed the sleeping giggle monster over; my head falling backwards once free.

After a few still moments, I made an exaggerated effort to stand back up, it caused my knees to creak— I'd have been more than happy to just drift into a deep sleep; I'm confident Morag knows her way out by now anyway.

'I canna lie, Morag, I don't envy you, I'm absolutely knackered. Thank God I can hand her back whenever I please.'

'I wish ah could!'

'Auch, you don't mean that. Are you biding long enough for a coffee?' Already shuffling towards the machine, I turned back to face my visitor; an exaggerated nod bounced its way over.
With Flora safely cradled in her arm, Morag stood up.

'Aye please, Isla, I think I need it.' A podgy hand ran up and over her face.

'Sorry I wis away so long, bloody funerals dinna half take up mare time than necessary. The dead dinna have much in the way o' patience considering they're nae going anywhere.'

My shoulders sagged— Granda's funeral had twisted its way back into my thoughts.
It wasn't like I hadn't been pondering it all day anyway, but still, there was an ache I couldn't shift.

'Oh Isla, I'm so sorry. I didn't mean...'
I shook my head in a, 'don't worry about it' kind of way.

Looking at my hands, the fingers were back to their silent knitting.

'Auch, Mo…' I started before she cut me off.

'Baby brain. It doesn't filter anything and my mouth certainly doesn't have a reset button.' Pushing for a small smile, Morag moved forward.

'Nah, you're fine.
I'm just feeling a wee bitty emotional this week, I'll get over it.' Popping another pod into the machine, it chugged out a beating thrum.

'Ah shit! It's Alistair's anniversary tomorrow.
Oh, for goodness sake Isla, I'm so sorry, why didn't ye say?'
Morag's free arm motioned for a coorie.

'Christ, I canna wait for this phase to disappear, I need my old brain back— That thing was rapid.
This replacement's like something out of the Jurassic era; everything's either buried away or completely extinct.'
Smiling a pained scowl, I moved into the one-armed embrace— It was probably the best offer I'd get for a while, so I'd be as well take it.

'Trust me to waltz in two feet deep. I should have jist taen Flora with me, given you some peace and quiet.'
Morag declared— her dark eyebrows meeting in the middle, cheeks pulled in tightly as the usual smile was replaced with a sullen grimace.

'You're fine, Mo honestly, I'm glad of the company.
I can't stand the silence, it drives me mad. It makes me think of everything I should, or could be doing.'
Pushing a ceramic handle into Morag's free fingers, she precariously balanced the baby in the other.
Tilting my head, I watched a potentially dangerous

game unfold. I mean, I could offer to help, but after being away for two full days, Morag could use the practice.

It seems fair.

Moving back towards the couch, we collapsed down. Morag only marginally more careful than myself.

I bounced with the weight of a Calanais standing stone.

The coffee creating waves against the deep and fragile ceramic coastline.

Turning to study Morag with Flora, my thoughts went sprawling across the room.

They were a perfect match; each one, building the other into an even better person.

Although children had never been in my plan... Or Paisley's, I couldn't help but admire their bond.

Should we have done that? Would it have strengthened our failures? Hmm, I doubt it.

Unintentionally, I let out a deep, heavy sigh.

'You really are a fantastic mum, Mo. That wee monkey's the luckiest girl in the world, and I can't believe how much she's changed you.'

Morag's eyes lifted to meet mine, noticeable signs of exhaustion darkening the lower lid.

I watched them both for a moment longer.

Bittersweet unease filling me— a hint of sadness and regret leached to the surface.

'Is that a good or bad change?' She asked with a surprised tone.

'Auch, good of course!'

'Honestly Isla, I'm scunnered all the time. I don't know if I'm a good mum, let alone a fantastic one.

I canna remember wit I'm doing or wit I've jist done.'

'Nothing new there then, eh?' I teased with a smile.

'Atch wheesht woman.

Last week I put Angus's socks in the dishwasher then drove to Armadale, got there and realised I'd left the buggy ootside the hoose. I'm absolutely puggled.' Morag pulled a short mouthful of coffee; obviously it was hot, she chewed her tongue for a second afterwards.

'Aye, I can see that, Mo, but you've stopped meddling in my affairs, so I don't mind…'

Morag's brows lifted, a smirk growing against her cheeks.

'…I'm glad your attention's on something else other than the great aunty Isla.' I teased in a hushed voice.

Glossary

Aboot — About
Affa — Awfully/Extremely
Afore — Before
Ah'hing — Everything
Awa — Away
Awa an bile yer heid — Away and boil your head/Go away
Aye — Yes
Baltic — Cold/Freezing
Bampot — Foolish Person
Bidie-in — Live in lover/ Non-marital partner
Bonnie — Pretty/Nice
Buff — Naked/Bare
Ceilidh — Get together/Dance
Clootie — Rag/Cloth
Coo — Cow
Coorie — Cuddle/Hug
Craic — Crack/Banter
Dae — Do
Deed — Dead
Dinna — Don't
Disnae — Doesn't
Dreich — Dreary/Bleak
Drookit — Wet/Soaking
Ein — One
Eejit — Idiot
Feart – Frightened
Fir — For

Fleg – Fright/Scare
Gie — Give
Guddle — Mess/Messy
Hackit — Ugly/Unattractive
Haeing — Having
Hame — Home
Heebie - jeebies — Unease/Nervousness/Disgust
Heid — Head
Heilan — Highland
Hiv — Have
Hoose — House
Hunners — Hundreds
Hurkle durkle — Lounge/Linger
Jist — Just
Lass — Girl
Lang — Long
Loch — Lake/Body of water
Manky — Dirty/Disgusting
Mannie — Man
Mare — More
Mawkit — Dirty/Unclean
Mibbe — Maybe
Michty — Mighty
Morn/The Morn — Morning/Tomorrow
Munster — Monster
Nae — No/Not
Niver — Never
Oor — Our
Oot — Out
Ower — Over
Radge — Crazy/Cross/Mad
Scoof — Stealing/Large gulp
Scud — Naked

Sgian Dubh — A small knife

Shindig — Party

Skelp — Smack/Slap

Skinny malinky — Thin/Lanky Person

Skirlie — Oatmeal (Scottish stuffing)

Skirls — Scream

Slainte mhath — Good Health (Cheers)

Sleekit — Sly/Cunning

Slever — Drool/Slobber

Spewings — Vomit

Stappit — Full/Stuffed

Stoater – Someone fantastic or excellent

Tae — To

Taen — Taken

Telt — Told

The gether — Together

Wee — Small

Wheechs — Steals

Wheesht — Be quiet

Wi' — With

Winna — Won't/Will not

Wouldnae — Wouldn't

Ye — You

Yer — Your

Yiv — You've

Printed in Dunstable, United Kingdom

67283621R00275